Published by Hot-Lanta Publishing, LLC

Copyright 2017

Cover Design By: Uplifting Designs

Cover Model: DesLaurier Media

Photo Credit: Jeff Kasser

This book is licensed for your personal enjoyment only. This book may not be re-sold or given away to other people. If you would like to share this book with another person, please purchase an additional copy for each person. If you're reading this book and did not purchase it, or it was not purchased for your use only, then please return it and purchase your own copy. Thank you for respecting the hard work of this author.

No part of this book may be reproduced in any form or by any electronic or mechanical means, including information storage and retrieval systems, without written permission from the author, except for the use of brief quotations in a book review. To obtain permission to excerpt portions of the text, please contact the author at meghan.quinn.author@gmail.com

All characters in this book are fiction and figments of the author's imagination.

www.authormeghanquinn.com

Copyright © 2017 Meghan Quinn

All rights reserved.

Tangled Twosome

USA TODAY BESTSELLING AUTHOR

MEGHAN QUINN

CHAPTER ONE

RACER

Why is it so goddamn drafty in here? I grip my hammer in my hand, my tool belt riding low on my hips, and my stereotypical construction hat rests on my head as I finish up the project I was hired to do.

Taking a quick look around, I search the bedroom, looking for an open window or AC vent that's blowing a cold breeze right against my dick and sac, making it almost impossible to look semi-decent in this scrap of fabric.

"Mmm, I think you forgot a nail on the ground over there," says the throaty, smoke-filled voice of Mrs. Sage, who is lying across her chaise lounge, wearing a silky pink robe that is barely tied around her waist. She makes it her mission to show me as much skin as possible, and as we're talking about skin showing . . .

I bend down to pick up the nail she's pointing at as the thin strip of man thong material rides higher up my ass crack than I care to admit.

Let's pause for a second.

Are you wondering to yourself, is Racer really wearing a man thong as he finishes building a solid oak shelf?

The answer is yes. Yes, I am.

I'm Racer McKay, and I wear man thongs for older, rich women while I work on simple projects around their houses. Excuse me, I mean mansions.

Don't worry. Yes, I'm also very much ashamed to admit the level I've stooped to in order to make some cash. I have my pride, but right now, when I'm offered three hundred dollars more to build a shelf in a man thong, I'm choosing to seize the opportunity.

Self-respect was thrown out the window two years ago when a pile of bills and responsibilities were thrust in my direction without any preparation or warning. Making money is as vital as breathing to me, so I will take it any way I can get it.

Cue the man thong.

"Oh, you're right. Here it is," I say, holding up the nail. "Thanks for the help, Mrs. Sage. I would hate to see you hurt yourself from my lack of attention to detail."

She waves me off and puffs her chest toward me, her robe slipping farther apart, showing the cleavage of a very saggy pair of breasts. I've seen my fair share of boobs, and even though I don't mingle sex with work, I can't help but want Mrs. Sage to remove the robe just so I can see what she has hidden under the silky fabric.

How saggy are we talking here?

I'm interested for exploratory reasons, for knowledge about every kind of breast out there. Because right now, Mrs. Sage looks like she's rocking a pair of pancakes that have been flattened by a steamroller.

"You would just have to nurse me back to health if that happened." Her finger trails up her varicose veined leg to her geriatric hip. I hold back the shiver that wants to spin up my spine.

All I can say is . . . can't unsee that.

I nervously laugh and tuck my hammer into its holster. "Not much of a nurse, Mrs. Sage. I might hurt you even more."

"I don't mind getting hurt." She starts to spread her legs and that's when I call it a day.

I turn around quickly, snag my jeans, and slip them up and over my legs, struggling around my tool belt. Once things are in place, I remove my hat, put on my shirt, and cover my hair with a backward baseball cap. The peep show is over.

Once dressed, I gather my tools, tuck my construction hat under my arm, and turn to Mrs. Sage. This is my least favorite part, getting the old bird to pay up.

"Leaving already?" She pouts, lipstick on her teeth.

"Unfortunately, I have another engagement I'm running late for." A lie, but it's the only way I know to get out of here.

"That's a shame. I really should book you for a whole day. That way you can't skirt out of here earlier than I'm ready for."

She walks out of the den and into the entryway where she opens her purse and pulls out a wad of one-hundred-dollar bills. My brain explodes from the amount of cash in her purse, as if it's chump change she's ready to throw around at a parade dedicated to her and her riches.

"What do I owe you? Six hundred?"

Fuck, it's five hundred, and if I wasn't a nice guy, I wouldn't correct her, but I believe in good karma. Especially considering where my bad luck has gotten me—trying to climb my way out of a large debt. I try to put as many good vibes out in the world as possible.

"We actually agreed upon five hundred, Mrs. Sage."

"Such a bargain." She flips through her cash, pulls out five bills —*damn*—and hands them over to me. "Shall I call for my next project?"

I pocket the cash. "Email is best, Mrs. Sage. I always feel awkward taking phone calls at work."

"Such a hard worker." She pats my face and leans forward, lips puckered, but I step to the side avoiding an attack from her old-lady lips.

3

As I depart, I wave my hand in the air and say, "Thanks, Mrs. Sage. I look forward to your next email."

Out of her reach, I toss my tools in the back of my truck, enter the cab, and place my hands on the steering wheel as I exhale a long pent-up breath.

My boys, Smalls and Tucker, can never hear about today's side job. There is no way they'll let me live it down if they knew. I know my two best friends—who I've been working with in construction for the last few years—have never had to put on a man thong and bend over for a client multiple times. And hell, if they found out I do—on occasion—I think they would question my sanity.

Although, they're aware of my struggles and try to help out where they can. Tucker, technically my boss, tries to schedule me as much as possible, but sometimes it doesn't feel like enough.

From the center console of my beat-up truck, I pull out my phone and see three text messages.

Tucker: *At the House of Reardon with Smalls. Come have a drink.*

Smalls: *Get your ass here.*

Adalyn: *Have you ever smelled burning skin before? It's nasty.*

I chuckle at the last message. I head toward the bar where Tucker and Smalls are hanging out and do voice text back to Adalyn.

"Try to avoid burning skin, especially on the worksite. I'm taking it you've had a fun shift at work today?"

Adalyn is one of my best friends as well. I met her through Tucker's fiancée, Emma. We spent one night together hanging out and we've been inseparable ever since. And before your mind starts racing a mile a minute about how we're going to get married and have little Radalyn babies, I'm going to cut you off right there. There is nothing going on between us. As Adalyn very honestly told me one night, she has no interest in starting any type of relationship with me since I'm not her type. Although, she said if I want to hang out with my shirt off it would be no problem with her. Such a horny little minx.

My phone rings in my hand. I put it on speaker.

"Addie sweetie pie snookum face."

"Racee pacey penis breath." God, I love her humor.

"What have we talked about?" I turn onto a main road, feeling a little more at ease knowing there is a beer in my near future.

"I can call you nicknames just not penis breath," she says in a monotone voice.

"Correct. I don't think that's all that hard to remember."

"I know," she sulks, "but ever since you taught me the insult, I want to use it all the time."

"Call your mom penis breath."

"Yeah, great idea. Next time my overprotective mom calls, I'll be sure to call her penis breath. I'm sure she'll love it."

I chuckle. "Maybe it's what your dad calls her in bed."

"I hate you. I hate you so much right now."

I full-on belly laugh, the rumble coming from the pit of my stomach. "You started it, Addie."

She lets out a long breath. "Note to self, don't call Racer penis breath ever again."

"I'm glad you learned your lesson." I turn onto State Route 17 and head toward The House of Reardon. "So what's going on, burning skin today at the office?"

"No, but I did watch someone get a mole removed and that smelled like absolute carcass. It was nasty."

"Why did you want to be a nurse again?"

"I don't know," she sighs. "Good benefits?"

"Good benefits? I would have sworn you were doing it for the free latex gloves."

"Well, there is my latex glove obsession," she says sarcastically. "Ugh, what are you doing tonight?"

"Getting a drink with the boys down at Reardon. What are you doing? Painting those gnarly toes of yours while drinking an entire bottle of peach schnapps?"

"Close, I'm clipping my toenails for you as a gift and drinking peach schnapps. Expect a package at your front door tomorrow."

"Aw, you shouldn't have." I switch lanes and speed down the highway, the froth of the beer calling my name.

"What did you do today?" Adalyn asks, changing the subject. "Were you with Mrs. Sage again?"

Adalyn is the only one who knows about Mrs. Sage and her "requests." I had to tell someone and Tucker and Smalls were not an option, given I work with them every day. But Adalyn was a safe second. She's cool and wouldn't say anything.

"Yeah," I huff. "It was extra drafty in her house today."

"Probably to cool down her old-lady hot flashes. Would she still get those at her age?"

"I don't know." I get off the exit, thankful I'm only a few minutes away. "You're the woman and the nurse; you should know a hell of a lot more about hot flashes than I do."

"Of course you would say that, sexist."

"Hey," I shout, seeing the parking lot straight ahead. "You know I'm the first fucking person to celebrate women and their rights. Forgive me if I don't quite understand your lady parts and the tubes that float around in your lower half. Do you know the intricacies of the penis?"

"As a matter of fact—"

"Scratch that, wrong person to ask." I put my truck in park, and I'm about to tell Adalyn I have to go when she starts walking toward me. "Well, hello there, pretty girl."

She smiles and pockets her phone, ending our conversation. Dressed in her scrubs, she opens my door and says, "You drive like a grandpa. Took you long enough."

I hop out and wrap my arm around her shoulder. "Crashing the dick party?"

"Can't resist."

When we enter the bar, we spot Smalls and Tucker immediately. They have a table off to the side with a pitcher in the middle and a plate of nachos. Thank fuck. I'm starving.

I pull out Adalyn's chair for her, like the gentleman I am, and then spin my chair around so I'm sitting in it backward. "What's up, men? Mind if the little lady crashes?"

"Only if she can hold her own," Smalls says, handing her a cup.

"You know I can." Adalyn winks and starts filling up our glasses with beer.

I pull a large chip dripping of nacho cheese and jalapenos from the center of the nacho plate and stuff the whole thing in my mouth. Damn, that tastes good.

"Help yourself," Tucker says. I'm sure that is *not* sarcasm I hear in his tone.

"Don't mind if I do. My belly boo was screaming at me for food."

Tucker is about to take a sip of his beer when he says, "Dude, you're a six-foot-three, grown-ass man; you can't say shit like belly boo."

I shrug his comment off and stuff more nachos in my mouth. Within a minute almost half the plate is gone and I have no regrets.

"Where's the fiancée?" I ask Tucker.

"She'll be getting off her shift soon. She's going to meet me here, and then we're going out for dinner. She has a bunch of wedding things she wants to talk about."

"Sounds riveting," Smalls teases.

"Hey, I will talk whatever kind of wedding stuff she wants to. She's marrying me, she said yes to me." He takes a sip of his beer, disbelief in his voice. "I'm one lucky fuck."

"This is crap. She better talk to me next," Adalyn huffs and crosses her arms, interrupting the loving moment Tucker was having. "I've been asking that girl about her wedding plans for months now, and she keeps blowing me off. Who does that? Someone who's trying to avoid me, that's who. I'm going to be her maid of honor, right?" She pokes Tucker. "Tell me I'm her maid of honor. End my misery and let me know." Tucker says nothing, which only fuels the fire. "Fine, don't tell me, but if she picks someone else, I swear to the yeast in my beer that I will start slashing tires." Adalyn stabs the table with her finger, showing us all just how her temper can skyrocket in a second. "All the tires will rue the day Emma didn't pick me as her maid of honor." She laughs sardonically and sips her beer while staring Tucker down. "This is all your fault."

Tucker holds his hands up in defense. "I have no idea what she's planning. You take that shit up with her . . . and leave my tires alone."

"Oh, I *will* take it up with her." Adalyn bounces her knee up and down, clearly still hyped up. It almost looks like she's about to explode . . . "Racer wears man thongs while doing his side jobs."

What the hell?

"Adalyn!" I give her a *what the fuck* look.

Frazzled, she covers her mouth. "I'm sorry. I needed to change the subject before I started running around the bar tossing drinks in people's faces."

"Talk about your fucking burning mole skin. Don't bring me into this. Christ." I lift my baseball cap off my head, run my hand through my hair and situate it back on, holding the top for a few seconds.

The table is silent before Smalls taps me on the shoulder. "What?" I snap.

"Are you wearing just the man thong, or is it one of those things where you pull the thong over your jeans to give the ladies a sneak peek?"

"Are we talking lace, silk, or cotton? I would assume cotton for breathability, but then again, I've never worn a man thong before," Tucker adds.

"How many do you have?" Smalls continues. "Do you wear them all the time?"

"Do you have a favorite color?"

"Are we talking thong or G-string? Because that's a big difference," Adalyn joins in.

"Huge difference." Smalls rests his chin on his hand and leans forward, batting his eyelashes as he waits for an answer.

My eyes fixed on Adalyn, I say, "I'm going to kill you."

She hides her smile and takes another sip of her beer.

She doesn't know what she just started.

But, oh yeah, she's going to get it all right.

CHAPTER TWO

GEORGIANA

"This raspberry gin rickey is to die for," Madison coos about her drink while swirling its paper umbrella. "Who knew adding raspberries would change my life?"

I take a sip of my own rickey and say, "Cookie makes the best gin rickeys. Daddy stole her from the Steadman Estate. Apparently he bribed her with the world because he had one of her rickeys while visiting with Wilbur Steadman and couldn't part ways with her talent."

Madison lifts her glasses off her face and turns toward me, shock in her eyes. "Your dad stole Cookie from the Steadman's? Oh my God! That's ballsy. What did Wilbur do?"

I shrug and adjust myself on my lounge, letting the sun bronze my skin. It's rare we get such a beautiful day like today in Upstate New York, so I'm trying to soak in as much as possible. "Daddy must have talked him down because I haven't heard anything since."

"Bet your dad gave old Wilbur a few stock options in the company to tide him over."

"I wouldn't put it past him."

Old Daddy Dearest is the owner of every lumberyard and concrete plant in the Tri-City area. He worked his way up from the bottom, starting at a sawmill in Pennsylvania, and through a lot of hard work and investing, he can now afford a mixologist genius like Cookie, a Rolls Royce he leaves in his five-car garage, and my mother's monthly "beauty" sessions.

But with his money comes your stereotypical rich-father syndrome: only the best for his kids. My oldest brother, Abraham, is the president of the company, Elizabeth, my older sister, married wealthy—*naturally*—and my second oldest brother, Spencer, is living off his inheritance he received when he turned twenty-eight. Typical playboy in New York City.

And what am I doing you ask? Well, I have a beautiful master's degree in business from prestigious Northwestern . . . and that's pretty much it. I have no money of my own—inheritance doesn't kick in until I'm twenty-eight, two years from now—my dad refuses to let me live on my own, get a job, or even think about lifting a finger to do any kind of work. This does not include the charity events I help my mom with. Daddy believes I need a man in my life to take care of me, to dote on me, and to "buy me all the pretty things." Insert eye-roll here.

Even though my dad thinks he has my life all planned out, even his top three "suitors" for his little girl, I have other plans. Big plans. Plans I've been dreaming of since I was a little girl in middle school and witnessed all things lacey, white, and pretty when my aunt married. Rolling around in bundles upon bundles of tulle became my dream. A dream I can now practically taste . . .

"So, are you ready for tonight?" Madison asks.

The heat of the sun intensifies with the mention of tonight. It's beating down on me, building up the pressure, circling me in an inferno of what's to come.

Tonight.

I don't think I've ever been more nervous in my entire life. Even when I was forced to go with Danny Leshay to senior prom because it was part of my father's business deal with a client. My dad buys out a lumberyard, and in return, I have to go with the guy's son to prom. Thoughts of being stabbed and murdered on the side of the road by someone I didn't know terrified me. Thanks, Dad!

"I'm prepared but so freaking nervous." I turn on my side and face Madison. "I have that sinking feeling he's going to say no."

"How can he say no, G? You've run through your presentation a million times. I've seen it. You are solid with all your numbers, with your projections; it's an easy yes."

"To any other businessman, my presentation is an easy yes, but to my dad . . . I have this horrible feeling it's going to be a hard pass."

And that's the honest truth. He's a good man, but when it comes to me, I'm his little girl, not an aspiring entrepreneur.

"You might be surprised." Madison takes a big sip from her drink. "He wasn't happy at first about you going to Northwestern and earning your master's in business, but he changed his mind about that."

I roll my eyes. "Yeah, because on paper, I'm more appealing to one of the 'husbands' my dad has chosen for me. An educated girl is a girl with goals and motivation, one that will be able to participate with knowledgeable commentary in dry, pointless conversations at charitable events. My entire life leading to this point has been a long and drawn-out finishing school run, and operated by my father, preparing me for the very moment I meet the one man I can stand at his side, woo his clients, and be the trophy wife I've been morphed into." I set my drink on the table between us and rest my hands under my cheek. "I want so much more, Madison."

"If you had red hair and was brushing it with a fork right now, I would think you were the little mermaid."

"I'm serious." I laugh just as cursing from a thousand men breaks up our little conversation.

From the side of the pool where renovations for the pool house are taking place, the lone construction worker is holding his finger between his jean-clad legs.

Madison sits up and lifts her sunglasses to get a look at the commotion. "Did you hammer a nail into your finger over there?"

The man who's been working on the building for a few weekends looks up at us. His head is covered by a backward black baseball cap, his chest is bronze from working many hours outside this summer, and it's hard not to notice the corded muscles wrapped around his entire body, from his chiseled stomach to his powerful biceps. To be honest, it hasn't been a chore watching him these last few weekends.

What's-His-Name looks up and pops his finger in his mouth, sucking on it as his body ripples under the brightness of the sun.

"Damn," Madison mutters under her breath just as the man pops his finger out of his mouth. "Mama likes."

Unable to hear Madison slowly discredit his self-respect, he gruffly says, "I'm good." Not giving us a second thought, he shakes his hand and turns back toward his project.

Never having spoken to the man—I've only seen him around—I cautiously say, "You sure? Kind of looks like you're hurt."

Slowly he turns his head in my direction, his eyes cutting me a look of indignation. "I'm good, Princess. No need to set your cocktail down to check on me."

Pardon me? Was that attitude?

I sit up, my legs straddling my lounge chair and tip my sunglasses up so he can see my dissatisfaction in his choice of words. "It's Georgiana, not princess."

Picking up his hammer, he shoves it in a holster attached to his side and says, "Could have fooled me."

"Oooooo," Madison says as if she's in grade school. "Burned." She sits back in her chair, taking a sip of her drink as if she's preparing for the show of a lifetime, one she might just get.

Slowly, I set my drink down and stand. I adjust the fabric of my swimsuit bottom so it's covering my ass and saunter over to the man, now sorting nails as he casually glances in my direction.

When I stand in front of him, I watch his eyes travel over my barely covered frame until he meets me head-on. His staggering height doesn't intimidate me, even though he towers over my petite frame. He appears strong and powerful with a hard set in his jaw.

"What did you say?" I ask, a hand on my hip.

Not giving me his complete attention, he says, "You heard what I said or else you wouldn't be over here trying to put on a front."

"Put on a front?" My voice sounds a little shrill from the accusation. "I'm not putting on a front."

"Yeah?" He pulls a rag from his back pocket, lifts his hat, and wipes his brow. His blond hair sticks up in all different directions with beads of sweat at the tips that aren't covered by his hat. "So you're not trying to act intimidating in front of your friend? You know, push around the hired help to make yourself feel better?"

"Excuse me?" Two seconds ago I was irritated, now I'm mad. "How dare you make such an awful accusation about me. You don't know a thing about me."

"I know enough," he answers and turns around to nail another board for the new siding. His incessant hammering has ensured a headache all morning.

"Hey." I poke his sweaty back, trying to ignore how amazingly tight it feels under my index finger. "I suggest if you want to keep your job you show a little respect."

Whoa, can we all say it together? Georgiana, you're a bitch. The words felt dirty leaving my mouth. I really don't act like this, like my—*gulp*—parents, but I'm tired, anxious about meeting with my dad, and irritated. It's a cataclysmic combination and when that happens, nothing good comes from it. I'm about to apologize when he starts to go off on me.

"Respect? You want to talk respect?" He spins on his heel and holds up his hammer. "What do you know about respect, Princess? From where I see it, you know nothing. Every weekend I've been here, you've ordered people around, watching them wait on you hand and foot, complained about not having any money, gossiped about every bad boob job in town, and have yet to be pleasant to anyone who stands an inch beneath you." He goes to hammer again but turns around once more and says, "And the heels you just *had* to wear out to the pool ripped a fucking hole in my nail gun hose, giving me no other option than to nail these boards by hand, adding on time I can't afford. So, Princess, excuse me for upsetting you, but I'm sticking with the nickname. It fits you to a T. Oh, and just so you know, sandals. Sandals are the proper footwear you should be wearing around the pool." He rolls his eyes, turns around, and starts hammering another nail into the siding of the pool house.

How dare he!

"That's what you think I am? Some whiney brat?"

"If the unnecessary high heel fits, Princess."

Unsure of what to do. I stomp my foot and say, "Well, I'm not." Pretty sure my reaction just solidified his assumption.

"Tantrums don't work on me; try your daddy." He continues to hammer away, his back muscles shimmering with each movement.

"Maybe I will. We'll see what he has to say about this little conversation."

He places another nail against the board and starts hammering. "Wouldn't be shocked if you did. You step on my hose, ruin my chances of getting this project done today, which only prolongs my time here, cutting down on my chance to make more money since I'm getting paid a flat rate, and now you want to get me fired. Sounds about right. Can't take the blame for anything."

No one has ever been so disrespectful to me.

"How was I supposed to know I stepped on your stupid hosey thing?"

"Maybe if you pay attention to people and objects around you, you may have noticed."

"You're a jerk, you know that?" *He has me all wrong, and it is really bothering me that he pictures me as a spoiled, inconsiderate, self-consumed brat. That's not who I am at all.*

"How do you figure? Because the way I see it, you're the jerk." His body fully turns around to face me, challenge in his eyes, maybe a bit of humor at the corner of his lips as he awaits my answer.

Holding my chin high, I say, "Because, instead of having a hissy fit like a petulant child, you could have come over to me and said, 'Miss Westbrook, sorry to bother you, but you seem to have poked a hole in my hose.' But instead you decided to stew over here and then pick on me when I was trying to see if you were okay from your inability to hammer a nail into a piece of wood properly. It's called being an adult."

He studies me, hands on his hips, not showing any kind of reaction. "Being an adult, huh? And you think you're an expert at that?"

"I would say I'm well-versed in the topic."

He nods, his teeth biting down on his lower lip as his eyes flick to where Madison is sitting. "Well-versed, interesting. Tell me, when did adults start eating dinosaur chicken nuggets for lunch?"

Just when I'm about to reply, Madison calls out, "Nuggies are ready, G. Come eat T-Rex's arms with me. Roar!"

I shut my eyes tight, willing for this moment to disappear, maybe praying for the ground to swallow me whole due to Madison's poor timing. The infuriating man says with a smile, "Your *nuggies* are ready, Princess. Don't want them getting cold."

He turns away, ending our conversation by putting earbuds in his ears and picks up his hammer. Apparently I've been dismissed.

I stomp toward my chair and flop down on the side facing Madison, who holds out the plate and a bowl of barbeque sauce. "God, these are so good. I love eating dinosaur."

"You couldn't have waited until I was done talking to him? God, Madison."

"What?" She shrugs and takes a bite of her nugget. "They were going to get cold."

On a frustrated sigh, I snatch a nugget from the plate and pop it in my mouth. What an insufferable, horrible man. How dare he? *He's listened to my conversations?* I don't talk about bad boob jobs. Well, Jessica Hahn's boob job was *very* unfortunate. I do not treat the staff here as if they're beneath me. I know all their names. But he's . . . he's obnoxious. What would he know anyway?

I hate that I had no recourse after he laid into me. I am never tongue-tied. Hopefully—*no, surely*—I'll be able to hold my own better when talking to my dad tonight.

∽

"Did you put together this presentation yourself, Gigi?" my dad asks. He sits back in his black leather and mahogany desk chair, his finger to his chin as he looks through the hard copy of my presentation.

"I did." I try to tamp down my nervous bouncing leg.

"All by yourself?"

"Yes." The annoyance in my voice is hard to control. What's so hard to understand? I designed and put together the presentation myself. I swear my dad thinks I'm still an infant with wobbly legs sometimes.

"Hmm." He rocks in his chair as he studies the plans, giving me no hints as to what he's thinking.

I just finished my twenty-minute presentation for Limerence, my all-in-one bridal boutique business plan. Not skipping a beat, I showed him the demographics in our area and the need for a shop like Limerence, how it would be unique and different from any other bridal shop in the area, even in the state. I gave him my five-year projections, my estimated start-up cost, the information of the storefront I already chose, reasons for the location, and ways he can invest as a partner. I approached the entire presentation like a businesswoman: professional, clear-cut, and to the point. My dad loves talking shop, he loves new ideas, and I played to his business tactics, throwing his strategies right back in his face.

Even though I'm nervous, I know I'm prepared. I know I can answer any question he might toss at me.

"These projections are sound. You were reasonable in your first three years."

"Thank you." For some reason, the urge to curtsey in front of my dad from the compliment is overwhelming.

"Start-up cost seems reasonable as well."

I point to the page he's looking at and say, "And that includes inventory and construction for the store. It's a great space, but it will need some refurbishment."

"Just like every other store out there." He flips to another page. His leg is crossed over his knee as he reads over everything. Excitement starts to boil deep in the pit of my stomach. He likes it; he just has to like it.

"Exactly. But I think with the discount I can get on supplies from one of your companies, I can keep costs low for construction. And collecting inventory, although challenging with my budget, I intend to offer space on consignment for designers until I can afford to purchase vintage dresses myself."

"Mm-hmm." He nods.

"And I will run the store until I can get my feet on the ground. Although, Waverly said she would love to help me with my marketing. I plan to utilize her great eye and photographic skills for social media and advertising."

Waverly is my oldest brother's wife. She and Abraham have been so incredibly supportive of my endeavor, my number-one supporters, actually. Madison runs a close second.

My dad clears his throat and closes the folder. He turns toward me and places my presentation on his desk. "Looks like you've thought of everything."

I nod. "I have. I didn't want to come to you until I had all contingencies covered. I've learned from many before me who've come to you with investment opportunities unprepared."

A small smile of approval passes over his lips. "Good girl."

Trying to hold back my excitement, I sit up straight and say, "What do you think?"

Smiling brightly, my dad folds his hands and lays them on top of his desk. "I think you've put together a solid business plan." My heart flutters in my chest. "You've considered all aspects of the economic terrain." Excitement boils inside me. "Your presentation and numbers are on point, your idea unique." My feet want to tap-dance in joy on his desk. "However..."

Look out, wet blanket incoming.

"You're twenty-six, you're a female Westbrook, and you're ready to start a family. Your priorities lie with your mother, helping with her charity until you're married and can start your own." He reaches for his Rolodex—yes, he still has one—and he thumbs through it until he pulls out a card. "I spoke with Chauncey McAdams, son of Barnabas, Wall Street mogul. He was telling me over a round of golf how he recently cut ties with his girlfriend and was interested to see if you were a good match." My dad starts to write a number on a thick card. "I told him you would be delighted to meet for a drink."

Is he kidding right now? This has to be a joke. First, there is no way some man named Chauncey is real. Second, my dad ignored my presentation then told me Chauncey *cut ties with his girlfriend* and was keen to see if I was suitable?

He tries to hand me the paper with what I'm assuming has Chauncey's number on it, but I don't take it. "Dad, I won't be going on a date. I'm not ready to start a family. I have a few years before I want to think about marriage. I have goals, and I want to accomplish them."

"Yes, having goals is a great attribute of yours, Gigi, but your goals are a little off."

"With all due respect, Daddy, I don't think it's appropriate for you to tell me what my goals are. Shouldn't that be a personal thing?"

"Not when it involves our family." The smile that was once on his face disappears and the stern set in his brows I've come to know very well appears. "You're a Westbrook. There is a standard you're expected to realize. You went to finishing school, you graduated from Northwestern like every other Westbrook, and now you're expected to marry like your sister, start a charity, and give back to the community."

"Why do I have to be married to do that? I can still start a charity, Daddy."

He shakes his head, his eyes cast down, disapproval in the set of his shoulders. "Not when you're trying to run a business that unfortunately might look good on paper but is a lose-lose investment. Low reward, high-risk, zero benefit to society."

And just like that, he sucker-punches me in the heart. One sentence. One sentence completely extinguishes the excitement that had been bustling inside. How can he use so few words yet smash my hopes and dreams completely? *How is it he knows so little about me and what my dreams are?*

With a droplet of hope left, I say, "I'm not asking for money from you, Daddy. You don't have to invest in anything, I'm requesting to have my inheritance released early."

"I worked hard for my kids to have an inheritance, Gigi, and I'm not about to watch you blow it on some pipe dream."

"Blow it? Trying to start a business, trying to become an entrepreneur isn't blowing my money, Daddy. It's following in *your* footsteps. If you want to talk about blowing money, why don't you talk to Spencer who is bleeding cash in the city?"

Spencer just received his inheritance. *He* is having a damn fine time wasting it away on menial things like expensive penthouses, over-the-top dates, and bad investments.

"Spencer is taking chances and learning from every experience he comes across."

"So why can't I take a chance then?"

"Because, it's not your role, Gigi. Your role is to assist your mother with her charities, find a well-respected man who can take care of you financially, and add to the value of our family name through a beautiful smile and a caring hand." *Add value. I can only add value by marrying and being taken care of? How can my father have so little faith in me as a person? How can he see me so . . . needy of being indulged. I'm not. I deserve to be respected . . .*

My teeth grind together, my ears turn hot, and tears of frustration start to fill my eyes. *Do not cry in front of him. Whatever you do, do not show weakness, because then he will never respect you.*

Knowing I have zero chance at winning him over, I hold my head high and stand from my chair, gathering my presentation materials. "Well, thank you for listening." The words feel like tar falling from my mouth. If I learned anything from my dad, it was never show your cards.

"You're welcome, precious." I turn toward his door when he says, "Oh, Gigi, don't forget this." Chauncey's number is extended toward me, trailed by a condescending smile from my father.

Carefully, without snatching the paper out of his hand, avoiding a paper cut to my dad's finger, I take the number and exit his office. In a steady pace, my heels clack across the marble floor and up the curved staircase until I reach my room where I quietly shut the door and sink to the floor. Chauncey's number is crumbled in my hand as defeat settles in my shoulders.

Deep down, that presentation went just as I expected it would —zero interest resulting in zero hope. Twice today, condescending men have *put me in my place*. One a consequential man I love, one an arrogant, *inconsequential* man I loathe. Surely I'm more than that.

What do I do now?

CHAPTER THREE

GEORGIANA

"AJ, go ahead, touch Mirabelle one more time, see what happens," Waverly, my sister-in-law, says to her eight-year-old son.

"I wasn't touching her," he replies.

"Was to," Mirabelle, the four-year-old, replies. "He was pokin' my arm."

"Was not."

"Was to."

"Was not."

"Was—"

"I don't care who was poking who," Waverly roars, looking like a classy version of fed up with pearls clasped around her neck and kitten heels gracing her feet. "There will be no more poking in this house or Daddy is going to start poking, and you're not going to like it." I lift my eyebrow at Waverly.

"Does Daddy poke hard?" Mirabelle asks, clutching her doll to her chest.

"Really hard. Incessantly until you end up screaming." Both kids' eyes go wide before they start to back away slowly out of the living room. "Believe me, Mommy is the only one who can handle Daddy's poking, so I suggest you shake hands and play nicely. Got it?"

They nod their heads just as Abe walks in, scaring both children. They run away and say, "We don't want to see Daddy's poker."

Loosening his tie, he turns to Waverly, "Do I even want to know?"

She giggles, presses a light kiss on his jaw, and shakes her head. "I don't think you do."

"That was horrifying," I cut in. "Everything about that threat was wrong. Mommy is the only one who can handle Daddy's poker? Come on, Waverly."

"What?" She smiles. "It's true."

"Jesus," Abe mutters in laughter and pours himself a snifter of brandy. "Mother of the year."

"Damn straight." She kicks off her heels and pulls off her earrings, which she tosses on the side table.

The moment Abe brought Waverly home to meet the family, I knew we were going to get along. I saw through her fake snob façade, her plastic pearls, and sweater sets and immediately knew she was different than any girl my dad would dream for his eldest son. She's independent, strong, armed with a beautiful mind, and knows how to work my parents into believing she's the picture-perfect wife for my brother; when in fact, she likes to eat a bag of chips in one sitting in her underpants, ride a bull with seven drinks in her system, and belch the alphabet louder than any person I've ever heard. She's real and perfect for my brother, who needs her kind of fun in his pre-planned life.

Their relationship hasn't always been perfect. They've had their dark moments, but being apart was more detrimental than being together, so they made it work. Waverly pulled on the sweater sets, and Abe adjusted to our father's demands . . . mostly.

"Drink?" Abe asks.

"Club soda with a slice of lime?"

"Yup." He nods and then turns to Waverly. "Anything for you, sweetie?"

Waverly looks between the both of us and shakes her head, amusement in her eyes. "Bud Light, none of this fancy drink shit for me. Give me the piss water."

Like I said, I love this girl.

"I know what my lady likes." Abe opens the mini fridge that rests under his bar and cracks open a Bud Light for Waverly. When he hands it to her, she takes a long pull from the can and then smacks her lips together.

"Man, that's good stuff."

Abe takes a seat next to Waverly whose feet are stretched out along the couch. He picks them up, sits down, and then puts them on his lap. He massages one foot while he drinks from his glass. Nodding at me, he asks, "What's new, G? Did you talk to Dad?"

I sigh and take a sip of my drink. "I did."

"From the way you're not beaming with joy, I'm going to say it didn't go well."

I shake my head. "It didn't."

"What did you talk about?" Waverly asks, looking slightly pissed that she's not in the know.

Abe turns to Waverly and squeezes her knee. "G was looking to score some dough off the old man."

"Oh?" Waverly lifts an eyebrow in my direction. "Wanting to get into the drug circle or something?"

"Yes," I deadpan. "I asked my rich, debutante of a father for money to start my own underground drug ring."

"And he said no? Blasphemy!" Waverly throws a hand in the air, a smile on her face.

"She wanted him to invest in her idea." Abe brings the conversation back to reality.

"Not invest, but give me access to my trust fund early." Would it have been nice for my dad to invest in his daughter's idea? Yeah, that would have been great, but I *believed* asking for my trust fund may have been an easier hill to climb. Clearly I was wrong.

"For what? Your bridal shop idea?" Waverly asks after she takes another sip of her beer.

"Yeah." I sit back in my seat and recount the conversation I had with my sexist father. "I had everything planned out to the nines. I didn't let one stone go unturned. I had graphs, charts, predictions, and every cent divided out so no money was wasted. I put my heart and soul into that presentation, and you know what?" I look up to the ceiling, remembering the look of pride on my father's face. "He was freaking proud of me. I could see it in his eyes; he was scoring my presentation. He asked questions and I answered them without skipping a beat."

Abe points his drink at me and says, "I looked over your presentation; it was one of the best I've ever seen."

"And I bet if you were the one who presented it, Dad would be asking how many checks he could write."

Waverly huffs and takes another sip of her drink. "I love you, Abe, but your father is a dick."

"He is," Abe agrees.

"Needless to say, he said no; he told me my place wasn't in the entrepreneur field but rather looking for a husband who can support me."

"He did not," Waverly protests.

I nod. I sip my club soda, wishing I asked for something a little stronger. "He did. He even gave me the number of Chauncey, his friend's son."

Waverly sits up now and stares me dead in the eyes. "Chauncey McAdams?" I nod and she rolls her eyes. "Oh my God, please tell me you didn't take his number."

"Don't worry, I won't be calling him. I'm not interested in any kind of relationship right now, especially with a guy my dad recommends."

"Yeah, I wouldn't want you dating any of those dickheads. They're just going to treat you like some kind of trophy wife, and you're so much more than that." I love that I have Waverly in my corner. *If only my dad saw me the same way.* I shouldn't have to grow a penis in order for him to agree to my business.

"Thanks," I sigh. "So, I guess that's the end of that."

"You can always wait until you turn twenty-eight and get your trust fund," Waverly suggests.

"I could, but there is no way the location I picked out would still be available. I don't think I'll ever find another storefront like that at such a good bargain. It's hopeless."

Abe clears his throat and leans forward. "It might not be hopeless."

I eye him. "What do you mean?"

"What if I gave you the money?"

Hope springs through my veins. "Are you serious?"

He nods. "I looked over your presentation, G. It was legit. You have a great business plan, and if you keep your start-up costs low like you planned, you could easily make this a thriving business in the first year. I would be happy to invest. Proud actually."

I lean forward in my chair and rest my drink on the coffee table. "You mean it, you would invest in my business, in me?"

"He would be a dumbass not to," Waverly cuts in. "Because if he didn't, he would be facing a sad few months of celibacy, and not by his choice."

"Nice to know where your head's at, sweetie."

Waverly pats his leg. "Just reminding you who wears the pants in this relationship."

I bite my bottom lip and glance at my brother who is nothing but happy. He really chose well when he chose Waverly. "It's five hundred thousand dollars, Abe."

"Psh, chump change," Waverly says, waving her hand. "Want it in cash?"

"Why don't you sit back and drink your beer, sweetie. Five hundred thousand in cash is not something we're going to do." Abe turns to me. "I can do a check. We can go down to the bank tomorrow and open a business account. It will be easier to do a quick transfer from my account to yours."

"This is real? You're really going to do this?"

Abe smiles brightly at me. "One hundred percent, G. I . . . no . . . *we* believe in you and don't want you to end up like our sister. You have ambition, and I don't want anyone to extinguish that, even our dad. You've paid your dues with Mom's charity. It's time you do what you want to do."

"Oh my God." Tears well up in my eyes. "I love you so much." I fling myself at him and wrap my arms around his body. "You're my favorite brother."

"There really is no contest, but thanks."

"I can't believe this. I'm going to make this happen. It's real."

"It is." Abe laughs but then straightens up and whispers, "Just don't tell Dad I'm the one who gave you the money."

Waverly snorts and mutters, "Fucking pansy."

"I'm going to give him the money back."

"What?" Madison sits up on the lounge chair in protest. "Why the hell would you do that?"

We've been sunbathing for the past half hour, chatting about the shop and the inventory I can stock up on when I received yet another email from a construction company saying they can't work with me.

You're going to be shocked. Word spread quickly that I found an investor and was looking for a construction company to help remodel the shop, and guess what? Daddy dearest found out. Being the amazing father he is—*hear the sarcasm*—he sent a warning to all construction companies in a one-hundred-mile radius that they mustn't accept a job request from me, and given he owns every lumberyard and concrete business in the area, no one would dare mess with their relationship. Leaving me with absolutely no one to work with.

"Because, no one will work with me. My dad has a monopoly in construction around here." *That* thought never crossed my mind.

"You're telling me you can't find one single person to do your remodeling?"

"No one." I faceplant into my lounge chair, hating every ounce of my life right now.

Madison is silent for a second as she sips on her drink. "What if we did it? I mean, how hard could it be?"

That makes me laugh—a little like a crazy person—but it makes me laugh nonetheless. "Madison, we know nothing about building shelves, let alone how to remodel. I'm sure if we attempted painting, we would mess it up somehow. Have you ever even looked at a hammer or tape measure before?"

"Uh yeah, I look at them all the time when that hot construction guy is using them. Where is he by the way? Shouldn't he be here by now?"

I look around the backyard but see no sign of him. I shrug. "I have no clue. Maybe he's done."

Madison points at the pool house. "The siding is half done. I don't think he's finished." She pauses and then lifts her head, her face looking maniacal. "Oh my God, hire the hot guy." *It's clear it's time for an intervention. Madison has been out in the sun too long.*

"You mean the hot guy who hates me because I poked a hole in his hose? Yeah, because I'm sure he's really going to want to work with me. Anyway, I think he works for Julius Parsnip Constructions. My dad is good friends with Julius, so there is no way hot guy will want to cross paths with that."

"You never know, maybe he's a rebel."

I think about it for a brief second when the side gate slams shut and hot guy comes stalking through the yard with a very unpleasant look on his face.

"Speak of the devil." Madison pokes me with her sunglasses to take hot guy in. "Go ask him."

Hot guy starts to pick up where he left off, looking aggressive in his every movement.

"I'm not going to ask him. He clearly is not in a good mood, and I'm pretty sure he's going to say no."

"You don't know that."

I look over at hot guy and then back at Madison. "I'm almost one hundred percent positive it's going to be a no."

"Ugh, where did your balls go?" Waving at hot guy, she says, "Yoo-hoo, hot guy, will you come over here?"

Under my breath, I yell at her, "What the hell are you doing?"

She whispers back, "Making things happen for you." She shouts again. "Hot guy, yoo-hoo, over here."

He turns toward us and says, "It's Racer, and I don't have time for your fucking games."

Racer. How can that name make every vein in my body tingle? And why does today's attitude turn me on? There is something seriously wrong with me.

Leaning toward Madison, I say, "Told you. He's not the guy. Don't bother him."

"Racer, come here. Come have a chat." Apparently Madison has other ideas.

He stares us both down, reaches into his pocket, and pulls out earbuds. Without breaking eye contact, he pops them in his ears, turns on his music, then turns around and starts working again.

"Well," Madison huffs. "He's rude."

"Did you not catch that from the way he first spoke to us? I told you he wasn't the guy."

"You don't know that. He might be the guy, he's just going to be a dick about it." Madison picks up a leftover orange on our tray of food, cocks her arm back, and throws it at Racer, missing completely but breaking the fruit on the siding he's working on. His shoulders tense from the surprise citrus. He slowly turns toward us where he finds Madison pointing a finger at me.

I swat her finger away and motion to Racer that I was not the thrower of the fruit, but it doesn't seem to work. He stalks toward us, anger in his eyes and rippling muscles in his chest about to bulge past the thin white cotton tee he's wearing. *Good Lord, the man is sexy.*

When he reaches our chaise lounges, he places his hands on his hips and says, "What the hell do you want? Just want to fuck around with the hired help? Have nothing better to do?"

"No." Madison holds her head high. "We actually have a question for you. If you weren't so rude and moody and just came over when we asked, Georgiana wouldn't have had to throw fruit at you."

"I did not throw the fruit. Madison did," I say weakly in an effort to defend myself. Racer eyes me for a brief moment and then turns back toward Madison.

"What's your question? I'm behind on my work, and I have Mr. Westbrook breathing down my neck to get it done today, I don't have time for this bullshit. The last thing I need is for his daughter and her spoiled friend to throw food at me because you have nothing better to do in your privileged life."

"That's not fair," I reply, sitting a little taller in my seat. "You can't make assumptions like that. You don't know us. We might have plenty to do, and you have no idea." It's a lie; I have nothing to do. Absolutely. NOTHING! It's one of the main reasons I want my shop so bad. I want to be responsible for creating happiness and purpose in my life, not sitting back waiting for someone to give me those things.

Racer raises an eyebrow at me. "You're right, you could have a lot on your plate. Tell me, how long do you think you're going to try to tan today? Is there a required amount of time each day?" He crosses his arms over his expansive chest. "I'm not well-versed on lounging, especially when it seems a necessity on your to-do list."

God, he's an asshole.

"I was thinking at least two hours," Madison responds while looking at her nails. "G, what about you?"

I hold back the knife-hand I want to deliver to my friend's throat. I love her, but Christ! "I have . . . things I have to plan." This causes Racer to snort and shake his head.

"Good to know, princess." He slips his hands in his pockets, his triceps flexing in the process. *Stop noticing his body, G. Stop. Noticing.*

"I don't want to hold you two up from your busy schedules, so I'm going to get back to work."

He turns to walk away, and I don't stop him. He is SO not the guy for me.

"Wait, you didn't hear how you can make more money."

"Madison," I groan quietly. "Let it go."

"Not interested," he calls out, putting his earbuds back in his ears, blocking us out from his little world.

"Just drop it, okay?" I beg of my friend. "He probably wouldn't do it anyway because he's working with my dad. I'm sure he's heard about the ban on any project with Georgiana Westbrook."

Madison turns toward me and lifts her glasses off her face. She holds them on her lap and gets serious. "You're just done then? You're not going to try to make this happen. You have the money, G. This is just a little roadblock. Maybe we can do it ourselves."

"Madison, I love you, but we can't do this ourselves."

"YouTube is a powerful thing." She winks at me.

"Not that powerful." I shake my head at my friend's idea, even though I'm so desperate, I might start making friends with all the carpenters on YouTube.

"Never know until you try. The good things are worth trying for, babe." She gets up and walks toward the house, empty drink in hand, leaving me to seriously think about her idea. *Could we? There are DIY YouTube videos on just about everything...*

CHAPTER FOUR

RACER

Fucking flying oranges. You would think one would have been enough. No. Princess's friend chucked two more in my direction just to remind me she was keeping her eye on me. How do I know this? Because, when Princess was in the house, her friend came up to me and made it known I was missing out on a huge opportunity to make some money and then slipped her phone number in my pocket. She then smiled and told me to call her when I didn't have my head "sandwiched between my testicles" anymore. *And here it is.* This *is the younger, less experienced version of every Mrs. Sage I've spent my* spare *time with. It's ingrained.*

Being that I just finished the pool house for Mr. Westbrook and was jilted out of one thousand dollars, thanks to being set back in my timeline by a holey hose, I refuse to do business with another Westbrook.

Fuck, I needed that thousand dollars.

The pile of bills I face every damn month is relentless. Sometimes I wonder if it's all worth it. I work day in and day out to preserve memories. And when I'm doubtful, when I'm tired as shit and ready to throw in the towel, I look around the house my dad and I built together and am reminded why. I'm busting my ass creating calluses on my blue-collar hands. I'm overusing my body, putting miles upon miles of wear and tear on my bones. But it's for him. He gave me everything from a sensible work ethic, to a caring soul and a humorous outlook on life. He taught me right from wrong, to respect others, and the responsibilities of being a good man.

"Christ, Dad," I mutter, shuffling through a new wave of bills. "How the hell am I going to pay all of this?"

I rub my forehead, my eyes going blurry from all the numbers staring back up at me while my mind runs a mile a minute. I look around my dwellings, the bare bones of the house remind me of all I've lost and sacrificed. I was able to keep a few pieces of furniture from what Dad left behind, but everything else I had to sell out of pure desperation. I had to say goodbye to his 1948 electric-blue Chevy half-ton truck he used to drive around in. I sold the rolltop desk he used to write his short stories on. And the jelly cabinet we refinished together? I sat on the kitchen counter and watched two men wheel it out of my life.

Now, I'm left with his ratty old recliner as the only piece of furniture in the living room, the small kitchenette table that seats four, and my bed. It works, but looking around under the dim light of the dining area, I realize this is not where I pictured my life at twenty-six: stressing about bills, a mortgage, and whether or not I can set aside the fucking cheap-ass bologna sandwich I have every goddamn day and instead splurge for a slice of pizza.

There is a knock at my door, pulling my mind away from the numbers in front of me.

I make my way to the entryway, not bothering to put a shirt on. It's summer in Upstate New York and humid as fuck. Given the bills, I don't bother with air conditioning, making the summers unbearable at times.

When I open the door, I'm greeted by my two my best friends, holding a twelve-pack of beer and three boxes of pizza. Damn, I could kiss them right now because if it wasn't for them, I would be eating saltine crackers and green olives for dinner, the only things left in my fridge.

"I want to put my tongue in your mouth so bad right now," I say while I grab the pizzas.

Smalls and Tucker don't even bat an eyelash as they follow me into the house, but once they step inside, they take a step back out.

"Dude, it's fucking hot in here."

"Yeah, I know. It's why I'm barely dressed, and I've been sucking on ice all night."

"Open a damn window," Smalls says, taking a step inside and walking around the house, flinging windows open. "The air is cooling down, use that to your advantage."

Not bothering to help him, I flip open the pizza box, snag a slice and take a huge bite, letting the grease and cheese swirl around in my mouth. Shit, that tastes good. My boisterous and hungry stomach is grateful.

"Why don't we eat outside?" Tucker suggests, still standing outside with beer in hand. They're both wearing shorts and T-shirts, but they're men. The shirts will go soon enough.

"Where do you plan on sitting outside? On the grass? Not sure I even have a blanket I could lay down for you."

Tucker shifts away from the door and calls out, "I'm putting down the tailgate on my truck. It's better than sitting in your humid house and eating ice chips like a pregnant woman in labor."

"He has a point." Before I can protest, Smalls grabs the boxes of pizzas and heads to the truck where Tucker is already setting everything up.

Reluctantly, I slip on a pair of flip-flops and follow them outside, but the moment I take in the cool night air, I realize they're right. It's much nicer out now than it was earlier. God, I'm stupid. We built this house with windows on both sides of the house to allow the summer afternoon breeze to cool it down. How have I not remembered that before now?

I hop up on the truck, pizza slice still in hand and ask, "What's with the dinner surprise?"

Neither of the guys say anything. Instead, they sit back in the truck bed and pop open some beers and start to take down a slice of pizza themselves.

"Is this a pity visit?" I ask. Both Tucker and Smalls know my situation, they've spotted me a few bucks when I've needed it, so it's no surprise to me if they came here tonight out of pity. It wouldn't be the first time, and I'm positive it won't be the last. *Wouldn't have made it this far without 'em.*

"Thought you might want a change in cuisine," Tucker finally answers. "Those bologna sandwiches are looking pretty stale, and I'm not the one who eats them."

I shrug. "White bread and bologna is pretty cheap, man. You get used to it."

"At least have peanut butter and jelly." Smalls chuckles. "Switch it up, man. Do you know the possibilities you can build with peanut butter and jelly, all the different varieties you can create? It would keep you busy for days."

"You could make a chart of all your different flavor combinations," Tucker adds. "That seems like a fan-fucking-tastic Saturday evening."

"Make sure you color-code it."

"I'm not a savage," I say. "If I made a peanut butter and jelly chart of course I would color-code it. I might be broke as shit, but I'm not stupid."

From the mention of my money situation, Smalls and Tucker tense uncomfortably and shift in their seats.

"So is it bad again?" Tucker asks.

I take a long swig of my beer and recollect the stack of bills resting on my table. I nod.

"What happened to the Westbrook job? I thought that was going to give you a little breathing room," Smalls says, looking concerned for me.

I sigh and look out toward the woods that flank the back of my house, providing the kind of privacy my father always craved, the kind of privacy I myself crave now as well. There's something so serene about drinking a cup of coffee in the morning and looking out your kitchen window to see nothing but nature surrounding you. It's one of the reasons why my dad chose this location.

"The Westbrook job was supposed to give me a little breathing room. That was until I didn't finish on time and for every hour I was past my timeline, Mr. Westbrook deducted two hundred dollars. Five hours later, I was out a thousand."

"Are you fucking serious?" Tucker asks, sitting up now, a pinch in his brow.

"Yeah. Apparently it was in the contract I signed." I roll my eyes. "Last time I sign a contract for a side job." I run my hand through my hair out of frustration. "I saw the price tag on the job, and I signed immediately without even reading it. When I went to talk to him about when I planned on finishing, he said it was fine for me to take my time; he'd just dock it from my pay. I *slightly* blew up on him, and that's when he pointed out the stipulation in the contract. I spent the rest of the day pissed off as hell while fruit was being thrown at me."

"Fruit?" Smalls asks.

I lean against the truck and shake my head while my beer dangles in my hand. "Westbrook's daughter and her friend found great pleasure in fucking around with me when I was working. Talk about a spoiled life. Those two, all they did was tan, eat chicken nuggets, and drink alcoholic beverages served by their maid."

"Chicken nuggets are the shit." Smalls sips his beer. "I have to eat them with honey mustard though."

"Nah, man. Barbeque all the way," Tucker interjects. "What about you, Racer? Honey mustard or barbeque?"

Not minding the rabbit trail, I say, "Neither. I like sweet and sour sauce."

"Ah, sweet and sour," Smalls groans. "I change my mind. I like sweet and sour too."

"What happened to *I have to eat nuggets with honey mustard?*" Tucker asks, a smirk on his lips.

Smalls shrugs. "I lied."

"Idiot," Tucker mutters and then points his beer at me. "So, flying fruit, huh? Did you toss it back?"

"No. I tried to avoid engaging with them, given the dollars going down the drain every hour."

"Sounds like they wanted a piece of your dick, man," Smalls points out.

I shake my head. "Nah, they wanted to offer me some way to make money." Smalls and Tucker chuckle, harder than I would expect them to. "What?" Irritation starts to grow inside me.

Smalls and Tucker exchange knowing looks. "Dude, they totally wanted you to strip for them."

"What? No way." I shake my head and finish my beer only to reach for another.

"Tell me this, were you shirtless?" Smalls asks. I nod.

"Were you wearing your tool belt?" Tucker adds.

"Of course."

"And they were trying to get your attention to offer you money?" Smalls asks, the wheels in his head turning.

"Yeah, they had some kind of job for me . . . what are you trying to say?"

Together, in unison, Smalls and Tucker throw their heads back and start to laugh, their voices echoing across the woods that surround my house. Fireflies blink in behind them, crickets chirp in the near distance, and my irritation skyrockets to a new level.

"Don't be douchebags, just fucking tell me what's so funny."

Smalls shakes his head in disbelief and drinks from his beer while Tucker clears his throat. "Racer, they want you to strip for them."

"Strip for them?" My brows pinch together. "No fucking way."

Tucker nods. "All the signs are there. When you're working, they're tanning. They've been trying to get your attention, and they have a way for you to earn money. Why would two rich girls have any other reason to offer you a chance at making money?"

I think about Tucker's question for a second. What would they want to do with me? Princess's friend wasn't specific as to what the job was; in fact, she was actually quite evasive about it. Shit . . . they want me to strip.

I run my hand over my face. "Jesus."

Laughter erupts again, this time, louder than before. Princess doesn't seem like the stripper-hiring type, although, given her status and her age, she's probably right in the middle of wedding hell where all her friends are getting married. And since it's summer in Upstate New York, the volume of weddings is higher. Is she in charge of a bachelorette party with her friend and looking for someone to bring the entertainment? I roll my eyes and down half of my bottle. At this rate, I won't be sharing the beer with my friends.

When their laughter calms down, Tucker picks up another slice of pizza and asks, "So, are you going to do it?"

"Do what? Strip?" Tucker nods and chews at the same time. "Are you kidding me? I would never do that."

"This coming from the man who likes to wear thongs for old women while building shelves."

"That was one fucking time. She was discreet and . . ." I take a deep breath and try to calm myself. "I'm not going to fucking strip for some rich bitches."

"How is stripping for a bunch of sweater sets different than wearing a thong for an old woman? I would think stripping would be better; at least you're stripping for someone your age." Typical Smalls—tries to make some kind of logic out of the situation.

"It's just . . . different. Okay? I'm not into making an ass out of myself."

Tucker smiles over his beer and says, "Too late for that, man."

S tripper.
No way in hell would I do that.

I scratch my chest as I sit up in bed, the sun beating down on the floor in front of me. It's past ten on a Sunday, one of the first Sundays I don't have a job to do. Most people would welcome the time off, but not having anything to do causes me to panic. I haven't had any new leads, and I'm starting to worry. Tucker can only schedule me for so many hours and with nothing to do on the weekends, my stressing over my lagging bank account increases. I *hate* having to work so much and see so little shift in that fucking balance. There has got to be more I can do.

Standing, I stretch and glance at the mirror in my bedroom, taking in my physique. I have to admit . . . it's totally stripper material.

Jesus.

Who says their body is stripper material?

A semi-desperate man considering lowering his standards for a dollar, that's who.

Now standing in front of the mirror, I run my hand down my stomach and watch as every muscle in my chest, stomach, and arm flexes. Hell, I could *possibly* do this.

Completely nude, I play a song on my phone and listen to the beat. I start with bobbing my head to the bass. "Good jam," I mutter, looking around the room as If I'm expecting someone to pop in and catch me red-handed.

Knowing the coast is clear, I widen my stance and look in the mirror as I start to do a move that resembles Danny Zucko while singing Grease Lightning. Quickly I notice what a tool I look like so I stop waving my arm about.

"That's not hot," I mutter and grab the back of my head.

Looking down at my semi-hard dick, I start to thrust my hips forward, watching my dick flop forward. The image makes me chuckle, so I thrust harder because, why not? I'm a guy and if I can flip my dick around, I will.

Hands on hips now, I stare into the mirror and thrust harder, willy flying about.

"Oh yeah, feast your eyes on that dick, ladies."

I run my hands up my body and link them behind my neck where I pump my elbows in and out and start to hop around the room, cock leading the charge. I could *so* do this.

Cock to the face.

Cock to the leg.

Cock against the arm.

Fucking cock everywhere.

"Such a beast," I say, really feeling the music now.

I thrust so hard that my dick starts to slap against my leg, my stomach, and . . .

"Fuuuuuuuckkk."

Cock and balls to the bedpost.

I crumple to the floor, cupping my moneymaker, and will the bile in my throat to settle as I catch my breath. Note to self: when feeling the music and thrusting hard, keep eyes open. At *all* times.

As I lie on the floor, hoping I can still have children one day, I think about my situation. Would stripping really be that bad? Is a stripper really what they want? I can be way off base here. They could just want someone to chat to about the opposite sex . . .

Who am I kidding?

If I wasn't so desperate, I wouldn't even consider it, but with the pressure of heavy debt at the forefront of my mind, I feel as though I don't really have a choice.

Just like my dad didn't. Medical bills from his Parkinson treatments were barely covered by insurance. And personal loans my dad took out to help pay off medical bills. Thanks to property taxes, the mortgage bills are crippling. But *he* didn't have a choice. We were fighting for him. For quality of life.

Once I regain feeling in my legs, I wiggle my way to my phone and my wallet that rests on my nightstand. I pull out the number Princess's friend gave me. Christ, am I really going to do this?

I roll onto my back and look up at the ceiling that is covered in beautiful stained wood planks. It was a touch my father was so proud to add. He believed in making every part of the house special, including the ceilings.

I squeeze my eyes tight and take a deep breath. I will do just about anything to keep this house, even if it means stripping for a bunch of rich women.

Reluctantly, I dial the number and turn the phone on speaker. It takes three rings before someone picks up.

"Hello?" I know instantly that it's Princess's friend. Her voice is beyond recognizable, as it's the kind of voice that sends a shiver down your spine, a memorably shrill one for sure.

"Uh, hey. This is Racer McKay. I redid the pool house for Mr. Westbrook."

"Racer, how nice to hear from you. Have you changed your mind?"

I swallow hard and nod even though she can't see me. "Yeah. I'm interested in your job."

"Fantastic. Can you come over now?"

"Now?" I look out the window, it's daylight. Err . . . aren't bachelorette parties at night?

"Yeah, now. Are you busy?"

"No," I answer, wishing I had an excuse I could fall back on even though I'm the one who called her.

"Great. I'll text you the address."

"Uh, yeah, sure. I just need to take a shower first."

"No need," she says casually. "You're just going to get sweaty all over again."

Jesus. "Understandable, but no one likes dirty dick in their face, so I'll take a quick shower."

"Dirty dick? That's a term I've never heard, although I've never hired someone like you before so I guess this is a learning experience."

Yeah, for the both of us.

"All right, well I'll be quick." I clear my throat and say, "Anything I need to bring? Props . . . music?"

"Props." She giggles. "Funny. We have music. Just bring your tool belt and body. See you in a bit. Oh and Georgiana doesn't know, it's a surprise."

"Ah, got it. Not a problem."

I hang up and stare at my phone for a second. Georgiana doesn't know? Does that mean she's the one I'll be dancing for? I sure as hell hope not. I'm already on rocky terrain where she's concerned; I can't imagine she would want me tickling her chin with my dick.

Shaking my head, I walk to my bathroom and start the shower. I have no doubt that my dad is laughing his ass off right about now. Yup, no doubt in my mind.

CHAPTER FIVE

GEORGIANA

"This was a bad plan." I still the rolling brush and look at the wall. "I mean, a really bad plan, you can still see the wallpaper."

Next to me, Madison chews her bubblegum and puts her hand on her hip as she studies the accent wall we've painted twice now.

"Hmm, should we have primed some more? Mr. Paint Stick on YouTube said we only had to prime once."

"Yeah, but he mentioned nothing about wallpaper. I knew we should have looked up painting over wallpaper."

"What's the difference?"

I point to the wall that is gloppy and gross. "Clearly there is a huge difference. This doesn't look like any of the walls in our houses."

"Because we don't have wallpaper."

"Exactly!" I sigh and put my paint roller in the pan of paint before I sit on the floor and put my head in my hands. "What the hell am I doing? I can't do these renovations on my own. I need to build cabinetry, break down walls—"

"We started on the wall," Madison points out.

I glance at the wall we tried to take down and inwardly groan. "Poking holes in the wall with the heels of our Manolo Blahniks doesn't count, Madison."

"It was working until you made us stop."

"Because you almost sparked a fire from hitting some kind of electrical thing on the inside of the wall. I think we were supposed to turn off all the power before we started banging walls."

"Hmm." Madison looks thoughtfully up at the ceiling. "You know, that sounds about right." She shrugs. "So we skipped a step. No biggie."

"Madison, that was a huge step. We could have gotten hurt or burned the whole place to the ground."

She pops a bubble and motions to the floor. "At least we know there isn't hardwood floor under the tile. We can rest easy."

I scan the floors we ripped up. There are patches of torn tile everywhere from where Madison wanted to "keep checking" for hardwood flooring. This is going to cost so much money.

"Yeah, now it looks like crap."

"I told you, just get some Gorilla Glue and patch it back up. Simple."

"And what do you suggest we do about that?" I ask, pointing to the wall behind me that we attempted to hang shiplap but failed miserably.

"I will admit that was a miss on our end. Apparently one of those stud finder things they talked about in the video was important. Who knew wood could be so heavy?"

Wood is very heavy, it's evident in the way the nails slid right out of the dry wall and made giant divots all along the side of the wall. Yup, it's a freaking disaster zone in here.

"I'm in way over my head, Madison. I should have never done this. I should have never taken your advice. What was I thinking?"

"Uh, that your best friend is a genius. Come on, look around." She spreads her arms and twirls. "You have your own shop. That's exciting." I know Madison is trying to be positive, but her cheery attitude is kind of hurting right now. How can she so easily dismiss something that means the world to me? How can she be so nonchalant?

I scan the room but can't feel any excitement. All I feel is nausea. Pure nausea over the situation I got myself into. I'm five hundred thousand dollars in debt, I've absolutely destroyed my store, and the only guidance I have are socially awkward men on YouTube trying to put in their two cents about home renovation.

Good job, Georgiana. Thumbs up.

I shake my head, failure taking over every positive thought I had about this experience. I really should have listened to my dad. Although, I wouldn't be in this mess if he didn't cock block me from all the construction companies within a one-hundred-mile radius.

"This is pointless. I should just throw in—"

Knock, knock.

If that is my dad, he'll take one look at the mess I've made and the look on his face will be anything but nonchalant. *I can't face that sort of humiliation.* But before nasty thoughts of my dad can take over, Madison claps her hands and runs to answer it. What is going on? I sit up a little and peek my head around the corner.

"You're here just in time. Come in," Madison says. "Are you ready to get dirty?"

"Uh, yeah, sure," a deep, familiar voice answers. Why do I know that voice? "I've never done this before though. So go easy on me."

"Oh I'm sure you're going to be fine given all your experience. And with those muscles I'm sure you can't go wrong."

"Okay," the man says timidly. "Do you have music? I brought my tool belt. Want me to put it on?"

"Yeah, whatever you're comfortable with. Is music necessary?"

"Uh, I mean, it would be kind of weird without it."

"Okay. Why don't you just play something you're comfortable with on your phone."

"No requests?" The man sounds nervous. Why would he be

nervous and why are they talking about music? I stand and brush off my bottom.

"I'm good with whatever. Hey, G, come out here, I have a surprise for you."

I turn the corner to see a man with his back toward me, his head bent forward. I know that backside, that tool belt . . .

Racer?

What's he doing here?

"Uptown Funk" by Bruno Mars starts to play, echoing against the bare walls of my construction nightmare. With his back toward us, he starts to snap with the music and shake his ass from side to side. I look at Madison who exchanges a glance with me and shrugs. With the beat, he spins around, grips the bottom of his shirt and starts to shake his body slowly as he peels his shirt up and over his head, showing off his very impressive body.

"Whaaaat . . . is happening?" I whisper to myself as Racer runs his hands up and down his stomach, his head cast down.

Looking at Madison again, she seems to be entranced as she stares straight ahead and claps to the music, encouraging Racer to continue with whatever he is doing.

Is this some kind of weird congratulations on your new store from Madison? It's unnecessary if that's the case. A new vase or flowers would have been just fine.

But more importantly, does my dad's construction worker moonlight as a stripper? My God, he does have the body for it.

Still, this is weird.

And it just gets weirder as Racer unbuckles his pants, showing off a bright red scrap of underwear. Oh God, is he going to take off his jeans? Do I want him to take off his jeans?

God, I kind of do, even though he's a mean bastard. But he has such a beautiful body.

"Take it off, take it off!" Madison chants, now reaching into her purse where she starts throwing coins, lipstick, and pieces of gum at him. She's not a cash girl, never has been.

With his hands now tucked behind his neck, he starts to

swivel his hips, making figure eights and thrusting in our direction. With each thrust, his jeans lower until they are pooling around his knees, revealing one hell of a well-packed pair of underwear.

"Yes! Look at that penis," Madison screeches. "Best carpenter ever. Who knew we would get a show with the job."

Racer's eyes snap to Madison where he pauses his thrusting and stands tall, pants still around his knees, a pinch to his brow. He fumbles with his phone before pausing the music and saying, "Carpenter? What are you talking about?"

"Yeah, what are you talking about?" I ask.

Madison glances between us, a guilty look on her face. She bites her fingernail and says, "I hired Racer to help out with the construction of the shop. I knew you wouldn't ask him, so I did it for you."

Pulling up his pants now and buckling them quickly, he asks, "You hired me to do construction?"

"Yeah, what did you think I was hiring you for?"

He grips his forehead in disbelief. "I thought you were hiring me to strip. Christ."

"Well, you did a good job." Madison gives him a slow clap. "I only have one tidbit of critique. Red isn't your color. I would stick with a black man thong."

"You have got to be fucking kidding me," Racer huffs, anger exuding him as he bends down and picks up his shirt. It almost looks like he's about to rip it in half as he puts it back on. Once his head pops through, he sends me the death glare of all death glares. "Did you have a part in all of this?"

"No," I say in desperation.

"A stripper." Madison chuckles, which makes Racer spit daggers at me. Crap. "Is that why you said something about dirty dicks in someone's face over the phone?"

"Yeah." He removes his tool belt. Anger controls his every move. "What the hell did you think I was talking about?"

"I don't know. I thought it was some weird construction term."

Madison shrugs, really not seeming to care about the mix-up. He looks humiliated, and I kind of feel sorry for him.

Shaking his head, he walks toward the door and says, "You could have stopped me before I started to unbuckle my pants." Looking at me as if all of this is my fault, he continues, "That's fucked up, Georgiana." He shakes his head, his eyes cast down, and in a sad voice, he buries his dagger into my chest. "Just another way you rich folk prey on those lesser than you." He tosses two fingers in the air. "I don't need this shit. I'm not that desperate."

The door slams shut, the loud sound reminding me of my problem. I have a shop with no one to help make it the way I want it to.

"He's so sensitive," Madison says as she picks up the paint roller and starts painting the wall again. "Can't take a little criticism on his underwear color." Oblivious, completely and totally oblivious.

"That's not what he was mad about, Madison," I groan. I waver between chasing after him and letting him go. A part of me knows I'll have to beg him to come back if I chase after him, and I'm not sure my pride can take that kind of hit. And yet, it seems like this irritated and volatile man is my last hope.

Crap.

Gah, am I seriously considering this?

"Dance, jump on it, if you sexy then flaunt it," Madison sings, the tune "Uptown Funk" still stuck in her head as she rolls the paint onto the wallpaper and dances in her own little bubble.

Rolling my eyes, I take a deep breath and run out the front door. I guess I am going to do this. What do I really have to lose? Pride? That was shot out the window when I started using my heels to bust open a wall.

I scan the main street looking for a fuming man and see an old rusted-out truck to the side, and Racer is stepping into. Bingo. Being safe, I look both ways before crossing the street, and reach his truck just as he slams the door shut. Lucky for me, his window is down.

"Wait." I grip the side of his window, startling him ever so slightly.

When he sees me, he lets out a long breath. "Come to boast? Throw some more gum at me?"

"Madison was tossing the gum, not me." *Really, Georgiana? Could you make the situation more awkward?*

"Whatever." He starts his truck and puts it in drive, but I hang onto the side of the window.

"Wait, you can't drive off with me hanging on to your window."

"Just watch." He looks out the side and starts to roll forward.

I screech and grip tighter. "Please don't drag me into traffic. Hear me out."

Leaning back in his seat, his eyes fixed ahead, he says, "Why?"

"That wasn't my idea back there. I had no idea you were coming or why you were coming to the shop in the first place."

"And yet, you still let me embarrass myself. Let me guess, you got it on camera and will be emailing it to all your friends to laugh over while you munch down on your . . . shrimp cocktail or whatever bullshit food you eat."

Growing more and more irritated over his assumptions about me, I fling open his door so he can't drive off. "You're an asshole, you know that?"

Now he looks me straight in the eyes and says, "Yeah, I know. If that's all you have to say, then I'm going to take off."

I should let him go. We already have a terrible rapport, and it would make for a bad working environment, but for some reason, I'm clinging to him. I can't seem to tear myself away. Maybe because the look in his eyes; I can see he's just as desperate as me. Or maybe because right about now, I would offer up my left boob for any kind of help. I hate to admit it, but I need him. I only hope that he needs me too.

"Work for me," I blurt out before I can change my mind.

"Work for you?" He shakes his head. "Sorry, Princess, but I'm not really in the stripper business."

"Not as a stripper." I exhale. "As my contractor."

"Your contractor?" He lifts his brow and puts his truck in park. He turns toward me, and it's hard not to notice how his broad shoulders take up the entire space of his cab. "What on earth could *you* need *me* to build?" And it's not the question he asks, but the patronizing tone in his voice. I get enough of that from my father.

Such a freaking asshole. I'm seconds from telling him to shove everything up his pee hole, but I bite my tongue and continue to move forward with my request.

"No. I need a contractor for my shop."

"Your shop?" One of his arms his draped over his steering wheel while the other lines the back of his seat. "What do you sell? Bitch pants?"

I grind my teeth together, hating every second of this.

"Your snark isn't appreciated. Maybe you should learn how to represent yourself in a more appropriate manner, then you might have more jobs, and you could afford a better car instead of this rusted-out piece of junk." I kick the side, which jars my toe. My goodness, what is this hunk of junk made of?

"Thanks for the advice, sweetheart." He taps his temple. "I'll be sure to remember that. Now if you don't mind, I'll be going."

He goes to put his truck in drive again when I lean over him and grip the gearshift. My breasts lay across his lap as I look up at him. Shock is registered across his face.

"What the hell?"

"You can't leave." I hate this. I hate that I'm begging. I hate that I am willing to do just about anything right now for him to agree.

"Why?"

Looks like pride is going to be pushed right out the door. Kind of where my butt is hanging at this mortifying moment.

"Because I need your help."

Taking a moment, he looks out the door, mulling over my painful request. He's pausing on purpose—to torture me—and I guess at this point I wouldn't expect anything else. When he scratches the scruff on his jaw, he asks, "Will I be paid?"

"Yes."

Mentally I cross my fingers as he deliberates over his decision. I've never wanted such a moody human to stick around and help me out before, but here I am, at the end of my rope, dangling out of his truck, lying across his lap, begging.

When I think he's about to shift his truck again, he reaches for his keys and turns off the engine. With a huge sigh of relief, I lift off him and brush off my clothes. I can almost see desperation coming off me in flakes.

"Why me?" His question is simple, but oh so complicated.

I decide not to beat around the bush. Might as well be completely honest. "You're the only one who's even given me a chance to ask."

He quirks his lip in understanding. "Build yourself a bad reputation there, Princess?"

Don't flip on him, do not flip on this man who might be your last hope, this man who can fix the paint on the wallpaper and the high-heel holes in the wall.

"No. My father has a monopoly on all construction companies. No one will help me per his request."

Racer nods his head. "Well, that poses an issue for me since I work for Julius Parsnip who is good friends with your dad. If he's telling people not to work with you, it doesn't seem like a smart idea to cross that line."

"He won't find out," I say quickly. "I'll make sure he doesn't know."

"Too risky."

He picks up his keys again and my heart starts to drop. "Please." I place my hand on his arm. "This shop means everything to me, and without your help, I won't be able to open it. I will pay you well, I promise. Name your price, and I'll make it happen."

The wheels in his head start to turn again. He nibbles on his bottom lip as he thinks. "What does the job entail?"

Hope flutters deep inside me. Please let him say yes. "Taking down a wall for an open-concept, adding new fixtures and moldings around the shop, installing a bathroom, shelving, dressing rooms, clothing racks, and a register stand."

He twists his lips to the side as I await his answer. He turns to me with a number. "Without seeing what I'm working with, fifteen thousand dollars for labor, the supplies are on you. Might go up depending on what I find. I will need a credit card from you to make all purchases, I don't do reimbursing shit, and I can only work nights and weekends. I will dictate my schedule."

"Done." I don't even flinch from his request. I can easily agree to all of that, mainly because I have no one else.

Shaking his head, he reaches for his tool belt and says, "Show me the space."

He said yes! Even though I don't want to, I need to thank Madison. I cannot believe that her weird, convoluted plan somehow worked. If he's here weeknights and weekends, does that mean I have to be here too?

It doesn't matter, G. You're going to achieve your dreams.

Let's do this.

Cranky carpenter and all.

CHAPTER SIX

RACER

I should have asked for more money. Not because Princess didn't a blink an eye when agreeing to my amount, but because of all the "renovations" I'm going to have to correct from the two debutantes attempting to do things on their own. Well, that's not entirely true. They had help. They had help from YouTube. Insert eye-roll here.

"And that's the shiplap wall," Madison points out.

Shiplap wall—more like pile of wood on the floor. I run my hand over my face and try to formulate a plan. Job number one, take the paint roller out of Madison's hand and tell her to leave.

"You have to go," I say to Madison, not sugarcoating my request. And yes, I might be irritated with her because of her misleading job request, but she really has to go. She's making this experience one hundred times worse than necessary with her constant jabbering.

She points at herself. "I have to leave? For what reason?"

I drop the paint roller in the tray and point her toward the door. "Because you're not helpful in any way. That's why. Say goodbye to your friend."

"Hey." She protests while trying to scramble out of my grasp. "You're just mad that you thrusted your dick at us for no reason."

Don't fucking remind me. Once again, no way in hell am I going to tell Smalls or Tucker about this incident, or Adalyn for that matter. With her big mouth, she'll have it spread through Binghamton that I'm offering up stripper services in no time.

And do you know what the worst part of all of this is? I was actually feeling the beat. For an on-the-spot performance, I was nailing that shit. And I don't care what Madison says, red *is* becoming on me.

"I couldn't care less about our little mishap." That's what I'm going to call it, no need for any other sort of definition. "You're a distraction, and we don't need that right now."

"Oh, I see what's happening." Madison continues to talk as I push her toward the door. "You just want some alone time with Georgiana."

"Not even a little."

"Are you saying you don't find her attractive?" Madison is now hanging on to the doorway of the shop, her claws digging into the sides, preventing me from pushing her outside.

Not wanting to deal with this, I turn to Georgiana and say, "Deal with this or I'm out."

She turns to Madison and pleads, "I'll call you later, okay?"

Madison huffs and snags her purse from the floor. "Fine, but just so you know, this isn't very good best-friend behavior. I will let it slip though, since you're under stress and on a timeline. Call me later, and for the love of God, don't play "Uptown Funk." Lord knows beefcake will take it as his cue to start stripping again." With a smarmy smile in my direction, she takes off, leaving us alone.

I rake my hands through my hair out of frustration and say, "She's not allowed in here when I'm around."

"Hold up." Princess walks up to me and stands tall, as tall as she can in those ridiculous heels. Who wears heels to take on renovations? I guess people who think they can take a wall down with them. "I'm the client here. You can't just start bossing me around."

"Pretty sure you need me more than I need you, Princess."

Not true, but she doesn't need to know that. Fifteen thousand dollars. Fuck, that would be life-changing. Literally life-changing. Eighteen monthly payments to the bank toward the loan to pay his medical bills. *That* would give me some breathing room.

"Are you going to be an asshole this entire time?"

I shrug and stick my hands in my back pockets. "Probably."

Taken back by my candid answer, her face grows angry before she spins around and mutters something under her breath.

"What was that, Princess? I didn't quite catch it."

She turns toward me, hands on hips, and says, "It's Georgiana, and I said I'm glad my dad deducted a thousand dollars from your payment. Seems like you deserved it."

Well, that ruffles my feathers and not in a good way. "I didn't fucking deserve that." I step forward, getting in her space. "I needed and deserved that thousand, but because you fucked over my timeline with your stupid heel puncturing my hose, I got screwed over."

Shit. The minute the words fly out of my mouth, I know I fucked up. A giant smile spreads across Georgiana's face from my admission.

"You needed that money, huh?"

"Uh, no." I step back. "Not really. I'm straight now. No need for money." Christ, this sounds bad.

She looks past me, out the window and to the street where my truck is parked, then her eyes give me a once-over. "I don't know, seems like you actually might need the money."

"I like cheap things. I don't need to flaunt my cash."

"That's if you had cash to flaunt. Don't tell me you do because it's clear by all the side jobs you take that you need the money, especially if you're working for Julius Parsnip, one of the premiere construction companies in the area. So what is it?"

"What's what?" I ask, feeling my face heat from embarrassment that she's called me out.

"What do you need the money for?"

"That's none of your fucking business," I snap. There is no way in hell I'm going to tell this woman about my money woes. First of all, I don't like her. Second of all, I don't trust her to keep her mouth shut, especially with her friend, Madison.

Her smile brightens even more; she knows she has me by the nut sack. The ball that used to be in my court, the upper hand I once held is now an even playing field. We both need each other and we know it, which means one thing: we're going to have to work together harmoniously to get what we want.

"You need me and I need you, so why don't we set aside our differences and get this work done?"

Clearing my throat, I look around and say, "You need me more."

She shakes her head and steps forward, closing in on *my* space. The smell of vanilla drifts toward me, and for a second—*only a second*—I think about running my hands through her hair. My mind is changed as soon as she opens her mouth.

"From the sweat at your temples, I'm going to assume you need me just as much, so let's not make this a commitment, because in the end, if this doesn't work out for me, at least I'll still have a roof over my head and a full bank account. What about you?"

What the hell?

She's just as arrogant as her asshole father.

Fucking bitchy comment right there.

"Are you going to act like a snobby bitch the entire time?"

"Are you going to be an asshole the entire time?"

I don't even blink before I answer. "Yeah. Plan on it."

She turns away from me and flips her hair over her shoulder. "Then plan on getting a lot of shade thrown your way."

"You're fist-fighting with fire there, Princess. You have no idea who you're dealing with."

She picks up the painting tools and says, "And neither do you." That fucking smirk, I wish it wasn't so damn cute.

～

"The bathroom can't go there. How many times do I have to tell you that?"

"I don't care. I want it there. It's better flow."

I massage my temples and look up from the plans I've been staring at for over an hour. I've never been more irritated in my entire life. I've worked with my fair share of privileged rich people who think they shit out roses, but Georgiana is by far the most infuriating client I've ever collaborated with.

"Prin—"

"Georgiana. It's Georgiana."

I roll my eyes. "Georgie." She grunts and crosses her arms. Too bad, she's Georgie now. "Do you see this right here?" I point to a wall full of plumbing on the blue prints.

"Yes."

"That's called plumbing. You need *that* for a toilet, unless you want everyone's piss spilling all over the brand new maple wood floors you install. Is that what you want? Shitter floors?"

"You're so crude."

"Just telling you like it is."

Looking at the plans, she studies them as if she actually knows what she's looking at and says, "Then just move the plumbing."

That garners a belly laugh from me. "You want me to just move the plumbing?"

"Yeah, why not?"

"Well, according to your timeline, you want this done in two months. Moving the plumbing will destroy that timeline and that precious budget of yours. It's not a simple fix, Georgie. You have to run new lines and everything. You're talking thousands on top of what you're already spending, not to mention labor. I'm not a certified plumber. There is no way I could do it. And I'm going to tell you right now, I'm a bargain. Go ahead, have someone on the outside come in and reroute your plumbing. You're not going to like the outcome."

"Ugh, you're just being difficult."

"I'm really not. As much as I love to make that vein in your forehead pop out in frustration, this is not something I'm being difficult about. It's called hard facts."

"What if we move the bathroom here?" she asks, not getting the point.

Grinding my teeth, I grip her chin and force her to make eye contact with me. "Listen to me and listen closely. The bathroom cannot move. I repeat, the bathroom CANNOT move. We can refinish the bathroom, but it has to stay put, so work around it. Got it?" The tail end of my sentence is said with more of a growl to get my point across. *I don't think I've ever been this harsh with a woman before.*

She snaps her head away and sits back in her chair. "Fine. We won't move the bathroom."

"Wasn't going to move it even if you asked with your top off while pinching your nipples." I shuffle the prints and remove my pencil from behind my ear. "Now, if you line up the dressing rooms with the bathroom, you won't have any odd jutting-out walls."

"I would never take my shirt off and pinch my nipples for you."

Jesus, this woman is going to give me an ulcer. I can feel it forming already.

I pinch my brow, a headache now pounding in my skull. It's been an hour, and she's already giving me an incurable itch to quit. "Focus." It's one word, but with the tone I say it in, it holds heavy weight.

"You were the one who brought it up. I just want to make it known I won't be taking my shirt off for you."

Or maybe I don't hold any weight in this conversation whatsoever.

I stand from my chair, knocking the damn thing over and roll up the plans. Her eyes widen from my abrupt movements. Is it wrong that I want her to be a little scared?

"I'm done for tonight," I announce. "I'll be back Wednesday. We can—"

"Wednesday? Are you kidding me? That's three days from now. How on earth are we going to stick to our timeline if you take three days off? No way, I expect you to be here tomorrow."

"I have a life, Princess. I can't be at your beck and call."

She stands as well, trying to match my height but fails miserably. "I have a life too, and it's been put on hold for two months until I can open my store. And think about it. The sooner you finish the project, the sooner you get paid and the sooner we don't have to be around each other anymore."

I like that way of thinking. Yeah, Georgie might be nice to look at, but she grates on my nerves way too much. Getting paid and vacating the premises earlier seems appealing to me.

"Fine. I'll be here tomorrow but on one condition."

"What's that?" She's bouncing in excitement now, probably because she thinks she won our little battle.

"You don't touch anything. Not one thing. I better not see you attempt to do any renovations, especially on work I've already done."

"I can help."

"No." I shake my head. "No, you can't. And do you know why? Because you tried to use high heels as a sledgehammer. That's why."

"It seemed like a good idea at the time."

"It wasn't. Terrible idea actually."

"I can still help." She stands tall, confident in her lack of construction skills.

"You can hand me tools and be my gofer."

"Gofer?" Her brow pinches together in confusion. If she didn't annoy me so much, I would almost think the look on her face was cute . . . *ish*.

"Gofer is someone who fetches things. You can be my fetcher.

But I'll be the one using the tools. I can't risk you fucking anything up. And when you come to the jobsite, you'll be dressed properly. No more heels or skirts. Jeans, shorts, T-shirts, and work boots. If you show up in anything other than that, I'm going home."

"Does a skort count?" She wickedly smiles.

"Thin ice, Georgie. Thin fucking ice." I put my pencil behind my ear and pull my truck keys from my pocket. "I'll see you tomorrow." I start toward the door when I remember something. I turn to her and ask, "What's the name of your shop going to be? I like to make sure I have a name for every project."

Her hands fidget in front of her and when she answers, she doesn't quite make eye contact. "Limerence."

"Limerence?" I repeat.

She nods. "Yeah, I kind of have this weird hobby where I collect words in a notebook that are beautiful to me. Limerence is my favorite."

"Yeah?" I kind of hate that this hobby of hers makes her seem more human, more down to earth. And I hate that I want to see this book to see what other kind of words are in it. "And what does limerence mean?"

"It means being in a state of infatuation with another human being. I figured if I'm going to have a bridal shop, it not only needs to have a beautiful name, but a meaningful name behind it as well."

I nod my head and turn away. "I like it."

Shame I don't like her as much as I like the word.

Fucking thoughtful, annoying woman.

CHAPTER SEVEN

GEORGIANA

"Plaid shirts, white shirts, jean shorts and . . . work boots? What's going on here?" Waverly asks as she looks in my cart. Yes, my cart. I'm not at the mall or a boutique store. I'm at Walmart, gathering work clothes because after looking through my closet, I wasn't terribly surprised to see I have nothing to wear when it comes to working on a construction site.

"I need some outfits for working on my store."

Beef stick in hand that Waverly pulled from an aisle, she motions to my cart. "You know the average person doesn't say they need outfits for construction. They just wear their rags they keep stuffed away for dirty days."

"I know but unfortunately I'm not the average person . . . not yet."

Waverly pats my shoulder and bites on her beef stick. "I love you, G, but you're never going to be average. It's cute that you want to try though."

"Why did I bring you again?"

"Because I know my way around a Walmart. Unbeknownst to your mom, I hit up Walmart once a week just out of spite."

I giggle to myself. My mom is the biggest snob ever and would never be caught dead in a Walmart, despite their amazing deals and vast selection of discounted items. She's more of a New York City shopper. She'll make special trips to the city just to pick up some clothes. So obnoxious. At least that's how I see it now. When I was younger—and it was my norm—I thought it was the coolest thing ever. But now, I've come to realize money isn't everything. It's having and achieving hopes, dreams, and aspirations; that's what's going to make you happy in life.

"Did you know I wore a shirt from Walmart once to your mom's monthly brunch, and she complimented it? Asked me where I got such a stunning blouse." Waverly chuckles to herself.

"You did not."

"Totally did. I was pissed about having to miss the Jets game, so I rebelled and wore a Walmart blouse. It's the most comfortable shirt I own and only cost me fifteen dollars. Doesn't get better than that."

"Where did you say you got it? Did you say Walmart? Oh please tell me you did."

Waverly sighs and thumbs through some activewear shirts, picking up a hot pink one and putting it in the cart. "I wish. Man, I would have loved to seen the look on your mom's face if I uttered the word Walmart at her Sunday brunch. She would have spit fire in my direction just to burn the damn shirt. I told her I got it at a Talbots outlet."

"You didn't say Walmart, but you said outlet? That's risky."

Waverly shrugs and adds another activewear shirt, this one blue. "I got some grief for shopping at an outlet, but I just shrugged it off. Told her I was with a friend and couldn't pass up this shirt. She then whispered in my ear and said she wouldn't have been able to either."

My laugh echoes through the women's clothing department. "She is such a snob."

"Do you know what the best part of this story is?"

"It's not over?"

Waverly shakes her head. "That following Monday, I went to Walmart, got my favorite honey-barbeque boneless wings from the deli section, cracked open a Sprite and walked around, taking in all the deals and when I spotted the treasured blouse, I got one for your mom."

"You didn't." I can't contain the smile stretched across my face.

"I did. I spent the rest of my day removing the tag in the shirt and replacing it with a tag from one of my Talbots shirts. I sewed it in, and then carefully swapped out the price tags as well. It was some of the most intense but satisfying work I've ever done. I gave it to her the following brunch as a hostess gift, and she practically died, she was so excited. She also told me it was our little secret that it was from an outlet. I zipped up my mouth and told her, her secret was safe with me."

My eyes are watering from laughing so hard. "Oh my gosh, how did you keep a straight face?"

"Barely made it through that whole conversation. Abe just shook his head at me. But you know what's so gratifying? It's your mom's favorite shirt."

"Wait, are you talking about the floral light blue blouse?"

"The one and only." Waverly takes another bite of her beef stick.

The laugh that bursts out of me garners attention from shoppers around us. "I love you so much. That's amazing." I wish I was as clever as Waverly, because I would have done this a year ago.

I walk us toward the food section and think about getting some snacks and water for the shop. Might be nice to have some food in case we get hungry while working. Look at me being a considerate boss.

"So are you going to fill me in? All I know is you're starting renovations, but you haven't said with who. Did you finally find someone brave enough to cross your dad?"

"I don't know if brave is the right word, more like desperate."

"Desperate works. Oh, gummy worms!" Waverly plops an obscenely large bag of gummy worms into the cart. "So who is it?"

I throw some chips in the cart and say, "His name is Racer McKay. He actually just finished up the pool house. I didn't want to ask him since we kind of don't get along . . . at all, but Madison slipped him her number and said she had an opportunity for him. I guess he really needed the work because he came over yesterday, and we established a timeline, budget, and payment. He's coming by tonight to start working on the place."

"Now when you say Racer, are you talking about the beefcake who spent a few weekends outside your dad's house with his shirt off, re-siding the pool house?"

"That's him."

Waverly nods nonchalantly and then says, "You know, I think I want to be a project manager. Just observe to make sure everything is getting done right."

"Oh, I'm sure. Don't get too attached; he's a real asshole."

"An asshole, huh? Why does that make me want to stare at him so much more?"

"Because you're weird." I sigh and grab a case of water and put it at the bottom of the cart. "He's really not pleasant. Insists on calling me Princess or Georgie. It's his way or no way at all, and he doesn't care for my social status."

Waverly pets the top of my head. "Poor little rich girl, a boy doesn't like you for your money. So sad."

"I didn't mean it like that. I meant he doesn't like it, throws it in my face a lot of the time. Little does he know, I couldn't care less about that status."

"Do you care about what he thinks of you?"

"No, not at all."

Maybe a little. Ever since I graduated from college, I've wanted to be someone else. I wanted to be free of the shackles coated in my dad's expectations. I wanted to live my life the way I dreamed of it, not the way my dad envisioned it. It's taken me a few years, but I can feel myself starting to separate from him, and it's never felt better.

The only bad thing about all this? My dad is unaware of my

continuation in perusing my dreams. He thought he shut me down, and I let him believe that. I had to, because if he knew I was moving forward, he would do something to jeopardize it, I just know it.

And how screwed up is that? That a father would try to stop his child from accomplishing her dreams. Shouldn't parents try to lift their kids up? Maybe he really doesn't have faith in me like I thought he did. Maybe he has zero belief in my ability. That thought might hurt more than anything. *But I'm sure I saw pride on his face when I went through the plan with him. Or did I see what I wanted to see? Needed* to see.

"Seems like you might care a little, given you're buying new clothes to do renovations in."

"It's not like that. He made it quite clear that if I want to assist in any way to make this process go faster, I'm to dress appropriately. I wasn't about to bust out my Ralph Lauren polos to paint in."

"The sheer idea makes me shiver," Waverly adds sarcastically. "Well, if you're going to dress the part, we have to make sure you fully fit in. Come on." Waverly grabs the cart and heads down the opposite side of the store. When she passes a giant bin of candy, she reaches her hand in like a vending machine claw and pulls out a few boxes of "movie theater" candy and tosses it in the cart as she says, "Bingo bango." She is so unpredictable, and it's one of the reasons why I love hanging out with her so much.

"Where are we going?"

"Just follow me. We pass a paint mixing station and turn down an aisle a few feet away. "Ah, here we are." Waverly bends down and picks up a pink tool belt. "Just what we need to top off the outfit. If your mother taught us anything, it's to accessorize properly. What's a lady going through renovations without a pink tool belt and matching hammer?"

I'm about to protest but then Racer's asshole tendencies pop in my head, and I can't help but let Waverly "accessorize" me for the job.

I can't wait to hear what he has to say about this.

~

He's late. He texted me earlier and said he would be here by six o'clock. It is now six thirty, and he's not here. I've sent him a few texts to see where he is but I haven't heard anything. Did he decide this job was too much for him? Maybe the money wasn't as important to him as I thought it was.

Did I read him all wrong?

Worry ticks at the back of my neck, and I start to chew on my nails when the door bursts open, startling me half to death.

I hold my hand to my chest and look Racer up and down. He's carrying a sledgehammer, gloves, and goggles.

"It's demo day," he announces as he slips on the glasses and gloves. Not even a hi, or a hey sorry I'm late, or even a courtesy glance in my direction to check out my outfit.

I mean, not that it matters or anything. I don't care if he notices my outfit.

Okay, maybe I care a little.

Fine, I care a lot. I specifically got this outfit because he told me to, and I would appreciate it if he noticed.

Hands on hips, I ask, "Where have you been? I've been texting you for the past half hour."

"I don't text and drive, Princess. It's against the law."

He lifts his sledgehammer, slings it over his shoulder, and walks over to the utility closet. He studies it for a second and then starts switching off power, leaving one light on in the front of the store. He flips the panel closed and stands in front of the wall where we attempted to heel poke the darn thing to death. In one giant swing, he starts taking it down.

I screech and step back as drywall starts to fly everywhere, spraying the air with dust and particles. Please don't let there be any asbestos in those walls, please, please, please.

I cover my mouth with my shirt and call out. "Do you know

what you're doing? What if there's asbestos in the walls? We could be sucking it all in since we don't have masks on."

Pausing for a second, back still turned to me, he says, "I did my homework, Georgie. This building was built in the early nineteen hundreds but was remolded in the nineties. They removed any remnants of asbestos way before you learned to stop crapping in a diaper."

With that, he starts attacking the wall again. He pounds on the wall with his sledgehammer and then sets it down, only to rip the wall apart with his bare hands. He's rabid in his movements, never taking a break, just tearing the wall apart as if he's on a mission, and it's to take down the entire building.

Not that I'm really staring, but from behind, his shirt clings to every muscle in his back, displaying the thick bulge of every strong section of his lats, arms, and shoulders, only to narrow down at his waist. I'm not ashamed to admit it; he has an amazing body, at least from what I could see of it over the past few weeks.

I think back to when he had his shirt off while working on the pool house. His tanned body glistened under the summer heat, his hair lightening ever so slightly from the sun, and his abs on full display, rippling with his every move.

The man has a workingman's body, and it's hot. It's hot as hell.

"You just going to stand there with your thumb up your ass, Georgie, or are you going to move some of this junk into that wheelbarrow over there?"

And then I'm thrown back into reality and his dickish ways.

Ignoring his dig, I walk over to the wheelbarrow and lift it up. Jeeze, it's heavier than I expected, so when I start to move it toward the pile of drywall, it tips over and slams into the floor, causing Racer to look my way.

It's the first time he's actually taken me all in. His eyes start at my work boots and slowly peruse up my legs to my shorts and then my shirt that is cut a little low in the front. What can I say? They didn't have many options at Walmart. I piled my hair on top of my head to keep it out of the way and pushed back the loose hair with a headband. When I see his eyes, they're full of heat, a look I haven't seen from him before. Usually his brow is pinched together, and his jaw is ticking out of pure frustration. But this look, this *I'm going to eat you* look, it's completely different.

"Um, the wheelbarrow is heavy," I say, trying to make this moment less awkward.

"What are you wearing?" he finally asks, removing his eyes from my breasts.

I twist in place nervously. "You told me T-shirt and shorts, so I'm wearing what you asked."

"That's not what I asked."

"Yes, it is. This is exactly what you asked for. And what does it matter? I'm not wearing heels or a skirt so you should be happy."

"I prefer the skirt and heels to this," he mutters as he walks over to me, eyes cast down, and transports the wheelbarrow with ease.

"You can't pick apart everything or this is not going to work." I cross my arms in defiance.

"And you can't wear sexy shit like that to work in."

Sexy?

I look down at what I'm wearing. Is he high?

"How on earth is this shit sexy?"

Racer starts to put drywall pieces in the wheelbarrow when he turns toward me and looks me up and down again. "To start, those shorts are entirely too short."

"It was the only kind they had."

"Well, they're too short. And that shirt, I can see too much tit. It's distracting." *What the hell? He's seen me in a bikini.*

"I can wear a camisole underneath tomorrow."

"And those boots with your socks, yeah, that's not going to work at all. It's like a fucking wet dream come true. Sorry, Georgie, you're going to have to change again."

Did he just call me a wet dream? I should be utterly appalled, but instead, my stomach is doing somersaults as I start to get slightly turned on. Good God, woman. Get it together!

"You can't be serious."

He nods. "I am."

I walk over to the drywall and start lifting pieces into the wheelbarrow as well. "Too bad, I'm not changing. These are my construction clothes, so deal with it. Be a grown-up and stop leering at women like some creeper."

"Not a creeper, Georgie, just a man. We notice shit like low-cut shirts, high-cut shorts, and toned legs in work boots."

Even though he's pissing me off, his compliments don't slip past me.

"Well, stop noticing and focus on the project. Think you can manage that?"

"I can handle anything." He winks, takes one more look down my shirt—pervert—and continues to rip the drywall down until there is nothing left but studs and a few wires. I'm amazed at how fast he works. But after his comments about my *tits,* my clothing, and my toned legs, I'm feeling just a smidge hotter. And that wink? It makes me all hot and bothered.

Together, without saying a word to each other, we work harmoniously picking up drywall, taking it to the dumpster I rented, dumping it, and repeating the process. Before I know it, I'm sweeping up the remaining dust while Racer drinks from one of the bottles of water I bought today.

"I'm going to call it a night. I have an early morning tomorrow at work and need rest for my muscles."

"Okay, will you be back tomorrow?"

"Yup." He lifts the hem of his shirt and bends down slightly, the flex of his abs showing off as he wipes his face with his shirt.

Damn.

It's all I can think as I stare at his impressive stomach.

"You know, Georgie, if I can't stare, neither can you."

Startled, I look to the side and fidget with the broom. "I wasn't staring."

He chuckles. "Okay, good cover." He caps his water, grabs his tools, and walks toward the entrance. "See you tomorrow, Princess.

Don't bother with the camisole; your tits revitalized my strength today. Thanks for the show."

The door slams shut on his last word, making me inwardly groan from how obnoxious he is. Just because I don't like to follow directions, I'll be making sure to wear a camisole tomorrow. The tit show is over.

CHAPTER EIGHT

RACER

Fucking bologna sandwiches. Some days they're appealing and sometimes they taste like rubber.

Today is a rubber day.

With my elbows on my knees, I look over the housing development I've been working on, and take it all in. Houses stacked on top each other, each building chosen from a selection of five model homes, sidewalks and parks ready to be installed, making it the perfect neighborhood for families.

Not so much for me.

I'm the kind of man who needs his privacy, a little breathing room from the people living next to me, just like my father. Although it's nice to have neighbors, I don't want my neighbors so close that I can share soap with them through the window in the morning.

But even though I would never live in this neighborhood, I'm proud of how it's turning out. There is something to be said about watching your hard work come to fruition. With my hands and the help of my coworkers, I've been able to build homes for families who will make a million memories.

Just like I did with my father. He wasn't much of a talker, but he always had words of wisdom to impart. "Never rush your work, son. Even if you are working for someone else, take pride and do your absolute best. Your name may never be mentioned when someone enjoys their new home, but you will know you gave it your all. You will be able to take pride knowing you made sure they got the best." I recall feeling angry when he said those sorts of things, because giving my all was fucking exhausting. But then at the end of the day, when we were both physically exhausted, we would laugh and joke and carry on as if we were both teenage boys. I found my first best friend on those nights. Now I miss his pearls of wisdom, his quiet ways, but mostly my friend.

I take another bite of my sandwich, trying to chew past the rubber and cardboard feeling in my mouth when a small box is tossed into my lap.

"Eat up, dude," Smalls says. "Before I do. I think I'm starting to put on some pudge."

A box of Oatmeal Creme Pies sits on my lap, and I thank Little Debbie eternally for being such a masterpiece of a woman and delivering such goods to the masses.

"I'm not going to be your nut fluffer and tell you you're not putting on pudge." I open the box, caring little about my bologna sandwich now, and stick a pie in my mouth, not even bothering to take small bites.

"A little return on the compliments wouldn't hurt you, you know, man. Tucker and I have spent hours pumping you up, making sure you feel comfortable with your testosterone levels."

Mouth full, I answer, "It's because I'm insecure at heart and you two are better people than I am." I pat his cheek and then say, "You're not getting pudgy, darling. You're the same size you were when I first met you."

"That means the world to me," Smalls answers, holding his heart.

"Knew it would." I wipe my mouth with the back of my hand. "So what's with the disposal of Little Debbie? Find a girl? Trying to trim and cut for her? Want her to see the pure definition of your ribcage?"

Smalls is the opposite of small. He's a giant. Huge, puts my muscles to shame, and you and I both know I'm ripped. You're picturing my biceps in your head right now, aren't you? Want me to kiss them for you? Want me to show you where the beach is, because I really—

"Dude, did you hear me?"

"Eh, what?" I sheepishly smile at him as he shakes his head. Oops.

"I'm cutting out sweets so I can outshine you in a tux at Tucker's wedding."

"What?" I whip my head around, panic starting to blossom inside me. "Did they set a date? Did he pick a best man? I swear to God if it's you, I will kill you in your sleep. Straight up, I have no qualms about offing the best man so I can claim the title."

"He asked me this morning. Sorry, man."

"What the ever living fuck?" I pop to my feet and march toward the house, Little Debbie snacks in hand, looking for the one man who needs some sense beaten into him.

When I swing open the door, I scour the main floor and ask, "Where the hell is Tucker?"

One of the electricians working on the hallway wiring points up the stairs. I take no time in climbing the stairs. "Tucker?" I yell, my voice echoing against the bones of the house.

"Back here," Tucker calls out.

I trudge through the space that will be the master bedroom and back to the en-suite bathroom where I stop immediately. Standing in the middle of the bathroom—that's full of black balloons—is Tucker, holding a basket of Little Debbie snacks—my favorite things in the world—and a two liter of Mountain Dew. Above him, written on the drywall is a note . . . for me.

Racer, be my best man.

"Racer—" Tucker starts, but I don't even let him finish. I scoop him up into a bear hug and spin him around the room, knocking balloons into the air.

"Yes, yes, yes. A thousand times, yes."

The claps of our fellow men, followed by eye-rolls and laughs, come from the bedroom as they surround the doorway.

"Put me the fuck down," Tucker mutters, clearly annoyed with my hysterics. When I set him down, he pushes me to the side and rights his shirt. "You happy I made a big deal? Is it everything you wanted... princess?"

I know this was for me, because I'm a dickhead like that. Making my friends do outlandish things to "please" me is one of my favorite pastimes, and the best part about it, the nut-sacks fall for it every time. The key to making it happen, to making them go above and beyond to prove their friendship: bitch. Bitch all the time.

For the past few months, I've been on Tucker's case about asking me to be his best man. He got engaged toward the end of summer last year, and I let him go through the holidays without harassing him, since they were taking the planning slowly, but I've really stepped up my annoyance. It totally worked.

I mean, the dickhead filled up a room of balloons and painted on the wall. Shit, if I wasn't afraid he would knock my teeth out, I would be rolling on the floor laughing right now. Oh fuck, this is fantastic. See what a little bit of nagging and persistence get you? A friend who will do just about anything to get you to stop, like a grown-ass man almost bending down on his knees to ask you to be his best man.

Classic.

"You've made my dreams come true." I go in for another hug, because why not, and he looks like he's on the verge of wanting to choke hold me. He steps away and clears out the room.

"The show is over. Get back to work." He turns to me and points to the balloons and wall. "It's your job to clean this shit up. Be rid of it before you leave, and prime the wall. Julius can't see that shit. Happy best man duties." Tucker smirks—knowing he bested me—then jogs down the stairs.

Hmm, maybe I wasn't as smart as I thought I was.

~

"Stop doing that."

"Stop doing what?"

I turn to Princess, wipe my brow, and say, "Stop fucking humming. It's annoying."

"I'm not humming."

I raise my eyebrows at her and start imitating her sound, exaggerating it a bit, because . . . I'm an asshole. "Is that not humming?"

She crosses her arms over her chest and juts a hip out. I've come to know this defensive pose over the last couple days we've been working together. "I do not sound like that. Clearly you tried to sound shrill, and I'm the least bit shrill."

"You like to think you are, Georgie, but you might as well be squawking with the birds. That shit hurts the ears."

"It does not."

I start tearing down another wall with my bare hands while she stands behind me and picks up the drywall pieces to place them in the wheelbarrow. After assessing the space, she decided to take down another wall. Lucky me.

I'm a pretty easygoing guy. I like to pull pranks, joke around, act like an asshole a lot of the times just to get a reaction from people, and I like to fuck and fuck hard. When one of those is off, I turn into an irritable bastard where everything annoys me to the point that I snap at the smallest of things.

Well, I'm irritated. I haven't fucked anyone in a long time because I've had no time to even pick anyone up. And why you ask? Because I'm working twenty-four/seven. When I'm not at the jobsite, I'm here, getting bitched and nagged at.

Oh, the fucking nagging.

This woman. Jesus, if she wasn't so hot, I might have quit by now. But seeing her tits bounce in her "construction shirt" gives me momentum. Does that make me sound like a pig? Slightly, but whatever, they're nice tits.

When I turn back around, I say, "How about we just don't make any noise? How does that sound? Hmm?"

"I can't work in silence. It's too boring. We could have a conversation, or will that be too difficult for you? Putting sentences together rather than talking like an ass-scratching ape?"

"Ass-scratching ape? That's the best insult you can come up with? Pathetic, Georgie."

"I'm not rude. I don't try to hit below the belt like you." Pieces of drywall are thrown into the wheelbarrow at a harder rate than before.

"I don't hit below the belt."

She snorts in disagreement. "You think you know me, but you really don't."

I rip another piece of drywall down, my muscles aching with every movement. Fuck, I need to take a hot shower after this and pop a few Ibuprofen as well. "Good thing part of the job isn't getting to know one another."

"What is your problem?" she yells, drawing my attention. "Why are you acting like such an asshole? I'm trying to be nice here when I really don't have to. I could be a total bitch. I could make your life miserable."

"Your bombinating has made me miserable enough."

Her brow crinkles. "My what?"

Picking up a piece of small drywall, I pull the pencil from behind my ear and scribble out a little lesson for the princess.

When I'm done, I hand it to her, place my pencil back behind my ear, and tap the piece of drywall. "Bombinate; to make a humming or buzzing noise. I know big, pretty words too, Georgie. Put that one in your little book."

She stares at the word for a few seconds before she storms off toward the back of the shop while saying, "You're so annoying."

I smile to myself, knowing once again, I gained the upper hand. I might be sore and tired and not in the mood to deal with the client of this job, but hell, a little "poking of the fire" is making these night hours go by a lot easier.

Why am I being a dick? Honestly, because it's a defense technique. I'm smart enough to know this. When I'm around people who intimidate me or who I know are better than me, I fall back on my ability to act like a total bastard. This way, I can keep them from recognizing my inadequacies, blinding them with a bitter personality.

Stupid? Oh yeah, big time.

But it's kept me from falling into a deep, dark hole where I know I would go if someone like Georgiana actually figured out who I really am: a poor boy hanging on to the last thread of his past.

And Georgiana, shit, she intimidates me. She's rich, gorgeous, and opinionated. It's shitty that what really intimidates me is her status. She's refined, polished, a fucking Rolls Royce that's never been touched. Whereas I'm the teal GEO Metro with no power steering and a flat tire that's huffing and puffing down the street, on the verge of breaking down.

We come from completely different lives, and I'm not blind to that. So instead of trying to be friends with this girl, of finding out down the road after we've bonded that I don't belong in her world, I use my strongest defense and dick her around.

Not the most mature way of handling things, but hey, I never claimed to be perfect.

"Do you want a soda?" she calls from the back, interrupting my thoughts.

Huh, maybe I didn't poke the fire as much as I thought I did. "Got any Mountain Dew?"

"Diet Coke."

"Not Coke Zero?"

"Just Diet Coke with lime."

Christ, fucking girl drink.

"I'll take one," I answer reluctantly. It might be a girl drink, but I'm thirsty.

Her boots clomp down the hallway. When she approaches, she's sipping from her drink and hands me mine. "Don't say I never gave you anything."

"Aw, Georgie, you're just the fucking sweetest." I wink at her, sarcasm dripping from my lips as I pop open the tab of the soda only to be sprayed up the nose and down the shirt by fucking Diet Coke with Lime.

Talking over her drink, she smirks and says, "Maybe if you start being nice to me, next time I won't shake your can for a minute straight."

Coke drips from my nose as I hold my arms out, trying to figure out what to do. Hate to admit it, but I'm kinda digging that Georgie has a little spice in her.

"You don't know what you just started, Princess."

She shakes her hands in the air. "Ooo, I'm scared."

"You should be." I take a step forward, closing in on her. "I'm a relentless prick, the king of driving people crazy, the master of pranks. I'm not afraid to open up my toolbox and bring down the hammer."

My words have zero effect on her. "Your metaphor is subpar at best, Racer. Your attempt at intimidation is sad, and frankly pathetic." She twirls her finger at the drywall. "Have fun cleaning up by yourself."

Still dripping, I nod and wring out my shirt. "It would be easier to take you seriously if your fly wasn't down."

On a gasp, she looks down at her crotch where in fact, her zipper is all zipped up. When her eyes meet mine again, they are full of murder. I can't help it, I laugh. I laugh fucking hard. "That was just a warm-up, Georgie." I tip her chin, and she slaps my hand away. "Wait until I'm fully warmed up, you'll regret ever shaking my soda."

Without a word, she heads to the back of the shop while pulling her phone out of her back pocket. I call out, "Don't bother searching the Internet for workplace pranks, they will have nothing on what I have in store. Don't waste your time, Georgie."

"I wasn't . . . go to hell!"

I chuckle to myself, take a sip from my half-empty can, and get back to work. Not a bad day in the office I would say, even if I'll be a sticky motherfucker until I can get home to shower.

CHAPTER NINE

GEORGIANA

"Don't touch that," I snap at Madison, who's twirling Racer's hammer around.

"You're tense." She drops the hammer on the floor and sits. "Do you need a snack? You're looking a little possessed."

"I'm not possessed. I'm just trying to look for something." Where is the godforsaken spreadsheet? Last time I had it, I was scrolling over my budget, making sure all updates had been entered. Mind you, all I'm entering so far is outgoings. *Sigh*. I like to work on paper once everything is set up, and update on my computer when necessary. I'm old school like that.

But being old school means you lose your shit. And since I have yet to make updates on my computer, only scribbled notes on my budget sheet, I need it.

"What are you looking for?" Madison looks around. "Sex? Because you need some, maybe it will ease some of the tension out of you." She flips a piece of wood over. "Nope, no dicks under here. Hmm."

"I don't need sex," I yell, a little louder than I mean to. Taking a deep breath, I place my hands on my hips and say as calmly as possible, "I'm looking for my spreadsheet. It has all my budget lines on it. I made some notes on it last night, and I want to enter them in the computer."

"You're not using your iPad? You should just use that. Paper is really becoming non-existent now."

"Your *helpful* commentary isn't appreciated right now, Madison." Go ahead, label me with the bitch card, I deserve it. I'm just . . . I'm high strung right now. Maybe I do need to get laid . . .

"Sheesh, last time I suggest something." She leans back on her elbows and stretches her legs out in front of her. "You should keep the place like this, see-through walls, electric stuff hanging around everywhere, and the floors, they're magnificent, you're really capturing the true essence of dirt."

"Madison, you know I love you, but I can't handle—"

"Hey, what's that?" Madison points to the ceiling and stares at it, a squint in her eyes.

Looking up to the ten-foot ceilings, I see a pencil stuck through the cracking drywall, pinning my spreadsheet to the top.

"Ahhhh," I scream as my blood boils. "That freaking man!"

"Is that your spready doo-dad you were looking for?"

"Yes," I groan.

"Racer do that?"

"Who else do you think would do this? God, he's so . . . he's so stupid."

Madison laughs and tilts her head back. "Good one, G. You really burned him with that comment."

Annoyed with everyone, I grab the ladder against the wall and drag it over to where my spreadsheet is hanging. Good Lord, this thing is heavy. "A little . . . help," I grunt.

"You seem like you're doing a fine job on your own."

"Why are you here?"

Madison shrugs. "Company I guess. I don't want to be around my nagging mother, plus once all this dusts settles and things are starting to look pretty, I'm going to help you hang things. My help is holding out until then."

"Glad you're waiting for the easy projects." I open the ladder and situate it on the floor.

"Hey, don't forget my attempt at painting wallpaper, hanging shiplap, and finding Racer. I think I've done my fair share of helping."

I sigh and start climbing the ladder, feeling unsteady and wobbly. "Can you hold the ladder for me, Mad?"

"You're not going to fall, are you?"

"If you hold the ladder I won't."

Being the semi-good friend she is, Madison makes a big deal about getting up and walking to the ladder. She holds the legs firmly to the floor, making my ascent slightly more sturdy.

"Why would Racer put your spreadsheet up there anyway?"

I reach the top wrung with my hands and look up at the ceiling. I'm going to have to climb a few more steps. "Because he's an asshole."

"Who's an asshole?" That deep, annoying voice I've grown to despise . . .

Madison turns toward the door, moving the ladder with her.

It happens too quickly. As I move to the next step on the ladder, it twists to the side, knocking my foot away and causing me to lose my balance. My hands flail in the air as I try to gracefully catch myself, but there is no hope.

Girl is going down.

An obnoxiously ugly cry for help rips out of my mouth as I twist my body awkwardly and start to fall, right into the barrel of Racer's chest. We topple to the floor, an oof coming out of him and girly cries ripping from me.

I find myself with my head awkwardly resting on Racer's jean-clad crotch and my lady bits tickling his chin with my legs on either side of his head.

We are casually prepped and primed in a sixty-nine position with Madison gawking over us. I can feel his breath between my thighs, which sends a shiver up my spine. The only thing resting between my face and Racer's penis is his jeans and I'm assuming briefs, but who knows, he seems like a man who goes commando.

Oh God, what if he's commando right now? My fingers itch to yank down his zipper and find out. Good Lord, my hormones need to take it easy.

But then his mouth is right against my arousal...

"Take a guy out to dinner first, Georgie." Racer pats my butt and chuckles, although I detect a strain in his voice from catching me.

I don't know what comes over me. Maybe it's the fact that my dad hasn't spoken to me since I started this project. Maybe it's the infuriating man that holds my future in his hands, or maybe it's the fact that I really do need sex, but before I can even stop myself, I whack Racer right in the scrotum and roll off him.

"Asshole," I mutter as he scrunches to the side and holds his crotch, small moans coming from him.

"Devil woman," he mutters.

I right myself and watch in amusement—sorry, I can't help but be a little pleased with my choice—as Racer's muscles strain while he takes deep breaths. Serves him right.

"Oh man, you got him right in the nads." Madison offers me a fist bump, which I match gladly, even though she was the reason I fell off the ladder. "I guess he won't be messing with your spready doo-dad anymore."

"I guess not." I wink at Racer and go back to the ladder. Hopefully Madison won't be distracted again this time.

∼

"Is the limping necessary?"

"You punched my balls, Princess, of course it's necessary."

"I did not punch them." I make sure my phone is in my purse and I have all the paperwork I need in my file folder for our trip.

"You sure as hell did. You punched them so hard, I felt them swing up my back and wink at my asshole."

I cringe. "God, don't be so vulgar."

"Don't be so stuck-up. I know it's hard to dislodge the pole that was stuck up your ass when you were born, but with a little lube, we can shimmy it out." He wiggles his eyebrows. "I don't mind taking it out for you and replacing it with my good-time pole."

Deadpanning, I ask, "Is that what you call your penis? Your good-time pole?"

He shrugs casually, pockets his phone, and stretches his hands over his head, revealing a patch of bronzed, toned skin on his stomach. "Haven't had a bad time yet."

"Pig."

Breezing past him, I walk to my car and unlock the door. When I go to open it, Racer calls out, "What do you think you're doing?"

"Getting in my car, isn't that obvious?"

"We're taking my truck." He points to his rusted piece of metal behind him.

I stare it down for a second and then shake my head. "I'm not riding in that thing. It's a death trap."

"I've had it for years; hasn't died yet."

"No, I'll drive."

"Yeah? And where do you plan on putting all of the sheets of drywall we need to get in that little BMW of yours? Strapping them to the top is not going to work, Princess."

Shoot, he's right. Righting my chin in the air, I say, "Well, we can drive separately."

"That's a waste of gas and more pollution than we need. Just get in the truck."

I shake my head. Stubborn woman that I am.

"Don't make me come and get you," he threatens, his chest puffing out and his eyes staring me down.

"You wouldn't."

He lowers his head and chuckles while he shakes it. "Have you not learned anything yet, Georgie? I do anything I want, and I follow through on threats."

"Just meet me there." I turn to get in my car when heavy booted footsteps come up behind me.

I have no time to move out of the way before he's flinging me over his shoulder and carrying me like an uncivilized savage to his truck. "Put me down, you ape."

The loud squeak of his truck door opening shoots through the air right before he plops me down on the seat, onto something crinkly.

"What is that?" I shift to the side and pull out a handful of wrappers, chocolate and cream-covered wrappers. They're everywhere. On his dashboard, on his seat, on the floor.

Oh my God! It's a rat's lair in here.

"Ewww!" I shake the wrappers from my hand and watch them float to the floor. "What are those?"

"Eh, yeah, haven't had a chance to clean out the old girl. Sorry about that."

"Why are there so many wrappers?"

He swats away the wrappers to the floor—yeah, much better. "Little Debbie is my sugar mama. I love that bitch hardcore."

"Little Debbie, as in the fat-filled snacks?"

"The one and only."

Scanning the compartment of his cab, I look at him and say, "There must be fifty wrappers in here. You've eaten all of them? Aren't you afraid of getting fat?"

Like the cocky ass he is, he lifts his shirt and pats his abs. "Not concerned, Princess. But thanks for checking."

He slams my door shut and walks around to his side. When he's settled, he runs his hand over the steering wheel and whispers something to his truck. Eyes closed, almost as if he's hoping and praying his truck starts, he turns the key in the ignition and a loud, strained rumble follows.

"That a girl." He pats the truck's dashboard and puts it in drive. The truck lurches forward, and I have to brace myself. Racer turns to me and says, "Seatbelt, please."

I reach behind me but come up shorthanded. "There is no seatbelt."

He looks behind me and snaps his finger. "Oh yeah, I had to cut it off Smalls when he got stuck last time he was in the truck. Fuck, that was funny."

Appalled, I reply, "I'm not riding with you in this truck without a seatbelt."

"No problem, Georgie, there is a seatbelt in the middle." He taps the bitch seat where the stick shift lies and winks at me.

"You've got to be kidding me."

"Not even in the slightest. Get that snooty ass over here so I can get this shit over with. I want to get home at a decent hour tonight."

Huffing my disapproval, I scoot over and buckle up. Racer wraps his arm around me and squeezes me tight to his chest; his cologne dangerously floats in my direction. God, he smells good. Why can't he smell like rotten cheese? That would be so much better, easier to not want to lick his neck.

"Isn't this sweet? All cuddled up together." His voice drips with humor.

"Just drive," I seethe.

"Not a problem." His giant man-hand grips the gearshift, which of course, is right between my legs. Nudging my legs, he says, "Spread them for me, Princess, you have to make room for me."

His voice is low, almost seductive with his request, causing me to catch my breath as I spread my legs wider to accommodate his hand.

"Look at that." His head tilts toward mine, his breath tickling my neck. "You do know how to follow directions."

My body ignites, aware of his strong presence surrounding me, enveloping me in some kind of messed-up, chocolate-covered-wrapper haze. There is no way in hell I'm going to allow myself to be attracted to this man.

Nope.

Not going to happen.

Job number one tomorrow? Call Chauncey McAdams. The last thing I want to do is go out with one of my dad's preferred choices in men, but after being close to Racer, I've realized something: I need a penis in my life, and I need it now...

Before I do something stupid like throw myself at the disgusting, pigheaded—*way too hot*—Racer McKay.

∽

Racer runs both hands over his face, the veins in his neck popping and the muscles in his forearms straining from our argument.

"We can't skip drywall, how many times do I have to tell you that?"

I cross my arms over my chest in response. "I'm not saying we skip it, I'm just saying we pick and choose where we put it."

"It doesn't work like that, Princess. It's a wall, it needs the proper materials."

"Well, it's not in my budget." I point at my spreadsheet, which he rips from my hands and pulls the pencil from behind his ear as he starts running over it.

He leans against the shelves that are housing the drywall and scrolls through my list. When he starts scribbling on my paper, I jump in.

"Don't touch that." I try to grab the spreadsheet from him, but his hold is too tight. "Stop, you're going to mess everything up."

"A thousand dollars for a chandelier? Are you fucking insane? Nope, that's gone." He makes a scratch across my sheet.

"I spent hours searching for that chandelier; it stays."

"Sorry to break it to you, Georgie, but the chandelier goes. Anyway, I have a friend who owns a light shop. I can hook you up with some cheap prices. You don't need that expensive Tiffany shit."

Caught off guard by his gesture, I back off, maybe I should let him—

"Five thousand dollars for a chaise? Are you losing your damn mind? No way in hell should you buy that."

"Hey, this is my shop. Not yours." With a strong grasp, I'm able to take the sheet from him and put it in my purse so he can't make any more adjustments.

He places his stupid pencil back behind his ear and says, "With that kind of budget, you're going to fail miserably."

"I'll have you know, my dad and brother both looked over this budget and saw great potential in my shop."

"Yeah?" Racer's face grows cocky, and what he's about to say next, I know I'm not going to like. "Do your dad or brother have any idea what goes into construction? Did they see that you didn't even account for the cost of nails, primer, or patch for the drywall? Did they see that there is no mention of paint supplies, wiring, or a replacement vanity for the bathroom because the one in there you couldn't bear to keep?"

"Well—"

"And what about the cost of redoing the floors or the scaffolding we have to rent because the ceilings in the space are ten feet tall?"

"They didn't—"

"Yeah, they didn't." He adjusts his stance, and I hate that I notice every muscle in his chest ripple with his movements. "Here's the deal, Georgie. You might know about business, but I know construction, and your construction budget is trash. If you want to do this right, let me do my work. When all is said and done, and I'm painting, adding the final touches, then you can reassess your budget and see if you can buy the fancy shit you want. Until then, hold your little purse strings tight because if anything, construction is unpredictable. You think you have it all figured out until something breaks, leaks, or flat-out surprises you. You should always allow for a fifteen percent variance. Trust me, I've seen my fair share of mishaps."

"That's reassuring."

He pinches my chin and smiles. "Don't worry, Georgie, I

haven't met a mishap I haven't been able to fix. You're in good hands."

Hands...

God, now I'm picturing his stupid hand between my legs again.

Chauncey McAdams is getting a phone call. He's getting a phone call tomorrow.

∽

"Yes, can you please tell him Georgiana Westbrook is calling?"

"Of course, please hold."

Lying on my bed in my parents' house, I twirl my hair while I wait for Chauncey to come on the line. Desperate times call for desperate measures, and I'm more than desperate right about now.

After watching Racer carry sheet upon sheet of drywall into the shop by himself, shirtless because would you know it? He got chocolate all over his shirt while eating a Little Debbie snack on the way back from Home Depot, and I went home dreaming of muscles. So many muscles. So many tightly wound, perfectly placed muscles.

Why can't he be one of those construction workers with a gut? Why does he have to be so incredibly ripped? And why does he have to eat like a man-child? What grown man smears chocolate all over his shirt while eating a Swiss Roll? According to him, it happens often.

How? How is that possible?

"Georgiana, what a pleasant surprise," Chauncey answers, his voice smooth, almost a rich tone.

"Chauncey, sorry if I'm calling at a bad time."

"Not at all. I'm glad to hear from you." I can just picture him with his feet up on his desk, a smirk across his face. "What can I do for you today?"

God, am I really going to do this? I glance over at my nightstand where my worn-out vibrator rests in peace and swallow hard. Yup, I'm really going to do this.

"I wanted to see if you were up for grabbing a drink some time."

"Grab a drink with Georgiana Westbrook? I would be an idiot to say no to that. I would be honored. When were you thinking?"

"I'm pretty open."

"How about tomorrow night? Does that work for you? Or does that make me sound desperate to see you?"

I chuckle. "Desperate would be asking to meet up in an hour."

"Thank God, I went with option number two then, huh?"

"Good thing."

"How about I pick you up at six tomorrow. If I make a good impression, maybe you'll allow me to take you to dinner too, not just drinks."

"Not making any promises, you better bring you're A-game, McAdams." I'm flirting.

"A challenge, I'm intrigued. I'll have my assistant give you my cell number. Text me where to pick you up."

"Sounds good." I flip to my stomach, a little excited about my date. Now how do I go about asking for sex without looking like a horny woman who puts out on the first date?

"I'm glad you called, Georgiana. I was getting nervous I wasn't going to hear from you."

Feeling a little guilty and hating my dad for letting Chauncey know about my "possible" phone call, I say, "Sorry I've been a little busy lately, but we can talk about that later."

"I look forward to it. I'll send you back to Mandi, my assistant. I look forward to seeing you tomorrow."

"Me too."

There, that wasn't too terrible. He actually sounded really nice on the phone. Lying back on my bed, I stare at the ceiling and cross my fingers at my side . . .

Please don't let him have a pencil dick; please don't let him have a pencil dick.

I don't think my vagina could stand the disappointment.

CHAPTER TEN

RACER

"Think you'll be done with the ceiling tonight? It doesn't take that long to wire lights, right?" Princess bounces below me, her impatience has truly grated on my nerves this evening. Electric isn't my specialty. I can put in the wiring, prepare where the cable lighting rails will go, but the electrician will have to do the final check and ensure everything is to code. But if there is one thing I know from years in building: never rush the electrics. It's protocol and can't be rushed. So yeah, I'm slow.

"It's going to take longer with your yipping. You know you don't always have to be watching over me while I work. You can go do other shit."

"I know. I just want to be a part of everything."

"Staring at me doing all the work is what you consider being a part of it all?" I wipe my brow with my forearm as sweat drips down into my eyes, stinging them. Fuck, it's hot up here and humid. So damn humid.

"Don't act like you want me to help you." She leans back in her chair and crosses her arms over her chest. "You can't have it both ways, Racer. You can't bitch about me not helping and then tell me I can't help."

Bringing the hem of my shirt up to my eyes, I press the fabric into the corners. "You must not know me very well, I bitch about everything."

"You're right, I don't know you well. What I do know is you treat your truck like a trash can, you snarl a lot, and you tend to take any chance you can get to show off your stomach."

"Sounds like you know enough, besides one thing . . ." I reach behind me and pull off my shirt entirely and toss it down at her. When the sweaty fabric hits her, she squeals and tosses it to the side. "I enjoy taking my shirt off around women who can't seem to stop staring."

"Gross." She wipes her legs and then her head snaps up at me, as if she just realized what I said. "I don't stare at you."

"All the time, Georgie." I twist two wires together and cap them off. "All the time."

"You're so full of yourself. You're not even my type." She crosses her arms and stares down at her perfectly painted pink nails.

"Handsome, rugged, and giant penis isn't your type? I'd hate to know what kind of man you like to drape yourself on."

"That's such a sexist thing to say. I don't drape myself on men. For your information, I've never made decisions in my life based on a man's suggestions. I've done everything in my life for me. I have a master's degree in business from Northwestern, graduated with honors, and have yet to truly dabble in a serious relationship because I've been focused on my goals."

"Master's degree, huh, Georgie? Impressive." More than I can say for myself. High school diploma and a good amount of work experience under my belt, that's all I have. She can probably guess that, no need to throw my subpar credentials on the table.

"Thank you." Her acceptance of my compliment is awkward, she doesn't quite know how to react, which is funny to me. I'm throwing her for a loop, and naturally, I like it.

"Still," I grunt as I install a canister for the recess lighting we decided on, "if you're not draping yourself over a man, I want to know what kind of guy is draping himself over you, especially if he's not handsome, rugged, with a big penis, because as you stated before, that's not your type."

"I never said big pe—" She pinches her brow and I chuckle to myself. "I never said that wasn't my type."

"You said I wasn't your type, Georgie, and those are obvious attributes I possess. To each their own. So, what is it? Boring with no sense of humor and a penis you can jack with only your index finger and thumb?" I make a tiny, itty-bitty motion with my finger and thumb to demonstrate.

"I'm glad you like to prove your stupidity on a daily basis."

"Excuse me?" I look down at her now. "Care to repeat that?"

"You can't associate the size of a man's crotch by their personality. Just because they might be boring doesn't mean they have a small penis. And most of the time, the men with all the muscles like yourself are overcompensating for what is lacking in their briefs." She smirks up at me. I skip right past her jab.

"You like my muscles, huh?"

She rolls her eyes while I get back to setting up the canister light. "You're just proving my point."

"And what point is that?"

"You are unable to hold an intellectual conversation. You love talking about your body, how attractive you think you are, and what you think is a big penis. Pathetic."

"I don't think I have a big penis, I know I do, Princess. You're cute for trying to bring me down a peg, though. As for my intellect, go ahead, ask me a question. I can hold a conversation."

I would prefer to hold a conversation of substance. It's more fulfilling to engage on a more personal level, and it's one of the reasons I try to ease the burdens that sit on my friends' shoulders. I want to be the guy they can rely on when they're in need. I take pride in it. Doing up Tucker's house for Emma and providing her with weekly Tucker-directed loving while he was away was one of the most fulfilling things I've ever done. Her face when she turned around and found him at her graduation? One of my proudest moments. *I helped put that there.*

I might not have all the riches or college degrees, or even the materialistic things that some people my age have, but what I do have is loyalty to the people close to me. I will do pretty much anything for them.

"Anything?" I can see the wheels turning in those questioning eyes of hers.

"Anything," I respond, hoping in the back of my head that I *can* hold my own against this woman. Fuck, I hate that she intimidates me, but she's so worldly compared to me, so much more refined, and one hundred percent out of my league.

"What's your favorite book? And why?"

"So proper," I joke.

"Just answer the question without being snarky."

She doesn't want snark? Fine, I can do snark free.

I make sure the canister is firmly in place before I sit on the scaffolding I'm on. I place my hands in my lap and make eye contact with her. I watch as she quickly scans my body, taking in my shirtless chest right before her eyes meet mine. She might think she's not into me, but it's obvious I do something to her; it's in the way her breath hitches with every once-over she takes.

"'Into Thin Air' by John Krakauer." I pause for a minute, remembering the words this broken man spoke of. "It's a memoir about the author's journey to conquer Mount Everest. Despite his preparations and knowledge of the goliath of all mountains, he didn't reach the top. A storm crushed his dreams. An unpredictable storm devastated him and everyone else on that mountain." I clasp my hands and look down at them. "Storms are a disturbed state in the environment that not only pertain to the weather, but in our personal lives, our personal state of well-being. And it's the eyes of the storm that are the most tumultuous, the eyes of a human that carry the most turmoil. When you're caught in a storm, it feels like everything crumbling around you is your fault. Just like John, I weathered an unpredictable storm, which left me bereft, lost, and struggling." I shrug. "I connected with the book on a personal level. I felt John's loss as if it was my own, which makes it a great book. If you feel it, feel the emotions of the characters rather than simply told them, you're living that book, you're not just reading it."

Georgiana is silent for a few seconds before she crosses her legs under her. "Weathering the storm, it's what can make or break you." I nod, not sure really what to say, not wanting to dive into details about my past. She doesn't need to know the specifics of my misfortunes, and it's bad enough I had to drive her around in my rusted-out truck. "I'm weathering—" Her phone rings, snapping us both out of the intimate moment, and without saying a word she answers it. "Hello? Oh yup, I'll text you the address. See you in a bit."

When she hangs up, she sighs and then puts on a mask of sophistication. "I have to get ready. If I leave you the keys, think you can lock up when you're done?"

Caught off guard, I stand and nod. "Yeah, sure. No problem."

"Thanks." She takes off toward the bathroom, well, where the walls of the bathroom are. There really is nothing in there besides a toilet and one roll of toilet paper on the back of the seat.

I guess that's the end of that conversation. And this is exactly why I need to keep my distance, because she's on a different level than I am. I'm the hired help; she's the boss with the checkbook. She's champagne and I'm nickel and dime beer. If we were living in the world of Jane Austen, I wouldn't even be allowed to talk to Georgiana Westbrook, let alone call her a nickname.

I drill the canister into the ceiling as I recollect our conversation. Did she think my assessment was stupid, my analogy? Did she actually find it interesting? And why do I really care in the first place?

Maybe because I need some sort of validation in my life. Validation for the accomplishments I've achieved, despite the major setbacks I've faced.

Before her phone rang, she was about to confess something. She started to say she was weathering something, but before she could dive deep, she stopped. What would she have shared? Do I really care?

A part of me fucking does. I run my hand through my hair, hating that I actually care. It's been a little over two weeks, and she's already burying herself under my skin. I couldn't be more annoyed.

I take my phone out of my back pocket and text the one person I know who can snap me out of this funk.

Racer: Drinks tonight. Your place?

I finish up installing the light, insert a bulb, and climb down the scaffolding so I can get a drink. I have one more light to install, which doesn't seem bad, but it will take me at least another twenty minutes before I can think about packing up.

I crack open the top of a bottle of water and let the cool liquid rush down my throat, clearing all the dust I've been breathing day in and day out. I look around the shop and can't help but count the number of projects we still have left. I'm busting my ass, but when it's just me, there is only so much I can do in a night. I'm wearing thin, and I think it's starting to show.

My phone buzzes in my pocket.

Adalyn: You always pick my place because you can drink my girly drinks without getting caught.

True, but I'll never admit it. She makes some of the best piña coladas ever and this guy is feeling a little coconutty today.

Racer: I'm taking that as a yes. I would ask if you want me to bring anything but you know it will just lead to me buying five boxes of Little Debbie snacks at the store, so spare me.

Adalyn: Because of your sick obsession with those snacks, I've gained five pounds. It's showing in my scrubs.

Racer: Sporting your very own Swiss Rolls now?

Adalyn: I hate you. You're no longer invited to my place. Have fun drinking in a ditch by yourself.

I laugh and lean against one of the walls, taking a small break from the wear and tear working like this puts on my body.

Racer: *Don't get sour on me. Remember last time I drank at your place? I fixed your leaky faucet, the one your landlord didn't care to attend to.*

Adalyn: *You also felt up my breasts and told me it was for science.*

Racer: *It was! As a man, it's recommended to be well versed in all things breastual. It's nice to have a variety of experience. No one breast is the same, you know? I think we learned that when I noticed your right one having more girth.*

Adalyn: *Don't talk about my breasts and them being girthy. God, you're never coming over again.*

Racer: *LOL. Fine, what if I promise not to touch your breasts?*

Adalyn: *I'm not making out with you either.*

Racer: *What about giving each other tender zone examinations?*

Adalyn: *Tender zone, what the hell is that?*

Racer: *And you're supposed to be the nurse. Eye-roll. It's where you keep your crotch, that's your tender zone. We can examine each other's, you know, to see if we're doing a good job cleaning. If you tickle my taint, I might very well be okay with that.*

Adalyn: *Sigh*

Racer: *What do you say?*

Adalyn: *Can I use a feather while I tickle you?*

Racer: *I wouldn't expect anything less.*

I wait a few seconds before she replies.

Adalyn: *Fine. But bring Zebra Cakes. We're going to get wild tonight.*

Racer: *You're on, sweetheart.*

Satisfied, I pocket my phone. Adalyn is the perfect friend. Yeah, we might fool around on occasion. We've never actually had sex, but fuck, just a little human touch never killed anyone. That's part of the reason we're such good friends. We get each other. We're both sexual creatures by nature. She knows how to scratch my itch, without sex, and I know how to scratch hers. Typical? No. Wanted? Absolutely.

I'm about to head back up my scaffolding when there's a knock on the front door. In the dim lights, I can see an outline of a man standing at the windowed door. Immediately the hairs on the back of my neck go up. What does this dude want? Clearly the shop is closed and under construction, so he can't be good news.

As I walk toward the door, a million thoughts of what would happen if I wasn't here and Georgiana was here all alone crowd my mind. Would she answer the door? Would this guy try to pull something on her? Very uneasy, I reach the door and shout through the glass, "We're not open, dude. Move on."

I stand tall, filling the space of the door, making sure to let this fucker know I'm not messing around.

"I'm here to pick up Georgiana Westbrook," the man calls through the door. "She's expecting me."

"Is she, now? And who the hell are you?"

"Chauncey McAdams."

What the fuck kind of name is Chauncey? Christ, his parents hated him at birth. Straight up, there is no love there.

Calling behind me, I yell, "Princess, you expecting a dickhead by the name of Chauncey?"

"Oh God, is he here?" I'm going to take that as a yes, a strangely unsettling yes. "Tell him I'll be right there."

Grinding my teeth together, I unlock the front door and open it wide, still filling the space. I take a moment to assess him. Under the streetlight, I can tell he's wearing a navy blue blazer with tan khaki pants and a white button-up shirt. His shoes look fucking expensive as shit as well as the watch on his wrist. His hair is slicked to the side and that fucking rich smirk on his face only makes me want to wind my fist back and clock it right off him.

Yeah, this is a simple assessment. I don't like him.

"Chauncey," he holds out his hand, which I reluctantly take.

"Racer. Nice to meet you. Uh, Georgie will be right out."

"Georgie?" Chauncey shakes his head as he steps inside the shop. "What an appalling nickname for such a beautiful woman."

Christ, she's not even in the room, and he's trying to shove his head up her ass. Cool it, Romeo, you'll have plenty of time to try to woo her.

Giving him another once-over, I decide to size him up, to see if he's the man I think he is . . . the boring, small dick of a man I spoke of earlier.

"Chaunce, can I call you Chaunce?"

"I prefer—"

"Chaunce it is." I hold back the smirk that wants to peek out from his indignation. "Tell me, what do you do for a living?"

"I'm in bonds." He gestures at my shirtless attire, "And you?"

"Stripper. Georgie lends me the space to practice. Want to see some of my moves?" I start to thrust in his direction, which causes his nose to visibly sneer. Fuck this dude.

"I'm good," he chokes out in distaste.

"Don't knock it until you try it, man. Girls touch your dick all night and give you money. How can you pass up such a lucky job like that?" I weigh my hands. "Bonds or stripper. Hmm, pretty sure I'll take stripper any day."

"You can't make a living off such a menial job."

"I beg to differ." I stretch my hands behind my back, flexing my impressive chest. "Just bought a Beemer the other day for the hell of it. I didn't need it, but I wanted it. Gregory at the dealership is my man. That dude is solid. Do you know Gregory?"

There is no Gregory . . .

"Oh yeah, sure, great guy."

Fucking douche nozzle.

I nod. "Next time I see him, I'll be sure to tell him you said hi."

"That would be great, thanks."

I nod at his pocket. "So what do you have in there? Billfold or money clip." I lean forward and say, "You look like a money clip kind of guy."

"You got me." Chauncey winks and pulls out a wad of cash held together by a money clip.

Typical Chauncey—not that I really know, but this tool bag has money clip wrapped in Benjamins written all over him.

"I'm a billfold guy myself, but that's only because I carry around condoms wherever I go. Never know when you're going to end up dick deep, you know?" False, but a perfect gentleman in this situation would just nod and change the subject.

Too bad Chauncey isn't the perfect gentleman. More like a skeeze. "You get a lot of pussy? I guess so since you're a stripper."

Cue the biggest eye-roll ever. I could have written down his response without blinking an eye and gotten it right.

"Who's a stripper?" Georgie asks, pulling both of our attention.

Standing behind me, Georgie walks up wearing a skin-tight red dress that is seared to her frame, defining her body perfectly, reminding me of just how amazing her body is. The top dips low enough to catch a small glimpse of her cleavage. The slit on the side of the dress runs dangerously high, but not indecently, just enough to drive a man like myself to thinking what it would feel like to slip my hand under the fabric, to test to see if she's wearing anything underneath.

To top off her non-construction clothes outfit, she's wearing nude-colored heels that turn her legs into fuckable sticks you want wrapped around your body as you drive deep inside her.

Fuck.

Fuck me, she looks good.

Fuck me, she looks too damn good.

"Your friend here, Razor. He was discussing his day job." Typical. It's fucking Racer . . . Chandler.

Georgie lifts a brow at me but doesn't question me. She's wised up—don't question me or else I'll just make it worse and more embarrassing.

From her purse, she pulls out a key and hands it to me. "Thanks for locking up. Will I see you tomorrow?"

I shrug. "Not sure. Pretty beat. I'll let you know." Her face falls, and like the asshole I am, I take pleasure in that.

"Oh, okay. Well, let me know."

"Ready?" Chaunce asks.

Georgie nods and starts to walk by me. That's when I whisper into her ear while snagging her upper arm. "He's got a small dick. Guaranteed."

"Racer," she whispers through her teeth.

"One tit grab says I'm right."

"Get a life." She blows by me but not before she glances at Chauncey's crotch and nibbles on her bottom lip out of concern. I can't help but chuckle. God, she's so easy to read. Although, right now, I hate that she is. She wants to get laid. The dress, the fuck-me heels? She's a horny girl in heat. *And she chose him? Small-dick bonds man?*

I turn toward them and watch as they walk out of the shop together. Before they shut the door, I call out, "Be careful, chlamydia's been making the rounds. Wear protection, kids, and abstinence is always a winner in my book."

I garner a giant glare from Georgie before the door is shut, causing me to laugh some more. Damn, I can only imagine the cogs spinning in her head right now. How to get Racer back . . .

She can try all she wants, she really doesn't know who she's messing with.

~

"Go ahead, smack my ass one more time, see where it gets you."

"I can smack your ass all I want."

I take a seat on Adalyn's couch and drape the hand holding my piña colada over the back. I face Adalyn and smirk. "I know this is going to be hard for you to believe, but you really can't smack my ass anytime you want."

For being someone who was very much against being physical

tonight, she's been super touchy. Hell, I wouldn't mind a little dry-hump session. If it happens, it happens, so be it.

She takes a long sip from her drink and says with lazy eyes, "Best friend privileges."

"Yeah?" I question her, "How come I've never seen these rules?"

"They're one-sided," she answers matter-of-factly.

"Seems a little unfair."

"Please," she huffs. "If I was licking your dick every time you passed, we would be having a different conversation."

"If you were licking my dick every time I passed you, I wouldn't be moving forward to my destination, that's for damn sure."

"Too bad for you, I would never lick your dick."

"Yeah, only snuggle it with your face."

Adalyn leans back on the couch and stares me down. "I rubbed my cheek against it once, Racer. Once! I was drunk and trying to look through your pee hole like a kaleidoscope. You can't blame me for being creative."

"I guess not. I think we have whiskey to blame for that night."

She takes another sip of her drink. "At least you were still wearing your pants. If I held your urethra up to my eyeball, I don't think I could ever look at you the same."

"Yeah, our friendship would be dead at that point." I tip my drink at her. "Thank God for pants, right?"

She clinks her glass against mine. "Yes, thank God for pants." She chuckles and then asks, "How's the new job? Seems like I never see you anymore. I mean, it's nine at night. Is this the new hour we get to visit? Or is this a booty call?"

"Has it ever been a booty call?" I ask seriously. She shakes her head and smiles sweetly at me, knowing I would never treat her like that. "New job is fine. Same old shit, trying to meet an impossible timeline by myself."

"Sounds normal. How's the boss? Still showing up in heels?"

I laugh. "No, she bought *construction clothes*."

Adalyn shakes her head. "Of course she did. Let me guess: boots, shorts, and a shirt."

I nod and take a sip of my drink. I press my lips together, savoring the flavor. "Not going to lie, it's hot on her."

"Not surprised by that either. If I know you like I think I do, you made some dickhead comment about her not being able to wear those clothes because you wouldn't get any work done."

"Pretty much." I shake my head, thinking back to that first day in her *new clothes*. "Hate to admit it, Addie, she's hot. Really fucking hot."

"Ahhh," she replies in a knowing way. "You're crushing on this girl?"

"First," I hold out one of my fingers, "this isn't middle school, I don't crush on people. And second, she's wicked hot but not my type."

"Hot is not your type? Huh, what are you looking for now? Snaggle face with burnt hair?"

I chuckle and nod. "Yeah, love that burnt-hair smell, really gets my balls tingling."

"Yeah, sperm-revving attraction? Never thought you would be a burnt hair kind of man."

"You learn something new every day." I wink at her over my drink.

She crosses her legs on the couch and gets serious, I can see it in the way she hunkers down. Damn, here we go.

"Enough with the joking. Why isn't hot your type?"

"Come on," I say. "She's on a completely different level than I am. There is no way she would ever want to date a guy like me, someone who works with their hands. I'm barely blue collar, and she's in the top tax bracket. Completely different lives. Plus, she annoys the shit out of me. She never does what I tell her, she always has to question everything."

Adalyn smiles and pokes me in the side. "You liiiiiiike her," she singsongs, instantly annoying me.

"I really don't. We couldn't be more different. But does she have nice tits? Yes." I nod my head. "Yes, she does."

"You're telling me if she came into her shop, completely naked and started thrusting her vagina at your dick, you wouldn't shuck your pants and give her something to ride?"

God, I love Adalyn. Never holds back.

"I mean . . ." I weigh out my options. "If she falls and I happen to catch her with my dick, that wouldn't be a bad thing."

Adalyn laughs. "I knew it. You would so fuck her."

"Yeah, I probably would." I shrug. "But it would be a huge mistake, because I know it would do nothing but make the working environment awkward. It's already awkward as is."

"Sexual tension?"

"No." I roll my eyes. "It's just weird between us. Like I said, there is the whole class thing there."

"This isn't the 1800s, Racer. You can date someone who makes more money than you. You can talk to someone who has gold bars sitting in a bank. You can be in the same room as someone who uses hundred-dollar bills as toilet paper. You don't have to segregate yourself."

"I'm not segregating myself. I'm just understanding and acknowledging my place."

"Why do you do that?"

"Do what?" I ask, even though I know where she's going with this.

She sighs and sinks farther into the couch. "Why do you make yourself seem less than you are?"

Avoiding the question, I say, "I know you like to believe everything is cupcakes and rainbows—"

"I have to." Her face turns somber. "I have to live in a far-off land because if I didn't, the shit I see in the hospital on a daily basis would destroy me. I have to try to see the positive in everything."

Shit.

"I'm sorry, Adalyn."

She holds up her hand. "This isn't about me. This is about you."

Knowing I won't be able to drop the topic, I say, "Not that I want there to be a chance with Georgiana, because I really don't, but if there was a minor chance I did, I know I would be completely wrong for her. And before you get on your high horse and start blowing steam up my ass, I'll tell you why." Adalyn crosses her arms over her chest and waits for an answer. "She had a date tonight, or what I'm assuming was a date. She got dressed up and some guy came and picked her up."

"A date, huh? How did that make you feel?"

A little weird...

"I couldn't care less. Like I said, I'm not interested. But what I did learn is that her type is the farthest thing from me. You should have seen this guy, Addie. Looked like every high-society douche nugget you see hopping around in the Hamptons. His hair was slicked back, he wore a blazer with khakis, and he even spoke like he was trying to squeeze as tight as possible to the stick shoved up his ass. And to top it off, the guy is a total creep. Think of a skinnier version of Glenn Gulia from The Wedding Singer."

"Ugh, that's such a good movie." Adalyn holds up her fingers and says, "Hey, wedding singer . . . aaarrooooo." She plays out one of the best scenes in the movie when the drunk brother falls off the curb and drops his drink.

"We need to watch that again."

Adalyn shakes her finger at me. "Don't try to change the subject with a movie date. But yes, we will. You bring the chocolate-covered raisins, and I'll bring the popcorn. But back to Glenn Gulia junior; you really think that's her type? Maybe she was going out with him because she had to. I think you shouldn't judge her from Glenn Gulia II. Who knows, she might be using him as a beard so she can forget about the hunky construction worker who's occupying her every thought."

I shake my head and answer sarcastically, "Yeah, that's it. Glenn Gulia II is her beard. Nailed it, Adalyn."

She clinks my glass with hers and gives herself a fist bump.

Ridiculous.

CHAPTER ELEVEN

GEORGIANA

"You gave him head, didn't you? You puckered up and gave him road head as he drove you back to the shop."

"God, no."

Madison scans the empty shell of a space and shakes her head. "You're lying."

"I'm really not. I would never suck a guy's dick for the hell of it while driving."

"Did you see his dick at all? Did you pet it for a few seconds, maybe wink at it, get it riled up?"

I don't even bother to look up at my friend as I go through my checklist on my iPad. "I did nothing to his dick last night. I didn't even look in the general direction of where his dick rested." That's a lie but Madison doesn't need to know that. I looked at his crotch when he first came to pick me up. And the only reason I did was because of Racer. He just had to bet on Chauncey having a pencil dick. It was all I could think of for the rest of the night. I'm surprised Chauncey wanted a second date after our rather drab conversation. I wasn't fully present. Instead of listening to

Chauncey, my mind kept going back to Racer and his shirtless, muscly self.

God, he ruins everything.

"Okay, so if no dicking was involved whatsoever, then why are there"—she starts counting with her finger—"ten bouquets? There are ten bouquets of red roses in this empty space. No man has ten bouquets of red roses delivered to a woman's place of work without thanking her for something. So what is it? What did you do? If you say anal I'm walking out this door right now."

I'm somewhat tempted to tell her it was anal only to get her to leave so I can get my work done, but I'm not that desperate for peace and quiet.

"Nothing." I shrug. "He came to pick me up, took me to a fancy-ish restaurant, told me all about his job, which was . . . boring. And then he brought me back here, kissed me and—"

"You kissed him?"

"Yeah." I turn my eyes to my iPad so my friend can't read my face.

"What kind of kiss? Was it a cheek kiss or lips?"

"Lips."

"You kissed Chauncey on the lips?"

"Why do you sound so disgusted? He's a very attractive, smart, and well-rounded man. Plus he had nice lips."

"Good God," Madison scoffs. "How long did you kiss him for?"

"Not very long. It was just a goodnight kiss. You know, *a thank you for dinner, I had a nice time* kiss."

"What does that even mean?" Madison starts to pace, as if the end of the world is coming. "Did you use tongue? Was there groping? Did he cup your ass?"

"No, nothing like that. Just you know, a fusion."

Madison seizes her pacing. She looks up at me with her head in her hand, bewilderment on her face. "A fusion?" She pauses and repeats. "A fusion? Well, if that isn't the least sexiest thing I've ever heard." Striking her hand across her neck, she continues, "He's done. If all you can say about his kiss is it was a fusion, then clearly this man isn't worth your time."

"Not all of us put out on the first night like you, Madison."

"I don't anymore. That was when I was young and flirty. I'm old and serious now."

"You're twenty-six," I deadpan.

"Yeah, almost halfway to fifty, I should just start digging my grave now." She sighs and sits on a five-gallon bucket of primer we still won't be using for a while. "I'm kind of disappointed. When I walked in to see all these roses, I would have guessed you at least got some last night. Nope, you just had a . . . fusion." Madison uses air quotes and rolls her eyes, clearly not hiding her disappointment in me.

"At least I got out there. That's more I can say for you. When was the last time you went on a date?"

Madison shakes her head and waves her hand at me. "Oh no, you don't. This isn't about me. This is about you. I get my jollies when I need them, don't you worry about me."

"Are you still seeing your parents' pool boy?"

Madison bites on her fingernail and looks to the side. "Trevor gets horny in the afternoons. I can't help it. He's all bronzy with muscles."

"He's twenty, Madison. You have to buy him beer with his pool-cleaning money."

Madison points her finger at me. "Don't you dare knock his pool money. He works hard for that. Do you know how hard it is to direct those pool-cleaning barracudas with those long sticks? It's not that easy. Believe me, I fell in the pool trying."

"You were naked, drunk, and had a bag of Cool Ranch Doritos in hand."

"Erroneous," Madison shouts and stands again, pacing the room. "So are you going to see this guy again or not?"

"Yeah," I answer casually. "I mean, I didn't have a terrible time. He was sweet and pleasant." Not to mention boring. Well, not the entire time. When we talked about our favorite Nirchi's pizza, I enjoyed that conversation *and* was surprised he was so passionate about it. "He did say he likes half-moon cookies."

Madison stops her pacing and turns toward me. "Chocolate or vanilla base?"

"Chocolate."

Madison winces and looks up at the ceiling. "Fiiiiiiine, you can go out with him again. But be sure to have him buy you a bouquet of half-moon cookies next time, especially if he wants to win me over."

"And winning me over has nothing to do with this?"

Madison shakes her head. "It's more important to win over the best friend, everyone knows that." She rubs her hands together and asks, "What can I help you with today?"

"Nothing. Racer is coming later tonight to put up the drywall and patch."

"I can help with that. When is he going to get here?"

"He's bringing his friend to help him. Pretty sure Racer doesn't want us to do anything when it comes to construction."

Madison's ear perks up. "A friend, huh? Is he hot like Racer?"

"No idea. I was just told to stay out of their way since Racer wants to get out of here as quickly as possible."

"More the reason to help them." Madison walks back to the bathroom and stops when she reaches the door. Her incessant walking around is starting to get on my nerves. "Whoa, what happened in here?"

"What do you mean? Racer tore everything out, we're going to re-tile, make it more chic and less scary-dungeon bathroom."

"Scary dungeon bathroom is the farthest thing from what I'm seeing. More like a weird . . . playful dream."

"What?" I look up from my iPad. Is she drunk again? "What are you talking about?"

"Come look."

"I've seen the bathroom, Madison. It's stripped down walls with holes in the floor for a toilet and plumbing."

"What does petrichor mean?"

My ears perk up from a word I have written in my special book, a word that's been in my book since high school. It's the second word I wrote down, right behind limerence.

Petrichor.

I can remember like it was yesterday. Being the youngest in my family, it was the first summer all my siblings were off living their lives, and I was left behind spending the summer with my society-enriched mother and workaholic father. It was quiet, a somber summer with an empty house of fading memories. It was the wettest summer we've ever had since I can remember and a part of me liked to believe it was the skies crying for me, setting the mood for what was to come: a consuming loneliness. Madison was in the Hamptons, my mom kept up her "best mom in the world" façade when in front of her friends. It was all about appearances.

But that summer . . . it gave me time to think, to think about the future I wanted to create for myself and how to find the pathway to achieve it. It helped me appreciate the small things, the things that matter like bringing out the happiness in your life, and it helped me appreciate the small things.

The small things like petrichor.

Have you ever sat back right before a rainstorm and watched the rain roll in, like a curtain closing over the sun?

Those first drops lighting up the ground with a fresh awakening.

The plants soaking up earth's moisture, drinking their share of nourishment.

And that smell of crisply fallen precipitation hitting the scorched summer terrain: petrichor.

Rising from my seat, I set my iPad down and meet Madison in the corner. When I turn the corner, the sight in front of me amazes me.

Splattered across the soon-to-be-tiled wall, which will be above the pedestal sink, is light blue paint in the form of rain, streaking down from the ceiling where it pools over the word petrichor, followed by a comment that says, "Can you smell anew?"

Stunned, I stand there, taking in the symbolism in front of me. He did this.

"Please tell me this isn't some bad potty humor. That would kill it for me," Madison says, interrupting my thoughts. "I don't think you should ever write something on the bathroom wall about if you can smell something."

Ignoring Madison, I step up to the wall and trace the word with my finger. I can smell the anew, I can feel the awakening within me; I can feel the impact of his words.

But my question is, why?

Why would he write this?

"I can," I whisper under my breath, tracing the letters one more time.

Leaning over my shoulder and whispering in my ear, Madison asks, "You can what?"

I chuckle and take a deep breath. "Petrichor is a way to describe the smell of freshly fallen rain. I don't know how he knows, but it's one of my favorite words, and it's the perfect way to describe the next step in this journey."

Knowing about my book, Madison nods. "Is it me, or does it make him that much hotter that he knows beautiful words?"

Like a hundred times hotter, which puts him at lethal levels. Chauncey might need another phone call. *Another attempt at being the man I need to relieve the Racer-induced desperation.*

The front door of the shop opens and male laughter filters in. I step outside the bathroom where Racer and, who I'm assuming is his friend, fill the entryway, broad shoulders making the space feel smaller than it is.

"She totally put out." Racer laughs and shakes his head.

"Roses are douchey," his friend adds and stretches his python-sized arms over his head. God, he's big.

Stepping into the main area of the shop, I feel like I need to defend Chauncey. "Roses aren't douchey, they're sweet."

Racer whips his head toward me and a lazy smile falls over his lips. For a second, an urge to run up and kiss him passes over me, but it's quickly washed away when he opens his mouth. "Roses are total douche-canoe status, Princess."

I put my hands on my hips now, ready for a fight. "Roses are romantic, but I guess you would never know that with the swill you drink and the lard you eat on a daily basis."

Racer squares up to me and crosses his bulging arms over his chest. "That lard I eat does me well. And I know romance, Georgie, don't question my ability to woo by what I eat and drink. Although, I guess the way you present yourself is more important to you than what rests in the heart."

I step closer, anger starting to boil inside me, all previous warming thoughts I had of Racer vanished. "It is about the heart for me. That's why sending a woman roses after a date—and that's all it was, a date—is romantic. He's telling me he appreciated my company. That's romantic."

Racer takes another step forward, closing the space between us to only inches. "No, what he sent you was a showboat, not romance. He was giving you a subtle reminder of what he can offer you materialistically, not what he can offer you intellectually."

I cross my arms now, a jut to my hip as I question him. "Yeah? You think you're so romantic? Fine, what would you have sent after a date? A text that barely spells out the word thanks? Maybe a coupon for a pony ride on your lap? Or an offer to get a front-row seat to the gun show?" I roll my eyes and shake my head, as if to say, "this guy."

Racer closes any space between us and leans forward so he's looking me directly in my eyes. I'm guessing his friend and Madison are watching with avid attention, waiting to see how this tête-à-tête will end. "You think so little of me." His eyes challenge me, looking past the surface, almost into my soul. Glancing past me for a second, his eyes land on the bathroom, and in that moment, I know he's questioning if I saw what he did.

"Prove me wrong." He already has in a way, but then he shows up, arrogance dripping off him in droves, and I can't help but rethink every kind thing he does.

"You really want to know what I would have done the day after *I* took you on a date?"

"Yeah, I really do."

He searches my eyes. There is a small squint to them, almost as if he's angry, but I don't break. I hold strong and wait for his answer.

Growing even more serious, Racer speaks in a quiet tone, so quiet I'm certain I'm the only one who will hear him.

"If I took you out on a date, Princess, I wouldn't send you roses the next day. You don't deserve them—"

"That's rude," I scoff.

"Let me fucking finish," he grits out. "You don't deserve them because they are a scapegoat flower. They're the type of flower men use because they know nothing about the person they're sending them to. Lover boy clearly doesn't know anything about you, because if it was me, I would have sent you a handful of variegated tulips."

"Variegated tulips? The multi-colored ones?"

He nods confidently. "Exactly."

"Those are like two cents," Madison chimes in.

Leaning past me, Racer says, "It's not about the money, sweetheart." Turning back to me, he adds, "It's about the meaning behind them." He tips my chin up with his fingers, his stare blazing a trail of heat down my spine. "Variegated tulips represent beautiful eyes, and if I took you out on a date, I know that's all I would be able to think about after I said good night."

A tingling awareness erupts across my skin as a cool mist of sweat coats me from his compliment. He leans forward another inch, his minty breath tickling my mouth. I subconsciously lick my lips, preparing for what's to come as my mind races; do I want this?

His thumb rubs across my lips and his head leans forward for a brief moment only for him to step away. Space and air, and everything heavy that's been hanging on our shoulders floats between us, reminding me that I'm in my shop, with my friend next to me, staring at my every move.

"Nice, man," Racer's friend says right before he fist-bumps him. "That's some wooing kind of shit right there."

Racer blows on his knuckles and then rubs them on his chest. "I do think so myself."

And once again, like a wet blanket tamping down my flame, I'm reminded why I can't stand the man in front of me. He's so freaking arrogant.

"You're annoying," I huff as I stomp away, unable to come up with a better comeback.

Madison starts to slow clap as I walk way. "Well played, Racer, well played."

"You're *my* friend, Madison," I yell.

"But that was so good," she says while chasing after me.

It was. Darn it, it was really, really good.

~

"Stop stroking his arms and let the man work," I yell at Madison once again.

"But look at them." My friend who has no shame stands in front of Aaron—aka, Smalls, but I refuse to call him that, especially since he's anything but small—stroking his arms while she flirts abhorrently. "I've never seen a man this buff."

"Have your eyes been closed when you've been around me?" Racer asks from on top of the scaffolding.

"Please," Aaron snorts. "You know you're nothing like me."

Racer points his hand that's holding a pencil at Aaron. "Don't you dare give me a complex again, man. Tell me I'm just as big. Tell me."

Aaron rolls his eyes. "You're big, Racer."

"Damn right." Racer goes back to marking something on the wall and says, "Get your ass up here, Smalls, I don't have all fucking night."

Having no self-respect, Madison asks, "Do you have a girlfriend, Aaron?"

He scratches the back of his neck and looks over to Racer for help.

"Better answer the question," I say while adding up some numbers on my computer. My eyes are starting to cross from the amount of digits floating around in my head. "She's not going to let you go until she finds out."

"She's right," Madison confirms.

"No girlfriend." Aaron steps away and starts to climb the scaffolding as Madison smiles brightly and sits down next to me.

"I like him."

"You like his muscles," I correct.

"Well, yeah. But I also like him; there is something he's hiding and I want to know what it is."

"He's hiding a micro penis," Racer calls out. "He's overcompensating with the muscles."

"And what excuse does that give you?" Aaron asks. He picks up a palette of patch and starts dragging it over the seams in the drywall.

"It's the opposite of you. I'm trying to keep up with my dick. It's hard to match my muscles to it because it's so big."

I snort . . . well, because, he's so ridiculous and obnoxious and full of himself.

"What's so funny down there, Georgie?"

"You're acting like you have a horse leg between your thighs."

"Who says I don't?" Racer picks up a spackle knife and joins Aaron in patching the ceiling.

"You don't," Aaron mutters.

"Dude." Racer holds out his hand. "Bro code. We all praise each other's dicks in front of women."

Aaron doesn't even bother to look at Racer as he continues to work on the ceiling. "First of all, there is no such thing as bro code for praising each other's dicks. Don't make up stupid shit. And second of all, if I'm, in your words, supposed to be your bro and praise your dick, then where were you two seconds ago when you were telling everyone I have a micro penis?"

"Ooooooo." Madison claps her hands. "Burned." With her hands on her chest, gazing up at Aaron, she asks, "Will you take me home with you?"

I slyly eye Racer who has a smirk on his face. "He got you there, horse leg."

Looking between all of us, Racer doesn't say a word, but he *does* start unbuckling his pants.

Oh Jesus . . .

"Whip it out, and I will spackle it to the ceiling. Close up shop, dude. No one wants to see your stank cock."

I laugh out loud and repeat, "Stank cock."

"It's not stanky," Racer says. "I wash my junk twice a day."

"Just keep working, stank cock," I call up. "I would like to get this place done in this century. Also, Aaron, you're allowed here anytime you want. I like how you put Racer in his place."

"He's just showing off." Racer elbows Aaron in the ribs and then climbs down the scaffolding.

"Where you going?" Aaron calls out. I was just about to ask the same exact thing.

Walking out the door, Racer calls out, "You all have upset me. I need to have a moment with my main squeeze."

The front door slams shut, sending a resounding rattle through the empty shop.

"Who's his main squeeze?" Madison asks. "I thought he was single."

Aaron sighs and continues to work. "Little Debbie. He's having a moment with Little Debbie."

I roll my eyes and get back to work. Why am I not surprised?

∼

"Do you need help?" I call out to Racer who's in the back of the shop, cleaning up his spackle spades.

"I'm good. I've got this."

"Okay." I shift on my feet and pull on the hem of my shirt.

Madison left a while ago, unable to score Aaron's number, who even though he *played* hard to get, snuck glances at Madison when she wasn't looking. And Aaron took off once they finished the ceiling, leaving Racer and me alone. "I guess I'll head out now. Do you want to lock up?"

"It's eleven o'clock. I'll walk you to your car, Georgie. So sit your ass down and wait for me to finish up."

"I'm more than capable of walking myself to my car."

There is a plop on the floor and the telltale sign of metal clanking together. "I know you're capable, Princess, but that doesn't mean you should go out there alone. So, like I said before, sit your ass down and wait a few seconds."

"You're so confusing, you know that?" I slide down against the wall and sit on the floor.

"How's that?"

"Because one minute you're sulking in the corner about some asinine thing and the next you're being an overprotective alpha who thinks everything he says is right."

"That's because everything I say is right." He pokes his head out from around the corner. "And you like it when I sulk. I've seen it in your eyes."

"I don't like it when you sulk. No one likes a man-child."

"Lying to yourself is only going to hurt you in the long run, Georgie. The sooner you accept your love for me, the better."

I shake my head and rest it against the wall. He's infuriating.

Twisted in a way.

Hot and cold.

Sweet and sour.

Like he can't make up his mind about how he wants to interact with me.

Stepping into the hallway where I'm sitting, he scans me up and down and adjusts his backward cap on his head. "Petrichor. Can you smell it, Georgie?" When I'm about to answer, thinking he's speaking of the new journey he spoke of on the developing bathroom wall, he nods toward the front door.

Rain floods the window, lighting up the dark streets with pelts of water, emanating the smell I've come to notice even on the inside looking out.

I take a deep breath and close my eyes, memories flooding my mind.

Loss.

Loneliness.

Abandonment.

Discouragement...

When I open my eyes, new memories waiting to be made in this shop wash away the old.

Can you smell anew?

I can't only smell it, but I can also see it.

"Come on." Racer reaches for my hand and pulls me to my feet. Without even giving me a second to catch my feet under me, he rushes me across the shop and straight into the road. He flings me into the empty street that is only lit by a single street lamp. I cover my head as cold, chilling rain drenches me.

"What are you doing?" I look over to Racer whose arms are at his side, his head tilted to the sky. Water cascades down his powerful body, soaking his shirt to his skin, making every contour and sinew visible through the fabric. But it isn't the muscles that are pulling my attention, it's the ease in his stature—an ease I've never seen in him before.

He's relaxed.

Carefree.

Complaisantly beautiful.

"Enjoy the moment, Georgie. Take it all in."

I shield the rain from pelting me in the eyes. "But I'm getting wet."

He spreads his arms out wide and soaks in more. "It's called living. Life is short, Georgie. You never know when your time is up, so spend every waking moment you have experiencing what life has to offer. Your clothes will dry, but your memory of this moment will live forever." *How can he know that this is one of the few moments when I've* experienced *life, and not* done *life?*

I pause, unsure what to do, and it must be too long, because before I know it, Racer is picking me up and spinning me around in the street as rain whips around us. I hold on to him for dear life and laugh when he starts to lose control, toppling us over into a puddle forming in a grass patch on the sidewalk. Mud splatters across the street and all over us, but I'm too consumed with Racer's position than with the mess I've become.

Hovering over me, drenched, is Racer with a devilish look in his eyes.

"Why are you so stuck -up?" he asks over the pouring from the skies.

I wipe my face with the back of my hand, trying to get a better visual on the man above me. "Why are you such a man-child?"

"You learn to live freely when you lose a piece of your heart. It's the only way to survive."

Caught off guard by his answer, I tilt my head to the side and ask, "Did someone break your heart?"

He runs a hand over his jaw, studying me for a second before he pops up and answers, "Something like that." He pulls me to my feet again and turns us toward the shop. "It's getting late."

The lightheartedness vanishes. The Racer capable of throwing wit my way at the drop of a hat is back.

Who broke his heart?

And why am I now so desperate to find out?

CHAPTER TWELVE

RACER

"Dude, don't burn my wiener."
"I'm not burning it."
I point at the hot dog I specifically chose and say, "See that black stuff, that's burning of the wiener skin."

"Christ." Tucker strokes the stubble on his beard and points at one of the outdoor chairs with his grilling tongs. "Sit the fuck down or leave."

"Talk about hospitality." I fold my arms over my chest and flop down on the outdoor couch. "If Emma knew you were yelling at your dinner guest, she would be pissed at you."

"Doesn't count where you're concerned. She's given me a pass when dealing with you. She knows what a little bitch you can be."

"That's not true. Emma would never let you treat me with such disdain." I point at my chest. "I'm the only reason you two are together."

The door leading out to the porch swings open and Smalls walks out holding three uncapped beers. He hands them out and sits on the rail of the porch, his feet perched up on one of the fence rungs. "Are you claiming responsibility for Tucker's fortune again?"

"I'm not claiming it; it's cold hard facts."

"The fuck it is," Tucker answers. "You were a glorified delivery boy."

"I used glitter!"

Last year, Tucker was an idiot and almost lost the best thing to ever happen to him: Emma. Not going to lie, she's hot as fuck. I was trying to get Tucker to set me up with her but the prick he is, he kept her to himself, and look what happened. He fucked up and little old Racer had to save the day. Insert jacking-off motion here.

Idiot.

I made things happen for them and subtle reminders of how I'm so great shouldn't hurt him. Hell, I gave him love again. You can't ever repay someone for that. At least that's what I keep telling him. Just secretly, seeing Tucker *in love* and hopeful was better than any repayment I could ever receive. So not telling *him* that though.

"No one asked you to use glitter, that was your own choice."

"It was a nice touch. It's called committing to the role you gave me. Will you never understand that?"

"Never," Tucker replies and then turns to Smalls. "Racer told me you were flapping your cock around at a girl the other day. Said you were really trying to hang it low over scaffolding. What's that about?"

You and I both know Smalls wasn't hanging his dick out, but sometimes when telling a story, exaggeration is required. So naturally, I turned the tables on Smalls and told Tucker he was practically masturbating over Madison when in reality, he was just sneaking glances. But only saying he was sneaking glances adds no drama. So pulling the dick out was the next best option. Always a winner in my book.

Smalls quirks his lip to the side when he looks at me and then shakes his head while taking a sip of his beer. "Yup, I totally jizzed all over her face from eight feet above. The accuracy I had was on point."

"He hit her arm, don't let him fool you. Splattered sperm everywhere."

"Dude," Tucker groans. "Don't fucking say splattered sperm. What is wrong with you?"

"Especially since your story is completely off base. Limits, man, you've got to know your limits," Smalls says.

Splattered sperm might have been pushing my luck . . .

"So what really happened?" Tucker shuts the grill and turns toward us.

I point at the grill and lift my head to look at what's happening in it. "Are you burn—?"

"I'm not fucking burning your hot dog. Calm your nut sack, man." Tucker runs his hand over his face, frustration clear in the way his neck veins pop. Something has to be going on with him and Emma. He doesn't normally get this irritated so quickly. It usually takes me a little longer than this to piss him off. "What happened with the girl?"

Sensing the tension, Smalls clears his throat and says, "It was a friend of Racer's client. She was flirting. That's it."

"Flirting?" I scoff. "She was practically humping Smalls's leg. The sad thing was, he didn't give her the time of day."

"Not your type?" Tucker asks.

"Totally his type. He was acting—"

"Hey, how about how we talk about Racer and how he's in love with his client," Smalls says with a smirk.

With a smarmy look on his face, Tucker folds his arms over his chest and sips his beer. "Oh, do tell."

"I'm not in love with my client. Where the hell did you come up with that?"

"Please." Smalls snorts and turns directly toward Tucker and speaks to him as if I'm not standing a few feet away. "You should see him with this girl, man. She's hot, and he doesn't hide the fact that he knows it. His eyes wander too much."

"Nothing wrong with looking." I chug my beer, getting myself ready for another one.

"And when he's around her, it's like they're in grade school. He's always pulling pranks on her."

"She's uptight. She needs to learn to relax so she's not always harassing me about her damn budget and timeline. It's for my benefit."

Ignoring me, Smalls continues, "And then he goes and pulls this philosophical bullshit by leaving special words around the project site that mean something."

"It's nice to . . ." Huh, what's my excuse for this one? "It's nice to be nice." There, that doesn't sound idiotic at all.

Smiling a little too brightly, Tucker repeats, "It's nice to be nice? When has that ever been your motto?"

I have nothing, absolutely nothing. When has my mind ever gone blank like this? I'm usually quick on my feet. I blame Georgie and her low-cut shirts; they flood my mind making it waterlogged.

I really don't like the look on Tucker's face right now. "So you like this girl."

"No." Maybe-ish, but we'll keep that between us. "She's annoying as shit, doesn't stop talking, and she's on a different playing field than I am. No way am I getting involved with that. Not even for a good fuck." It would be a good fuck. I know it would be. Sometimes the stuck-up ones are the best because when they get a chance to unleash pent-up aggression, they go crazy in bed. Knowing Georgie, I know she would consume me in the sheets. No doubt about that.

Tucker and Smalls exchange glances, the kind of glances that speak a thousand words between them, and I don't appreciate it.

I point my finger at both of them. "Don't do that. Don't look at each other as if you know something I don't know. I'm aware of that look. There is nothing going on. She's hot, gorgeous actually, I'll give you that, but that's it."

Smalls doesn't even acknowledge what I just said. "He likes her, you can see it all over his face."

"I don't like her. I tolerate her."

Leveling with me, Tucker says, "Let me ask you this. Have you shared a Little Debbie snack with her yet?"

"Hell, no." Lies! I've thought about it. Shit, I thought about stocking the shop with a crate full of them, possibly playing a game where we close our eyes and have to eat the first one we pick and then guess what it is. Hell, I want to play that game right now. I would dominate.

"Do you want to?" Smalls asks, smiling too damn wide.

"She wouldn't eat them if I offered. She has caviar taste, man. She's fancy as shit. Our lives clash." Growing serious for a second, I grab the back of my neck. "She's paying me to fix up her shop. I'm desperate for the money, and she knows this. I know what I look like to her." *And I fucking hate it.*

"And what's that?"

"A man who can't provide for himself. A penniless man with no education, no savings, and nothing to offer someone like her. Hell, she sees me drive up in a rusted-up truck every day, wearing a rotation of two pairs of jeans with the same paint marks on them. I have nothing to offer a woman who has everything. So there's no reason to even visit the topic if I like her or not, because whether I do or not is a moot point. The feeling would not be returned." That is something I know.

"Racer," Tucker starts to say but I shake my head.

"Don't bother trying to talk me up. Just drop it, man." It doesn't matter.

They are silent for a second, their gazes drawn down. They get me. Enough said.

"You're so much more than how you describe yourself," Smalls says, breaking the silence. "You're the first to tell us it's not about the possessions in our lives, but the experiences."

That's true, I am. I'm all about living life because it's way too damn short to fixate on menial things, but with Georgie, it's different. It feels different. *She* deserves more.

"I agree, but not everyone does." Especially if Georgie goes out with a dickweed like Chauncey Rose Giver.

"So I take it you won't be sharing Debbie with her," Tucker says, adding some light to the conversation.

"Not anytime soon." I nod at the grill. "Are you paying attention to that?"

"Stop questioning my grilling abilities." Tucker puts down his beer and opens the lid; smoke billows out, filling the air around us. Tucker waves the thick smoke out of the way only to reveal charred and blackened hot dogs.

"For fuck's sake," I yell while standing. "I told you, you were going to burn the hell out of my wiener." I snag the tongs from Tucker and pick up my hot dog. I shove it in his face and say, "It looks like a shriveled-up dead dick." I toss it back on the grill and return the tongs. "Grill master, my ass." I turn toward the house with one mission on my mind. "I'm raiding your cabinets. I know you have some Swiss Rolls around here somewhere."

"You'll never find them."

"Challenge accepted!"

～

Another long-ass day on the job, and another long-ass night in front of me. Sore and tired, I pull my haggard body out of my truck, snag my tools, and head to Limerence. The lights are on, shining brightly through the front windows that Georgie covered with purple paper yesterday so people couldn't see the changes. She wants to have a grand reveal when it's all finished.

I don't know if it's the conversation I had with my boys the other day or how tired I am, but I have no energy for tonight. The project is moving along quickly. We have the walls and floors done. I still have to work on that godforsaken bathroom, install shelves, build her consulting office and front desk, but for the most part, things are starting to come together.

But today, today is going to be hard. Not physically hard, but mentally.

I have to ask for money.

I got this month's round of bills and once again, I'm fucking scraping by. I need a reprieve from the stress, and there is only one way to get it.

I pull on my baseball cap and then quickly spin it around on my head so it's backward. Might as well get this humiliation over with.

The door to Limerence is unlocked, which I don't like. I've told her many times to keep it locked up when she's here alone. Not that she's in a bad area, but you never know what kind of creep will walk by and try to pull something.

When I walk in, I'm greeted by Georgie—no Madison today—lying on the floor, staring at the ceiling, her trusty iPad next to her. But for once, her eyes aren't fixed on it.

"I thought I told you to keep that door locked," I say while setting my tools down and locking the door.

"I just unlocked it because I knew you were coming and thought I'd make it easier on you."

"Thanks, but keep it locked." I scan her up and down and notice she's not wearing her "construction clothes." Instead, she's in a pair of tight-fitting skinny jeans, some kind of black fitted top that hangs off her shoulders with her heels resting next to her. "What's up, Georgie?"

"I don't want to work today." Her voice sounds distant, sad, not the Georgie with sass and spice I know.

"You don't have to. You can go home if you want. I can handle it." There is no way *I* can go home today. Despite the pain in my body, I'll be working. I need to be paid.

Ignoring my suggestion, she squeezes her eyes shut and sighs. When she opens them, they shine with sadness. "Supine," she softly says.

Drawing closer, I ask, "What?"

"Supine. To lie facing upward. It's how I used to think over major life changes. It's the seventeenth word in my book. At the time, I had no idea there was such a beautiful word to describe something I did daily, but there it was, sitting, waiting for me to write it down." Quietly she whispers, "Supine."

A little worried, I squat down to her level, ignoring all the creaks and cracks my body makes as I edge closer to where she rests. I'm tempted to push a stray hair behind her ear but I resist. That's an intimate move and right now, that would be inappropriate. "Georgie, you seem tired. Go home, take a long bath or something, and relax. I've got this."

She shakes her head from side to side. "I can't go home."

I know I shouldn't ask. I know I need to keep this relationship as professional as possible, especially if I'm going to ask what I need to ask today, but the look in her eyes—the emptiness, a look I know well—I just need to find out why it's there. What's stopping her from snapping at me, from using that sassy mouth of hers?

"Why can't you go home?"

She closes her eyes and a tear falls down her cheek.

Oh hell . . .

"I don't have one. My dad had the maid pack up my stuff today and put it in storage. I was left with two suitcases and a note attached to them saying that if I were to go against his wishes and disrespect him, then I'm not welcome to live under his roof."

"He kicked you out?" Georgie nods her head, more tears falling from her eyes. Shit, I don't know what to do.

Scratch that, I know what to do. I know how to console a friend. But a client, someone I'm trying to keep at a distance? What do I do in this instance? Do I pat her shoulder and say, "There, there, everything will be okay"? Do I try to show her the bright side? At least he didn't go psycho ex-girlfriend and burn all her things. Or do I just ignore her and get to work? Technically my job is to redo the shop and nothing else. I'm not required to sit around and work out her problems with her. That's what Madison is for. I had a good dad. There would never have been a time where

I would have feared being kicked out. Even when I was a tool at times.

And yet . . .

Fuck, my heart reaches out to her.

"Shit, I'm sorry, Princess," I say softly. Not knowing what else to do, I join her on the floor and lie face up, our shoulders bumping, our hands inches from one another.

Don't grab her hand. For the love of God, don't grab her hand.

My pinky brushes against hers and ever so slightly I hook mine around hers. She doesn't pull away so I leave it at that. Just a little bit of comfort, that's it.

Swallowing hard, I ask, "Do you need a place to stay?" Please say no, please say no.

Tucker did that, offered a girl a place to live and ended up proposing to her later on down the road. It worked out for him but pretty sure that was a rarity.

Luckily, Georgie shakes her head. "No, my brother, Abe, is taking me in."

"Well, there you go. No need to be upset." Hell, my empathy needs a little help. I'm struggling here, trying to walk this fine line, and I'm doing a shitty job at it. I can feel it.

"It's not about my living arrangements, it's about my dad's belief in me, about—" She sighs. "You don't need to know about the drama that is my family." Before I can answer, she says, "I need to get out of here. I need to breathe." She sits up and brushes the hair out of her face. Glancing down at me, her eyes full of need, she asks, "I don't know how to do that though."

"To breathe?"

"To let loose. To throw caution to the wind. To run without shoes. To enjoy life." She bites her bottom lip as I sit up to join her. "Show me, Racer. Show me what it's like to spend one night without a worry or care."

"What makes you think I know how to do that?"

She studies me, her gaze traveling all over my body until they settle on my eyes. "Because, you have adventure written all over you." She places her hand on my forearm, hope in her eyes. "Show me, Racer. Please."

Fuck.

Fuck me.

"What about the shop?"

She shakes her head. "Not tonight. Just give me this, please. Tomorrow we can go back to bickering, but tonight, please help me see happiness, help me know what it's like to be free." *I just wish I knew what that was like as well.*

No doubt in my mind, this is crossing the line. Going out with her, showing her a good time, that's not even blurring the line, that's taking an epic long jump over the line into dangerous territory. But when she pleads with me, those sad, yet beautiful eyes of hers begging, fuck it's hard to say no.

I take off my cap and run my hand through my hair. When I secure my hat back on my head, I ask, "Do you think you can keep up?"

A beautiful sense of ease crosses over her features. "I'll do my best."

Looks like my request for money is going to be put on hold for the night. I'll survive another day, I always do. I always make it work. If anything, I'll take yet another loan out from the bank of Smalls and Tucker. Fuck, not Tucker, he's saving for a wedding. I really hope Smalls doesn't mind.

Resigning to what my night has become, I point my finger at her, making sure she understands me completely. "No arguing? You do as I say?"

Slyly she says, "Within reason. I refuse to go streaking or show my naked bits."

A lazy smile stretches across my lips. "Where's the fun in that, Princess?"

"No naked bits." She points at me, determination set in her jaw.

I stand and bring her with me. "We'll see about that."

"You're not doing it right."

"Clearly. If I was, it would be skipping." Her frustration is getting the best of her. There is no way she's relaxed, not even in the slightest.

"You have to loosen up, stop being so stiff."

"This is your idea of fun? Skipping rocks? How is this supposed to be enjoyable?"

Turning toward her, I slowly invade her space so she has to tilt her head back to look me in the eyes. I pinch her chin with my index finger and thumb and say, "Letting loose starts with the simplest of things. Breathing, smelling the air around you, experiencing a moment rather than trying to overpower it. Skipping rocks is for the lazy, the young at heart, the people who have not a worry or care in the world. The people who get great joy out of soaking in nature around them while using the raw materials of this earth to have fun. Keep it simple at first, relax your shoulders, and soak it in."

Letting out a long puff of air, she closes her eyes for a second and then pops them open, showing me those mossy-green pools that have stunned me from the very first day I saw them.

"Show me. Show me how to do it right."

The determination vibrating off her is contagious, so once again, I take charge.

"First, you need to take off those heels. They're not suitable for skipping rocks."

"I thought men like heels." She bends over and slips them off, revealing perfectly painted toes. I don't know why that's hot to me, but it is.

"We do, but we like them best when you're wearing them while wrapped around our waist."

"Such childish fantasies," she scoffs and stands tall once again after she sets her heels on a large rock.

I take her chin in my hand again and with a deep, sultry voice,

I say, "It's not childish when I envision my cock driving into a woman wearing heels. Where her heels pierce my back with such force that I know I'm doing everything right to see wild abandonment cross her face."

Swallowing hard, Georgie holds my stare for longer than I expected and then steps to the side. Clearing her throat, she asks, "So how do we do this?"

Needing a second myself—visions of her wrapped around my fucking waist clogging my mind—I bend down to the ground and start picking up rocks. I choose a variety so I can teach her the good from the bad.

"This is what you've been throwing."

"Yeah, what's wrong with it? Looks like a perfectly fine rock to me."

"It looks like a miniature boulder. It's going to sink immediately, because there is no way it will skip across water. You need a smooth surface." I show her the perfect kind of rock to skip and let her hold it. "See how smooth that is on both sides?"

Her fingers glide across the smooth surface, drawing my attention. She works the rock in her hand, really taking it in, and all I can think about are those hands, those perfectly polished and soft hands fondling me all the right ways. Fuck, it's been longer than usual since I've had sex, and it's showing.

Fuck is it showing.

Starting to grow hard, I will myself to calm the eff down. She's off limits. Completely and utterly off limits. Focus on the damn rocks and that's it.

"Okay, so it needs to be smooth. Makes sense for better gliding."

Christ. I swallow hard.

And here I thought skipping rocks was going to be innocent fun. Somehow my convoluted mind turned it into something dirty. Really, really dirty.

"Yeah, uh, so it's all about the angle," I continue, trying to rid the image of me gliding smoothly into Georgie. Not a good idea to focus on that. Focus on the task, teach her how to skip a damn rock, and get this night over with. "You want to make your arm parallel with the lake and grip the rock like this." I take the rock and wrap my index finger along the edge. "When you go to throw it, keep even with the surface and let her rip like this." Smoothly, like I've been doing this for years—which I have—I let the rock go, and we both watch it skip across the lake with precision until it loses momentum and falls into the lake.

Georgie turns to me and says, "That was kind of hot."

My brow pinches together. "Skipping rocks? That's hot to you?"

She shrugs. "I don't know. It just was. Don't make fun of me, I'm trying to loosen up."

"You're right." I hold my hands. "I apologize. I shall take the compliment. Fuck yeah, it was hot. Want me to flex now?" I hold up both my arms and flex my biceps, then with one hand, arm still flexed, I point at the lake and say, "You want to throw the rocks that way."

Her laugh filters through the air as she shakes her head. "Oh my God. You're so lame."

I wiggle my eyebrows. "Got you to laugh, so it's a win in my book. Go ahead, Princess, give it a shot."

"Okay." She places the rock in her hand like I taught her, gets in a wide stance—which I did not tell her to do, but whatever is comfortable is fine with me—and she cocks her arm back. "Ready?" she asks while looking over her shoulder.

"Let it rip, Georgie."

With a deep breath, she winds up and throws her rock . . . right into the sandy mud in front of us with a resounding plop. I can't help it. I bend at the waist and start laughing hysterically.

There it rests, the perfect skipping rock, buried in the mud of the shore, never fulfilling its rock-skipping duties. My laugh echoes against the lake and from my peripheral vision, I can see Georgie standing next to me, arms crossed. If I know her like I think I do,

I'm going to assume there isn't a happy look on her face. When I stand, my assumption is correct.

"It's not funny." She looks like she wants to pout.

"Oh it's fucking funny, Princess." I wipe a little tear from my eye and poke at the corner of her mouth. "You were so determined, and man, I've never seen anyone shove a rock so hard in the mud." I start to slow clap. "Hell, you win the award for best rock burier."

"You're an ass." She pushes my shoulder, and I grab her hand. I spin her into my chest and wrap both arms around her small shoulders.

Leaning over, speaking into her ear, I say, "And you need to remember to lighten up. Look at that rock, Georgie, look at what you did to the poor thing. You fucking showed that thing who's the boss."

I can feel her shoulders ease, so I continue, "So when you go to pick it up, it will know, it will shake in its little rock boots that if it doesn't skip for you, you're going to raise hell."

She's quiet for a second and then adds, "So much hell."

"That a girl." I bend down, pick up the rock, rinse it in the lake, and then hand it back to her. "Can you feel him quivering? He knows, this is it, he better fucking skip for you."

"Do rocks pee? Because I think he just peed in my hand."

I chuckle, loving the life returning to her eyes. Seeing her so upset was weird for me. I've seen her angry . . . and sassy. But this? Light? Fun? She's almost cool.

"No fucking idea, but I'm going to say yes, that rock has just pissed its stone pants in your hands."

"Good." She winks at me, and fuck if my stomach doesn't flutter.

What the hell?

"Okay, you little pants-peeing rock, are you ready? Show me what you're made of." Getting in position again, she angles her arm back and glances in my direction.

Once again, I repeat, "Let it rip, Georgie."

She flings her arm forward, the rock sailing past the mud and straight into the lake where it sinks drastically on the first attempt to skip.

She stands there staring out at the lake as I hold back my chuckle, trying not to make the situation any worse than it is.

Shaking her head, she grabs her heels and says, "Eff this. That rock had it out for me from the very beginning. I'm glad he's drowning in the pits of lake hell." Laughter erupts out of my chest.

"I'm going to take your retreat as a sign that rock-skipping is over?"

"You got that right. Next activity."

Next activity is it. At least she's a little looser, because what I have planned is going to require to be a lot looser.

∼

"You have got to be kidding me." Georgie bites her bottom lip and looks behind her.

"I'm not, Princess. It's either dance or no drinks."

"Just hand them some cash." If only it were that easy for me.

I make her look at me and hold her still. "Those heels are going to come in handy now, so use them to your advantage. I'll help you up." I go to lift her when she swats at my hands.

"What the hell are you doing? Do not lift me up on that bar."

I chuckle from the panic in her face and lean forward so my cheek grazes hers, and I'm speaking directly into her ear. "Nothing is going to happen to you, Princess. I wouldn't allow it." I press my hand against her hip and pull her closer. "You're safe when I'm around. But if you want your drink, you're going to have to work for it."

Eyes wide, she pulls away and asks with a shake in her voice, "Do I really have to dance on the bar?"

Seeing how nervous she is, I shake my head. "You don't, Princess. You really don't, but tonight is about letting loose. Tonight is your one night to step outside your comfort zone and live it up. If there is ever a moment to throw caution to the wind, it's now."

Her hand slides into mine, and I refrain from closing my eyes, from showing how much I like the feel of our palms connecting. God, it feels good, so damn good. "You won't let anything happen to me?"

Leaning forward some more, I press my forehead against hers, the intimacy between us growing to dangerous levels. "Never. I promise." I step back and clear my throat. "Now go get us some drinks, we have some darts to play, and I'm not doing it empty-handed."

"Oh God, am I really doing this?"

"You tell me, Georgie."

She looks back at the bar again, contemplating her decision. And before she changes her mind, she presses her hand against my chest and says, "Help me up."

"Fuck, yeah." I scoop her up and whisper in her ear, "Make me proud."

When she stands on the bar, the music changes, the crowd cheers, and all eyes are on her. A slow beat starts to channel through the joint. Looking unsure, Georgie starts to move from side to side, doing the "grandma sway" and I try to keep my face neutral so she doesn't see me laughing. It's taking a lot of courage for her to be up there, so I know not to fuck this up with making her feel insecure . . . even if I should hand her a shawl and cane to go with her sway.

When the crowd quiets down, confused as to why she's acting like a geriatric up on the bar, I shout up to her. "Let go, Georgie. Just fucking let go."

She makes eye contact with me.

And does the sexiest thing I've ever seen. She turns in my direction, as if all her focus is on me and me alone and starts to feel the beat of the music through her body.

The "grandma sway" is gone. Instead, Georgiana Westbrook drops her socialite and stuck-up snob persona and becomes an entirely different woman. A vixen with eyes for me and me alone. Hell, I'm instantly entranced.

Her body moves flawlessly with the music, her eyes trained on me, her hands running up and down her body, until they run through her hair. Her shirt lifts up with her movements, revealing a small patch of skin. That patch of skin I saw many times while she was tanning out by the pool, but right now, in this moment, that little patch of skin is doing a hell of a lot more for me than her bikini-clad body ever did.

Fuck, she's so hot.

No . . . she's not *just* hot. She's beautiful.

She's beautiful in the way she moves, in the way she's so unsure but also confusingly confident. It's almost like she's innocent *and* naughty at the same time, if that's even possible.

The crowd around me starts to cheer, mainly the men, who are seeing exactly what I am—a gorgeous woman moving her body seductively to the erotic-sounding music. It's devastating to all dicks around, because she's a wet fucking dream but so unattainable.

Men around me bump each other and draw closer to the bar, closing in on Georgie. A slightly worried look crosses her face but she has nothing to worry about. I elbow my way forward just in time for the music to stop and for her dance to be over. Everyone around us cheers, but I'm focused on one thing and one thing alone: making sure Georgie isn't touched by any man that isn't me.

I reach my hand up to her, which she takes, and I yank her down into my arms. She squeals and then safely falls into my chest where she wraps her arms around my neck. She squeezes me tightly, giving me an unexpected hug, and then pulls away when her feet hit the floor. Her hands skim down my back, trailing a desperate yearning through my thin cotton shirt. Fuck . . .

She rests her hands on my hips and her eyes meet mine. "Thank you," she whispers just as another man comes up behind her, placing his hands on her hips.

I'll never know why men think it's okay as a random stranger to approach a woman like this. It's creepy and just fucking wrong. Get to know her name first, dickhead. *Although in this situation, there will be no getting to know her name.*

"Want to dance?" he asks loud enough for everyone around us to hear.

I yank Georgie into my chest and wrap both arms around her, shielding her from the creep. "She's with me, dickhead, and unless you want my fist decorating your face, I suggest you leave her the fuck alone. Got it?"

The man holds up his hands and says, "I don't want to cause any trouble."

"Then beat it before my fist flies through your teeth."

Not even bothering to bid us a goodbye, he flees and thanks to talking loud enough for everyone around us to hear, no one in the vicinity even looks our way. Just the way I like it.

"Here you go," the bartender says as he hands us the drinks we ordered before Georgie got up on the bar and danced. "On the house. Thanks for the show, sweetheart." He taps the counter and then assists another customer.

In awe, Georgie hands me my beer and then sips from her girly drink. "I won these for us."

Chuckling, I shake my head. "I wouldn't say *won*, but you did get them for us. Thanks, Princess."

"I can't believe it." She's smiling brightly, bouncing in excitement. "I want to do it again." She starts to get back up on the bar when I grip the back of her jeans and pull her down.

"Don't even think about it. Once is enough; I don't want to get in a bar fight with every man in the vicinity."

"But it was so exhilarating."

"I'm sure it was, but you can dance on the bar on your own time. We have other things to do. Come on, Princess."

She loops her arm through mine and follows me to the back room. God, *that feeling. Of a girl on my arm.* Been a long time. But it's not just that it's a girl on my arm. It's because of *this* girl. This hot, complicated, beautiful, off-limits girl. Shit. Maybe I should have stayed back at the shop to work. I wouldn't be in this predicament—a hard dick with the urge to take this woman back home with me—had I stayed away.

~

"You hustled me."

"I did not."

"Don't even fucking lie to me right now." I point my beer at her. "You've played before. There is no way you can shoot that well and never played before."

"Beginner's luck."

"Bullshit," I say, calling her out. "You hustled me to get your way. Just admit it."

Looking over her exposed shoulder, she smiles at me, a devastating smile that's been eating me up all night. "I will never admit to anything. I won fair and square. It's time to pay up."

"You won under false pretenses. I went into our bet knowing fully well I was going to win, or else I never would have shook hands on your ridiculous request."

She presses her lips together. "Sounds like your problem, not mine."

I lean back in my chair, observing her in her tight fucking jeans, sexy-as-hell shirt, with a provocative smile plastered across her face that says, "I got you." I like it. I like it a lot. *I like her a lot.*

"I demand a rematch."

She shakes her head. "That would be your fourth rematch."

"Best out of five."

"No." She laughs. "We're done. You need to pay up."

I sit up in my chair and hang my beer between my legs. "What if I don't?"

"What if you don't pay up on your bet?" She thinks about it for a second and then says, "Then I'll purposefully let a box of Little Debbie snacks lay out in the sun right in front of you."

"You wouldn't," I answer back, loving how playful she is.

"I so would. Swiss Rolls, death by sun."

"You evil witch," I sneer, standing over her.

She carelessly shrugs. "I take my bets seriously. I'm not opposed to take your unsettled debts out on your friends, Little Debbie being the victim."

"Heartless." I shake my head. "So fucking heartless."

"Pay up, Racer."

Sighing, I set my empty beer bottle down. "Fine." I shake my head in disbelief. I can't fucking believe I'm about to do this. "I should have bet something different."

"You're the idiot who agreed."

"Because I didn't think—" I take a deep breath and settle myself down. "Doesn't matter, you're a sea wench and that's that." I head toward the bar, hating every minute of this. When I turn to see Georgie talking to the DJ, a giant smile gracing her face, lightness takes over me. Yeah, I might just humiliate myself right now, but seeing her happy? Yeah, it seems I'm cool with that.

The beat of "Uptown Funk," the same song I "stripped" to in front of Georgie and Madison when I first went to the shop, plays over the speakers.

That's my cue.

Rolling my eyes, I jump up on the bar and shuck my shirt, tossing it straight at her.

Go big or go home, that's my motto.

∼

"You're a savage."

"Am not."

"Are to." Georgie is shaking she's so upset. "How could you possibly do that? What is wrong with you?"

"Uh, nothing. I'm hungry." I take another bite and Georgie brings her hand to her forehead in shock, her eyes transfixed on what is in my hand.

"Stop. Stop! You're ruining everything."

"What?" I asked confused, lifting up my Kit Kat. "What the hell am I doing wrong?"

"You're biting into the whole thing."

"Correct, it's called eating it."

"No." She shakes her head and shows me her Kit Kat. "You're supposed to peel the bars apart, not just bite into the whole thing. Who does that? Savage beasts, that's who."

I observe her Kit Kat and mine and then shrug my shoulders and take another bite. "It all tastes the same, doesn't matter how it goes down."

"It matters. It matters greatly. I don't think I can handle you right now."

"Because I'm biting into my Kit Kat differently than you."

She sits up on the bed of my truck, her face a mask of seriousness. "You're not just eating it differently than me, you're eating it differently than EVERYONE. No one eats their Kit Kat like that. No one."

"Never been someone to run with the crowds." Not caring, I pop the rest of the bar in my mouth and lean back in my truck bed to look up at the foggy night air. We're parked in front of Limerence, eating our gas station snacks we picked up. "And you can't be mad at me. I introduced you to not only the glory goddess that is Little Debbie, but I also showed you how to properly fill an Icee." I nudged her leg with mine.

"I wouldn't say that makes up for eating your Kit Kat improperly."

"You were not putting the top on the cup first. I just got you a half-cup more of Icee. I taught you all you need to know in life."

She sips her blue raspberry Icee and nods her head. "That was a pretty clutch lesson."

"See." I toss my empty cup in the back of my truck and soak in the night we had. Weird, random, but fun, almost too much fun. "Stick around me, Princess, you'll learn everything you ever need to know."

Silence spreads between us until she shifts on the truck bed and faces me. With her legs crossed, she puts her hands in her lap and speaks softly. "Thank you for tonight, Racer. I had to get my mind off things."

"No big deal." I shrug it off even though I know it was a big deal. It was a huge deal for me, because not only did I not earn the money I desperately need, I spent too much time with this woman. I spent too much time watching her loosen up. I liked her before tonight, and now, after our time together, I fucking really like her.

And what do people say? Never get involved with your boss? Yeah, I just very well might be fucked.

I check my watch and even though it says midnight, for a second I think about trying to get some work done. From the way she's yawning and the way my body is screaming at me for Ibuprofen, I know it's a lost cause.

"It's a big deal to me. I know you didn't have to take me out tonight. I appreciate it."

I sit up and stretch my back right before hopping off the truck bed. Time to get back home so I can get a little sleep before tomorrow morning. Taking a day off is not an option.

"No problem." I stick out my hand and help her off the truck. When she lands on the ground, she stumbles for a second, gripping my waist for balance. When she catches it, those green eyes stare up at me, something unfamiliar passing over them.

"Thanks." Her hand slides up my back, her fingers dancing over my spine, spiking my body with chills. "Are you coming tomorrow to start working on the shelves?"

Her fingers dance with my shirt and I can't help but wonder what the hell she's doing. Is she trying to drive me crazy? Because job well done.

"Yeah, I have to." I grip my hat, immediately hating that I answered her in such desperation. She has me out of whack. She shouldn't be touching me like that. She can't touch me like that or else I'm going to do something I regret.

"Because of the deadline?" Her hands run to the front of my

waist where they play with the hem of my shirt barely covering the waistband of my jeans. My dick hardens in seconds from the light brush of her fingertips.

"What?" I breathe out, my hands now finding her hips, trying to steady myself.

"The deadline." Her finger curves into the top of my belt loops as she steps closer. Fuck me I'm hard as a rock right now. Her fingers are so damn close to my hardening cock, dangerously tempting me to the point of no return. "You need to work tomorrow because of the deadline."

Deadline, she keeps saying that word but it's not registering. All I can think about is the way her fingernails feel against my skin, how they're just inches away, so fucking near, that I can almost feel her getting closer with each breath.

The deadline. Yes, the fucking deadline. I need to work because of the deadline, not because I need the money—yeah, that's all she needs to know.

"Yeah, the deadline. I don't want to have to charge you more."

She shakes her head and steps closer. "I hired you for a fixed cost. You can't charge me more." Her hand slips under my shirt and runs across a little patch of skin. I almost topple over from the contact, contact I haven't had in a long time.

Where the hell is this coming from? Why is she touching me tonight? Seeming into me? Just yesterday she was telling me to go to hell. None of this makes sense.

"What's happening?" I ask, not sure why I just let that slip out of my mouth.

With uncertainty in her face, she shakes her head. "I'm not sure."

We search each other's eyes, our hands moving on their own. God, her skin is so smooth. So soft. It's not until I notice a sparkle on her neck, a light shimmering off the necklace she's wearing that I'm reminded why this is a bad idea. We are worlds apart and no bridge will ever connect us.

Stepping back, I grip the bill of my hat, trying to rein in my emotions. "I should get you to your car. It's getting late."

Her face falls flat, all the sparkle in her eyes vanishing. And just like that, with one brush-off from me, she puts up her wall.

"I can make it to my car. I'm fine." She steps away. "Thank you for tonight. I had fun. Back to work tomorrow." Awkwardly she pats my shoulder and starts to walk away.

I snag her hand before she can get too far and say, "Where do you think you're going? I said I'll walk you to your car."

"My car is just around the corner in the back, I'll be fine."

"Like hell I'll let you walk around the corner of the building at midnight. I'm going with you. Stop being stubborn and just let me do this."

"Fine," she huffs and walks, once again on her own. Leaving me to follow behind.

Annoyed, I chase after her, wondering if she's hurt from the way I pulled away. *Surely she didn't really want me to kiss her. Does she want me? Physically, yes. But not in any other way.* "You don't have to walk so fast, you know." I catch up to her but she doesn't look in my direction.

"Just trying to get to my car, that's all."

"Seems like you're trying to ignore me."

"Why would I do that?" she asks, picking up her pace. Damn she's a fast walker.

I jog to make up her pace. "Because maybe you wanted to kiss me, and you didn't get a chance so now you're embarrassed."

Listen, I don't know why I said it. Words slip out of my mouth before I can stop them. Are they the most intelligent words? Nope, not even in the slightest, but that's me.

Georgie halts, causing me to knock into her back. When she turns around, she's screaming mad and I'm nervous what will happen but also intrigued. "I didn't want to kiss you."

I decide to push my luck. "I think you did."

"Don't flatter yourself, Racer. I had no intention of kissing you."

"Sooo, your hand up my shirt was because you were cold? In this muggy New York summer heat?"

Looking flustered, she steps back and says, "You know what?"

"What?" I step forward again, closing the space between us, because frankly, I can't help but like getting her all riled up, even though I know I should back down.

"You're . . . you're," she stutters, searching for her words.

"I'm what?"

Raising her chin, she lifts her hand and just when I think she's about to stick it under my shirt again, she brings her fingers together to form a point and jabs me right in the sternum, sending me back a step. I rub the spot where she jabbed me, shocked from her weird attack. "Hey, what was that for?"

"That's for being annoying. Get a life, Racer. I would never even think about being intimate with you."

I don't believe her, not one bit. Since my ego is *slightly* wounded, I want to prove her wrong, so as she goes to jab me again, I stop her and wrap my arm around her waist, pulling her right into my chest. Her hands fall against my pecs, her legs struggle to balance on her heels. Surprise is clear in her eyes.

I tilt her chin up so her lips are in direct line with mine. Instead of struggling against me, her body melts, molding against mine, creating the kind of friction *every* man desires. Still unaware of my next move, she holds her breath in anticipation.

Doesn't want to kiss me, my ass.

From the way she wets her lips to the position of her hands clinging tightly to my chest, there is no doubt in my mind she wants to kiss me.

And fuck, I want to kiss her.

Just a little taste.

Just a little indulgence, something to get me through these next couple days. That's all.

That's all it will ever be.

Pinching her chin with my thumb, I bring her close and lower my head. Before I press my lips against hers, I pause, waiting for her to push me away, waiting for her to change my mind, but when she makes no move to stop me, I move forward and press our lips together.

Soft, warm, fucking intoxicating. Her mouth is exactly as I imagined it . . . addicting.

At first, she's tentative, almost unsure, but then her hands grip my shirt and pull me closer, molding our bodies together. A smile dares to peek out, but I hold it back. I'd be an idiot to ruin this moment. And an I-told-you-so kind of smile would one hundred percent ruin this moment. Right now, I want nothing to get in the way of Georgie's mouth on mine.

Her vanilla scent floats around me, spearing me in half as I pull her closer and run my tongue along her lips, parting them ever so slightly. For a brief second I think she might hold out on me, denying me entrance, but then she surprises me when her tongue meets mine, dancing, tangling, caressing.

Fuck, yes.

My hand that's around her waist slips up her back as I deepen our connection, not wanting this to end. Ever since I first laid my eyes on Georgie, I've wondered what her mouth tasted like, what she would feel like in my arms . . .

She tastes better than I imagined.

She feels better than I imagined.

She's a fucking goddess in my arms.

I want more.

I need more.

I can feel my hormones starting to lose control, my heart beating rapidly, knocking down the reservations I had about this woman, at least for this moment. It's just her and me, nothing resting between us.

Soft and velvety, her skin is so fucking smooth under the palm of my hands as I continue to lift them up her back and then to her ribcage. She moans in my mouth, disconnecting our lips for a second. Sadly, that's all it takes to break the moment.

"Oh my . . ." she gasps as she pushes me away and puts her

fingers to her lips. "Wh-what are you doing?"

Surprised and shocked all in one, mouth still agape, hopefully tongue not hanging out, I look her up and down and say, "Uh, kissing you."

I'm feeling the loss of her in my arms, the feel of her pressed against me, the way she desperately clung to me. Did she feel it too? Did she feel the connection?

"Why were you kissing me?" She's still pressing her fingers to her lips, trying to make sense of what just transpired between us.

"Uh, I wasn't the only one doing the lip-locking. Not to be a total jackass, but weren't you kissing me back?"

Eh . . . wrong thing to say, I know it the minute she hears what I say by the way her surprise switches to fury.

"You *are* a jackass," she snaps, and then stalks toward her car without saying another word. Hot and cold this woman. I like it.

Thankfully I can see her car from here, so I watch as she angrily gets inside, slams her door, and starts the engine with such precisely psychotic movements it makes me chuckle.

Didn't want to kiss me. She's such a sassy little liar. At least I know I can call her on her bullshit. The only problem now . . . what will tomorrow bring?

Truthfully, there isn't just one problem though. Because fuck, I want to kiss her again. A lot.

Shit.

Even though it felt so good to have one little taste, it was more detrimental than I expected it to be. As she drives off, I want to chase after her, beg for one more kiss.

Frustrated, I rake my hand through my hair. I need to focus. I have to let tonight go, drop it, and push past the way she felt entirely too perfect in my arms. I hate that it's true, but preserving my father's memory has to come before *any* wants or desires I might have. I need to narrow down my work, and fuck . . . I need to ask her for my money.

That won't be awkward at all, especially after that mind-blowing kiss.

CHAPTER THIRTEEN

GEORGIANA

The door opens and I look up from my list of things we need to get done today. Racer strolls in with a wide grin on his face, the kind of grin that's sexy, yet beyond annoying, because I can easily read his face. It's saying, "I told you so."

I didn't want to kiss him last night. I really didn't.

What about my wandering hands, you ask? Okay, they were a little incriminating, but in my defense, I have poor circulation so I was trying to keep them warm. That's all.

Cold fingers needed warming up. That's my reasoning as to why they were sliding around under Racer's shirt, caressing his abs and reveling in just how built the man is.

Not because I wanted to feel his skin.

Not because I found him attractive last night.

And not at all because I like him and his carefree spirit.

And not because he is one of the sexiest men I've ever known.

Nope.

I don't like him one bit.

He's kind of an asshole actually. No. Not kind of. He *is* an asshole. He is a relentless prankster, enjoys poking fun at me, and believes his opinion is the only opinion anyone should ever take.

Don't get me wrong. I know what your little pitter-patter heart is thinking . . .

He took you out last night, showed you how to have a good time that didn't involve anything more than five dollars per person. He leaves beautiful words around the shop. He wants to make sure you stay safe by walking you to your car.

I get it!

I don't need to be reminded. Believe me, I know.

I think about it all the time. Way more than I care to admit.

All right, I'll be frank. Between us ladies, I can't get him off my mind. I *really* think about him all the time and not because he's completing the renovations on my shop. I think about him in all the wrong ways. Like what kind of shirt is he going to wear? Is he going to take it off at any point in time? Does his tan continue past his waistline? What about his hat, is he going to wear it today? Backward like always?

God, a hat shouldn't turn me on. I shouldn't be frothing at the mouth waiting to see if a man is going to wear his hat backward on a daily basis. And yet, here I am, inwardly clapping my hands frantically while my leg bounces in place, beyond excited that Racer just entered my shop wearing that worn-out hat, backward. Of course.

Sigh . . . I could stare at him all day.

"Morning, Georgie. Lips chapped from last night?"

And then he opens his mouth.

I have never in my life met a more infuriating man. And yet, he's charming-ish? What is that about? It's really not fair. It's not fair that I can want him so badly, yet want to throat throttle him the next minute.

He's exasperating.

Staring down at my papers in front of me, I avoid eye contact and say, "I'm actually nursing some abrasions on them. Try using ChapStick; might help with those razor-blade lips of yours."

His lips are actually incredibly soft and perfect and wonderful and . . . sigh.

"Sassy this morning. You must have remembered to take your laxative."

What in the ever-loving hell?

My head snaps up, and when I see his shit-eating grin, I want to punch him in the throat. It's going to be one hell of a long Saturday, that's for sure.

He gives me a thumbs up and adds, "Good for you." Clapping his hands together, louder than necessary, he looks around and starts listing off the things we need to do as if we didn't just make out last night. Scratch that, not only make out but feel each other up in a PG way. How can he act so cool when I'm burning up inside? "Tiles are in. I'll start on the bathroom next week. I really want to get these shelves constructed today, it will make—"

"The bathroom needs to be tiled today." I shake my head, trying to avoid fanning myself in front of him. *Focus on work, G.*

He raises his brow at me and puts his hands in his pockets, his arms flexing drastically with the movement. "Is that so?"

"Yeah, it is." I point behind me with my pen. "So get to work." Yeah, get the hell out of here before I shuck my bra and throw it at you with an attached invitation that says, "Go to town, big boy."

God, my nipples are hard.

Studying me—please don't look at my nipples—, he says, "All you need is some leather and a whip and you would be one hell of a dominatrix. Although, I'm not really into being topped." He stares at my breasts—shit—and then smiles. "Eh, one night wouldn't kill me."

I set my pen down and fold my arms over my chest. His eyes automatically go to my cleavage where he blatantly stares. He's so aggravating. I wish I could teach him a lesson. He licks his lips, his eyes still trained on my chest . . .

Bingo.

My breasts. Racer's weakness. In my head I rub my hands

together, because two can play at this little game he's created. Frenemies it is.

"Bathroom first. The toilet needs to be installed. I'm done going over to the deli across the street, buying a pickle and then peeing. We need a bathroom."

"Just do what I do, pee out back in a bush."

"Ew." I cringe. "You do not pee in a bush outback."

He shakes his head and laughs. "I don't, but hell, seeing your disgusted face was worth it. Bathroom it is, Princess, but don't get mad at me when you're ready to start stocking your shelves and they're not ready."

"I'm mad at you right now because I have nowhere to pee, so it's not like my feelings for you are going to change."

"Aw, not even after last night's lover's connection? I thought your little hand exploration up my shirt would have gathered me some points." My nostrils flair and I grind my teeth. Yup, he's going to get messed with today, no doubt about that.

"We didn't have a lover's connection." I stand and put away all my papers besides my to-do list. I will keep that out as a reminder to Racer that we have a lot to do today. Well, he has a lot to do. I have some teasing to accomplish. *Payback is a bitch, Racer, and she's coming for you.*

I walk back to where the bathroom is and he follows closely behind. "Pretty sure we did. Your hand was down my pants."

His exaggerations are obnoxious, and I've realized the more I deny them, the more he jokes around. What happens when I toss them right back at him? We will just have to see.

"My hand was down your pants?" I cross my hands over my chest again, giving him a great view of my cleavage; too bad I'm wearing my camisole. No worries. That will be tossed shortly.

"Right down there." He makes a gesture with his hand to imply cuppage.

"Oh yeah," I snap, "you're right. My hand was down on your pants. I guess it wasn't really memorable."

"And why not?" He steps forward, total confidence in his face, as if he's ready to call me out.

"Because, I wasn't finding anything down there and I got nervous I was going to have to start digging. Having to dig for dick isn't the best way to try to impress a lady."

His face falls flat. "Bullshit."

"Truth. But hey'"—I step up and tap his cheek—"at least you have the muscles." As I walk away, I call out, "Let me know if you need help with the tiling."

Grumbling behind me, Racer starts preparing to work. I chuckle to myself and step to the side, out of sight. When I hear him lifting the tile boxes, I quickly take off the camisole that's under my V-cut, white T-shirt and put it in my purse. Like the whore I want to act like, I stick my hand in the cups of my bra and readjust myself so the ladies look plump and fresh. Looking down, I'm pleased with the view, so I go in for the kill, well, the partial kill.

When I enter the bathroom, with his beautiful word still on the wall, I find him on the floor situating himself. I grip the sides of the doorway and lean forward.

"You know, maybe we should do the shelves first."

Racer looks up at me and before he can even make eye contact, he's greeted by the gape in my shirt, giving him a serious view down my shirt. He sits back on his feet and clears his throat. "Uh, why's that?"

This very well might be too easy.

"I don't know. Maybe you're right. It might be easier to see what to order if I have the shelves done." I bend down and start to retie my construction boots right in front of Racer.

His eyes are fixed on my breasts. He's not even subtle about it.

Men.

So easy.

"Then again, once the bathroom is finished, we just have the shelves and painting to be done before I can start stocking. You can finish up my consultation room after that while I make things pretty. Hmm . . . what do you think?"

"I think you need to make up your mind so I can get started."

"Okay, let's stick with the bathroom."

"Fine. Now get out of here, this space is too small for two people."

"Oh yeah, sorry. Shout if you need anything."

Smiling, I leave and grab my iPad where I start perusing different vintage dress sales to see if there is anything I can buy to put in my store. I want to provide room for vintage and new, both local and worldwide.

My phone rings as I'm flipping through pages.

Madison.

"Hey," I answer.

"Did you get the invite?"

"What invite?"

Madison huffs on the phone. "For Bitsy's Ball in the Hamptons. It's in two weeks. Kind of tacky that she waited two weeks before the event to send invites. Although, she has it the same weekend every summer so maybe she's assuming she's conditioned us all to keep that weekend free."

"Shoot, I bet my mom got one." I bite on my nail. I've never been into the parties my parents attend, especially ones in the Hamptons, since they're all about showing off how much money you have and how you can drip it off your body in the summer heat. Bitsy's Ball, though, is a must for me.

Every year she has a fashion show. It's one of the many activities she sponsors throughout the weekend and this year, it's wedding themed. There are going to be at least a dozen local designers attending, designers I would die to have represented in my shop.

"Just ask her."

I swallow hard. "They kicked me out yesterday."

"What do you mean?" Madison's tone grows more serious. She

might be fun and flirty most of the time, a bit of a ditz on occasion, but she's a solid friend, a person I can trust, loyal to the core.

"My dad wasn't happy about me going behind his back and starting my shop, so he said if I was going to disrespect him, I was out."

"God, he's such a drama queen. Do you need a place to stay?"

"I'm with Abe and Waverly right now. It works for the time being until I can get on my feet and find a place of my own."

"It sucks that you don't get your trust fund for another two years."

"Tell me about it. At least I have my brother supporting me, and once Limerence gets up and running, I can start supporting myself, which is what I really want."

"My girl G, such a little entrepreneur."

"That's me." I sigh into the phone. "Maybe Waverly and Abe got an invite. I'm sure they don't want to go. I can take their spot."

"That's a good idea. Because you know who's going to be there, right?"

"Natalie Roman," I answer, knowing exactly who is on the lineup. "Believe me, I'm well aware. I just want two seconds of her time to see if she will sell to my shop."

"And we can get you those two seconds. We just need to get you into the event first."

"Let me call Waverly and see what she says."

"Okay," Madison responds. "Text me when you're done."

"I will."

I hang up and quickly pull up Waverly's name in my phone. The phone barely rings before she picks up.

"This better be good. I'm shaving for my afternoon quickie with your brother and have about ten minutes before he's lubed up and ready to go."

Groaning, I say, "How many times have I told you not to talk about sex with my brother to me? It's so disturbing."

"I just said quickie. It's not like I talked about the fantasy we're playing out. But if you must know, I'm the flight attendant and he's—"

"Stop! Please, don't say another word. Let me just ask my question so you can finish shaving."

"You're on speaker phone. I'm multi-tasking. What can I do for you?"

Why do I envision a piece of licorice hanging out of her mouth as she's shaving in her giant, jet-powered bathtub? Maybe because that's how I found her one time.

Wanting to get this conversation over with so she doesn't start telling me about what she has in store this afternoon, I ask, "Did you get an invite to Bitsy's Ball?"

"Ugh, yes. That ragged old hag sent me another one. Doesn't she realize I have better things to do than sit around and hobnob with her fake friends and talk about all the lawn parties I won't be attending?"

"So you're not going?"

"I would rather shove a butt plug up your brother's ass and pull it out with my teeth."

A shiver runs up my body from the gross visual. Although, I will forever be grateful to Abe for bringing Waverly into my life. She gets it. She's real . . . and slightly vulgar, but boy, does she turn it on for my mom, completely different woman. It's amazing to watch.

"What would you say if I took your invite?"

"Why the hell would you want to go to that thing?"

I try not to show the desperation in my voice when I say, "Natalie Roman is going to be there."

"Ahhh," Waverly says. "And you want to get her to sell in your new up-and-coming shop."

"Exactly."

"And if you show your face at Bitsy's party it will hold more weight than just contacting her. I see where you're going with this. Smart lady. Yeah, take my invite for sure. I'll call Bitchy . . . oh I mean, Bitsy today and let her know we unfortunately can't come but are sending you as a replacement."

"Think she'll get mad?"

"No. She's all about the numbers. The more people the better, and hey, if your last name is Westbrook then she's going to want you there anyway." Clearing her throat, Waverly speaks in an uppity voice. "Let me call the dried-up beef jerky right now. Call you back in a second."

"Okay."

I open my iPad back up and search Natalie Roman on the Internet. When her website pops up, I click on it and instantly marvel at her dresses. They're not the type of wedding gown you see at Klinefelds. They're not showboaty at all. They're simple, beautifully crafted, and so elegant. They're the exact look I want in Limerence; they'd be the perfect window display as well. Very eye-catching. Reaching into my file folder, I start flipping through my contacts. The last few weeks, while Racer was at his day job, I went to every wedding venue, florist, DJ, bakery, photographer, and even hotel to introduce myself and the concept I'm aiming for. I explained to them that I would offer clients the opportunity to shop through my associates—them—for other wedding services, so they could avoid running around town trying to determine who's best.

With an exciting amount of interest in partnering with me, I now have leverage. I can pick and choose who I want to advertise in my store, and thereby offer my clients the best.

I start sorting through the business cards I gathered when my phone rings again. That was quick.

"What did she say?" I ask.

"She was upset because clearly the life of the party won't be there, but she said she would love to have the littlest Westbrook attend."

"Ahh, really? That's so great. Do I need anything from you? Like the invite?"

"Yeah, when you come home tonight I'll give you the obnoxious box she mailed that includes an itinerary for the entire weekend. You must really be committed to this venture if you're willing to torture yourself like this."

"Anything it takes."

"That's my girl. Now let me be. I need to get my freak on. See you tonight."

"Thanks, Waverly."

"Oh . . . wait. I almost forgot. There was one stipulation."

"A stipulation?"

"Yeah. She's a fucking nut bag that one."

"What is it? Do I have to bring her a certain kind of flower or something?"

"No, nothing like that. You just have to bring a date."

"A date?" *What the hell, Bitsy? Why is that even something she cares about?*

"Yeah, she doesn't like single ladies lurking around, says they do nothing but cause trouble and try to steal husbands."

"I don't steal people's husbands."

Racer chooses that moment to walk into the main part of the shop. He raises an eyebrow at me, but I turn so I can't see him. I don't need his judgmental expression in my line of sight right now.

Whispering so Racer can hopefully not hear me, I say, "I don't steal husbands." Something whacks me in the back of the head. When I turn around, Racer is shirtless, drinking a bottle of water and letting it slowly leak out of his mouth and drip down the column of his neck. His bronze skin is already glistening and rippling under the recessed lighting he installed.

That son of a bitch!

He's trying to get me back for my no-cami show. *And I hate that it is hot as hell, that I'm enjoying his show.*

Just wait, just you freaking wait, Racer. When he makes eye contact with me again, he winks. I can feel the steam build up inside of me, waiting to explode. Infuriating!

"I didn't say you stole husbands, but you get the point,"

TANGLED TWOSOME

Waverly says, breaking me away from my anger ogling. "But it's required for you to bring someone if you want to come."

"That's so ridiculous. If I have to bring someone, maybe I'll bring Spence."

"Your brother? You want to bring your brother, the immature asshole who would rather spend five hundred dollars on one single shoe than fill his fridge?"

"He loves stuff like this."

"And he will ruin every connection you make. Don't bring him. Hiring a male escort would be better than Spence."

I hate that she's right. Any leverage I gain during Bitsy's Ball would be quickly washed away the minute Spencer opens his mouth. Not a good idea.

"What about that guy you went out with the other day? Chandler. He could be an option."

"Chauncey."

"Oh yeah." She makes a shivering sound. "That name alone makes my clit shrivel up like a raisin. He fits the bill, though. Bitsy would fawn over him."

"God, she would. She might even like *me* more if I brought him."

"She's that kind of lady. I say go for it. He might be a really good guy, and he could be clutch at getting Natalie Roman on your side."

"I think you're right. Okay, I'll ask him. Might be weird since we only went out once, but he might be okay with it. Thanks for all the help. I'll see you tonight."

"I'm making lasagna!" It's all she says before she hangs up on me without even a goodbye. I should be confused, but it's not the first time she's ended a conversation like that, and I'm sure it won't be the last.

Wanting to inform Madison, I shoot her a quick text about what's going on then stand, making sure to kick Racer's shirt to the side, despite my curiosity of what it would feel like if I wore it.

It's time to turn up the pressure cooker in here . . .

Is that the right term? Who cares? I'm using it.

Scanning the room, I try to find something that could possibly . . . ah ha! Spackle. Won't be too damaging, but damaging enough that I might need some "help."

I bust open the top, take a glob out with my finger and OOPS, look at that, I got it on my shirt. Now to test out my best acting abilities. Here goes nothing.

"Oh no. Shoot," I yell out loudly, trying to get Racer's attention. I don't hear anything so I speak louder. "Ugh, I got spackle all over me."

Still nothing.

Okay. Time to step it up.

"I just wanted to spackle this hole myself—"

"What the hell are you doing out there, Princess?" Racers asks as he shifts around in the bathroom.

"Just fixing some of your work." I try to contain the smile that's spreading across my lips because I know he doesn't like me going anywhere near his "work."

His heavy construction boots stomp across the floor as he comes into the main space. His eyes look wild as he glances around to see what I'm up to. Still shirtless, obviously, with his hat backward, his muscles flex and twitch with anticipation of yelling at me.

"Don't touch my work. What have I told you?" He scans the walls. "There is nothing wrong with the walls. Why are you trying to fix something that isn't broken?"

I point to the wall next to me. "There is a little speck here that needs to be filled. It's driving me crazy."

"What speck?" He comes over to where I'm standing and examines the wall. "There is nothing wrong with this wall." Turning to me now, he puts out his hand. "Give me the spackle . . . now."

With a roll of my eyes, I hand it over and then, without even thinking, I grab the hem of my shirt and pull it over my head. Racer pauses in his attempt to take away the spackle and watches as I remove my shirt . . . in slow motion. There is no hiding his perusal. He takes me in from the tips of my work boots to the top of my ponytail. He observes every inch, and Lord, I feel the heat of his observation, like a whip of lava right up my spine.

Holding my shirt out, I say, "I got spackle on my shirt."

I'm wearing a white lace bra and from the look on Racer's face, he likes my garment of choice today.

"Uh," he scratches the back of his neck, "just put some water on it."

"What about my bra, did I get some on that as well?" I stand on my toes and angle my breasts in his direction. His chest rises and falls rapidly as he weirdly tries to sidestep me but also help at the same time, as if his mind is delivering conflicting reactions.

"It's white, I can't tell."

"Feel it to see if it's wet." I lean forward some more and he takes a step back.

Hold back your smile, G. Hold it back!

"I'm not feeling your breast for spackle. You can do that yourself." Racer sticks his hands in his back pockets, restraining himself. But it doesn't go unnoticed the muscles contracting in his chest from his position, it almost makes him look that much stronger.

"I guess I can feel for spackle." Taking the opportunity to feel myself up in front of Racer, I seductively run my hands over the cups of my bra and close my eyes. From the clearing of his throat, I can tell I'm having an effect on him. *Poor man. Not.* That's what he gets for every prank he's pulled on me since he's started working here.

Sex. Sex always does it to guys and after last night, after the way he kissed me, how he looked at me, I know there is an attraction.

"I don't feel anything." I open my eyes and all I see is Racer gripping tightly onto the back of his neck, his biceps flexing, and a tight clamp to his jaw. He's holding back, so it's time to go in for the kill. "Maybe it fell into one of the cups of my bra." I start lifting the cup to peek in when Racer grunts and holds my hands down.

"You have to stop fondling yourself."

That's it. I can't hold it back any longer. A laugh pops out of me before I can stop it. His eyes narrow on me and realization hits him.

He's been played.

"There is no hole you want to spackle, is there?" It's as if he growled those words at me. *God, so sexy.*

"Not so much." My smile stretches farther.

Grunting, he moves forward, pinning me to the wall, one hand on my hip and the other pressed against the wall behind me. There is no humor in his face, just pure frustration. I've seen that look before, and this can either go two ways. He will lecture me about messing with him . . .

He leans forward. Heat pours off him, surrounding me with tension, my body instantly becoming aroused.

Or he will close in on me, sucking in all the air around us, leaving me breathless.

His hand starts to slide up my side to my ribcage. Awareness of the feel of his hand on me tickles my spine, awakening every erogenous zone in my body. I want to pick up where we left off last night. I want to get lost in his lips, in his touch, in the way his strong body presses against mine.

"You trying to get my attention, Princess?" His voice is low, sultry, infiltrating my brain.

"No." I shake my head. Don't waver in your voice; don't show how much he affects you with just his presence. "Just trying to teach you a lesson."

"A lesson?" He raises a brow and positions his foot between mine, his body leaning forward, his hand skimming my skin, so close to my bra. "Why do I need to be taught a lesson?"

To keep some distance between us, I press my hand against his bare chest to let him know that's as far as he's going to get, but it almost seems useless when I feel the beat of his heart and the pull of his muscles along my fingertips.

"Be-because," I stutter. "You can't go kissing people whenever you feel like it."

A lazy smile draws across his lips. "Ah, upset about last night? Wished I went further?"

"No."

"Liar." He smiles. "Don't worry, Georgie, that was a one-time thing." Why does my stomach plummet from the thought of his kiss being a one-time thing? Did I really like it that much? That shouldn't even be a question, of course I did. "You and me"—Racer reaches up and plays with a strand of hair from my ponytail while still propping himself against the wall—"we're like water and oil. We will never mix. We're too different."

"Why do you say that?" Not that I want us to mix. Ugh, that's a lie, I wouldn't mind "mixing" just one night.

"You're caviar, Princess, I'm Spam."

I can feel my forehead scrunch in disdain for his comment. "You're not Spam, and I'm sure as hell not caviar."

"Please, Ge—"

"No. You have no idea who I really am. All you see is Westbrook attached to my name, and you think you know me. You don't. I'm the furthest thing from how my family wants me to be. So don't lump me in with caviar when I lean more on the Spam side of life."

That might have sounded a little classier if we weren't comparing ourselves to processed meat in a can.

Sighing, he lowers my hand from his chest and holds it in his. His other hand caresses my face, his thumb trailing along my jaw. God, he feels so good, so strong and warm. So intimate, everything I want from him, everything I crave.

"I'm sorry. You're right, I don't know you very well." He steps even closer and presses his body against mine. I'm instantly drowning in his masculinity with no life raft to save me. He's inches from my face when he licks his lips. His cologne is sucking me, pulling me closer, egging on all the emotions raging through me. Kiss me, touch me, feel me... love on me. "Maybe we should get to know each—"

The front door opens, cutting Racer off. We both turn to see Chauncey standing in the doorway holding a bakery box and another dozen roses. He takes us both in, topless, intimate, practically on top of each other, our hips ready and willing to thrust at one another.

Oh boy, this doesn't look good.

Quickly, Racer and I separate as if we're teenagers and our parents just caught us. I scramble to put my shirt on while Racer picks up the spackle on the floor and starts spackling the wall that doesn't need to be spackled.

"Chauncey, hi. What are you doing here?" Everything comes out high-pitched as my cheeks redden and Racer whistles and spackles next to me. Not obvious at all.

"Uh, am I interrupting something?"

"Nope, not at all." I pull on my shirt making sure it's in the proper place. "Just doing some, uh," I peek over at Racer and continue, "some spackling."

With the flowers, Chauncey points at Racer. "I thought you were a stripper."

"What?" Confused, Racer looks at me, and then a wicked smiles spreads across his face. "Oh yeah, I do the stripping. They love me down there at Bologna Beaters. Have you been to that joint?"

Chauncey steps back, insulted by Racer's question. "I've never been to a strip club, let alone an all-male one."

Racer snorts under his breath and mutters, "Bullshit." From behind, I smack his abs and hate that I liked the feel of it. Having never dated someone in such incredible form, it's as if my hands are just drawn to his body.

To him.

"Racer also does some construction-type things." The look Racer gives me is comical. Well, it would be funny if I wasn't sweating so much right now. "He's been helping around the shop. But he's really a stripper. Loves taking his clothes off." I don't know why I'm going with the stripper story, other than protecting him. If my dad found out one of Julius Parsnips's employees worked for me, Racer might be fired. I wouldn't put it past him.

"I love taking my clothes off. I don't even know why I still have my pants on now." Racer goes to unbuckle his belt but I glare at him, halting his process.

"You're working with a stripper?" Chauncey doesn't look happy about it, and if I'm going to ask this man to go to Bitsy's Ball with me, I'm going to have to ease the discomfort in him.

"You have nothing to worry about. Racer's gay."

"I'm not—" I elbow Racer in the stomach casually. "Oh, yup. I'm gay. Bring me all the dicks. I just love those things, can't get enough of the Lincoln Logs God graced this earth with." Overdo it much?

Chauncey looks skeptical, and I don't blame him. Who refers to the male genitalia as Lincoln Logs? "Last time I was here you talked about loving women who touch your penis."

"Did I?" Racer twists his mouth to the side and then shrugs. "You caught me. I was trying to bro out with you, dude. Feel you out, you know . . ." He coughs and looks down at the floor as he runs his foot over the cement. "Because, I uh, I thought you were cute." That last sentence sounded like he swallowed razors while getting it out. "You're totally my type."

Once again, Chauncey looks confused. "I'm your type?"

"Totally. Love the whole businessman vibe. You got my dick twizzling around in my panties." Why did he have to say panties? Honestly. "But don't worry, I won't hit on you, or Georgie for that matter. Look, I can even honk her hooters and not get turned on." Reaching from behind me, Racer does just that. He honks my right breast, his thumb skimming my nipple with precision before he breaks away. "Go ahead, man, feel my dick, limp as a wet noodle. He's a sad boy, doesn't like ladies. But put your penis in my—"

"I think he gets it, Racer; you're gay. You can go back to the bathroom," I grit out, trying not to show how uncomfortable I am.

"Not a problem, boss lady." He turns to leave and then quickly comes back and says, "Honk, honk," while squeezing my left breast. "Didn't want the old girl feeling left out. Nice seeing you again, Chaunce." Racer blows a kiss at him from over his shoulder and takes off toward the bathroom.

Oh my God. I hate him so much.

"Sorry about that." I turn to Chauncey who still looks unsure. "He gets a little crazy if he doesn't have sugar every hour."

Staring at the spot in the room where Racer was leaning against me, he recollects what he walked in on. "When I came in here, it didn't seem like he was gay." That's because Racer is the furthest thing from gay, but Chauncey doesn't need to know that.

"He was practicing a scene from a play he's doing this summer. He has to play a straight man and wanted to see if he was convincing." Okay, that slipped out of me way too easily.

"A play?" I nod my head but I don't think Chauncey is buying it. "Georgiana, I don't have time for games . . ."

"No, I'm not playing games," I say quickly. "You have nothing to worry about when it comes to Racer." I move closer and reach for the flowers just as Racer shouts from the back.

"Hey, sugar tits, is that twinkie dick gone yet? I was hoping to get at least three quickies in before lunch."

My nostrils flare, my skin flames red, and anger boils deep in the pit of my stomach.

I'M. GOING. TO. KILL. HIM.

"Nothing to worry about?" Chauncey shakes his head. "I don't like to be dicked around, Georgiana."

"I'm not, he's just . . ." What is he? Being an ass? Trying to make my life a living hell?

"Pants are off," he shouts some more. "The good-time pole is out, and I've got your favorite lube in the warmer. Come aboard the Racer Express, next stop Georgie's wet vagina. Choo Choo!"

Murder. Murder is in my future. Limerence was a nice idea, but it looks like it will be prison time for me, unless I can insert him into a wood chipper without getting caught.

"I'm out." Chauncey sets the flowers and bakery box on the floor and without a goodbye, takes off, slamming the shop door shut.

I stand there, my hands curling at my sides, steam billowing out of my ears, death threats going off in my head. There goes my date for Bitsy's Ball; there goes my chance to possibly have a relationship with a good man—*boring but good*—and there goes my chance to show off a refined man to Bitsy.

Death.

Murder.

Imminent.

I spin on my heel and run right into a solid brick wall.

"Watch it there, Georgie. You almost gave yourself a black eye on my nipple."

Steadying myself, I set my hands on his hips for a brief second before snapping them away and flicking him in the middle of the chest. He laughs, so I flick him again.

"Yikes. Hold off there, metal fingers, you might put a divot in my sternum."

"What the hell do you think you're doing? You just ruined my chances with that man."

Racer rubs his chest where I flicked him and stares at the bakery box behind me. "Pastries, yes!" *What the hell?* He ignores everything I just said and flips open the lid? "Fuck yes, bear claws." He bites into one and talks with his mouthful. "Did you know it's almond paste that's in the middle of these things? Fuck, they're so good. This one seems to have a hint of lemon. Want to try a bite?" He holds it out to me and before I can stop myself, I slap it out of his hand.

With a resounding plop, the bear claw has hit the floor.

Pastry down.

Man next.

CHAPTER FOURTEEN

RACER

Have you ever been there when a joke goes too far? You know the moment you should have pulled back but didn't? The point when you've pushed the person past their limits and you're staring down the barrel of a wrath of hell flying at you in waves.

That's where I am right now.

But instead of a wrath, I'm about to have a front-row seat to a full-on conniption.

I'm just sorry my bear claw was caught in the middle of it all.

"I'm going to kill you." With her arms aimed at my neck, Georgie charges after me, straight-up crazy in her eyes.

See what I'm talking about? Pushed the little tart way too far. Note to self: she chokes when she's angry. Cripes!

I grip her wrists so she can't strangle me and even though I'm holding her back, her fingers try to claw at me, wiggling at me, trying to inch forward.

Vicious.

"He wasn't worth your time, Georgie. You can do better." It's true. That dude is most likely a two-pump chump with a Napoleon complex and bushy pubes. It's the impression I got anyway. No way does a man named Chauncey shave his balls.

"Who are you to make that assessment?"

"Just looking out for you."

"I don't need you to look out for me." She starts pacing the room. "You have no idea what you just did."

Drama much? Jeeze, I saved her a night of boring conversation. She should be thanking me.

"Calm down. There are many other fish in the sea."

"I don't care . . . ugh, it's not about the relationship. It was about . . ." She pauses and grips her forehead. Damn, she really does look distraught. And here I thought I was really doing her a favor. Maybe I was wrong.

Once again the shop door opens and this time the visitors walking in aren't for Georgie.

What are they doing here?

"Is it okay we come in?" Adalyn asks, followed by Emma, Tucker's fiancée.

"What are you two doing here?" They smell of trouble.

Before they can answer, Georgie cuts them off. "I would appreciate it if your bimbos didn't come visit you during your work hours. This is so unprofessional, Racer. I have the mind to fire you after everything you did this morning."

Well, this took a nasty turn. I can usually smell it when I fucked up and boy does the air smell foul right now. A serious stank scent of fuckery.

"Maybe this isn't a good time." Adalyn starts to back up when I stop her.

"Give us a second." I snag Georgie's arm and pull her to the back of the shop where I pin her against the wall. She struggles, but I stop her. "Cut it out and stand still for a second," I whisper.

"Get off me."

"Georgiana," I snap at her, which gets her attention. "Listen to me carefully. Those two women in the other room are my friends, not my bimbos, whatever the hell that means. One of them is getting married next year to my best friend, so if I were you, I would put on your professional pants because she could very well be your first client." I have no idea if that's the truth but anything to get this woman to calm down would be perfect right about now. "I know you're pissed at me, but try to act like a professional for the next few minutes. In the long run, it might help you out."

Straightening up, her face morphing from anger to somewhat pleasant, she pats down her shirt and whispers, "I still hate you."

"Yeah, tell me something I don't know."

I follow behind her as she makes her way back into the main space. With a smile plastered on her face she goes up to Adalyn and Emma and holds out her hand. "I'm so sorry about my comments earlier. Can you imagine Racer makes me blood-red mad to where I black out in anger?"

Damn, Pencil Dick was that important?

"Sounds about right," Adalyn answers while shaking Georgie's hand. "I'm Adalyn, and this is my friend, Emma. No need to apologize. What did he do this time?"

"Nothing." I can't defend myself, so I'll just stay quiet.

Not buying it, Adalyn and Emma turn to Georgie. "Tell us everything."

"Hey look at that, Georgie, it's time to tile the bathroom." I say to the girls, "Thanks for stopping by, but you best be going now."

"Oh, it must be really good if he's trying to kick us out." Adalyn rubs her hands together. "Tell us everything."

Traitor!

Georgie smirks at me. I'm so not going to like this. I feel like they're all twiddling their fingers ready to rag on me. I'm about to be thrown to the wolves and get a verbal beatdown by three women with a vendetta against me, and most likely my Little Debbie snacks.

Secretly I pray for them to leave Debbie out of this; she did nothing wrong.

"I'm really not in the business of throwing Racer under the

bus." Ah, there's some loyalty. Thanks, Princess. "But then again, he did just ruin a huge opportunity for me." Maybe not . . .

"What kind of opportunity?" Emma asks, giving me the stink-eye. God, she's going to tell Tucker, and he's going to give me shit. Perfect.

"Well, you see, in two weeks I need to attend this big weekend in the Hamptons. It's where all the important people are going to be who I need to network with to get this shop up and running. The invite requires I take a date. I *had* planned to take this guy who would have been perfect, but Racer deliberately scared him away."

Cue the light bulb. That's why Georgie was so upset. Well, now I feel like an ass. BUT, if I had to be honest, Chauncey doesn't deserve to go anywhere with Georgie. He's a nitwit and she's . . . hell, she's something special.

"Why would you do that?" Adalyn walks up to me and smacks me in the back of the head.

"Ouch." I rub the spot she hit me and scowl at her, but it makes no difference. "I was sparing her from a boring night. I didn't know she had a weekend planned."

"Doesn't mean you should meddle in her business," Emma adds.

"This coming from the person who tries to meddle in my personal affairs every chance she gets."

Emma rolls her eyes and crosses her arms over her chest. "Sorry that I want you to find a girlfriend to keep you from man-crushing on my fiancé."

"Ha, Tucker would be so lucky if I even glanced in his direction."

"You're absurd." Adalyn asks Georgie, "So what are you going to do? Do you have to take a date?"

Georgie nods. "It's required. And normally I wouldn't really be into going, but so many influential people will be there, including Natalie Roman, and I have to try to get a one-on-one with her."

Emma claps her hands. "Oh my God, her dresses are to die

for!" Returning her fury back on me, Emma whacks me in the back of the head just like Adalyn. "Way to ruin everything."

"I didn't know." Why am I bothering? One male against three women. Whatever I say isn't going to get me anywhere.

"Take Racer," Adalyn suggests with a wicked smile.

"No," Georgie and I say in unison.

"I have a lot of work I have to do here, so I can't afford to lose a weekend of work. I don't know anything about tea and crumpets. I'd be a horrible choice."

Adalyn scoffs at me. "You're not meeting the queen, idiot, you're just going to the Hamptons. You owe her this."

"No, it's really not a good idea." Georgie shakes her head as if Adalyn's suggestion is the craziest thing she's ever heard. Not to be sensitive, but she could tone down the no. I wouldn't be the WORST person to take. Close to it, but not the worst.

"Agreed. Not a good idea."

"Do you have anyone else?" Adalyn asks, really trying to find a solution.

Georgie shakes her head. "I even thought about asking my brother, but that would be humiliating."

"Oh, what about Smalls?" Emma suggests. "He would do it, I bet. He's a good guy. Have you met him?"

"Aaron, right?"

"Yeah. Want me to ask him for you? He's really chill, I'm sure—"

"No," I grit out. Fucking Smalls; no way in hell is he doing it. Sending him off on a weekend getaway in the Hamptons with hot-as-fuck Georgie? Yeah, no thank you. I might not be able to have her but to hell if I'm going to let my friend get a shot.

What's that?

I might not be able to have her . . .

I'm acting like some controlling alpha male?

Yup. Nailed it.

"You don't get a say in this," Adalyn says, dismissing me. She pulls out her phone. "I'll give him a call right now."

She barely makes it past the home screen on her phone before I yank it out of her hand and pocket it. "Smalls isn't an option."

"And why not?" Emma puts her hand on her hip. Just from the look on her face I know I'll be hearing from Tucker later. Fucking fantastic.

"Because . . ." I swallow hard and take the hit. "I'm going." The loss of money is going to hurt me but honestly, how much more can I really lose at this point?

"You're not going," Georgie says.

"Like hell I'm not. I already have my outfits picked out in my mind. How do you feel about hockey jerseys and pants with hamburgers on them?"

"You have got to be kidding me. You're not going. I can find someone else."

"Hate to point out the obvious," Adalyn states, "but with only two weeks, it doesn't seem as though you have many options. Unless your brother has a friend? Don't worry, with our powers combined, we can housebreak him. He just needs a little training."

"I'm not doing any kind of training. I have work to do."

"Do you really think we can train him?" Georgie asks while biting on her nail.

"Uh, did you not hear me? I'm not doing any training."

Ignoring me, Adalyn and Emma nod. "Oh yeah, he's trainable. But it won't be easy. We only have—"

"Two weeks."

Adalyn cringes and says, "It will take some long nights—"

Frustrated, I blurt, "I don't have time for long nights. I need to finish this job so I can get onto the next one. I have bills, ladies, and flouncing about with the wealthy in the Hamptons is not going to pay them."

Georgie gives me a sincere look of understanding. Shit, I didn't mean for that to slip. The last thing I want is pity, especially from her.

"What if I paid you?"

And there it is.

Pity.

I run my hand over my jaw, scratch my neck for a second to calm down the anger boiling inside me. Putting an end to this conversation, I finally say, "I'm going, there will be no paying me, and no fucking training. That's the end of it."

I walk back to the bathroom, ready to fucking bust some tile with my bare hands.

I really fucking hate pity.

∼

"Come on out. I don't have all day."

"Go to hell," I shout from behind the curtain.

"Racer, don't make me ask again. I'm not opposed to whipping that curtain open." Adalyn has been a pain in my rear end ever since she showed up at the shop five days ago. And of course, after she and Emma roped me into this Hamptons weekend, they've been hanging out with Georgie, talking about Emma's wedding and planning it all. Which means for the past five days I've had to deal with not just one testy female, but three.

I stare at myself in the mirror. This has to be some kind of sick joke. There is no way guys wear this. At least no self-respecting guy wears this.

"Come on, Racer. Just show us."

Us . . . yup, you heard that right. Us, as in not just Adalyn but Adalyn and her squad, which consists of Georgie, Georgie's sister-in-law, Waverly, Madison, and Adalyn herself. The only reason Emma isn't here is because she has to work, but fear not, they're sending her updates. Why Waverly and Madison have to be involved is beyond me. The minute I step out of this dressing room I know they're going to do their girly squeals and make a big deal out of everything, and that's the last thing I want to hear right now.

Fuck. I run my hand over my face. All I wanted was to make a little extra money. The price tag Georgie and I agreed to when we first made a deal about her shop was too good to pass up. If only I knew it would lead to this: blue balls, no money in my pocket, and a gaggle of cooing women on the other side of a curtain ready for me to put on a "fashion show," I never would have signed up.

And what's even worse is I haven't been able to find a good time to ask Georgie for an advance. The last few days have been consumed by my day job and Georgie's attention being stolen by Emma and Adalyn, leaving me to myself when it comes to the work in the shop. Not that I'm complaining about the silence.

"Racer, you have three seconds to open that curtain."

"Or what?" I ask Adalyn, who's making empty threats.

"Or I'll tell everyone about the time you got drunk at my house and started putting on—"

I whip open the curtain and stare her down, mentally telling her to shut her trap. No one needs to hear about how I tried on her dresses that were far too small for me. That's a story that stays *between* friends.

When the girls take me in, they all have different reactions. Adalyn giggles, Waverly fans herself, Madison nods her approval, and Georgie? I can't really tell what she's thinking.

"Pink is your color." Madison claps.

Pink is not my fucking color. "I look like a giant penis." Adalyn snorts, loving this way too much. It was the first outfit they wanted me to try on, and I know why. They want to torture me. I'm wearing a pink polo shirt with matching pink and green plaid shorts that cut me mid thigh, and to top it off, they made me tie a *mint* green sweater around my shoulders. I'm a far cry from my typical holey jeans and plain T-shirt.

My dad is rolling in his grave right now.

"There is no way in hell the guys at this Hampton weekend thing will be wearing this." I motion at the outfit. "This is ridiculous."

Waverly steps in. "Sorry to say, Race-Man, but they will be dressed exactly like this."

"She's right," Madison says. "They all wear this exact outfit with variations of colors."

"This tight?" I adjust my crotch, feeling the pressure on how small the clothes are on my masculine body.

"Well, not all of the men are built like you." Waverly scans me up and down. "But yeah, they wear their clothes tight."

"I think my balls are losing feeling."

"You're such a baby." Adalyn rolls her eyes.

"You're going to have to suck it up. This outfit will make you fit right in," Madison adds.

"Agreed." Waverly nods again. "I say we get three outfits in different colors."

Madison starts pointing at the outfits behind me. "Yeah, blue and yellow, red and orange, and this pink ensemble. He will be the talk of the town."

"The bell of the ball." Waverly laughs.

"Hold still so I can take a picture for Emma," Adalyn demands.

I grab the back of my neck, my frustration ready to explode, as Georgie steps up to me and removes the sweater. She gently feels the fabric of my shirt and shakes her head. "It's not him. He needs something different."

"Of course it's not him. He wears a tool belt for a good percentage of his day, but he can't wear that to Bitsy's Ball," Madison adds.

"I know." Georgie stares into my eyes, and I get a sense of protection somehow. She speaks softly but firmly, "He's doing me a favor, so he needs to be somewhat comfortable."

Fuck, I want to kiss this woman so hard right now, not just because she's not going to force me to wear this hideous outfit, but from the gentle way she's shielding me. It's a different side of her I haven't seen, a side I could easily become addicted to. Scary. It's how she's acted toward me over the last few days. And without vocalizing it, I can tell my attendance to her weird weekend is softening her a bit. And it's also making me feel vulnerable.

I have bills to pay. Everyone heard it, especially Georgie. She doesn't know all of my struggle, but I think she's starting to get the idea, and to hell if her gentle side isn't slowly picking away at the wall I'm trying to keep between us.

But with her light touch, the way she sees me, rather than the mannequin she's bringing to the Hamptons, but as a man, fuck, I'm having a hard time separating my reservations for this woman with my feelings.

"Madison, grab me a pair of grey chino shorts in his size as well as a white button-up, athletic fit." Grabbing my hand, she leads me into the dressing room and shuts the curtain, giving us some much-needed privacy. "I know you don't want to do this, I can see it all over your face." She looks up at me. "Just tell me right now if you're out. I won't be mad. You're already doing so much for me with the shop. I know I guilted you about Chauncey, but if you're going to be miserable, I don't want you to go."

Well, shit. I never saw that coming. Georgie and I are usually battling in a game of wit. We're not the type to have sensitive moments, so to say she's catching me off guard is an understatement.

Do I really want to go to this Bitsy Ball that seems like a total nightmare, a weekend feeling out of place? No, not even a little. I'll be losing out on precious time I don't have to spare, but for the life of me, when I look at her pleading—*and fucking gorgeous*—green eyes, I can't say no.

She might drive me crazy. She might make me want to punch a wall at times with her asinine thoughts on construction, and she might make me feel inferior not by her doing but by my own, but hell, there is something about this woman that makes me want more with her.

You don't know me at all.

She's said it to me so many times. Maybe it's time I truly find out who Georgiana Westbrook is.

Intimately, I tug on a strand of her hair and say, "I'm in, Princess." I run my thumb along her jaw, and she leans into my touch, her eyes fluttering. "Just don't make me wear this."

She laughs and shakes her head, "I won't."

"Here you go." Madison sticks her hand through the curtain and hands us another set of clothes, a set I could *possibly* get on board with.

"This might be better." Georgie passes me the clothes. "Let me know what you think." She goes to leave when I snag her hand and twirl her back toward me.

"Stay. I don't want to walk out there again if I look like another giant penis. I'm already self-conscious as it is."

She twists her mouth to the side in confusion. "Why are you self-conscious?"

This is neither the time nor place to get into this conversation so I say, "Don't worry about it, Georgie."

I release her hand and take off the pink shirt and toss it to the side. I'm not afraid of pink, but hell, that looked like shit on me. Next I shuck the tiny shorts. Georgie turns away, but not before I notice her face turning red. It's not like I'm naked; I have boxer briefs on, but I *am* enjoying her reaction.

"Don't be afraid to look. Get your eyeful in now, never know when you might get another chance."

"Just put the clothes on."

I chuckle and slip the shorts on first. They hang loose on my hips but hit me at my knees, a more comfortable location. So much better than mid-thigh.

"I have pants on. You can look now."

Turning around, she eyes them and smiles shyly. "Those are much better."

"Help me with my shirt." I slip it on and start to roll up the sleeves. I can't stand long sleeves; I feel like I'm suffocating in them.

Pausing for a second, I can see her considering helping me but unsure if she should. After what I'm assuming is a deliberation in her head, she gives in and starts buttoning up the shirt. I love the way her fingers barely graze against my skin. I can feel my abs flexing with each pass of her fingertips, almost like a feather caressing me. Feels good. My breath picks up, and I'm super aware of just how close she is. When she finishes, she taps my chest but doesn't step away.

"This looks much better. Very handsome," she whispers.

"Handsome, huh?" I lift an eyebrow. "I endure a little humiliation dressed as a giant plaid penis and now you're throwing compliments in my direction. Damn, I should have asked to be humiliated a while ago."

She rolls her eyes and steps away. "Don't push your luck."

"Never dreamt of it, Princess." I wink and then look at myself in the mirror. Much better. I actually look like I can pull this off. "I might need a haircut." I run my hand through my shaggy top.

She comes up next to me and assesses my hair. "Just a trim on the side. I like it a little longer on top."

"Is that right? Good to know." I wrap my arm around her waist and pull her in close. What surprises me is how she seems at ease with how I touch her. I know how much I like it, but does she feel the same? "What do you think? Do we look like a couple?"

For a moment she's silent, taking in the reflection in front of us. What I wouldn't do to find out what she's thinking right now, what her true thoughts are, because all I can think about is how good she looks by my side. Is she thinking the same thing? Or is she thinking she masked *me* well enough to show off to her society friends? Fucking hope it's not the latter.

"What are you doing in there? Come on!" Madison calls out. For someone who probably spends a lot of time shopping, she's sounding incredibly bored.

Not wanting to cause any more of a scene than we have, I open the curtain and strut it for the ladies. They hoot and holler as I spin and shake my ass for them, Georgie in the background smiling at my antics.

To be a dick, I announce to the room, "The outfit is so not wearing me. I'm wearing the hell out of this outfit."

"Get it, girl!" Waverly snaps in my direction, egging me on.

"Don't encourage him," Georgie says. "He has a big enough

head as it is." Her arms are crossed as she watches me from the dressing room, but the smile on her face speaks volumes.

She's not hiding anything. She's enjoying herself and damn if I don't like that.

～

"You've been quiet the whole ride back. Is everything okay?"

Everything was fine until I went to pay for the damn clothes Georgie wanted me to get and realized it was a little over six hundred dollars. I stood there, stunned, unable to even pull out my wallet.

Six hundred dollars on three outfits and a pair of fucking boat shoes. What kind of fucked-up thievery is that?

To my chagrin, Waverly stepped in and put her credit card on the counter before I could even think about pulling mine out. She said since it was her invite she was going to pay up. Although it was a kind and unexpected gesture, I can't help but feel weird. *I bet no man in their world would ever balk at six hundred dollars for clothes. Fuck, they probably spend more than that on shoes. God. I just feel . . . demeaned.*

Feel like *I* am the charity case.

Hell, I walked into the shop wearing work boots, jeans with holes, and a plain green T-shirt. I was so out of place that if I hadn't had the "squad" with me, I would have been *Pretty Womaned* and told to leave.

"Fine," I mutter as I pull onto the street that leads to Limerence.

"You don't seem fine." From the corner of my eye, I notice her uncap her drink and take a drink just as I hit a pothole. Oh shit, she's spilled her drink down her face and neck. "Shoot. Do you have napkins?" She reaches for my glove box and before I can stop her, she pops it open and is inundated with my overdue bills.

Fuck.

The one day they're in my truck. The one day. I'm so done with pity. I'm so done with debt. It's bad enough I was going to take them to Smalls to see if he could loan me some cash. But this? Georgiana fucking Westbrook, my part-time boss seeing my reality? *My drowning-in-debt reality?*

"Can you fucking shut that?" I snap at her as the word OVERDUE in red stares at her.

"I'm sorry." She stumbles with trying to shut the bills back in the glove compartment, but there's no use. She's seen what they are.

I pull into a parking spot right in front of the store, put the car in park, and quickly slam the glove compartment shut. Facing forward, I grip the steering wheel, my knuckles turning white as heat runs up my spine.

She saw them all.

Fuck.

"Racer, I'm sorry."

"Drop it, okay?" I pull the keys from the ignition and exit the truck, waiting for her to do the same but when she doesn't, I look inside the cab, hands gripping the top of the truck, propping me up. "Are you just going to sit there?"

Not answering me, she stares at the street, her eyes watering. Shit. Just when I think she's about to cry, she digs around in her purse and pulls out her small purple notebook. Quietly she flips it open and starts searching through page after page until she stops, finding what she's looking for. She runs her fingers over the words written on the paper and then turns it toward me. I'm so angry and humiliated but the sincerity in her features surprises me.

"Flawsome," she says, as she scoots into the driver's seat. With her spare hand, she carefully runs her fingers over my scruff, examining me carefully. With a nod, she repeats, "Flawsome. Someone who embraces their flaws and still believes they're awesome." On a deep breath, she says, "Be flawsome, Racer, because honestly I wouldn't expect anything less from you."

Scooting past me, she presses her hand against my chest in

reassurance, exits the truck, puts her notebook away, and goes straight into Limerence without looking back.

Emotionally paralyzed, I sit back in my cab and chew on the side of my mouth.

Be flawsome.

Accept your flaws and be awesome.

Fuck if that doesn't ring true, but my biggest flaw bruises my pride.

Growing up, my father always instilled in me that hard work was the only way to work, telling me I'm to provide for not only myself but the family he dreamed of me having one day.

"Be the better man," he would say to me every day. At night, before bed, he would read me a story, kiss me on the forehead, and as he hovered over me, looking me in the eyes I inherited from him, he would kindly say, "Make mistakes, tell the worst truth rather than the best lie, love hard, and be the better man."

I've strived to be the man my dad raised me to be, but with bills pounding me from every direction, with each roadblock after roadblock knocking down my ego, I fear the solid foundation he tried so hard to build has been bruised. *Crushed.* How can I be the better man when I can barely make ends meet? How can I accept my flaws when the woman who catches my eye is miles apart from me? *And will remain so. I* have absolutely no doubt. She will soar even further away from me with every minute her dream becomes her reality. Her *successful* reality.

Her smile is rich, her eyes bright with the future not far ahead of her, her lips, fuck, so luscious that I could spend hours worshipping them. She's searching for perfect—*she deserves perfect*—and I'm far from that, something that will be more abundantly clear the minute she enters the stately Hamptons mansion with me at her side.

Flawsome.

I lean my head against the truck, my eyes cinched shut. She's seen it now, my biggest—*humiliating*—secret. There's no denying the evidence in my glove compartment. She's not stupid, she'll link everything together. My need for money, my desperation to get the job done, my dilapidated truck, the clothes I couldn't fucking buy . . . the bills. It's all there. She knows I'm broke.

Tell the worst truth rather than the best lie . . .

Words of wisdom from the man who taught me to be the better man. *Who was the better man.* I can either go in there, deny everything, act like a dickhead—because as she already knows, that's what I'm best at—or I can walk into Limerence with my head held high, be the better man, and be fucking flawsome.

I run my hand over my face, take a deep breath, and once again exit my truck. Nerves tangle in my stomach as I approach Limerence. From the window in the door, I can see Georgie sitting on the floor, her legs propped up looking at her iPad.

I'm not naïve in thinking she's way out of my league, but fuck if her last comment doesn't have me thinking otherwise. *"Be flawsome, Racer, because honestly I wouldn't expect anything less from you."* She has moments, little moments where I can see past the thick veneer she's put up to shield herself, moments that show her true inner beauty, her grace, and unexpected tenderness. *A far cry from the elitist, bikini-clad, nugget-eating hellcat I first thought she was.*

Even though I love fighting and joking with her, it's the tender moments that have me fucking wishing I could scoop her up into my arms and show her another side of fun.

Taking a deep breath, I walk through the door, pulling her attention away from the iPad. When she looks up at me, she softly smiles and pats the floor next to her. I take a seat and bring my knees up so I can rest my arms on them. I stare down at my linked hands and say, "I'm sorry I snapped at you back there."

"You don't need to apologize, Racer."

"I do. I shouldn't have gotten angry at you. It wasn't like you were intentionally snooping. Just wrong place at the wrong time." Not able to look at her, I continue, "I've, uh, I've had some money issues. It's the reason I took this job because the paycheck will really help me out. I . . . uh, I was actually going to ask for an advance."

Fuck, this is hard. I can feel sweat start to pool at my lower back from how uncomfortable and awkward I feel.

"Why didn't you ask sooner?"

"Because." I slouch more against the wall. "It's fucking humiliating. I mean what kind of irresponsible asshat do I look like asking you for money?"

"You're not asking me for money, Racer, you're asking to be paid for the job you're doing."

"Still, it's you."

"What is that supposed to mean?" She's not angry, which is helping, only needing clarification.

I glance in her direction. "Come on, Georgie. You have the world at your fingertips. Not to sound like an asshole, but you don't know what struggling is like, the concept is foreign to you."

She laughs sarcastically. "You couldn't be more wrong."

"Georgie . . ."

"Remember how I said you know nothing about me? Well, you really don't. I am nothing like my family believes me to be. The Georgiana you met while you were working on the pool house for my father? That's the girl my parents want me to be. The socialite who runs charity events and walks on the arm of men like Chauncey McAdams. But I'm not that girl." Looking around the empty space, she continues, "Limerence has been a dream of mine for a long time. I went to college, completed a master's in business so I could open this shop. I spent some time after school helping my mom with her charity events, helping her improve them so the events benefit the needy more than the rich attending. And during that time, I spent hours putting together my business plan, making sure everything was in place so that when the time came, I could ask my dad to release my trust fund early so I could take a step toward accomplishing my dreams."

"And you did."

"Without any help from my dad." Her voice is sullen; it makes my heart ache for her. "He made me believe what I came up with was worth his time, that I actually put together a business plan he could be proud of, but in the end, he used words to put me in my place. In *his* deemed place. He told me to get my head out of the clouds and to pretty much accept my role."

"Your role?" Anger starts to blossom inside me. "What do you mean he told you to accept your role?"

Georgie fiddles with the hem of her shirt, her shoulders deflating. "My dad is the biggest chauvinist you will ever meet. He couldn't care less about the women's movement, about equal rights and equal pay. He believes the man is the one to provide and the woman is the one to stay at home and look pretty. Growing up, my mom would wear heels in the house just to put on a good show for my dad. I don't think I've ever seen her wear anything comfortable. She's always dressed to the nines, polite, and proper in every scenario. My father expects the same from my sister and me as well as my brother's wife, Waverly."

"You've got to be fucking kidding me. So suppressing not only his wife, but his daughters is part of his agenda?"

"Yup. Ever since I can remember he's always been like that. My brothers could run off and be boys while my sister and I had to sit and look pretty. It was *the Westbrook way*. We are professional eccedentesiasts."

"What's that?"

Once again, she pulls out her little notebook and flips to the middle. She takes her time looking for the page, but when she does, she smooths her hand over the word and then follows the doodles around it. The word and definition are small, almost too tiny to read, but surrounding them are all different shapes and sizes of faceless smiles.

"Eccedentesiast. It's someone who hides their pain behind a smile. We learned quickly how to become masters at this repressive art." She shrugs and stares at her notebook. "It's one of the main reasons I started this notebook. It was a way to escape, a way to find beauty in the world around me that was so fabricated, so stifling at times. It gave me hope. It made me happy."

And just when I thought this woman was two-dimensional, she

reveals layer after layer. I was wrong. She is nothing like the woman I thought she was.

"The shop, you still moved forward with it despite what your dad said?"

"Yeah. Luckily, Abe, my oldest brother, is like a second father to me. He looked over my plan and asked how much I needed. He's been supporting me ever since my dad said no and kicked me out of his house. There have been three people who've been the driving force behind me when it comes to Limerence, and he's one of them."

"Who are the other two?" I ask, curious for some reason.

"Waverly and Madison."

I nod and look down at my hands. "You sure it's just three? Pretty sure I know a guy who would love nothing more than to see you succeed."

Glancing in her direction, I give her a shy smile; she returns it in spades. God, she's beautiful.

"You want to see me succeed?"

I don't even have to think about it. I do. I want to see her succeed and shove her success in her dad's face. I want her to be the woman she deserves to be: free.

I reach over and grab her hand, entwining our fingers together. "I want nothing more than for you to have everything you've ever wanted at your fingertips, Princess."

And that's the God's honest truth.

CHAPTER FIFTEEN

GEORGIANA

The last few days have been weird. That's the only way to describe it. Just . . . weird. Ever since we went shopping for clothes, it's as though our dynamic shifted. We're cordial to each other, almost afraid to make the other mad. For some odd reason, I don't like it.

I don't like it at all.

Instead of bickering, we ask each other if we need help. Instead of pulling pranks on one another, we kindly bring each other a bottle of water. And instead of fighting over what project to do next, Racer asks me what I would like him to do. *And starts it.*

I miss the tension, the push and pull between us; it was fun. And if I'm reading him right, like I think I am, he misses it too. Because instead of flowing harmoniously together, we're awkward. At least when we were fighting, we were passionate, now we only touch the surface of the bond between us and it's . . . boring.

How messed up is that?

I want to fight with this man. I want to see how far I can push him. I want to see that sexy smirk of his when he's teasing me. I want the light banter, the fun jousting nights where we push each other to our limits.

It's so twisted, our relationship, but ever since he's started working here, I've become accustomed to his relentless teasing and nit-picking fights. I need them. They make me feel alive. *He* makes me feel alive.

"Would you like me to paint the bathroom today?" he asks as he walks up to me freshly off his day job. I don't know how he does it personally, how he has enough strength to continue doing manual work day in and day out. Perhaps when you have no other option, you grin and bear it.

Before our little chat, the chat we have yet to acknowledge since that night, or the way we held hands and stared at a blank wall for over an hour without saying anything, Racer would never have asked me what I wanted done in the shop. He would have barged into Limerence, Little Debbie snack in hand, with his mind already made up on what he was going to do. There would be no discussion; it was what he wanted. *And invariably, he was right, but I never acknowledged that.*

He's different now, and I know it has to do with what I told him about my father being a demanding ass. Racer is trying to present me with options, options I never had growing up. And even though I appreciate it, I want the old Racer back. The one who drove me crazy but also made me smile every day with his antics.

"Up to you," I answer him. "Whatever you think is best."

"Not my shop, Georgie. You have to let me know what you want. You're the boss."

Sigh, yup, giant sigh. "I guess finish up the bathroom so we can check that off the list."

He winks in my direction. "Sounds good. I'll be in the bathroom if you need me."

When he leaves me, I sit on the floor and try to think about what this coming weekend is going to be like. Racer and I sharing a small cabin and being super awkward with each other in the

Hamptons. Not only will Racer look and feel out of place, I'll be stressed from the potential of what the weekend can bring to me, so we'll be an awesome pair to be around.

God...

I rub my temples, trying to ward off the headache threatening to take over just as my phone rings. Since I've been getting lots of out-of-town phone calls from sellers, the strange number doesn't throw me for a loop.

"Hello?"

"Hello, am I speaking with Georgiana Westbrook?"

"Yes, can I help you?"

I don't recognize the voice on the other line so I'm wondering if I'm speaking with a possible vendor.

"Yes, this is Gerrick from Yamine Olaff, my colleague talked to you on the phone the other day about ordering stock for your store."

Quickly, I pull up my spreadsheet on my iPad and look up Yamine Olaff and what I wanted to order from them.

"Yes, I spoke with Pauline. We discussed a new line of vintage-inspired gowns I could possibly sell in the shop."

This is huge. I was hoping to hear back from them about their new line. Yamine and Natalie Roman are my girls. I want them in Limerence. I know they would sell well and represent everything I want for the bride I picture as my client.

"Ah yes, Pauline, she's lovely. She passed on your information, and after I reviewed everything, I decided to follow-up with you."

"Fantastic. How can I help you?"

"Tell me a little bit about your shop."

"Well, it's going to be a one-stop shop for brides looking for a specific—"

"Are there going to be cats?" Err... what? Did I just hear that right? Did he ask if there are going to be cats?

Confused, I ask, "Cats? What do you mean?"

"Sorry, I didn't think it was a confusing question. I just wanted to know if you will house cats in your shop."

Okay, so I did hear him right; he's asking about cats, little meow meows. Weird.

"Uh, no. No cats."

"Hmm, okay. Any live animals at all? It's important to Yamine to make sure there will be no live animals near the dresses."

What kind of bridal boutique would have live animals? That is just asking for a disaster. Then again, there are some shops that want to be different. But still, live animals around white dresses? Just stupid.

"No live animals at all. I can promise that."

"So no doves?"

"Uh, nope. No doves."

"Not even ones used for ceremonies." *Is there a difference?*

Trying not to sound sarcastic, I say, "Nope, not even ceremony doves."

"Okay. Can you tell me a little bit about your fridge space? Do you have a state-of-the-art industrial cooler?"

What? Why on earth would I need a cooler? I'm not running a restaurant. There won't even be any food available to clients.

"No, no cooler in the shop."

"Really?" He sounds stunned. "Are you planning to install one?"

Don't act rude; do not act rude, G. This is a huge opportunity, just put up with his weird questions.

"No. We are not planning on installing a cooler at this time."

Without skipping a beat, the man asks, "Then how do you plan on keeping the dresses fresh every day?"

Excuse me as I start to wrack my brain for answers. I've done my research. I've researched everything you could possibly think of when it comes to this industry, *especially* selling dresses, so I'm caught off guard when he asks me how I'm going to keep the dresses fresh.

"Um, dress bags."

He tsks at me over the phone. "You plan on putting Yamine Oloff's dresses in a bag? Please tell me you're joking."

I shift on the floor. This guy is most definitely a bit of a jerk, and he's making me rethink everything I know.

"I'm sorry, Gerrick, but I'm new at this. Does Yamine have a specific way she would like her dresses stored?"

"Yes, in a cooler." I roll my eyes. I'm not getting a cooler for dresses. "How else would you store her organic collection?"

Organic collection? Say what?

"I think our lines may have crossed. I was interested in her vintage-inspired collection."

"I'm well aware. But like Pauline explained on the phone, you can't just sell one collection. If you want the vintage line, you're going to have to take on the organic line as well."

"Oh, um, Pauline never mentioned that. I'm sorry, I was unaware."

"I'm positive Pauline would never neglect mentioning that to you. Maybe you weren't paying attention."

Okay, now he's just being an ass, which is completely unnecessary. I need to stay professional. If I learned anything from my dad, it's always stay professional.

"I apologize if there was any kind of confusion, but I was unaware of the organic line."

"If you want to carry the vintage line, you must take the organic line as well."

"And the organic line requires a cooler to preserve the dresses? What are they made of? Lettuce?" I try not to laugh from my question.

"Two of them, yes. But most of them are hemp."

Lettuce dresses? I've heard of dresses being couture, but lettuce, really?

"Oh. I don't believe I'll have the resources to maintain those kind of dresses."

"So let me get this straight," the man says, raising his voice. "You call the design studio of Yamine Olaff begging to carry her dresses, and when we decide to give you a chance, you disrespect Yamine as a designer?"

"No, I wasn't disrespecting her, I was just—"

"You're trying to work with Natalie Roman as well, right?"

Sweat coats my upper lip, my stomach starts to churn, and then I realize that a couple salad dresses that need to be stored in a cooler are going to ruin this entire opportunity for me.

"Yes," I answer, swallowing hard.

"Well, Natalie and Yamine are very close, you wouldn't want Natalie to find out about your inability to work with a designer, would you?"

"I don't want anyone to think that of me," I barely squeak out.

"Well then, I suggest you think twice about installing a cooler."

Oh my God, Oh my God, Oh my God. I don't know anything about dress coolers, is that even something I can find more about on the Internet?

"Can I ask you, how much do they usually cost?"

He huffs into the phone. "To house dresses, we're looking at about fifteen grand plus a five-hundred-square-foot space."

My eyes bug out of my head. That's a third of my shop. For for a cooler. A *dress* cooler. There is no way I'll be able to fit it in the plans. Plus a cooler for fifteen grand is going to break my budget. I start to gnaw on my nail, worry etching all the way down to my toes. I guess a regular Igloo roller cooler from Walmart wouldn't be appropriate.

"Oh okay, I guess I need to think about it."

"What's there to think about? This is Yamine Olaff." *I'm well aware.*

"It's just a lot of money," I answer. I hope I don't sound cheap.

"I know of someone who could possibly help you out. Have you ever heard of Danny Kaye and the Morning Show?"

"Danny who?"

The guy's voice eases as he repeats, "Danny Kaye and the Morning Show. They're known for their morning prank phone calls." My mind takes a second to process what he's saying and then . . .

You have got to be freaking kidding me.

"Are you telling me this is a prank phone call?"

"Yup." The guy laughs obnoxiously while sounding off some siren as if he caught me. "Your friend Racer called us and set up the whole thing." He laughs some more.

Fire starts to spit out of my eyes as I look toward the bathroom. There he is, leaning against the wall, arms crossed over his impressive chest, and the most gorgeous smile I've ever seen gracing his handsome face.

"He did, did he?" I answer, looking straight at Racer.

"Yup, said to give you a hard time. Hope you're ready to kick his ass, sweetheart."

"Don't you worry, I am."

I give them the right to play the phone call on the radio and when I finally hang up, I stand and walk toward him. And so far, that same smile hasn't left his face.

"You're going to pay for that."

"Not interested in carrying lettuce dresses in the store? Thought you wanted to be different, Georgie."

I push his chest but he doesn't move an inch. "I thought I was going to lose both of my biggest designers . . . over a five-hundred-square-foot cooler to house salad dresses. I'm going to kill you!"

He throws his head back and laughs so I tap his stomach out of anger. Not even flinching, he continues to laugh.

"Oh hell, you should have seen the look on your face during that entire conversation. Priceless."

And just like that, the twisted twosome is back. Even though he just put me through the wringer, I don't think I've ever been happier, because right now, the all-American boy who's consuming my thoughts is smiling and joking with me. And hell, if I don't thrive off it.

He opens his arms and I fall into them. When he wraps those strong arms around me, I realize something else just as true. He's my friend. I have another friend in my corner, and with a flawsome man like Racer McKay in my corner, I know I'm extremely lucky.

"Thanks for lunch, I haven't had a fine peanut butter and jelly sandwich in quite some time." Racer takes a giant bite from one of three sandwiches I made him. The man can eat; I just want to know where he puts it all. "What is this, crunchy peanut butter?" He looks over the sandwich, studying it intently.

"Yes, it's crunchy with mixed berry jam."

He nods and takes another bite. He talks with his mouth full, which for some weird reason makes him oddly adorable. "Nice touch, George. The peanuts add a nice texture."

"Are you going all food critic on my PB and J skills right now?"

Lifting his shirt, he dabs away some of the sweat that's collecting on his forehead, beneath his backward hat. His abs flex with the movement, drawing my attention. Each divot calling out to me to touch, to examine . . . to lick.

"I think every human should be judged on their PB and J skills."

I pull my eyes away from his stomach just in time not to get caught staring. "Why do you think that?"

"Because," he takes another bite, "I think building a peanut butter and jelly sandwich is in everyone's repertoire, but only the truly skilled know how to make a proper one. And I want to be friends with the truly skilled."

"Is that so?" I take a drink of my green tea and study him for a second, watching the way the muscles in his jaw move with each bite and swallow. It's sexy.

His neck is sexy? Is that possible?

"So where do I land on your scale of sandwich artists?"

He smiles from my term, and I realize how much I adore his boyish charm. Pulling his eyes away from me, he examines one of the sandwiches I made him and starts assessing it. "Good ratio of peanut butter to jelly. Nice choice in bread. The crunch you added has been a pleasant surprise, and the mixed berry jam is fucking delightful." I giggle from his girly term. "But . . ."

I perk up; there's a but? "But what?"

He quirks his mouth to the side, almost to say, "*Sorry, but you're not quite perfect*." "The bread, it should have been toasted. Toasting it would have taken you to boss level when it comes to the PB and J."

"Toasting it?"

He nods and takes another bite. "When you don't toast a peanut butter and jelly sandwich, the peanut butter and bread form a paste on the roof of your mouth. Even though it tastes good, it can get quite irritating."

"But I didn't have a toaster."

"Rookie mistake."

"Well, If I knew I was going to be critiqued, I would have sprung for bacon."

He pauses mid bite and stares at me over his sandwich. "You're a beast for bringing up the option."

I polish off the rest of my sandwich and wipe my fingers. "Well, maybe next time you'll communicate expectations better. I'm not a mind reader, Racer. Frankly, the fact I didn't make boss level is on you, not me."

I stand and gather my trash as he stares me down. "Don't you turn this on me. You didn't have a toaster. The toaster is what's key. This is on you, Georgie. This is on you!" he calls out as I make my way to the back, laughing to myself the entire time.

∽

"What are you doing?"

"What do you mean?" Racer asks while he strokes the middle fork sitting in front of him.

"Why are you touching the fork like that? It's like you're trying to turn it on."

"Everyone likes to get forked, Georgie." He winks and I roll my eyes. Lame. "Plus, it feels nice. It's so smooth. I like it when things are smooth." He lifts his brow in my direction, indicating he isn't really talking about the silverware.

"Don't look at me like that." I palm his face and turn it downward so he's forced to focus on the place setting in front of us. "Pay attention. This is going to be important. There will be an actual ball we'll attend after the runway show. It will be a sit-down, and you're going to want to know the place settings and how to use them."

"Can't I just watch you? Do I really have to learn this shit?" He runs his hand through his hair, his frustration starting to show. We've been working on the shop all day and now, with plastic ware and paper plates, I'm trying to teach him proper etiquette. It hasn't been as easy as I thought it would be.

"What if I'm talking to someone and you want to eat?"

He leans back against the wall. Between us is a makeshift table made from a cardboard box, our throw-away table settings carefully on top, and a cup full of nails in the middle to represent a centerpiece. It isn't the classiest, but it works.

Racer carefully scratches his jaw and says, "You know, I'm not the degenerate you perceive me to be. I promise, I won't sit at the table, prop my leg up and start scratching my balls. I'm house-trained."

"House-trained? I watched you pick up a Swiss Roll from the floor, dust it off and swallow it whole."

"That's living by the five-second rule, Princess. It helps build immunity, nothing wrong with wanting a strong immune system."

I cross my arms over my chest, ready to challenge him. "When it's raining, you go outside to get wet and when you come back inside, you say you just partook in nature's shower."

"Nothing wrong with saving on the water bill." He smiles devilishly.

"You think boots are everyday shoe wear."

He stretches his legs out, showing off his worn footwear. "When you carry a hammer seven days a week like me, Georgie, they are everyday wear."

Wanting to prove my point, I move closer, crawling across the floor to reach him. With every inch forward, his ravenous eyes travel from my face, to my neck, to my breasts. There is no shame in the way he blatantly stares at me, just pure heat. It makes every nerve in my body tingle in excitement. Never in my life have I had a man stare at me like he does, as if I nodded at him, he would tear my clothes off in a second and have his mouth all over my body.

And honestly, I would *not* stop him, not even a little.

I want him to touch me. I want to taste his lips again. I want to know what it's like to be held down by his strong arms as he buries himself deep within me. I want to see his face when he's feeling euphoric. I want to see the veins in his neck pop, and his muscles ripple above me as he tries to hold back. I want to see it all.

When I reach his stretched-out body, I kneel next to him with my hands on my lap. I place my hand on his cheek, only to feel him lean into me. My thumb gently caresses the scruff on his cheek while I try to envision how it would feel rubbing against my inner thigh.

His head turns slightly, enough for my thumb to touch the corner of his lip. What I wouldn't give to have his lips on mine again, just one more taste. I lean forward and move my hand to his ear where I caress his hair before plucking out the pencil he hides behind his ear. I lean forward and speak softly into his ear. "And this pencil, you always keep it behind your ear." Before he can respond, I flip the pencil behind me into the pile of trash we have to take to the dumpster.

I await his snarky reply but instead of coming back with his cunning wit, he panics. Every ounce of the mischievous man I've come to know vanishes, and it's almost as if a twelve-year-old boy takes over. He looks genuinely scared. Horrified.

"No." He scrambles up, moving me to the side in the process, and launches toward the pile of garbage, digging through it. "Fuck. Fuck!" he yells, as he starts to throw trash around the shop.

Uh, is this another one of his pranks?

"What are you doing?" I get up from where he knocked me over.

"Where did it fucking go? Where did you toss it?"

"The pencil?" I ask, so freaking confused.

"Yes, the pencil."

"Uh, I don't know. Over there somewhere."

His hands move rapidly over the trash, plucking through it like a crazed man. "Where the fuck is it?"

"Jeeze, calm down, I'll buy you a new pack tomorrow. It was a joke, Racer."

"It's not fucking funny." He sits back on his heels and grips his forehead.

Okay, this is a different side of him.

He's not just acting like an asshole.

He's panicking.

My gut is telling me I did something very, very wrong. Needing to right this, I crawl over to him and press my hand on his back; he shutters away and scowls at me.

Oh God. *I did something really bad.*

"Let me help you find it. It might help if we just carefully go through everything. We know it's in here, we just have to find it."

Not saying a word, he carefully starts picking through the trash, setting it to the side so we know what we've looked through and what we haven't. Quietly, we work together, the tension between us growing exponentially with each piece of trash turned with no sight of the pencil.

"It's in here, it's not like it could just disappear," I say, a little worried some mythical force came and stole the pencil. My hands shake as we get to the bottom of the trash and there is no pencil in sight.

What the hell? I turn to Racer who almost looks white, he's so pale. I need to find this pencil. Crawling around on my hands and knees, I scour the floor. It couldn't have gone that far.

I start making my way around the edge of the shop when I spot it. Thank you, Jesus. I hold up in the air and announce, "I found it."

Feeling silly and embarrassed, I walk over to him and hand it back. For a brief second, I considered putting it behind his ear for him but thought better of it. With the way he's looking at me, I'm going to assume he doesn't want me touching him, let alone getting anywhere near him.

"Thanks," he grunts out before getting up and dusting his jeans off. "I'm going to get back to work."

And just like that, without any kind of explanation, he leaves the "training" session and starts putting his tool belt back on.

Crap. *What the hell did I do?*

CHAPTER SIXTEEN

RACER

I have never felt more awkward, more uncomfortable, and more fucking turned on in my life. It's a lethal combination that's doing weird things to my body.

First of all, I'm driving a Porsche right now. Yup, a fucking black convertible Porsche. Why, you ask? Because it's all part of the illusion we are trying to portray this weekend. It's one—yes, one—of Georgie's brother's cars, and he has no qualms in letting a complete and total stranger drive it. And I'll tell you right now, I'm enjoying every second of it.

Second of all, I'm not turned on by the car. I know that's what you were thinking. No, I'm turned on by the hot-as-fuck girl sitting next to me. Georgie and I met at Limerence. I parked my truck in the back and when I came to the front, there she was, fidgeting in her tight white dress, her golden hair in wavy tendrils cascading over her shoulders, and her lips lined in a subtle pink, highlighting every goddamn gorgeous feature on her face. This is not the Georgie I know, or at least, the Georgie I've come to know. I've become used to her construction clothes, which, don't get me wrong, are hot, but Georgie in a dress with heels and lipstick? Fuck

TANGLED TWOSOME

me, I'm hard. Needless to say, my dick has made the trip extremely irritating.

And finally, it's awkward and uncomfortable. Why? Because, I fucking freaked out about her chucking my pencil. We have yet to really talk to each other. We've only said what's been necessary like meeting time for this weekend, what to pack, and what needs to be finished in the shop. But that's about it.

Ever since we started driving toward the illustrious Hamptons, the car has been dead silent, the only noise filtering between us the occasional blinker and roaring engine. And what makes this worse, when we arrive at the bungalow we're renting, we'll have to act like we're a couple.

Christ.

This is all my fault. I shouldn't have freaked out on her, but then again, I had no chance of reining back my emotions the minute she tossed the pencil away . . .

Knowing I have to do something, I clear my throat and grip the back of my neck with the hand that's not steering. "Uh, I want to apologize about the other day." Hearing my voice after not talking so long sounds weird. It's scratchy but almost timid. Fuck, when have I ever been timid?

"Oh, no need," she says, not even turning toward me.

Yup, this is awkward. She probably thinks I'm some psycho who has a sick love obsession with his pencil. Hell, that's what I would think if I were her.

I need to clear the air, even though it's not something I really want to explain, nor talk about. The only problem is, we can't go on like this. There is no way we'll be able to make this weekend somewhat authentic.

Up ahead there's a rest stop so I take advantage of it. I don't want to be driving when I explain everything to her.

"What's going on?" She looks around the rest stop. "Is the car okay?"

I put it in park, far away from all the other cars in the parking lot to give us more privacy. I turn to her, my eyes fixed on the steering wheel in front of me. "Nothing is wrong with the car. Georgie, I need you to hear me out."

"I told you, it's fine, Racer. We don't have to talk about the pencil."

What a weird thing to say. *We don't have to talk about the pencil.* Almost seems like there is some kind of sexual innuendo in there.

"I want to." My index fingers rub the genuine leather steering wheel. It feels like butter, it gives me just enough of a distraction to open up to the woman who intimidates me more than anyone. "Two years ago, my father passed away."

"Oh, I'm so sorry." Without even thinking, her hand slides into mine, our fingers locking together. I stare at our connection, drowning in the feel of her palm against mine. *You never realize how much you need touch until it's given to you as a surprise gift.* God, I love the feel of her soft hand in mine.

"It's taken a toll on me. Emotionally and financially. I lost my best friend. I also *inherited* his medical debt, which was not small, and it's the reason I'm struggling; it's why taking on this job was so important to me. I would do anything to preserve the memory of him because he is the man who taught me everything I know. He taught me how to work with my hands, how to be a good man, a respected one. After he passed, I clung to every little thing I could, every possession of his that I could, until I *had* to sell it to try to stay afloat." I run my hand through my hair, messing up how carefully I styled it this morning. "I was only able to keep a few things; the house we built together, some random memories, his chair, and the pencils he used to collect on jobsites..."

"Oh my God." Georgie leans in close to me. "I had no idea, Racer. I'm so sorry. I would never have disrespected your father like that if I had known."

"I know, Princess. You had no idea. I just needed you to know why I freaked out so much. I only have a few pencils left. I barely use them anymore, but I feel the need to carry one around with me whenever I'm on a job. It's like he's with me, watching over every brick I lay and every nail I hammer, just like he used to."

"Racer . . ." Leaning in even closer, she slips her hand over my jaw and forces me to look her in the eyes. They're brimming with tears, sorrow for my loss obvious. She's feeling what I'm feeling. She understands, and fuck me if at this very moment, this intimate moment that's enveloping us, I'm crushing on her. Fucking big time.

All it takes is a little humanity to help you fall for another soul. And I'm falling, I'm falling hard. I'm not sure if any kindness would do, or whether it's simply the gentle and sassy woman in front of me.

"I'm so sorry you've had to endure so much pain, so much heartache, and so much insufferable responsibility all at the same time. Losing a loved one is heartache on its own, but to lose your father and inherit his debts as well . . ." She shakes her head. "You're one extraordinary man because I would never have guessed you were harboring such pain."

"It's because I'm flawsome," I joke, which makes her smile. Her hand slides down my jaw to my chest where she puts some unwanted distance between us. I want her to come back. I want her to rub her thumb across my lips. I want her to rub her fingers across the scruff on my jaw while she stares into my damn eyes. Fuck, I want her so damn bad.

We're so different. We come from different worlds. We come from different upbringings. So how is it possible that we're both so fucking similar? *Aligned.* Driven. Perseverance is our middle name. I refuse to drown in the debt my father left me so I can preserve the one thing that means the most to me: my house. And Georgie, she's a motherfucking train, plowing forward, determined as hell to make Limerence a household name, to prove her father wrong.

At first I didn't see it. I didn't notice the same strong set in her jaw, speaking of true determination, but now, since she opened up to me about her dad, I can't see anything but a strong, goal-oriented woman on a one-way track to make her dreams come true. And that's fucking sexy.

"We should probably go so we get there at a decent hour." She breaks the silence and squeezes my hand. "Thank you for sharing. You didn't have to, but I truly appreciate it."

"No need to thank me, Georgie. I couldn't take the heavy breathing coming from you anymore, and I know you were chomping at the bit to ask." And just like that, I break the spell. I did it on purpose, because I couldn't take her small, intimate touches anymore. My dick is already hard, and I don't need it to pop out of my hundred-dollar khaki shorts. Christ.

"I was not breathing heavy." She fully sits back in her seat, clearly irritated.

I impersonate a heavy breather and put the car in drive. "It was like you were trying to suck a pipe down your throat but were choking on air while you did it." I do another impersonation, which garners a swat to the arm from her.

"I did not sound like that."

"You so did. Should we stop by a pharmacy to get you some saline spray, clear out your nose a bit?"

"Yeah, sure, let's do that," she deadpans. "And while we're at it, why don't we take a quick break at a strip club so you can finally take care of the hard-on you've had this entire time."

. . . . .

Busted.

Not able to give someone else the last word or show my shame, I say, "Staring at my dick, Georgie? If you want to see it that bad, just ask. I'm not opposed to driving with dick out. It's refreshing in a convertible especially. Cocks like feeling the wind in their head as well." I tap her quad with my finger. "Here's an idea. We put the top down. I unleash my cock and you push your dress down so your tits are out and I blow down this highway. You never know what total freedom is until you feel the wind in your nipple hair."

The visual is too much for me, I chuckle to myself. Wind in your nipple hair . . .

"I don't have nipple hair," she answers, clearly offended.

I waver my hand. "Eh, I'm going to have to be the judge of

that. Whip them out, I'm really good at making a proper assessment on nipple hair."

"Just freaking drive and leave my nipples alone."

She looks out her window as I continue to chuckle to myself.

Ahhh, that's much better. A pissed-off Georgie is the best kind of Georgie. Fucking fiery and perfect in every way.

~

"Well . . . it's cozy," I say with my hands on my hips, assessing our little bungalow. Scratch that, the bungalow Georgie rented. Makes me wonder why it's so small, hmm . . .

"Cozy is not how I would describe it."

"Yeah, how would you describe it?"

She spins around, taking in the miniscule space and shakes her head in disbelief. "A sardine can. The mini fridge they spoke of is under the bathroom sink, which is sandwiched between the shower and the toilet. How is that functional?"

"Are you telling me you're opposed to using your toilet seat as a kitchen counter where you make you're not-quite-boss-level peanut butter and jelly sandwiches?"

She shivers. "Toilets should never be near the food . . . ever." She looks around again and makes an annoyed sound. "And there is no door to the bathroom. It's all open."

"That's usually what a studio is, Georgie. Every room is combined into one small space. My favorite thing in this place is the bed. I hope you're not a sheet hog, I don't need my toesies getting cold."

She gives me an odd look. "We're not—"

I place my hand over her mouth. "I'm going to stop you right there. No, I will not sleep on the floor, nor will I sleep in the chair in the corner. I'm chivalrous, but I also have a bad back from my job, so the bed will be where I'll be resting my head. Deal with it."

Instead of fighting back, she spins on her high-ass heels and starts to unpack her bag, annoyance in each movement. She's so damn tense, and I can't help wonder why.

Wanting to poke the fire—because I can't get enough of that burning spirit of hers—I walk up behind her and press my body against hers. She immediately stands ramrod straight. I wrap my arms around her waist intimately and talk into her ear, slightly leaning over her shoulder to do so.

"Sharing a bed could be fun, Georgie. We can play games. Like pin the condom on the dick, and donut toss, and nipple barber shop. I did promise a thorough exam."

I span my palm over her flat stomach and bring her right up against my body. Her breath does a quick intake, a gasp so sweet I'm tempted to spin her around and suck it right out of her mouth. I shouldn't give in to temptation, but with her in this dress, in this small room, I can't not make a move.

"And you know, I'm really good at snuggling." I nuzzle the side of her neck, brushing the scruff on my jaw against her silky skin. "I'm also very good at fucking."

She leans her neck to the side, indicating that she doesn't plan on pulling away any time soon. Fuck if I can hold back now.

"Are you good at fucking, Princess?" I trail my lips along her neck, slowly, oh so fucking slowly.

"You don't want to know," she breathes out heavily. "The truth will only hurt you in the end."

"Why's that?" I ask, now kissing the spot on her neck that rests below her ear. Goosebumps spread over her skin. There is no denying my ability to make this woman squirm, but the truth is, she can make me squirm just as much.

"Because, despite my ability to blow your mind in the bedroom, you'll never get to see it." She spins in my arms and presses her hands against my chest. She glides them up to the collar and grips tightly. Licking her lips, she pulls on my shirt, bringing me closer to her mouth. Talking seductively, she says, "It's just pretend this weekend, so don't get any ideas."

"I've had ideas way before this weekend, Princess. The question we have to face now is: will you be able to resist me?"

"Easy." She brings me closer, her hand wrapping around my neck. Her thumb caresses my hair, lightly stroking it, putting me into a trance where I can't think of anything else but the relentless pounding in my hardening cock. "It isn't about if I can resist you, it's if you can resist me, Racer."

A challenge.

If I were a stronger man, I would accept that shit and turn her upside down, showing her not to mess with me. But hell, I'm hard as fuck, I've wanted this woman since I saw her in a bikini, busting a hole through my nail gun hose, and I have zero willpower left.

Fuck our differences.

Fuck our partnership.

Fuck this weekend.

There is one thing I want, and I'm not waiting anymore.

"Are you asking me to try to resist you when you're wearing this fuck-hot dress? Impossible," I growl just as I push her against the wall and press my hips against hers. She gasps as her hands tighten on my collar. I press my knee between her legs and cup her cheek. Looking her square in the eyes, I say, "You have one chance to say no. Right now. If you really don't want this, tell me no."

"No," she answers me, causing my stomach to bottom out. Maybe I read her completely wrong. Maybe the sexual tension I've been feeling is really only on my end. I go to step back, totally confused. "No way I can say no," she finishes with a devilish smirk on her face. *Thank fuck.*

Point to Georgie.

Grinding my teeth, I shake my head. "Get a little enjoyment out of that?" Fucking sassy trickery.

"Just a little." She cutely scrunches her nose.

I remove her hands from my collar and press them up against the wall, pinning her in place with my knee still between her legs. I press my lips along her jaw and up to her ear where I whisper, "If I *didn't* want you so much right now, I would be walking away with plans of pure torture in your future."

"Seems like you're the one who would be tortured, not me." Her breath caresses my skin, sending chills down my spine. Fuck if she isn't right about that.

"Are you trying to tell me I have no effect on you whatsoever?"

"None," she whispers as her fingers curl over mine when I move my knee up to the juncture between her thighs.

"None whatsoever?" I take one of her hands and lower it only to slip it under my shirt that's billowing forward. I press her palm against my abs and watch as she bites down on her bottom lip.

She shakes her head and I move my knee in small strokes. On a little moan, her head falls back and she says, "None."

Shit, that was sexy, so I repeat the move. Slowly, I rub my knee against her pussy and watch her unmistakable arousal. Her eyes flutter briefly, her mouth opens, and with one glance down I see how hard her nipples are.

Such a beautiful little liar.

"Well damn." I rub my nose up the column of her neck and back down until I reach her collarbone. I nip at it, lightly biting along the bone and kissing each nip. Her hips start to move back and forth slowly on my leg, and hell if I don't grow harder in seconds. "I can't believe I don't even make your nipples hard." I release her hand that is now freely caressing my stomach and rub my thumb across her hardened nipple. Lifting my head, I catch her gasp on my lips as I'm millimeters away from her mouth. "Oh wait, your nipples are hard. Looks like I'm going to have to fuck the lies right out of you." I lick my lips, move my leg up just little bit more, and . . .

"G, are you in here?" The door to the bungalow flies open, and Madison walks in wearing a ridiculously large sun hat and navy-blue sundress. "Oh my God." Madison covers her mouth with her hand.

"Oh my God," Georgie repeats as she pushes me away, barely getting any space between us.

"Oh my God," a male voice adds, a voice I haven't heard before.

"Oh . . . my . . . God," I draw out, trying to turn around so my erection isn't poking the intruders in the eye.

"We weren't doing anything," Georgie says like an idiot. Yeah, we weren't doing anything. Insert eye-roll. It was obvious we were about to devour each other. Fuck, I can still feel the sexual tension between us.

"Oooo, I'm telling Dad on you." Dad? I turn around and place Georgie in front of me as she tries to shoo me away but I keep her still. The boner has yet to ease, even from the intrusion. Listen, I've been hard all fucking day, it's going to take a few seconds to let the guy wilt.

"What the hell are you doing here, Spencer?"

"I brought him with me as my date. I couldn't find anyone else," Madison answers. "The real question is what you're doing in here?" She wavers her finger between the two of us.

"Practicing," Georgie says, her voice all high-pitched and squeaky. "We want to make sure we look like a real couple, you know?"

"Uh-huh." Madison crosses her arms over her chest and juts out her hip. She's not buying it. It's written all over her face. "So having your hand halfway up Racer's shirt is helping you practice being a real couple?"

"Mm-hmm." Georgie nods. "It's all about practicing intimacy. We don't want to look awkward when Bitsy comes to talk to us. You know how cutthroat she can be."

"And what about Racer? He had his hand on your boob." Madison looks at me and so does Spencer, both of them waiting on an answer as Georgie elbows me, trying to get me to play along.

Not sure what to really say and hating this ridiculous lie, I shrug and answer truthfully. "I really wanted to touch her boob. Her nipple was hard—ooof."

Georgie elbows me harder this time, right in the stomach, which you think I would be mad about, but seeing how pissed she is only makes me laugh. I wrap my arms around her waist and pull her into my chest. Madison's eyes widen as I lean over and nibble on Georgie's neck. She scrambles to get away, but there is no use, goosebumps spread across her skin giving her away.

Pulling away for a second, I wink at Madison and ask, "What do you think? Convincing?"

She nods, mouth slightly agape. "I would say. I'm frankly impressed, G, that you can make your nipples hard on command like that."

"I hate all of you," she says, pulling away and heading into the bathroom with no door.

Unfortunately, we all laugh at Georgie and her inability to throw a proper fit. From the corner of the bathroom, she stands defiantly, looking sexy as hell. I adjust my sleeves while staring her down and just for her benefit, I give her a wink to let her know this little interlude isn't over.

And I'm shocked as fuck when a brief smile passes over her lips. *Practicing* my ass. This weekend is going to be more fun than I expected. *And hopefully I'll be able to alleviate the worst case of blue balls ever seen this side of New York.*

CHAPTER SEVENTEEN

GEORGIANA

"We didn't get properly introduced. I'm Spencer." Spencer holds out his hand that Racer takes in his while he still keeps one arm wrapped around me.

"Racer, nice to meet you. I'm your sister's boyfriend." Oh Jesus . . .

"Pretend boyfriend," I add.

Racer squeezes me closer to his side and whispers in my ear. "We'll see, Princess."

We make our way down Main Street in East Hampton, headed toward Rowdy Hall for dinner. Madison thought it would be "fun" to all go out to dinner. Me, not so much.

Not because I'm not hungry or don't want to hang out with Madison and my brother—well, Spencer is questionable—but because I'm freaking charged up right now. I can't even begin to describe the ache between my thighs. And it worsens every time Racer touches me, speaks in my ear, or looks me in the eyes with that heated gaze of his. I want nothing more than to flip Madison and Spencer the bird and sprint back to the bungalow with Racer at my side to finish what we started.

Madison has the worst timing ever by far. Then again, I'm kind of glad she walked in at that point because if she didn't she would have seen way more skin than she'd probably prefer. Note to self: lock the bungalow the minute you step inside it.

And what the hell is she doing here with Spencer? I know she needed a date, but my brother? She couldn't have found anyone else to bring? She has a Rolodex of men in her phone, including the pool boy. I hope they're not staying together because that would be just too weird for me.

"Boyfriend, huh?" Spencer asks, eyeing Racer for a second. "You're not her usual type."

"What's my usual type?" I ask.

"Douche," Racer answers for him and then pats my shoulder. "Your usual type is douche, Princess."

"It is not."

"He's so right." Spencer laughs and claps his hands as we arrive at Rowdy Hall. "I don't think I've ever seen you with a guy that's not a douche. Granted, I don't know Racer yet, but so far, I like his style."

I scoff. "Racer is the biggest douche of all." Not true, but honestly, my comebacks are very weak right now. I blame it on the fact that all I can think about is Racer's dick pressed up against me. *Inside me. Everywhere . . .*

Leaning close to my ear, he whispers, "Biggest, yes. Douche, never." He bites on my earlobe and yup, my nipples are hard once again. Oh, and the mention of him being the biggest, yeah, that doesn't divert my attention away from his dick at all. Not one bit.

"Four please, and can we possibly sit in the courtyard?" Madison asks the hostess.

"Of course, follow me." She glances at Racer and smiles with a wink. A wave of jealousy rolls over me and clouds my vision. I snap my arm around Racer's waist and let her clearly see that he's "taken." Well, *pretend* taken, but she doesn't need to know that.

Madison and Spencer walk in front of us while Racer takes my hand and leads me in the direction of the whore-y hostess. He pulls me in close and says, "Easy there, tiger. I only have eyes for one woman and like the good little girl she is, her nipples are hard and waiting for me."

Get it together, nips! *Christ.*

"Stop staring at my nipples," I whisper at him.

He squeezes my hand and says, "Not a chance, Princess."

We are seated in the back of the courtyard surrounded by brick, twinkle lights, and a beautiful, shady tree. The bistro set we are seated at offers a bench loveseat and two chairs. Naturally Madison and Spencer take the chairs while Racer and I are left with the loveseat. It wouldn't be such a big deal if Racer didn't take up more than half of it and I wasn't so turned on by his . . . *everything.*

Racer wraps his arm around my shoulders as I take in the ambiance. It's quaint, with stars shining above us and the au naturel feel of the perfectly potted plants expertly placed around the courtyard. The lights crisscrossing over us makes the space feel almost magical and the man sitting next to me brings the whole experience to the next level.

"Beer, I need beer," Spencer announces while grabbing the drink menu. "Are you going to get one of those girly drinks you like so much, Madison?"

"Why? You're going to ask me for a sip, aren't you?"

"You know a man of my stature can't possibly order one for myself. Oh, look at this one"—he points to the menu—"it has grapefruit in it. Get that one."

"You're absurd." Madison leans over to look at the drink. "Damn, that does sound good."

These two. I'm not going to lie, I'm still shocked Madison decided to bring Spencer since they've had history. Do I like my friend getting involved with my brother? Not so much, especially when the last time they interacted—I use that term loosely— Spencer left for the city, leaving Madison behind. She told me time and time again they were friends and had never truly been serious, but I saw it in her eyes. She hurt when he left.

So can you imagine my surprise when I see him here with my best friend once again?

"Are you going to get a drink, Georgie?" Racer asks, his fingers twirling a strand of my hair, his breath tickling my ear.

Yes, yes I am getting a drink. I am getting all the drinks with all the booze.

"Yeah, are you?"

"Eh, I'll probably just get water."

Water. That doesn't sound like Racer. I've seen him drink beer with Aaron before.

I'm about to question him when it hits me; water is free. My heart immediately starts to ache. I completely forgot to tell him this entire weekend is on me. I know how tight things are for him, and the last thing I want is him thinking he has to pay for all our outings. He's doing me a favor. But how can I say it in a way that doesn't offend him? I don't want to wound his pride.

Needing to let him know he doesn't have to worry about money, I try to distract Tweedle-Dee and Tweedle-Dum. "Hey, did you see the appetizers, Madison?"

"God, I love a good appey." Madison fists-bumps.

"Don't even think about getting artichoke dip, no one likes that shit."

Madison pops her head up over her menu. "Everyone likes it."

"No one," Spencer counters. They face off, ready to throw down the gauntlet over appetizers. They're too easy.

While they fight, I turn toward Racer and carefully run my hand up his chest—trying to look as intimate as possible—and grip the side of his face. Quietly I speak into his ear. "Get whatever you want this weekend. It's all on the business card." I didn't say it's on me, because I didn't want him to feel emasculated, instead I said the business.

"Geor—"

"No, I'm serious. This is a business trip, okay?" With my face so close to his, I gently press a kiss against his cheek, trying to reassure him . . . or more like trying to sneak in any kind of intimacy. His kisses drove me mad at the bungalow. I don't think I've ever felt so turned on. But it wasn't just that. It was as if he couldn't stop kissing and touching me, as if he *needed* to show affection. It was erotic, hands down. But it was also . . . extraordinary. I'm thinking Racer is a man good with all his tools. *God, G. Settle. Not here. Not . . . yet.*

He clears his throat and brings me in a little closer by wrapping his arm around me tighter. "What about at night, when I'm hard as fuck and sharing a bed with you? Is that still business, or will that be pleasure?"

Oh God, I feel like I can't breathe. His other hand glides across my thigh and moves up toward the hem of the dress. I can't even tell if Madison and Spencer are still arguing, because all I can focus on is the man slowly destroying me with every caress and soft-spoken word.

I swallow hard and caress the hardened scruff on his jaw. "Pleasure," I whisper, just before I pull away and straighten myself. When I look over at Madison and Spencer, they're now sharing a menu and pointing at the different appetizers they can agree on.

I pick up my menu to somewhat concentrate on what I want to get when Racer leans in again, his hand still on my thigh and traveling higher. "I want to, no I need to fuck you so bad right now. I just need a little taste. Give me a little taste, Princess."

Is he serious? His hand slides up even higher now. Thankfully our bench is pushed in and there is a cloth over the table or else Madison and Spencer would be getting quite the show.

Talking very quietly, he grits out, "Spread for me."

Oh my God, he is serious. I keep my lips sealed and casually shake my head. No way are we doing this right here in front of Madison and my brother.

"Spread your legs, Georgiana," he grits out. The use of my full name hits me hard and miraculously my traitorous legs spread only slightly, but just enough for Racer to move his hand to my panty line where he casually strokes me. "Are you wet?" He's so quiet, so seductive. I know only I can hear him but with viewers a mere few feet away, I've never felt more exposed. *And hot.*

I nod, unable to answer him with my voice. There is no way I can speak right now. Not with the way Racer is playing my body, as if he knows every single button to press at the right time.

"Oh salmon. I haven't had a good salmon in a long time," Spencer says.

"You are not getting the salmon. It's going to make my hair smell."

"If I can't get the salmon then you're sure as hell not getting potato skins."

"We agreed," Madison protests and once again goes back to the menu. Honestly, these two are like children.

I can't even think about food right now. Not with Racer caressing my panty line. "How bad do you want me, Princess?"

Nope, not answering that question. Just going to look at the menu. Going to study it real hard. Oh look at that, the soup of the day is French—oh my God, his fingers are under my thong. My legs spread even wider without even being able to stop them. I swear they have their own brain. With the new level of access, Racer starts to caress my slit and I feel my eyes roll in the back of my head.

"Fuck," he breaths into my ear. "Fuck, this was a bad idea." *You think?* I could have told him that the minute he put his hand on my thigh.

My clit is pounding now, a light sheen of sweat coats my skin, and all I can think about is the unyielding need ripping through my core. There is no question. I want him and I want him now.

I turn toward him and whisper quietly, "I'm so wet, Racer. I don't think I can . . ." His finger presses against my clit, and I almost slip out of my seat. I bite my bottom lip, stopping myself from moaning at the table I'm sharing with my best friend and brother.

"Touch me, Princess. Feel how hard I am right now."

No, I can't. There is no way I can do that. If I do, I have no idea what will happen next. I might lean over and start sucking him. I have zero willpower right now. *Zero.*

Instead, I stand quickly, pull my dress down, and snag my clutch from the table. "I have to pee," I announce very unladylike to the table and race off to the bathroom, thighs clenched.

Legs pressed together, I sprint-walk to the bathroom where I lock myself in a stall and lean against the wall, trying to catch my breath. My body is ignited, sparking with electricity, so freaking alive that I can't stop shaking. My phone beeps with a text. It can only be one person. With a shaky hand, I pull my phone from my clutch and read the text.

Racer: *You can run all you want now, Princess, but just know this. You're. Mine. Tonight.*

I lean my head against the stall wall and try to calm my racing heart and raging hormones. He's just a man, a very interested man, a very attractive and interested man. *You can do this. Think about all the times he's pissed you off.*

Blank.

Nothing is coming to mind.

All I can think about is his lips on mine, his hands caressing me, his hand in my hair, his deep voice whispering in my ear.

My phone beeps again. I look down to see a picture. Racer took a selfie of him sucking on his fingers. The fingers that were intimately touching me.

Racer: *I'm eating your pussy at least three times tonight because damn, you taste good.*

Heat erupts all around me as I quietly moan. Okay, it's worse away from him. Retreating to the bathroom has done nothing but turn me on even more. Damn him.

He always has the upper hand, always. Twisting my lips to the side, I think for a second, because surely two can play at this game. Garnering enough courage, I pull up the camera on my phone and turn it around in selfie mode. I fluff my hair, make a kissy face and pull down on my dress while pressing my boobs together for massive cleavage. I take a few shots until I get one I know will do the job. Instead of sending it right away. I take a second to gather myself and as I exit the bathroom, I send it.

I make my way through the restaurant and head toward the courtyard where Madison and Spencer are still bickering. Racer glances down at his phone he's holding in his lap and I know the minute he sees the picture. His face goes hard and a muscle in his jaw ticks. I take the moment to walk up to the seat and say, "Scoot over."

His eyes sear through me as I sit down, and satisfaction bursts through me. Just to tip the scale in my favor, I slide my hand up his leg as I situate myself on the bench and barely run my fingers over his obvious erection. I'm not going to lie, the feel of him has me practically panting, but it's pure satisfaction when Racer shifts high in the seat and clears his throat.

I pull my hand away just quickly enough when Madison looks up from the menu. "Oh good, you're back. Racer suggested we get oysters. You cool with that?"

Of course he would suggest oysters. The man has a one-track mind right now and it's all about sex.

"I love sucking down oysters." I smile, making sure to emphasize the word sucking. I know Racer hears me loud and clear by the way he tugs lightly on a strand of my hair.

God, I hope he tugs harder on it tonight.

～

"Can you not rub your belly like that? You look like an ape," Madison snaps as she hangs on to Spencer's arm. She's just as bad, leaning into him as we walk down Main Street. They both ate their body weight in food tonight, trying to take each other down, seeing who could eat more.

Spencer went for the win.

"It helps me digest," he answers.

"You look ridiculous. Tell him he looks ridiculous, G."

I'm barely able to process what's happening. Instead of holding

TANGLED TWOSOME

hands or walking with his arm around my shoulders, he's walking next to me, his hand casually gripping the back of my neck, his thumb caressing my skin. Who walks like this? Who in their right mind thinks this is the proper way to walk?

Racer, that's who.

"You look ridiculous." I appease my friend who is walking in front of us.

"Thank you." She sighs and leans more into Spencer. *Please don't get attached, he will only leave again.* "Are you excited about tomorrow, Racer? Ready to be thrown into the society life?"

"I'm more excited about tonight," he whispers into my ear. Christ, man. Just focus on being normal for two seconds.

"What?" Madison asks while looking behind her.

"Yeah, super-duper excited. Peed my pants at least three times so far today over it. I just can't contain my excitement. Think there will be a conga line at one of the parties? I love a good conga."

Smart-ass.

"No way, man," Spencer answers. "But if you start one, I'll be right there behind you."

"There will be no starting of conga lines." I lay down the hammer. "You two will be on your best behavior."

"Ooo, let's go into Tiffany's!" Madison squeals, pulling Spencer into the store with her. Because we're a group, we follow closely behind.

Madison drags Spencer over to the engagement rings. I can't even begin to process the train of thought she might be having, instead, I casually walk around with Racer.

"Do you like jewelry, Princess? I don't see you wear it very often."

Casually, he releases my neck and grips my hand instead. There's something that makes my stomach flip upside down when his large hand takes mine. It's such a simple move, an easy way to say I like you, but it hits me hard.

Focusing on his question, I shake my head. "Not really. If it is the right piece, something meaningful, then yes. But other than that, I'm not really interested."

He hums into my ear. "You're really not like your family, are you?"

I look up at him, enthralled by his handsome features. Those blue eyes of his sparkle under the light of the showroom and eat me up. I've always thought Racer was hot, but seeing him tonight, his affection toward me, his longing, my perspective has done a one-eighty. There is no way I won't let this man take me. There is no way I can deny him anything. He has me eating out of the palm of his hand.

"I'm not." I shake my head.

"You're genuine. The real deal."

Flirting, I run my finger along the glass enclosure and look behind me. "Took you this long to figure it out?"

"Took you this long to show it."

"This one, this one." Madison jumps up and down and claps her hand. "We found it, G. Come watch Spencer propose."

Say what?

I turn around quickly to see Spencer and Madison with huge grins on their faces nowhere even near the engagement rings anymore. Talk about having a heart attack.

"That's not funny."

They both fist-bump and laugh. "The look on her face was priceless. Could you imagine us getting married? What a nightmare." Madison pushes off Spencer and starts toward the door.

"It wouldn't be a nightmare." He chases after her. "It would be a fucking pleasure."

Rolling my eyes, I slip my hand into Racer's and lead him out into the street where Madison and Spencer are bickering.

"There isn't another guy, is there?" Spencer scoffs.

"Oh, there is. His name is Aaron, and he could beat you up with one flex of his pinky finger. Trust me, he's huge."

"Steroids will do that to you," my fit and rather muscular—*but naïve*—brother pushes back.

"He's not on steroids." Unsure, Madison leans toward Racer and whispers, "He's not on steroids, right?" Racer shakes his head. "He's not on steroids."

"Probably has a small penis." Spencer adjusts his watch on his wrist casually.

"It's giant actually. Biggest penis in the land. Touches his knee actually. They call him Knee-Deep at work."

"His nickname is actually Smalls," Racer cuts in only to receive the death glare from Madison. "I mean, yeah his nickname is Knee-Deep."

Spencer laughs and walks away with Madison's hand latched in his. "Nice try, babe. There is no guy."

We make our way back to the bungalows and luckily I watch Spencer and Madison part ways with a high five and good night. Relieved, I follow Racer to our room, nerves starting to shoot up my spine, coating my body in goosebumps. Everything has built to this moment, to what's going to happen next, and even though my body is ready, I'm not sure my heart is.

The bungalow is just as we left it for dinner, small yet comfortable. Racer shuts the door and, like a smart man, locks it. When he turns to face me, I fidget in place. I feel awkward, exposed, unsure of what to do. Do I make a move? Do I fling myself at him? Do I start stripping, hoping he follows suit?

Instead of saying anything, Racer unbuttons his shirt and walks toward the chair in the corner. He doesn't say anything when he sits down, shirt open revealing his magnificent chest, defined and mouthwatering. With a raised finger, he motions for me to come toward him. I slip out of my heels and walk over to where he's sitting.

He laces our fingers together and pulls me down so I'm sitting across his lap. With the hand that's not connected with mine, he caresses the back of my neck, occasionally twirling his finger in my hair. He's innocent in his touches, never once indicating anything other than a little light flirting. *Actually, it's more like adoration. He's intent on making me feel incredible.*

"You look beautiful tonight, Georgie. I don't think I told you that."

"Thank you. You look very handsome yourself," I answer back, unsure how to take his compliment. We're usually fighting, trying to pull one over the other, so compliments feel a little odd. Yet, they're nice on the ears . . . and nerves.

"Do you know what I found out about you tonight?"

Unsure where he's going with this, I answer, "That I take good bathroom selfies?"

He tugs on my hair lightly and chuckles. "Fuck, you do, but that's not what I was going to say."

"Then what did you find out?"

He flips our hands around over and stares at my palm as he traces it lightly with his index finger. "Do you have your word book with you?"

"Always."

"Grab it and a pen."

When I get up, he taps my butt and smiles sheepishly at me. Oh God, he's so cute. That boyish charm is burying itself in my heart.

Quickly, I grab my notebook and a pen and sit back down on his lap, resuming my position. Without skipping a beat, his hand is twirling in my hair again, an action I'm becoming accustomed to. No one has done that to me before. It's affection, but not to score. It's just Racer. A gentle yet alpha lover.

"So you want to know what I found out today?"

"Yes." I move on his lap, loving how I fit so perfectly. Surprised how easy this seems with him.

"Do you know of the word oenomel?"

"No." I shake my head.

He nods at my book. "Open it up, Princess. You have a new word to write down." I do as I'm told and uncap my pen. I actually love how invested he is in my book. Not once has he ridiculed it. Not once has he teased me. Rather, he's given to it. Provided a part of himself. He runs his fingers along my leg as he speaks. "I watched you tonight, Georgie. You spoke of Limerence with such passion, such unbridled strength, that I couldn't help but be enamored. And when your older brother praised you, you took his compliments with such grace. It was beautiful." I've always known Abraham was on my side, knew what I dreamed of. But Spencer hasn't been that brother. He's more aloof and egotistical.

"I'm the youngest child in an accomplished family, Racer. I feel as though I *need* to make a big statement to impress my family. I don't think it should be important, but it is. I want to make something of myself. I want them to be proud of me . . . as well."

"And that's so fucking sexy, watching a woman of your talent and strength accomplish what you're meant to do. Hell, you're making me ache for you and you alone."

I'm caught off guard; I don't quite know how to react.

Releasing my hair, he tilts my chin down so I'm looking him directly in the eyes. "Oenomel." He takes my pen and starts writing in my notepad on a blank sheet. His writing is chicken scratch, but it's endearing. He glances up at me, his eyes serious and . . . earnest. "It means something that combines strength and sweetness. That's you. That's what I found out tonight, Georgie. You're the definition of oenomel . . . with a dash of sass."

Turning away from me, he writes the definition in my book and signs the bottom, "Entry by Racer for George."

My heart melts.

Never in a million years would I have thought the asshole who refurbished my parents' pool house would be a man I would desire. But here I am, my heart flipping, my stomach dropping, and my brain telling me to do everything in my power to keep this man around. Even if he drives me crazy sometimes. There are so many facets to this man, so many ways he's impressed and surprised me. And he gets me. He wants me. *Me.*

He's utter perfection.

When he closes the book, I press my hand against his cheek and slowly straddle his lap so I'm facing him head-on. "Thank you," I whisper. "That was so sweet."

"It's the truth." His hands gently glide up and down my thighs. "You surprised me in every way possible. I just want you to know I see you. I see how hard you work. I see you putting in your time. I see you reaching to achieve your dreams. And I will do anything possible to help you get what you want. What you deserve."

"Like dress up in preppy clothes and act like my boyfriend all weekend?"

He grips my waist and situates me so I'm flush with his lap. He leans his head back on the chair cushion and smiles at me. "No acting here, Georgie. I'm your boyfriend, like I said earlier."

"Yeah?" I laugh. "Just like that? You're my boyfriend, end of discussion? When a few hours earlier we were barely talking to each other?"

"Technicality." He smirks.

"Well, who's to say I'm ready to commit?"

"Playing hard to get? Fair enough. I can charm the fuck out of you. By the end of the weekend you're going to be begging me to call you my girlfriend."

"You're so sure of yourself. Well know this, Racer, I don't beg."

Removing his hands from my legs, he places them behind his head casually and stares at me. At the same time, he spreads his legs forcing my legs to spread as well. *Torture.* "Funny, your body was begging for me to ease the ache between your legs at the restaurant."

Of course he brings that up. I'm surprised it took him this long.

"That was because I was hungry," I counter.

Smiling wickedly, he responds, "Yeah, hungry for my dick."

Cue the biggest eye-roll ever.

"Lame. So incredibly lame." I hop off his lap and start rummaging through my suitcase for my pajamas, taking a deep breath trying to calm my heart. *I want him so badly. But I also need to fight him. It's us. It's how we roll.*

When I find them, I feel Racer behind me, slowly unzipping

my dress. Caressing my skin with his deep, velvety voice, he says, "In this bungalow, we sleep naked, Princess."

And just like that, my dress slides off my shoulders and pools to the floor, leaving me in just my thong and bra.

Oh God . . .

CHAPTER EIGHTEEN

GEORGIANA

Strong fingers glide up my sides, barely caressing my skin until they rest on my shoulders. He steps closer behind me. His heat so searing it vibrates. Sex is in the air; it's present, it's going to happen, and I can feel the electricity bouncing between us, igniting a flame deep inside me that hasn't been lit in a while. *If ever.*

"What do you want me to do tonight, Princess?" He presses his lips gently over my neck.

I shift my head to the side to give him better access. Still holding my shoulders, he works his way up to my jaw while his fingers play with the straps of my bra.

"Everything," I whisper, loving how tender he is, how he can magically make me feel his every breath, every caress, every vibration from his voice. It's like there is nothing around us, just the anticipation.

He moves the straps of my bra off my shoulders, letting them fall naturally. The weight of my breasts are barely held up. He trails his hands down my arms and pulls on the straps until the cups of my bra are forced to flip down, exposing my breasts. He deliciously groans in my ear as he leans forward over my shoulder.

"Fuck, you're gorgeous."

Releasing the straps, he kisses my jaw and carefully brings his hands to my ribcage where he rests them for a brief second. He's so close, so freaking close to touching me exactly where I want him. The ache for him to squeeze my breasts is overwhelming, to feel his fingers pluck and tug my nipples. I'm tingling with need.

He moves another inch upward, now nibbling on my ear, his breath hot on my skin, his groans making me more turned on than ever.

His hands don't cup me. Frustrated, I spread my palms across the back of his hands and move them up to my breasts where I make him grip me. He groans loudly in my ear, an animalistic sound that hits me right between my thighs.

"Yes," I moan as my head falls back on his shoulder, and he starts to squeeze my breasts upward. His fingers run over my nipples but never quite pinch them. It's a gentle stroke, but I want more. "Harder," I demand, shifting on my feet.

"Fuck, Princess." Racer clears his throat and then brings my body completely against his. The first thing I notice is his erection, and oh God, it feels so good.

I stop his hands from squeezing and glide his fingers to my nipples. "Pinch them. Make me feel. Take me somewhere else."

Without replying to my demand, he grunts and snaps my hands to my side, the straps of my bra tickling my skin, heightening my senses. He reaches behind me and with one flick, my bra comes undone and slips off my body. Even though my breasts were already out of their confines, I feel more exposed.

Thinking he's going to go back to my breasts, I prepare for his hands but instead, he runs his fingers along the waistband of my thong, digging into my sides, and sliding awfully close to where I'm desperately wet for him. My breath hitches when his hands splay across the front of my torso, his fingers dancing where I ache, to where I'm burning with need. I feel like I've wanted him for so long, even though I'm only recognizing it. Him. It's him. I'm not simply horny. It's Racer. He sees me. Wants me. Needs me.

"You're so soft," he murmurs while pressing kisses along my shoulders. "So fucking silky. I could caress your skin all fucking night and be a happy man." And he does just that; he doesn't touch me where I want him to, where I think I'll explode, but instead he relishes in the way my skin feels under his fingertips.

Across my stomach, down my thighs, across my ass, up my back, to my arms, across my collarbone, to my arms again, followed by my stomach. It's a circle he keeps on repeat while relentlessly pressing his lips against every erogenous zone along my neck, shoulders, and ears. Goosebumps are deathly high on my skin, my body's on fire, and my clit pounds uncontrollably. My stomach bottoms out with each pass of his hands that don't touch my arousal and then flips upside down when he barely skims my panty line or the underside of my breast.

It's torture.

Magnificent torture.

I reach behind me and grip the back of Racer's neck, latching on to something. I play with his hair, letting him know just how much he's affecting me, how much I want him to continue. I grip tighter when he passes over the underside of my breasts again, moaning with his tense fingertips.

Barely able to speak, I breathlessly say, "I'm so wet, Racer. For you, I'm so wet for you."

"Fuck, Princess," he groans as his pelvis carefully starts to grind into me. "You can't say things like that to me when all I want to do is take my time."

"Please don't. I need you, Racer. I need you now."

Without saying a word, he glides his hands up my stomach and cups my breasts. I moan louder than expected and melt into his chest for support. Every inch of me is focusing on two things: the way Racer is squeezing my breasts and the unyielding pounding in my clit. Never have I known this level of pleasure. I've never felt such a strong burn inside me, a need so heady I may cry if I don't find release. I want release. I want him.

And when I think he will never give it to me, he pinches my nipples with his forefingers and thumbs. I cry out loud and lean my head against his shoulder, my hands holding on to the back of his neck for support. "Yes," I cry and he pulls and rolls my nipples, never giving in, always taking. "Touch . . ." I take a deep breath as he pulls again. My eyes snap shut, my body trembles, and for a moment I think I may orgasm, with one more pull . . .

"Touch . . . me." He pinches harder and I scream his name. I'm pulsing, a heartbeat of pure white-hot pleasure in my core knocking to be released. Tension builds, blood flows to one part of my body, and a lonely tear leaks out the side of my eye when I don't think I can take any more pressure.

"Please," I beg, as I try to hold on. My resolve is breaking, there isn't much more I can take.

And then he moves one hand down the front of my stomach. With each pass, my clit pulses harder. My thong is soaked. He did this to me; he brought me to the point where I'm balancing on the apex of one hell of an orgasm. I *need* him to blissfully push me over.

His breath against my skin is like a warm blanket as he continues to travel his hand downward until it's lifting my thong and touching my pelvic bone. He pauses causing me to cry out. *Please don't stop now. Please don't do this to me. I don't think I can take any more.*

He softly kisses my cheek, forcing me to turn my face. We meet halfway, and the moment our lips connect he presses two fingers inside me. I gasp into his mouth, and I'm silenced with his tongue. His tongue and fingers working in unison; he works me, sending me into a frenzy of sexual bliss. With two fingers inside me, he presses his thumb on my clit and applies pressure while his lips mold with mine. He's such a good kisser; his mouth should be illegal. I could get lost in his lips for hours.

He starts to pulse his thumb and when he curves his fingers

upward, I stand on my tippy-toes as I moan into his mouth. My vision starts to tunnel black, my feet go numb, and all I can focus on is what this man is doing to my body.

One thrust, two... three, and oh God!

"Yes," I cry out, moving my hips on his hand. "Oh God, yes." I fall apart and come on his fingers, my orgasm ricocheting through me until I can no longer stand. My legs wobble and before I can even think about falling to the floor, Racer is scooping me up into his arms and taking me to the bed.

A white, fluffy comforter surrounds me as I try to catch my breath from one of the most powerful orgasms I've ever experienced. *Who is this man? How did he know every fantasy I've ever had? How can he give me... that?*

Racer stands above me, his erection straining his pants. His shirt is tossed aside, and he rakes his hand through his messy blond hair as he takes me in with those devastatingly sultry eyes of his. In his work gear and boots, his backward hat, and treasured pencil behind his ear, he is all male and obscenely hot. But this side of him? This side of him is sexy sinister, suggesting wicked things in our future. *And I'm ready. So, so ready.*

The muscles in his chest ripple as he leans forward and grips both sides of my thong. He doesn't give it a second thought when he pulls my underwear off, leaving me completely naked. He pockets my thong and stares down at me, pulling on the back of his neck. He smiles wickedly.

Even in my lust-induced haze, I ask, "Why are you smirking like that?"

"Because"—he leans forward and hovers over me on the bed—"you're so fucking gorgeous and about to get fucked every which way. I hope you're ready."

I bite my bottom lip and say, "I hope that's a promise."

"I can guarantee it is, Princess."

To solidify his promise, he bites down on one of my nipples and pulls up on it. On a gasp, I lift my chest to his mouth as he nibbles and then releases me. "You're so receptive. I fucking love it."

He pulls away and leaves me on the bed breathless. I watch as he reaches into his bag and pulls out a box of condoms. He sets them on the nightstand, and if I wasn't desperate to have him climb on top of me, I would tease him about how sure he was about this weekend. But I have no strength, so I leave it and watch him undress instead. *Which is not a chore.*

When he removes his shorts, I'm greeted with the finest man I've ever seen in a pair of boxer briefs. His skin is smooth and tight; his shoulders are broad, strong, powerful; his pecs flex with every move he makes, reminding me that I'm about to be with a dream man. When my eyes trail down, I'm reacquainted with the abs I've seen on many occasions when he lifts his shirt to dry sweat off his brow, but this time, I get to stare. Admire. *Touch.* The V that cuts his waist defines his body, pointing all my attention to the erection pushing at his briefs.

He bites the corner of his lip as he stares me down, his eyes blazing. Hooking his thumbs in the waistband of his briefs, he brings them halfway down, teasing me as his arms flex in anticipation. I'm about to lean forward and pull them down for him when he slips them off and pushes them to the side.

I stare.

I stare so hard.

Standing in front of me is pure male perfection, from his predatory heated stance, to the thick and long penis between his legs, and even the smirk on his face. I have no other option but to stare, to take him all in, to memorize this moment, because I doubt I'll ever see someone as perfect as him in my lifetime.

"You're making me harder by the way you're looking at me, Princess." His voice . . . it's rough, scratchy . . . needy.

"Is that even possible?" I answer quietly as my legs instinctively part.

"Seems like it." He nods at the box of condoms. "Put one on me." The demand sends shivers through my veins because he didn't ask. He growled it, and hell if that didn't make me more wet. More ready.

I tear open a packet as he steps toward me. Instead of putting it on right away, I decide to tease him a little. I place my hands on his thighs and smooth my palms over the strength in them. His cock jolts in front of me and as I edge closer to him, pre-cum glistens his tip. Leaning forward, I press my tongue against the head of his cock. He groans, but I keep my hands still, only letting my tongue barely touch him. I flick my tongue back and forth, causing him to groan and steady my head with his hands.

"What are you doing?" he asks, his breath heavy.

"Giving you a taste of your own medicine."

"You're going to make me come if you keep that up."

I smirk up at him. "Isn't that the point?"

His eyes go dark and a growl pops out as he lifts me up and tosses me on the bed. He quickly follows and hovers over me. My hair fans out around me and he grabs a chunk of it, twirling it in his fingers. "No way am I coming in your mouth. I'm coming inside you," he whispers inches from me. "I'm going to come inside you while you're wrapped tightly around me, my name rolling off your tongue."

His lips descend onto mine. At first he's soft, gentle, exploring as his hand plays with my hair, his erection casually rubbing along my leg. It's so carnal, my mind doesn't quite know where to focus. I want him inside me, I want him to kiss me deeper, I want him to pull harder on my hair.

Moving my hands to the back of his neck, I pull him in closer and swipe my tongue across his. A feral growl escapes him and seems to set him on fire. Mouths open wide, our tongues tangle, search, seek for release. He pulls on my hair a little harder, and his cock moves toward my entrance. I spread my legs farther until he's now resting between them. I move my hips, seeking his length. When it hits my slit, I buck up and feel the long smoothness of his cock run along my throbbing clit.

"Oh, yes. God, yes," I moan into his mouth as my body melts.

"Christ." He tenses. "So fucking wet. So goddamn wet and hot."

His tongue retreats from my mouth and starts working its way down my body where he nibbles on my nipples, biting harder than I expected. *Holy shit . . . this man.* I dig my fingers into his back with every bite and pull. On the last one, my chest lifts off the bed as I use him as an anchor. "So good," I cry, wishing he would spend hours worshipping my breasts. Before I can ask for more, his head disappears between my legs and his tongue is running along my clit.

My legs fall completely open and my hands grip the sheets beneath me. He presses down on my inner thighs, keeping them wide as he buries his face between my legs. Using his entire mouth, he kisses me up and down, flicks his tongue along my clit, and sucks it in with such magical precision that I'm panting, sweat coating my skin, a darkness of pleasure looming above me. *Never. Been. This. Good.*

I'm going to come . . . again.

"Racer," I start to breathe out heavily, "I'm going to—"

"Not yet." He pulls away, takes the condom I unwrapped for him, and sheathes himself. "On your stomach, Princess."

"Wha—" Before I can finish my sentence, he flips me onto my stomach and hovers above me.

On either side of my head, his hands prop him up as he leans down over me to speak into my ear. "You like your hair pulled, don't you?" I nod, not ashamed to admit it. "Good, because I'm going to need something to grip on to as I bottom out in that sweet pussy of yours."

He lifts his face from my ear and presses his lips down my back, his tongue running the length of my spine along with little nips from his teeth. When he gets to my butt, he pauses for a second and then kisses my tailbone. It's a sweet, intimate move that has me panting, gripping the sheets, waiting. *Wanting.*

"Lift this beautiful ass up for me." His body is no longer over mine, instead he's directly behind me, and surprisingly without embarrassment, I lift my butt and angle it high in the air. "Fucking sexy."

His hands smooth over the roundness of my butt, almost in a massage-like motion as I feel him pull me closer to the edge of the bed where he stands. One of his hands runs up my back, along my spine, and tangles in my hair. Carefully he pulls back so my head is lifted from the mattress. My entire body is arched from my position, and I couldn't be more ready.

The touch of his sheathed cock presses against my entrance and as I breath out a long breath, he enters me . . . slowly.

From the urgency of him flipping me on my stomach, I thought he'd be fast, that he'd fuck me right off the bed, but he's delaying gratification in the best way possible.

"Fuck, you're tight, Princess," he mutters as he continues to bury himself inside me. "You okay?"

"Yes," I squeak out. "More, give me more."

He grunts and moves in deeper until I feel him fully inside me. With one hand gripping my hip and the other in my hair, he pauses and catches his breath. "You feel good, so fucking good." I move my hips, trying to urge him but he holds me still. "Give me a second, beautiful. Let me—" I move again and he grips my ass tighter. "Fucking hell, hold on one second."

"Can't. Please . . ."

"Hell." He pulls back on my hair some more, leans over and pinches one of my nipples. "Hold on, Princess."

With a grip on my breast, he pulls out and then slams back into me. The power behind his thrust shakes my bones, sends shivers through my nerves, and causes my toes to tingle. This isn't going to take long at all.

His fingers are relentless on my breasts: plucking, squeezing, pinching. His hand in my hair never lets up: pulling, tangling, yanking. His thrusts shake me to my core: hard, powerful, deep.

This is nowhere close to making love.

He is fucking me, and he's fucking me hard.

I want this to last forever. I want to capture this feeling and hold on to it. He's so robust, overwhelming, consuming. I'm lost. I'm lost in this man's touch, his words, his grunts, his cock buried so far inside me I'm confident I will never catch my breath.

He pounds into me as sweat coats my skin, and my vision starts to blur. Throbbing, everything is throbbing. With every thrust, his groans become louder and louder, my cries grow until finally he buries himself so deep I fall over the edge.

Everything around me goes black as a searing wave of ecstasy washes over me. I fall; I fall hard as Racer thrusts three more times and then quietly grunts my name, my full name. Hearing it roll off his tongue in the moment of sweet bliss makes my heart flutter too damn hard.

"Fuck, Georgiana," he breathes out. "Fuck that was . . . perfect."

I couldn't agree more. I just hope that wasn't a one-time thing. I've never felt so full . . . or satisfied.

In a haze, I hear Racer take care of his condom and quickly return to bed where he turns me over, greets me with a lust-filled smirk, and then scoops me into his arms only to lay us back down in bed. He covers us up and holds on to me tightly as he rests his cheek on the top of my head.

"Georgie . . . Fuck. I'm lost. We fit. We fit so fucking well. Not letting you go now."

Not letting you go. I feel exactly the same. He told me he'd fuck me into forever, and he did. Was it his physical strength that made that so good? Was it his stamina? His lust for my body? He's right. We fit, all right. It was perfect, and I want more. But in this moment, in his arms, I want this. I want to be held.

"You do like to snuggle," I tease, loving the way I feel protected.

"Told you I did." And he doesn't say that in a smug way. He seems just as amazed and surprised as I am.

I dance one of my fingers across his chest casually and listen to his heartbeat slow down. "This still doesn't mean you're my boyfriend."

He chuckles, and I love the deep rumble he makes. "I'm not worried, George. I have all weekend to change your mind."

Does that mean he actually wants to?

He snuggles me closer and plays with a strand of my hair. All weekend? If I wasn't so stubborn I'd be asking for the title right now. Begging for it actually.

Because one thing is sure, Racer is a man I will never forget. It's possible he may have ruined me. That's the effect of absolute bliss. That's the effect of an unrestrained Racer McKay.

CHAPTER NINETEEN

RACER

Shit.

Shit, shit, shit.

Last night, fuck, it was amazing. It was more than amazing, it was . . . indescribable. Never in my life have I connected with another human being like I connected with Georgie. The oenomel Georgie I cherish swept me into her little world, peppered kisses all over my body, and gave me a piece of her I wasn't sure I would ever have.

And I didn't want any of it . . . That's what I told myself going into this weekend. *Don't get wrapped up in the woman. Don't let yourself lose track of what this is all about.* But hell, sitting next to her in the car, being awkward toward each other, I needed it to change. Once I opened up, I was a goner, especially after I saw understanding in her eyes.

I lectured myself on staying away but I can't. I'm drawn to her. I'm enchanted by her sweet and caring side and then mentally walloped by her sass. The pushmi-pullyu is addicting, the sense of raw magnetism we feel for each other, the fights, the fucking . . . the cuddling, shit.

I want it all.

"Are you ready for this?" Georgie holds on to my hand for dear life, wearing a white sundress, high-heeled red wedges, and a giant look of concern . . . for me.

"Nothing to worry about, Georgie. I've got this."

She cringes. "Do you mind calling me Georgiana around these people? Is that too much to ask?"

Smiling at her, I pinch her chin and bring her lips to mine where I press a light kiss on them. When I pull away, I caress her jaw, and she leans into the touch. "Georgiana it is."

"Thank you." Clinging to my arm, she says, "Gosh, I'm nervous."

"It's just a little afternoon cocktail party. Nothing to worry about, Princess. Plus you have some pretty decent arm candy with you. If anything, you're going to have to beat women off me with a stick."

"They will be too consumed with showing off their 'picture-perfect' lives." She grips me even tighter. "Just stay close to me, okay?"

"How close are we talking here? Want to pull my pants down and mount me? We can enter reverse cowgirl style, might be hot."

"That would not be hot."

"It was last night." I wiggle my eyebrows at her, remembering how her long blonde hair floated down her back as she rode me with her hands braced on my thighs. Yup, that was really fucking hot.

"Racer," she reprimands with a little slap to my stomach.

Chuckling, I pull her into my chest and kiss the top of her head. "What? It was. Remember how hard and fast you came? I do, because you milked my cock so fucking hard."

"Oh my God." She buries her head in my chest, probably out of embarrassment. "Please don't talk about me coming."

"Who's coming?" Madison walks up with Spencer at her side.

"No one." Georgie pops her head up, her cheeks flushed. Well, this isn't obvious at all.

From above, I point down at her head and mouth, "She was coming . . . hard."

Madison covers her mouth and laughs while Spencer twists his face in disgust. Catching on, Georgie looks up and finds my pointing finger. "Racer!" She elbows me this time, making me laugh even harder.

"What? My dad always taught me to be truthful. Plus, they should know you couldn't resist me last night."

"You lied to me." Madison walks up to Georgie and flicks her arm. "I asked if you boned and you said no, he slept on the floor and you slept in the bed."

I raise an eyebrow at Georgie. "You told her I slept on the floor? Harsh, Princess." I direct my attention to Madison and quickly say, "Spencer, you might want to cover your ears." He groans and walks away. "There was no sleeping on the floor. In fact, we had sex four times. She came, I would have to guess probably around nine times, and she really liked it when I sucked on her nipples and plowed into her simultaneously."

"Oh sweet Jesus." Madison fans her face.

"What the hell is wrong with you?" Georgie is spitting fire. One of the many ways I like her. Maybe with her being angry at me, she won't be so nervous. "What kind of man gossips like that?"

"Not gossip, Princess. Straight-up facts. I pride myself on being an informer. I want to make sure your best friend has all the facts when you talk about me later and tell her I was above and beyond the best sex you've ever had."

With her arms now crossed over her chest, no warm feelings floating in my direction, she says, "You think you were my best." She scoffs, but I don't buy it.

I lean toward Madison and cup my hand over my mouth. "I'm the best. Her leg shook like a dog's when I touched her nipple."

"It did not!"

"And when I pulled out my cock for the first time, her exact words were 'hummina hummina, snarffle snarffle . . . mmm cock'."

Madison claps her hands together and laughs while Georgie

looks like she's about to pull a knife from her back pocket and murder me. But just to push my limits to the max, I throw in one more *crucial* piece of information.

"And I plowed into her so spectacularly last night that when she got up to go to the bathroom, her legs were just wobbly enough for her to fall into her suitcase, ass up."

That is true.

A gasp comes from Georgie. "I told you not to say anything."

"Sorry, beautiful. Can't have you spreading lies about our night together."

"You fell into your suitcase? Oh, that's classic." Madison laughs some more. "He fucked you silly, G."

"Straight-up baby fawn legs."

"You're dead to me," Georgie says and then calls out to Spencer. "Spence, come walk me into this event, you're my new date." As if she's punishing me.

"Not a problem." I lend my arm out to Madison. "I do believe Madison and I have some more catching up to do." We start to walk toward the party when Georgie separates us and latches on to me.

"I would rather put up with your idiocies than have you two hang out together. That's just asking for a living nightmare."

I kiss the top of her head and wink at Madison. "Catch up with you later."

She does a fake-gun motion at me with a returning wink. "Gotcha."

"I hate you two," Georgie mutters.

I squeeze her to my side and whisper, "No, you don't. You especially don't hate me because I'm the one who is going to take you back to the bungalow after all this and eat you so hard you're going to come three times all over my face."

Her breath hitches, but that's her only tell as she straightens her spine and guides me into the party.

I'll take it.

"What is your line of work, Racer?"

"He's a president at a local bank," Georgie cuts in for the fifth time. Yup, got it, I'm a president at a bank. I don't need the reminder.

"Is that right? Fascinating business." Really? Banking is fascinating? Man, I don't want to know what this guy's day job is.

"Love those numbers." I wink and tip my tumbler at him.

It's been pretty easy to slip into Georgie's hoity-toity crowd. All they do is brag about the next latest and greatest things they bought, name-drop, and discuss the latest gossip. All three things I've had a hand in so far, something Georgie hasn't been thrilled with, but come on, I'm not going to sit back and listen to all this bullshit. If I have to pretend, then I'm going to pretend the fuck out of everyone. Hence why I'm currently harboring a Dufour Grand Large sailboat back home, waiting to take her out to sea with my very good friend, Stefani Germanotta—aka, Lady Gaga—and discuss the latest happenings of the pop world, most recently the feud between Taylor Swift and Katy Perry. Everyone I've told this to has fawned over me for more details but I zipped up my lips and stated my loyalty to Gaga.

Georgie was less than thrilled. I think it's the reason she keeps answering the questions asked of me before I can even open my mouth.

"Dante, will you come help me over here?"

"Sure thing." Dante, the man who thinks banking is better than sex, excuses himself and takes off to help out Mr. Salmon Pants with the matching sweater. The dress code here is absurd.

When he's out of earshot, Georgie turns to me with a not-so-happy look on her face. "Love those numbers?"

I shrug. "I didn't know what else to say, and I wanted to say something because you keep talking for me. It's starting to look weird."

Leaning in closer, she whispers through her smile, "It's because you started telling everyone you are Lady Gaga's best friend and helped her pick out the meat dress."

I chuckle to myself. I did say that. "But did you see the looks on their faces? They were in awe. Now look at you. You're the cool girl who brought the guy who knows Gaga."

"But you don't know her, and when Mr. Fennel comes around looking for the backstage passes you promised him, what's going to happen then?"

"Feud," I answer simply. "Gaga and I will be on the break-ups, simple as that. It will be her fault, of course, spilling her wine all over my brand new boat deck. It will go downhill from there. It will be all the rage in Hollywood, and then she will write a song about me, and I will cry every time I hear it on the radio."

Georgie stares at me for a second, really trying to process everything I'm saying. "There is something seriously mentally unstable about you."

"Ah, you love it, Georgie." I wrap my arm around her and bring her into my chest where I place a kiss on the top of her head. "I make things interesting and that excites you. Don't deny it."

"I want to," she mumbles while relaxing in my arms.

"But you can't. It's okay. I suck people into my web. It's what I do best. I bury myself deep and you have a hell of a time getting me out. Just ask Tucker and Smalls, there is no escaping from me."

"You're oddly proud."

"Georgiana Westbrook, what a pleasure to see you." We are interrupted by a refined voice standing beside us.

Georgie turns and smiles brightly. She holds out her hand to the lady who spoke. "Bitsy, it's such a pleasure to see you again."

"Pleasure is all mine." Bitsy sizes me up with one sneer of her upper lip. "And who is this tall drink of water with you?" There is no way she means that, not by the way she looks like she's about to stab me with her own handcrafted machete.

"This is my boyfriend, Racer. He works in banking."

"Ah, the man who knows Lady Gaga." Ha, my reputation precedes me. I'm in the gossip ring. I feel oddly proud.

"The one and only." I lend out my hand that she takes casually. "Nice to meet you, Bitsy. Great event. Your grounds are gorgeous, appetizers mouthwatering, and the company is superb. Very delightful afternoon."

Yeah, all that dribbly bullshit just flew out of my mouth. I'm impressed with myself. Looks like I can hang up my construction boots up for a weekend, after all.

"How sweet of you to say. I'm glad you're having a nice time." Turning back to Georgie, she continues, "I heard about your shop. It sounds charming. You're looking to sell Natalie Roman's dresses?"

"It would be an absolute dream of mine," Georgie gushes, her eyes lighting up.

"You would be very lucky. I was actually talking with Natalie, who is preparing for the show right now. She's looking for an assistant. Would you wish to help?"

Georgie presses her drink against my chest and steps forward. I fumble with her glass for a second and watch as she about loses her mind. "I would love to."

"Good. Let me show you the way. The show is in thirty minutes. You don't mind if I steal your girlfriend, do you, Racer?"

I shake my head and hold back all inappropriate comments. "I wouldn't dare stand in the way of my girl and her dream designer." I give her a wink and watch as Georgie lights up even more.

With a quick peck to my cheek, she takes off with Bitsy, leaving me awkwardly alone. Hopefully we don't have a sit-down lunch in the next thirty minutes because I would be totally fucked as to what silverware to use.

She wasn't supposed to leave my side, and yet, I couldn't be more thrilled for my girl.

My girl.

Yup, that's exactly who she is. My fucking girl.

~

Well, that was . . . weird. Who has a fashion show in their backyard for the hell of it? Especially a fashion show featuring bridal gowns when almost everyone attending is already married. From what I gathered, these people don't have any interest in buying wedding dresses. The only person this event was remotely beneficial for was Georgie, who's been missing for over an hour now, leaving me to fend off the feisty party goers who only want Lady Gaga tickets.

Guess what? You're rich, so buy some!

Honestly. I wish I fucking said that. Instead, I owe Gemmey Planks, Russell Mariano, and Mrs. Robichois backstage passes. I gave them my phone number so when they call to pick them up, they'll be directed to Woo Fong's Chinese in Greene, New York . . . oops. Hopefully they don't come after Georgie because she will have my head.

And you would think since I divulged my secrets to Madison about the wild romping Georgie and I took part in last night that she would feel obligated to stick close by me. That's a no. She's been hanging out by the cheese display all afternoon bickering with Spencer who's three drinks past his decency quota. Talk about a hot mess, but then again, as I look around, I start to notice everyone is a hot mess. Drunk, sticky from the humidity, and full from crudités, these socialites have seen better days. The men are drowning in cigar smoke, the women are standing on wobbly legs, lipstick smeared in the corner of their lips, and the staff continues to feed the alcoholic beasts charging this weirdly possessed party.

I top off my lemonade—I stopped drinking a while ago—and place the glass on the tray of a waiter walking by. Pushing up my rolled-up sleeves, I look around for Georgie but still don't see her. Maybe she's talking with the designer. I can only hope.

"Do you have a moment?" a voice asks from behind me. Ugh, more Lady Gaga tickets to hand out that I don't have.

When I turn, my heart hitches in my chest and my stomach

bottoms out. This is the last person I expected to run into at Bitsy's drunk fest.

Georgie's fucking father.

Oh.

Shit.

I swallow hard and pray to whoever is listening to make me unrecognizable to this man. Let him be so pompous that he has no idea who I am.

"Yes, what can I do you for?" I ask, trying to sound like the banker type.

"I've seen you walking around with my daughter today. Are you two together?" His face is lined with angry wrinkles, the ones near his eyes the scariest. He holds his drink to his chest as he speaks and doesn't falter when making eye contact. He's probably one of the only people here who isn't drunk.

Fuck, does he recognize me?

Just play it cool.

"Yes, sir. Georgiana is my girlfriend."

Casually, as if he's calculating his next move, Mr. Westbrook brings his glass to his lips, takes a tiny sip, and then nods. "Donald Westbrook." He extends his hand and I take it quickly, giving him a strong handshake. "Everyone is talking about the charming date my daughter brought here."

Charming? Ah shucks.

I smile graciously. "That's good to hear. I'm the lucky one she brought though. I'm honored to be here with her."

"What's your name, son?"

Hell, he doesn't remember me. Do I tell him my name? It's not like it's a common name like Michael or Jim. Would he recognize it?

Going for the truth, I answer, "Racer, sir. Racer McKay."

"Racer." My name rolls off his tongue and not in a reassuring way, as if he's trying it on for size. "I heard you were the president of a local bank in Binghamton. That's commendable. Tell me, is that where you met my daughter, at the bank?"

Fuck. We never went over details of our relationship and the main reason was because we weren't supposed to be split up. That went terribly wrong. Where the hell is Georgie? I fidget and try not to tell him the truth; he doesn't need to know I met —and ogled—her at his property while I worked on his pool house under the blaring summer heat. Probably not best to insult him.

Think. Think of something . . .

"Charity event." I nod, liking my answer. "She was wearing a green dress that caught my eye, and when she turned and I saw those gorgeous eyes of hers, I had to introduce myself."

A small smile passes over Mr. Westbrook's face, and I'm unsure if it's a good smile or a smile that says I caught you in a lie.

"I remember the event, and yes, she looked stunning in that dress."

Okay, I really had no idea if the dress thing was true, I made that up on the spot, and now I'm confused as fuck because I can't read this man. Is he playing with me, seeing where I will falter, ready to call me out on my Lady Gaga and pinky-out bullshit, or is he trying to pretend like he knows what his daughter has been doing? Please, for the love of fuck, let it be the latter.

"Unbelievable." I swallow hard. "But then I got to know her, and I knew there was no chance I would be leaving the event without securing her number."

"Smart man." Mr. Westbrook tips his glass in my direction. "I had a similar meet-cute with my wife. She caught my eye from across the room, and I spent the entire night trying to win her over."

"Seems like your charm worked."

He laughs and shuffles on his feet. "That it did. Thirty-five years and four children later, and we're still going strong."

"Wow, thirty-five years, that's quite the accomplishment. Any secrets I need to know?"

Throwing back the rest of his drink, he steps forward and looks around, before whispering, "Keep her in line."

I scratch the back of my head. Did I hear that right? Did he just say keep *her in line*? That can't be right. Can it?

"What?" I laugh nervously.

Acting like we're buddies now, Mr. Westbrook saddles up next to me and says, "There is something you need to know about the Westbrook family, Racer. The men provide, they lead, and the women follow." I heard him right. That's fucking great. Way to be a sexist, misogynistic asshole. Wow! "Mrs. Westbrook is the perfect follower. My son Abe found a woman who falls in line with my wife and eldest daughter, doting, classy, and a devotee to her beloved."

Waverly? He thinks Waverly is a follower? Hell, she really must put on a good act around her in-laws. I make a mental note to experience that in person, because Waverly clammed up is something I have to see.

Clearing his throat, he leans even closer. "But Georgiana has some work to do. I'm sure you've noticed her stubborn personality." Ha, stubborn, yeah, one can say that. I fucking like it. "She has this idea in her head that she's going to provide for herself. That her *silly* business will keep her busy." He chuckles. "Fairly sure it's going to turn over in a few months after opening because, let's be honest, we're in Upstate New York; it isn't a metropolis for eager brides." Man, this guy has some balls. *Or perhaps he doesn't have any, which is why he feels he needs to overlord women. Ass.*

"Are you serious about Gigi?"

Ew, Gigi is a horrible nickname. Caught off guard, I answer honestly. "Dead serious." And it couldn't be more true. Evidently, Georgie has wiggled her way into my life, and I have no intention of saying goodbye anytime soon.

"Then between well-respected men, you have a responsibility. You need to shut down this bridal shop idea of hers before it becomes an embarrassment to the family." I blink a few times. He's so unsupportive, so fucking awful. My dad would never have treated anyone so disrespectfully. "She's had her fun, but it's time for her to get back to reality, to be put back in her place. Her mother needs help with her charities, so Gigi can dive into that. But it's your job to help her see that." Mr. Westbrook puts his hand on my shoulder. "If you want to be a part of this family, it's best you ensure Gigi realizes where she belongs. It's best you show her how absurd her shop is and how it will shut down in a few months. Rein her in, son. Rein her in."

Son.

Fuck that, I'm the farthest thing from this man's son and honestly, I would be ashamed to call him my dad.

Stepping aside, I brush him off my shoulder and watch as his jovial expression turns into a sneer. Hell, he's not going to like what I have to say next, but fuck if I'm going to stand by and let him talk about Georgie like that. *Rein her in*. Fuck that, I want to set that beautiful woman free.

"Pardon me, Mr. Westbrook, but the only thing that needs *reining in* is your shitty fathering. You should be ashamed of yourself, because frankly, I'm disgusted listening to your nonsensical, chauvinistic dribble. Your daughter, the one you want to repress, the brilliantly talented, intelligent daughter, doesn't need to have her wings clipped. Her father should be uplifting, cherishing, and supportive. But *you* see zero worth in your daughter's abilities, and that's not only pathetic, given you're the man who raised her, but sad. You have no fucking clue what you're missing." Shaking, I step into his space and stare down at him. "Georgiana Westbrook is simply *more*. She's brilliant, funny, quick-witted, and doesn't back down. She's tenacious, yet cautious when she needs to be. She is proud, but also sweet and caring. And above all else, she's strong-willed because she's had to fight through the years of bullshit *you've* handed her. When she prevails, when she proves your small mind wrong, fuck, I wouldn't want to be you. She's going to make me so damn proud, and she will have no one to thank but herself." Leaning in closer, I say, "Stay the fuck out of her way because she's going places, and if anyone, and I mean fucking anyone, tries to put a speed bump in her way, I will personally make it my mission to bulldoze over that sorry motherfucker. Got it?"

Being the arrogant SOB he is, he doesn't acknowledge me, so like the classless man *I* am, I roll up my napkin, plop it in the cup in his hand, and take off.

What a pitiful, sorry excuse for a man. No man should ever be allowed to father a child when they're as prehistoric and vile as Donald Westbrook. Moments like these make me realize how incredible my dad really was. He gave me everything I needed for life. I only hope I'll get the chance to pay that forward one day.

And fuck, I couldn't be more turned on by how strong Georgie is. *Rein her in.* I shake my head.

No way in fuck.

I will do everything in my limited power to ensure that incredible girl finds her wings and soars. She not only deserves to succeed because of that dickhead, but because she is phenomenal *despite* that dickhead.

Fly, Georgie . . . fucking fly.

CHAPTER TWENTY

GEORGIANA

"What is going on? He's shaking in there and won't say anything to me. He hasn't said a word to me since we left the party."

I'm standing by the ice and vending machine, a dollar in hand for some "chocolate" as I secretly meet up with Madison. I had one of the best days ever, secured not only Natalie Roman for the shop, but some of her high-designer friends as well. I was floating on cloud nine until I found Racer pacing back and forth by the side yard shrubs. When he spotted me, he asked me how everything went, I told him my good news, he nodded, congratulated me, and then said we were getting the hell out of there.

That is all I know. And thanks to his stubbornness, he won't tell me a darn thing, and we've missed the rest of the day's events.

"Ah, G. It's not good."

Great, his Lady Gaga lying got the best of him. I told him not to go too far, but then again it's Racer, and he really never knows when to stop.

"Did he get caught? Did someone else know Lady Gaga?"

"No, this has nothing to do with Lady Gaga." She takes a deep breath and looks me straight in the eyes. Oh crap, this can't be good. "G, he saw your dad."

Oh God.

Oh GOD!

I shake my head in disbelief. This did not happen. Please tell me this didn't happen. I look for a seat, but there is nothing around, so I lean against the wall enclosing the vending area.

"My dad was there today?"

Madison nods. "He was. I saw him talking to Spencer, which pissed me off. I mean, I know he's your dad and everything, but like I told Spencer, he should extend his loyalty to you. We fought about it for quite some time, which I won't get into, but once we were finally able to calm down, we spotted your dad talking to Racer."

They talked? Oh crap . . . OH CRAP!

Knowing my father, there is no way he would recognize Racer. He barely acknowledges our staff, so a weekend-only laborer wouldn't cause a blip on his radar. *But he talked to him?*

"Did you hear anything he said?"

Madison bites her bottom lip. "Only the last half. I hid behind a lawn statue, posed like the damn thing so I wasn't caught, as if I was in some spy novel. Missy Richards caught me and asked me what the hell I was doing. I told her challenging myself for the charity posing I do for art classes. And for some odd reason, I blurted out to her that I do it in the nude." Madison rolls her eyes. "I would never pose nude unless I asked Leonardo DiCaprio to draw me like one of his French girls."

Still bewildered, I say, "Madison, you know I love you, but please, no rabbit trails. What did they say to each other? Was Racer caught? Did my dad know who he is?"

My stomach is churning in knots, flipping all over the place, making me so incredibly nauseated I don't know if I should step outside for some fresh air or barf in Madison's ice bucket.

"No, your dad didn't recognize him, but he did tell Racer to *rein you in*."

"Rein me in?" I pinch my brow.

"I'm assuming from your shop. Missy was talking to me then so I couldn't hear that well. She'll be getting a fruit cake for Christmas, that's for damn sure."

"What did Racer say?" I'm shaking, so scared.

"He let your dad have it." My body seizes from her words. When I look up at her, she nods. "Big time, G. He told your dad off, called him a horrible father, and beautifully stuck up for you. The things he said, God, he likes you, G, and he likes you hard. If you weren't my best friend, I would have thrown my body at him. It was sexy."

My stomach continues to flip but now in an entirely different direction. "He told him off?"

"Yeah. Donald Westbrook ate his freaking words tonight. I've never heard anything like it. Honestly, I was a little turned on when he was done. He told your father he would personally bulldoze anyone who got in your way. Like . . . how freaking sexy is that?"

Beyond sexy.

"He believes in you, G. Straight-up, that man is a keeper. I know you're guarded, and you have every reason to be. But Racer? Even though you've never looked for or needed a knight in shining armor, that is what he is. Not as a rescuer, but as a believer. *In you.* He is completely and unashamedly there for *and with* you." Leaning in, Madison gives me a hug and then takes off toward her bungalow with an empty ice bucket.

He defended me.

Even though I shouldn't be surprised, I am a little. Not because it's out of character for him, but because of who he stood up to. *For me,* he stood up to the most intimidating man in my world, the man who could take Racer down with a flick of his wrist. Truthfully, it scares me a little that he will still try.

My heart just expanded a few inches for a blond-haired, cocky, fun-loving, *loyal,* and insufferable prankster.

After I quietly shut and lock the door, I spin around to see Racer already in bed, shirtless, with his hands behind his head, casually watching the TV. I hear the low hum of announcers talking about a home run. Baseball.

Since I'm ready for bed, I stick the Milky Way I purchased at the vending machine—so I didn't come back empty-handed—into my purse. I kick off my shoes and undo my hair, letting it fall over my shoulders. From the corner of my eye, I can see Racer staring at me, watching every move I make, so I give him a good show.

I start with my shorts and slip them off. Since I'm not wearing underwear, Racer is getting one heck of a view now. I hear him lightly growl just as the TV is turned off and the moonlight becomes the only source of light for the room. Next, I slowly lift my tank top over my head. Completely naked, I turn toward him and slowly walk in his direction. As I draw closer, he sits up in bed, his eyes fixated on my body, chest rising and falling rapidly.

When I reach him, I carefully stroke his face, loving the way the scruff of his jaw prickles under my exploring fingernails. "Thank you," I whisper, unsure how to broach the subject.

He looks back and forth between my eyes for a few seconds before realization hits him. He helps me move on top of his lap and under the covers and slowly runs his hands up and down my thighs.

"I meant every word I said."

I cup both of his cheeks now, not minding that I'm naked and he's still in boxer briefs. "Why didn't you tell me?"

"Because you were on such a high from connecting with those designers. I didn't want to ruin it for you." He shakes his head. "You didn't need to know."

With all the intentions of keeping things innocent, I lean forward and press a light kiss on his lips while I grip his cheeks. I speak softly. "Thank you for sticking up for me."

His hands caress my back now, tangling in my hair occasionally.

"No need to thank me, Georgie. I believe in you. You're going places, Princess; don't let anyone stop you from taking your dreams and making them your reality. Got it?"

This man.

How could he be so insufferable at times and then the next minute, so capable of stealing my heart with one sentence? He believes in me. It's such a simple thing, to believe in another human being, to look at them and say, you're capable of accomplishing your dreams. But that simple act can change the outcome of someone's life. It can change the outcome of your heart.

With heartfelt encouragement comes monumental accomplishments.

I can feel it. My dreams, my goals, they're right in front of me, ready to be steered in the right direction. Prior to this stranger coming into my life and making my goals his, the only encouragement I've received is from Abe, Waverly, and Madison. It's like we're . . .

"Seelenverwandt," I whisper quietly with my head down.

"What?" Racer asks, tipping my chin up.

"It's German. For short, it means kindred souls." I take a deep breath and say, "We're two of a kind, Racer. Both reaching for goals, both needing support, both yearning for an end to the relentless speed bumps we've been forced to roll over each day."

"It was like you were meant to step on the hose to my nail gun." His smirk catches me right in the heart. When everything around me seems so cruel, it's a beautiful smirk that can pull me from diving into a deep dark hole head first.

"I didn't do it on purpose."

He chuckles and grips my hips, situating me on his lap better. "Lies, Princess. You had your eyes on me the moment I lifted my hammer from my tool belt. You thought to yourself, *how could I possibly get this man to notice me?* Oh, I know. I'll dress nonsensically in heels and a bikini and strut around the pool."

I roll my eyes and deadpan, "Yup, you caught me."

"I know." He answers with such cocky finality in his voice it grates on my nerves . . . almost. "It's what you're doing now. Strutting around here, naked, tits fucking perky as hell, trying to entice me to do naughty things to you."

"You're so full of yourself. You're the one who pulled me onto your lap. I just came to say thank you and then take a shower. You're the one turning this into something else."

"You kissed me."

"Without tongue. It was a simple kiss to say thank you." I shrug my shoulders. "Face it, you're the one making this naughty. Not me."

"Uh huh . . ." He studies me, his entrancing eyes devouring me. "Then tell me, why are you moving your wet pussy along my hardened dick."

I smile wide and place my hands on his chest. "Because I love the way your dick feels when I slide over it."

Laughing, he pushes me backward and hovers above me. Brushing a strand of hair off my face, he meets my gaze. "Fucking stubborn woman."

"Why am I stubborn?"

He starts to slip his boxer briefs off, and I can't help but look down as he reveals his erection. A shiver runs up my spine from what's to come. I want nothing more than this man to be buried deep inside me, his arms wrapped around me, protecting me from the outside world.

"Because you can't admit when you're attracted to me, that you want me."

"It's because you already have a huge ego, no need to inflate it."

He pushes his briefs to the side and slips on a condom right before he spreads my legs open. "Sometimes having a big ego is all show, Princess."

"Are you telling me you're insecure?" I'm joking but from the wave of seriousness that passes over his face, perhaps he's not. "You're insecure?"

"Intimidated." He says the word quietly and then starts moving the tip of his cock over my wet slit. "I have to keep up with you, with your strength and courage. I want to make sure I'm doing right by you."

"Seelenverwandt," I remind him. "I'm with you and you're with me. We're one of a kind, Racer. Kindred souls." He inserts himself inside me. My head falls back and I gasp. So full, so right.

"Kindred spirits," he whispers as he leans down and cups my cheeks, his elbows next to my head.

I kiss him and nod. "So different, yet so much the same."

His thumbs stroke my face lovingly, as if he's truly seeing me for the first time. "So beautiful, so stubborn, but so strong." He presses his lips softly against mine and gently moves his hips, making sure I can feel his entire length.

Our hands connect, our fingers twine together, and our chests collide—his pressed against mine—as our lips remain locked. He grunts into my mouth, I moan back into his. I wrap my legs around his waist, his hips move faster, harder.

Our lips search each other out. Our tongues mesh, our sweat mingles, our skin smacks. It's erotic, yet real. I can feel his need for me deep in my bones with every thrust, every kiss, every grip of his hand on mine.

This isn't just a fling; this is something else, something brewing that has the potential to knock me out.

"Yes," I moan.

His hips take over the rhythm and I let them, holding on, never wanting to let go.

"How close, Princess?" he grits out.

"I'm there."

Grunting, he swivels his hips and slams into me one, two, three times. Everything around me fades to black. The only thing I can hear is Racer. The only thing I can feel is pleasure racing through us.

"Fuck," he moans, his hips stilling as my entire body throbs while I tilt over the edge and fall into complete bliss. I wiggle my hips up and down, riding out my orgasm over his thick cock.

"God, yes," I mumble as I open my eyes and look at the most

handsome man I've ever met. His blond hair is a mess, his deep green eyes heady, and his lips swollen from mine.

So sexy.

So mine.

He leans in and kisses my lips softly. "Give me a second." He hops off the bed and cleans himself up. When he returns, I escape to the bathroom for a quick second. When I walk back to the bedroom, the covers are pulled back and his arm is inviting me to have a naked snuggle. Don't mind if I do. Clothes are useless at this point. I know I'm in for a long night of his body moving inside of mine, and I wouldn't change it for anything.

"Snuggle up, George."

"Calling me George doesn't freak you out?" I ask while I fit myself into his embrace.

"Not even in the slightest. It's kind of cute actually. Fits you."

I chuckle. "An old-man name fits me?"

"It does." I feel him smile into my hair right before he kisses my head. "So I have a question for you?"

"Yeah? What's that?"

"We go back to Binghamton tomorrow. I want to know, have I deserved the right to be called your boyfriend? Did I do the title justice?"

A part of me wants to continue to joke around with him about the title, to wait until we get back to Binghamton to let him know. But I can't do that, not after the way he stuck up for me to my father, not after the confidence he has in me. I would be so lucky to be able to call him my boyfriend, and he needs to know that.

I sit up, place my hand on his chest, and look him in the eyes. "I would be the luckiest girl in the world if I could call you my boyfriend, Racer. Which seems so bizarre to say, given where we began, but in the time we've spent together, I can't think of another person who has helped me learn to live, to follow my dreams, and to feel cherished. You've done so much for me, Racer. I can't let you go."

He studies me for a second. "It's because you don't want to say goodbye to my dick just yet, isn't it?"

"Oh my God." I swat his chest. "Can't you be serious for a second?"

"Where's the fun in that?" He sweeps me back onto the mattress and caresses my cheek. "You're beautiful, Georgiana. I can't believe you even looked my way. I'm the lucky one, and I promise to carry the title with pride. You're mine to protect, to watch over, and I promise to make sure no one gets in your way."

I melt right there on the spot, my stomach fluttering with a million butterflies. *How did I get so lucky? How did he look past my walls and see what he sees?*

"You're an amazing man, Racer." *And I'm so glad you're mine.*

CHAPTER TWENTY-ONE

RACER

"Look at him, he's all fidgety and nervous looking. How cute," Smalls says from behind me.

"I know. It's good to see him shiver in his boots for once." Tucker laughs.

"Kind of want to shove a Zebra Cake down his throat just to calm him down."

"Nah, it's good to see him like this, almost like he's about to piss himself."

"Can you two fuck heads shut up?" I grit out as I start to pace the length of my kitchen. Voices trail in from the backyard of my home where I've set up a fire pit, brews, and lawn chairs. "I don't need you working me up even more."

"Do you realize, whenever we're nervous, you sit back and poke the fire?" Tucker points out.

I hold up my hand. "I'm fucking aware. And you know I can dish it but I can't take it, so either leave or come fluff my nuts, because I'm about to be fucking sick here."

"Dude, you've been together for two weeks now. She's cool."

Smalls is right, Georgie is cool, but she's never seen this side of me. She's never been to my place in the two weeks that we've been officially together. It's made being together interesting, that's for sure. We've had some "late nights" at the shop, breaking in different counter space and making sure the walls are sturdy.

But tonight is the first night she's coming here, to my empty space, where I live with bare minimums.

"She's going to look at this place and laugh," I say, voicing my fears. "Fuck, I don't even have curtains. Shouldn't I have curtains? Should I hang up a flannel shirt or something? Make it look like there is something there?"

"That's some tacky shit," Smalls says. "Don't hang anything up. You're good, man. She's going to love your place."

"Dude, she grew up in a mansion. I've been in her house. They have marble fucking floors. Marble fucking floors!" I pull on the strands of my hair as I begin to pace again.

"And yet, she still talks to us lame peasants. Imagine that," Tucker deadpans. "Come on, man, you're the first person to tell us she's nothing like her family, so why freak out now? The way I see it, she's going to love everything about this house because it represents who you are and the relationship you had with your dad. It's built from love, sweat, and camaraderie. She's going to sense that the minute she walks in. Don't doubt her. And for fuck's sake go change your shirt, your armpits are all nasty with sweat."

"Fuck." I lift my arm and see the giant sweat stains under my arm. "Shit, that's ugly."

"It really is. Go change." I walk away when Smalls calls out, "But maybe leave the shirt, we can try to pin it up as a valance." His smirk causes me to flip him off, which only makes him and Tucker laugh. Assholes.

Making quick time, I jog to my room, change out my light blue shirt for a white one with a dark green pocket—some fancy shit there, look out, Cam from Modern Family—check my hair in the mirror to make sure I didn't make a wreck of it, and head back out into the grand room just in time to see Smalls open the door for Georgie.

TANGLED TWOSOME

From a distance, I get to see her initial reaction and fuck if it doesn't hit me in the chest. She looks at the cathedral ceilings her mouth agape and stars in her eyes. *She's in awe?* "Gosh, it's beautiful in here."

They're her first words and they're simple, but they cause me to fall for this woman just a little bit more.

When I make myself known, Smalls just gives me an *I told you so* look, grabs his beer in the kitchen, then heads off into the backyard with the rest of the guests. Tucker joins him.

"Hey," I greet her lamely with my hands stuffed in my pockets, feeling shy as fuck.

"Hey Racer." She gives me one of her gorgeous smiles and walks toward me in a pair of tiny shorts and a thin, flowy tank top that's showing off too much cleavage for her to be seen in public. Fucking vixen.

When she reaches me, she wraps her arms around my waist and stands on her toes to give me a kiss. I grant her one but then tug on her shirt, it doesn't move up.

"What are you doing?" She chuckles.

"You're showing too much tit."

"I am not."

"You are. I can see your nipple."

She looks down at her shirt and then back up at me with a twist to her mouth. "Did you develop X-ray vision overnight that I'm unaware of?"

"I did."

"Stop it." She laughs and swats at me. "My shirt is fine."

"People are going to stare."

She shrugs. "Let them, you're the one I'll be straddling tonight, and that's all that should matter to you."

And fuck. I'm hard. *What's new around this woman?*

She scans the room and says, "Are you going to give me a tour or am I going to have to show myself around?"

"Depends, did you bring an overnight bag with you?"

"I have my toothbrush in my purse, no need for clothes

259

because I plan on being naked all night." She winks and walks down the hallway toward my bedroom, her fingers running along the walls. "The woodwork is beautiful." The girl has class and an incredible eye for beauty and detail, so her opinion really matters to me.

I can think of something a hell of a lot more beautiful than the damn woodwork, and it's shaking away from me in a pair of tiny denim shorts.

Fuck me.

∼

"These chicken wings are so freaking good." Georgie cleans off the bone in her hand and drops it on her plate in front of her. Barbeque sauce is covering her face as she licks her fingers, and oddly, it's adorable to watch. My girl knows how to eat off the bone, something I should be very pleased about.

Thankfully, Tucker and Smalls brought over food to grill, because they're fucking amazing friends like that. I had a few bags of chips and it was a BYOB deal because to hell if I could afford for everyone to drink beer. Not going to happen. Georgie brought the ingredients for s'mores, giving us a proper campfire dessert. *She's so damn cute.*

"Need a wet nap there, George?"

She shakes her head. "Who needs a wet nap when I can lick my fingers clean?" Seductively she starts sucking on her finger and I take about three seconds of that bullshit before I pop her finger out of her mouth.

"Act like the lady you were taught to be," I tease. "Use a napkin for Christ's sake. I'm getting hard just watching you do that."

She giggles and starts wiping her fingers off with a napkin.

"I kind of liked it," Adalyn chimes in. "It's fun watching you squirm, Racer." Apparently that's the popular consensus tonight among my friends.

"Watch it, you don't want to offend him. He's a sensitive bear tonight," Smalls says, wrapping his arm around Adalyn.

"I'm not sensitive, just aware of my feelings."

Tucker snorts from the side where Emma sits on his lap. The only ones left are Georgie, Emma, Tucker, Adalyn, Smalls, and my friend Hayden, who plays hockey professionally. He's rather quiet, like usual, just taking everyone in.

Tucker clears his throat and says, "Georgiana, did Racer tell you he made me propose to him to be my best man at my wedding?" Of course. It's rag time. I see how this night is going to go. Fair enough.

"Or did he tell you about the time he cried when he was watching *The Bachelor* because the girl he wanted to win wasn't handed a flower?" Smalls adds. Fucking Raven should have been proposed to! Nick, what an idiot.

"Or how about the time he ate a plastic cupcake from a kid's play set because he thought it was a Little Debbie snack?" Adalyn asks. Booze will do that to you.

"Hey, that shit looked real, and it was dark," I say, attempting to defend myself. It's not my fault Fisher Price makes legit-looking food items.

"What about the time he was so upset he wasn't able to finish spelling out his name in the snow because he ran out of pee?" Hayden shakes his head, piping in now, of course. "Always get the twenty-ounce, man. Always the twenty-ounce."

Aren't these assholes a good time?

"I was unaware." Georgie hides behind her smile with a napkin. I can see mischief in her eyes. "Seems like he gets upset a lot. Which makes sense since he cried in bed in the Hamptons because he forgot to say '*Mother, may I?*' after I told him to lick my nipple. You face the consequences when you don't play the game right."

Everyone around us erupts in laughter as I purse my lips.

Fucking *Mother, may I?* She wishes she was in charge. That will never happen. I own her in the bedroom.

"Laugh it up, dickheads." They don't stop, so of course, I slip on my immature pants and give them a taste of their own medicine. "Tucker used to brush a plastic unicorn's hair before he went to bed every night because he said it soothed him."

"Dude!"

"Smalls once wore heels and said they made him feel pretty."

"My legs felt sexy," he says.

"Adalyn can queef on demand. She's actually doing it right now; that's her queefing face." Everyone turns to her as she shoots daggers at me. I'm really not sorry about that one.

"Hayden went through a box of condoms before he figured out how to put one on."

Hayden just shrugs. "They were too small for my giant dick."

"And Georgie here"—she stares me down, waiting to hear what I have to reveal—"squirts."

"Racer!" She slaps me in the arm which makes me laugh . . . hard. Looking around the camp, she pleads to the group. "I do not squirt, there is no way in hell I ever could, not with the below-average orgasms Racer delivers. Really a three-point-five."

I stand quickly. "It's a solid nine-point-five and you know it."

"What's the point five knock for?" Hayden asks, looking more alive now.

"Couldn't find the landing zone initially."

"Lies!" I raise my arms in the air. "All fucking lies. Spread your legs, I will find the landing zone no problem. Come on, spread them." I get my fingers ready.

Laughter erupts around me. This is crap. I gather empty bottles and plates and announce, "This night is over. I demand you leave at once."

"Come on, man, stop being a little bitch." Tucker nods toward the fire. "Enjoy the night and be happy you have a girl who will stick around even when you lie about her squirting."

Everyone agrees with Tucker, which annoys me even more, but reluctantly I sit down and pull Georgie onto my lap. She wraps her arm around my neck and kisses the side of my head.

"I still think you're handsome when you're all in a tizzy." She ruffles my hair and kisses me again.

I melt right into her side as everyone starts talking about Emma and Tucker's wedding. Georgie chimes in with excitement, mentioning all the discounts she can get them and how excited she is to have Emma come in and be her very first client.

I sit back and watch as Georgie very easily slips into my group of mismatched friends. I get why I thought we were so different at first, but right now, with her sitting on my lap relating easily with my friends, it's like she was made to be with me, like all the puzzle pieces in my life are finally starting to fall into place. *I never knew I'd want that. Or find that.*

It couldn't be more perfect.

~

"This room is magical." Georgie is resting in my arms, her bare chest against my side as her fingers dance across my pecs. "It's so beautiful. I can't believe you built the entire house with your dad."

I admire the tall ceilings covered in old barn wood, giving the room a very rustic feel. I remember nailing those into the ceiling. I wasn't happy about it, more annoyed actually because it was tedious, time-consuming, and having to constantly stare at the ceiling to ensure everything was straight, my neck ached. All I wanted to do was quit, throw in the towel, and tell my dad I was done, but he wouldn't let me. Instead, he lectured me about the small things, about paying attention to detail, and putting my hands to work to create something of beauty, something unique.

I'm glad I stuck it out, because looking at the ceiling now, I'm not only reminded of that day, the day my dad made me grit down and prevail, but I'm reminded of the beautiful craftsmanship my dad put into every project he took on. His attention to detail is something I've taken on myself. If he wouldn't do something half-assed, neither will I. He would love Georgie. Her tenacity, her vitality and passion. God, I miss him sometimes, and now is one of those times. I want him to hug my girl, tell her how proud he is of her, and pass on one of his many time-learned wisdoms. I want him to laugh with her and applaud her drive.

"It was an honor to build it with him," I answer. "Don't get me wrong. I had days where I wanted nothing to do with this house, but every day was a new day, and then watching my father slowly deteriorate in front of me, I knew I had to soak up every last moment I had with him, even if I wanted to rebel and do something other than work on the house."

"Can I ask about your mom? Was she around?"

"Nah, I shake my head. She divorced my dad a while ago. She lives in the Florida Keys where she sings at different local joints. She's not good enough to go anywhere, but good enough to appease the drunks. She's happy."

"Oh, do you ever see her?"

"Not really. She calls me on my birthday and holidays but that's it. I'm not upset about it. I would rather her be upfront about not wanting to be a mom than pretending and making an ass of herself. I know she's there if I really need something, but it's better this way."

"That's sad."

"I accepted it a long time ago. Not all women are maternal. I have Tucker and Smalls; they're my family. And I guess Emma, who dotes on me like a mom would. I would rather have family by heart when they're interested in me as a person, rather than family by blood who just pretends. You know?"

"Makes sense." She pauses and rubs her cheek against my chest as I play with her long hair. "My mom pretends and I hate it, so I understand where you're coming from. You almost wish they wouldn't try, because when they want to pull the parent card it's hard to listen to them; it's hard to take them seriously."

"So true." I take a deep breath and kiss the top of her head. "I'm sorry your parents are shitheads. You deserve more."

She chuckles. "They really are shitheads, aren't they?"

"They are; it's surprising you're not a shithead yourself."

She playfully pinches my side. "Gee, thanks a lot."

"Hey, that was a compliment." I squeeze her closer. "I'm glad you're here, Georgie."

"I'm glad you finally invited me."

"I know. To be honest, I was freaking out right before you got here. The boys had to calm me down."

"Why were you freaking out?" She lifts up from my chest to look me in my eyes.

Wanting to feel her, I caress her cheek, loving the way her soft skin feels under my touch. "I was kind of ashamed that I don't have much in the house. I had to sell so many things when my father passed because I needed the money. I kept the bare minimum and haven't really been able to replace what I lost." I pause and bite the corner of my lip. "You come from extravagance, so I guess I was just ashamed."

"Racer." She climbs on top of my lap, her naked body rubbing against mine, causing all kinds of things to dance inside me. "None of that matters to me. What matters is who you are as a person, how you're respected, and how you carry yourself. Yes, you're a smart-ass most of the time and drive me crazy every chance you can, but you're sweet and full of heart."

"Heart, huh?"

She places both her hands on my chest and leans forward. "Such a beautiful heart, Racer."

That means a lot to me, but I think she has that the wrong way around. This girl has broken out of the boundaries that served to constrain her. She could have been the snobby, spoiled bitch I initially thought she was. She could have had the douche prep boy to dine and woo her, providing her with the extravagance she was accustomed to. But, no. She's more real than I expected, and I'm still fucking amazed when she sticks by me. *She gets me.*

"It's you with the beautiful heart, George. But you need to know something about me. You're mine now, and since you're in my little circle, I will do anything for you. *Anything.* It's hard to get in my circle, but once you're in, you're protected."

"And that's something I will never take for granted."

Her lips meet mine, spiking my arousal in seconds. Fuck, I can't get enough of this woman, this painfully suppressed, strong-willed, beautiful woman.

CHAPTER TWENTY-TWO

RACER

When I worked on projects with my Dad, he would tell me to take a moment, to step back and to appreciate the hard work I've put in with my own two hands. He always told me it's a subtle reminder of what I'm capable of.

The shop is silent with Georgie out getting dinner for the both of us so it gives me a chance to reflect.

I take it all in, from the refinished floors, to the crown molding, to the custom-built shelves I'm finishing. It's impeccable. I'm damn proud, and I'm damn proud of the girl who's put this all together. She's the one with the vision; I've just followed her plan. Well, and I've added my two cents where I've needed to.

We have some painting left to do and some final touches like doorknobs then we should be good, ready for her to start filling the store with stock. And it's a lot. When I was having dinner with her, Waverly, and Abe the other night, she showed me everything she's been hoarding, and I was seriously impressed. This girl is ready and I couldn't be prouder.

Getting back to work, I run some wood glue along a piece of wood and clamp it together with another. I would have to say one of my favorite things about building is working with wood. It's fascinating how we can manipulate it into practically anything we want. And the smell of it, the smell of freshly cut wood, sawdust in the air, a project before me, it reminds me of my dad, which brings fond memories. *Even when they make me sad.*

The door opens, and I smile as I look up expecting to find Georgie. Standing before me is Mr. Westbrook and the look on his face doesn't necessarily read happy, especially when he notices me. It's when he takes a step forward that I see realization cross his face.

"You're the boy who worked on my pool house." I prefer man, not boy, but I'm not going to mention that at this time, especially since Mr. Westbrook looks like he's about to pop a vein.

"Uh," I pull on the back of my neck, "yeah, that's me."

He takes another step forward. "Have you been helping my daughter?"

There are two ways I can answer this question. I can cower and say no, that I'm just visiting and still planning on going back to the "bank" tonight to finish up some work, or I can nut up and be the man my dad taught me to be.

I set the wood glue down and dust off my hands. "Yes, sir."

His eyes light up with distaste. "Is she paying you?"

"I don't think that's any of your business."

"It is my business. She's *my* daughter."

I take a step forward, prepared to use my height and brawn to intimidate. He might have money, but I have power. "Pretty sure she stopped being your business when you kicked her out of your home for chasing her dreams. And since we started dating, she's become my business. I have no intention of letting you come into her sanctuary and destroy it with your hate. So tell me, did you come here for a reason or just to cause trouble?"

He twists his lip to the side in disgust and steps back while repositioning the blazer on his shoulders. "I suggest you step away from this project."

"You suggest? Thanks for the suggestion, but I'm a man who can make my own decisions."

"Do you have any idea the kind of power I possess?"

Christ. Men like this aren't really men. They're inconsequential. They bring no value to human life and only project greed, skewed values, and bestow negativity on those trying to grow. In my eyes, this man is worthless and to hell if I'm going to let him push me around.

"With all due respect, Mr. Westbrook, I could give two flying fucks what kind of power you possess. The way I see it is you have two options: you can continue to be a dickhead and lose your daughter forever, or you can man up, put on your *quality father* jeans, and be the encouraging father Georgiana deserves."

"I don't need parenting advice from someone who poses as a banker to try to gain respect," he seethes. I don't have to "try" to gain respect; I earn it through hard work and loyalty.

"Sure you do." I'm tempted to pat his cheek but I refrain, as I don't want him to charge me with assault. Knowing him, that's exactly what he would do. "Because you're doing a shitty job. Georgiana deserves more than what you're offering her. Look at what she's put together." I wave my arms out to the side. "This is her. This is *all* her. She has designers lined up to sell their dresses in her shop. She has inventory to sell, and brides knocking on her door every day asking when she's opening. She's done all of this despite your attempts to wash her away into a world of nothing, where she can't shine." I shake my head. "You need to hop on board, man, because if you don't you're going to miss out on a front-row seat to something beautiful: your daughter's success."

He purses his lips, his nostrils flaring in anger against his beet-red face. He's either going to explode or punch me in the face. If he does try to get physical, I won't fight back. There is no need to beat up this old man. Pointless.

Gearing up for his fist to meet my face, I hold my breath when he slowly backs away and points at me. "You're going to regret this."

"Not as much as you're going to regret not being a part of your daughter's life."

When the door slams shut, indicating his exit, I take a deep breath and shake out my arms. Fuck, I'm tense. My shoulders feel like stone, my neck is stiff, and a headache starts to take root at the base of my skull. In the matter of seconds I feel wrecked and all from one man and his inability to be a decent human.

How is it fair that such a vile man can exist and corrupt and bully, when a good man like my father was taken away so early? Life isn't fucking fair.

Feeling a little sick to my stomach, I get back to work, trying to rid my memory of that awful conversation. He's not worth my time, and yet, I honestly wish he would listen to me. I wish he would drop his arrogance and be proud. Be proud of the woman he created, because she's perfect, and he has no clue.

The front door swings open again and this time, instead of seeing an angry man ready to cause trouble, I see my brilliantly beautiful girl holding a take-out bag and carrying a giant smile on her face. "I got two free tacos!"

She launches into my arms, as if her taco score is the best thing to happen to her all day.

"Awesome, Princess," I answer but with a little less gusto than I wanted.

And she notices. "What's wrong?"

"Nothing." I shake it off. "Tired, that's all."

"Want to take a break? You've been working really hard."

"That would be great." She hops out of my arms but not before placing a kiss on my lips.

She heads back to the private office where she has a mini fridge now. "Want a Diet Coke Lime?"

I grit my teeth. "Yeah." And before you get all judgy on me, I like the shit, okay? It's all she ever buys so I've been forced to drink it and hell if my taste buds haven't welcomed the beverage. The lime is subtle but good.

I pull up the stools I nailed together with extra wood and the matching table. I was sick of sitting on the floor. They aren't pretty, but I've had some of the best dinners of my life at this little kiddy set. Yes, kiddy set, we are about a foot off the floor. It works.

"I splurged," she says as she walks back in the room. "I got guacamole. It called to me."

"We're splitting it this time. Last time we 'shared' guac, you left me with maybe two bites."

She smiles and pulls the contents out of the bag. "I said I splurged, Racer. We both have our own."

I shake my head in disbelief a smirk passing over my lips. "God, I could fuck you so hard right now."

She winks. "Later, handsome. Later."

And just like that, the tension inside me dissipates. *She* gets me. Like she said, kindred spirits. Never knew I'd want it, but sure as hell glad it found me.

~

"It looks amazing."

We sink to the floor and lean against the wall. I have my arm wrapped around Georgie as we both take in the finished shelves. They really do look amazing. Just a few touch-ups and they should be good to go.

"I can't believe we're almost done. It seems like yesterday I was throwing myself across your lap in your truck so you wouldn't drive away."

"You can still throw yourself across my lap if you would like."

She nuzzles into my side. "Fat chance. There will be no sex tonight."

My hand that is rubbing her back pauses. "Uh . . . I don't remember agreeing to that."

"Racer, what did I say earlier?"

"I don't recall." She pinches my side making me laugh. "I'm still not sorry."

"You cut the straps of my camisole . . ."

"I thought I saw a bug on your shirt. It's not my fault my scissors got out of control. Plus, you don't need to wear those things, you look better without them."

"Because you like to stare at my cleavage."

"Exactly." I kiss the top of her head. "So that should be a check in the good box that leads to sex."

"You're ridiculous." She sighs into me and starts to play with a hole in my jeans. "Can I ask you something?"

From the tone of her voice, I know it's going to be serious. "Of course."

She's quiet for a second as her finger plays with the frayed strings of my jeans. "Will you be honest?"

"Always, Princess."

"Do you think Limerence will be successful? Do you actually think it's a viable idea?"

I don't even skip a beat when I say, "One hundred percent. No doubt in my mind."

She looks up at me, unease in her features. "You're not just saying that?"

I cup her chin and shake my head. "Never. You should know me by now. I don't bullshit when it's important. What has you doubting yourself?"

She rests her head against my shoulder and stares at the shelves again. "It's so close, the grand opening. I'm almost at the end of this marathon I've been running, and even though I thought it was a great idea at the beginning, I'm nervous it's going to flop. I'm nervous I won't be able to follow through on my projections. What if I fail, Racer?"

"Then you fail," I answer matter-of-factly. "But don't give up before you even get a chance to succeed. Have faith in the business plan you've put together, in the connections you've made, and the product you've put together. Look around you, Georgie, you created this—"

"No, you did."

I shake my head. "I built it, you created it. Visualized. I just followed your blueprint. Everything you see in front of you came from that pretty little head of yours. Be proud of what you accomplished and go into this final mile with a second wind. Don't drag your feet, fucking spring forward into your future, because I know it's going to be amazing." I squeeze her tight.

And that's the God's honest truth. I can feel the buzz, I can smell the petrichor, anew is right around the corner, and I'm excited to see what's next in store for Georgie.

∽

"Go ahead, level it. I bet you twenty bucks you're going to eat your own words." I cross my arms over my chest, knowing I one hundred percent leveled out the mantel for the house we're working on.

"I don't know, looks crooked," Smalls adds.

"That's because you're tilting your head to the side, jackass." I smack the back of his head. "Stop fucking around, and let's clean up this shit so we can go home."

"Go home, or go see your girl?" Smalls lifts an eyebrow at me.

"My extracurricular activities aren't your concern."

He chuckles and then grows serious. "How's it going? You really like her?"

I think over the last two months we've spent together working on Limerence. We've fought, pranked each other, and somewhere between we fell for each other. At least I fell for her. I'm hoping she's feeling the same way.

"Yep." I nod. "I like her a lot. She keeps me on my toes, doesn't put up with my bullshit, and she's inspiring. That girl has drive, man. It's sexy."

"A lesser man would think of her drive in a different light," Smalls counters while picking up our tools.

"Yeah, tell me about it. The other day—"

"McKay!" My name is screamed through the newly painted walls. Julius Parsnip, my boss, is stomping in my direction, not looking happy at all. Shit, did he see my Little Debbies and get pissed I didn't share them? The man is round and wobbly and froths at the mouth if he sees alcohol or sweets.

I stand to my feet and brush off my pants. "What's up, boss?"

"My office, now." He stomps away as my stomach starts to sink. This can't be good.

I turn to Smalls and say, "Let Tucker know."

Tucker is our project manager, so he runs the show since Julius is usually drunk off his ass in the office. If anything happens, I want Tucker to know.

"On it." Smalls pulls out his phone as I chase after Julius.

While I follow behind Julius, I try to find any reason I'd need to follow him into his office. It's not a raise; I know that. The man is a stingy bastard. Tucker had to threaten to leave to make more money, and luckily for him, he's a huge asset to Julius, and he couldn't lose him. Me, not so much. I'm good at what I do, but in Julius's eyes I know I'm replaceable.

I don't think I've done anything stupid on the worksite like I used to when I first started. I work more than everyone besides Tucker and Smalls, so cutting hours short can't be it. And there is no way in hell my work is shoddy. I take pride in making a good product, so that can't be it either.

When we reach his office, I shut the door just in time to see him fall into his office chair with a sickening plop.

"Turn in your badge, hat, and vest. We're letting you go."

My heart immediately drops as my stomach starts to turn in rapid succession, bile rising into my throat.

"What?" I ask, my voice shaky. I mean, I thought I might get in trouble for something, but fired? That thought never crossed my mind.

Julius looks up at me, his eyes rimmed with red, dark circles lining the anger in them. "I said turn your shit in."

My body goes numb. I can't even begin to comprehend the impact this will have on my life . . .

Trying not to stutter, trying to be strong, I pull on the back of my neck, my knees wobbling beneath me. "Can I ask why?"

Julius shuffles through some papers and leans back in his chair. "You mouthed off to one of our distributors. I expect my employees to properly represent this company and unfortunately, you didn't do that."

"What are you talking about? I don't talk to any of our distributers." The minute the words leave my lips it feels like a pound of lead sinks down in my stomach.

Donald Westbrook.

Fuck.

"From the look on your face, I'm going to assume you know who I'm talking about."

I need to save my job, set Julius straight, plead if I have to. I can't lose this job.

If I lose this job, I lose my house.

If I lose my house . . . fuck, my throat clogs up.

If I lose the house I lose my dad forever.

I lose . . . everything.

"Julius"—I hope he'll actually hear me—"that was a personal issue when I talked to him. It had nothing to do with business. You and I both know I would never do anything to jeopardize this company."

"Interesting, because Donald called me this morning to let me know about your little spitting match. He told me if I wanted to continue to work with him, I had to get rid of the smart-mouthed know-it-all. And since he owns every lumberyard in a one-hundred-mile radius, I can't lose that relationship. Sorry, kid. Next time I suggest you hold back whatever you want to say to distributors."

Desperation oozes out of me as I step toward his desk and put my hand on it for support. Swallowing hard, I say, "Julius, I need this job. I can't lose it. Please give me another chance."

An evil smirk crosses over his face and for a second I think he might let me keep my job with some added bonus that would appease him.

"You're out. Turn your stuff in . . . now."

My breathing starts to escalate, my fate slipping from my grasps as I remove my gear slowly and pile it on Julius's desk. Once I turn in my badge, I go to plead one last time but he points to the door, dismissing me.

Fucking hell.

I walk out of his trailer with my head down, holding back tears. I fucked up everything. Everything lost. Everything I've ever wanted.

My dreams of raising a family in the house my dad and I built . . . eviscerated.

Trying to preserve my father's memory . . . gone.

The life preserver I've been hanging on to, making it month by month was shattered, leaving me to drown.

One man has stolen everything I've been working for.

"Fuck," I mutter as my throat closes in on itself and my eyes start to water. I walk quickly to my truck so I don't have to talk to any of the guys, but when I reach my wheels, both Tucker and Smalls are leaning against it, waiting to hear what happened. I don't have to say anything. Just one look and both their faces are curtained in anguish because they know . . .

"We'll figure this out," Tucker says as I climb into my truck and rest my head on the steering wheel. "I'll figure this out, man."

I shake my head and shut my door. I start my truck as tears fall onto my white work shirt. There is no figuring this out.

It's over. I just lost.

I don't regret what I said. I would say every word again to that bastard. He told me how powerful he was, and I knew it too. But fuck if I would allow him to belittle my girl with his shit.

Georgie needs to know I would do anything for her.

Even if it means leaving her side so I don't tarnish her brilliance.

I want her to win.

To succeed.

To soar.

I can't fucking face her, not with this. Not when Limerence opens in a week.

She deserves so much fucking better.

Not someone drowning in their dead father's debt.

She'll always have my heart. She'll *always* have my support.

But I won't be someone who drags her down.

She will win.

Even if I lose in the process.

CHAPTER TWENTY-THREE

GEORGIANA

"G, do you want this rack over here in the corner?" I look behind me where there is a rack of seven dresses in the back corner that needs to be in the front. "No, can you bring those up here and put them next to the D. Herman dresses? The beading is similar so it will be nice for brides to compare both designers next to each other."

"I knew they didn't belong back here. Are you almost done with the jewelry?"

"Yup. Just finishing up a quick polish and I should be set." It's past lunchtime and Madison and I have been organizing the shop since six this morning. Needless to say, she wasn't too thrilled about the early start, but with the combination of excitement for the opening in a few days and gallons of coffee she's functioned well.

"I can't believe it's almost here. It was like yesterday you were throwing fruit at Racer to get his attention."

I give Madison a look. "You were the one throwing the fruit, not me."

"Eh, you see it one way, I see it the other."

"Your way is false." I place the last necklace on display and then stand away, stretching my arms behind my back and moving my neck from side to side. I went with simple, vintage-styled jewelry trees to display my stock. At first I wasn't too sure about it, but now that I see it all together, I know it was the right choice. It looks so pretty and everything is accessible.

"Looks good." Madison stands next to me, taking in my display. "I'm proud of you, G. You really made it happen."

"You helped me, Madison. Without you pushing me and getting Racer to jump on board I never would have done this. So thank you."

"Aw, I love you." Madison wraps her arms around me and squeezes me tight. "Just remember I require an hour-long lunch break." She winks when she pulls away. Yeah, she won't be getting an hour for lunch. Not going to happen.

We bag up the plastic trash on the floor and clean up. Once I add price tags we will be all set. That will be tomorrow's hell. Inventory. But even though it will be hell, it's the good kind of hell that I can't wait for.

"Where is Racer? I haven't seen him since he wore that cut-off shirt where the sleeve holes extended down to his ribcage. God, that was a hot shirt."

It really, really was.

"Uh, he has some kind of work thing in Syracuse. He's been staying up there. Thankfully he was called up there after all the construction was finished."

"Have you spoken to him?"

I shake my head. "Not really. We are kind of on opposite schedules right now. I've sent him a few texts but haven't really heard back from him. I don't want to disturb him."

"That's weird. He can't respond at night?"

"Madison"—I give her a look—"you know how important work is to him. I'm sure he has a good reason. I'm not worried."

She huffs out her displeasure. "Is he at least going to be here for the grand opening?"

I pause, not really sure. I guess I always assumed he would be. "Huh, I really don't know. I never thought of him not being here." The thought of him not holding my hand when I open the doors of Limerence to the public breaks my heart. He would know that, so he will be here. *We* built this place together. I can't wait to see his face when he sees it filled with stock. It's perfect.

"Well, you better get in touch with him. He has to be here, if anything to accept all the compliments people are going to be handing out when they see this place."

"Yeah . . . I'll call him tonight." In the back of my head, I hope he answers this time. I didn't want to make a big deal about it to Madison, but I've been concerned that I haven't heard from him. With both of us consumed by work, we haven't been able to catch-up. What kind of person does that make me?

Crap, now I feel really bad.

Madison points her finger at me and says, "You better." Walking backward to the private office, she asks, "Can I get you a drink?"

"Yeah, Diet Coke with Lime."

"Shock alert." Madison rolls her eyes and takes off. When she's out of sight, I quickly grab my phone and send a text to Racer. My nerves are getting the better of me, and I type out a desperate text.

Georgiana: Hey, are we okay? I haven't heard from you in a bit and with the shop consuming me, I'm getting nervous that we haven't talked in a few days. Can you call me tonight? I don't care what time it is. I miss you.

The front door opens and Emma and Adalyn walk in. Their initial reaction to the shop is complete awe. They are the only ones allowed in early because they're friends obviously. The rest of the shop is closed to the public, even the window displays, hence the GRAND opening.

"Georgiana, it's beautiful in here." Emma spins around, taking everything in. "Wow, you've really turned this place into a fairy tale."

"It's gorgeous." Adalyn takes it all in as well and starts reading my beautiful words I've painted on wood planks and hung around the shop. "Coruscate: to sparkle." That one is hung by the jewelry. "Tarantism: the uncontrollable need to dance." Above the shoes. "Serendipity: a fortunate happenstance." Above the cashier desk. "Felicity: a sense of happiness." In bold by the dresses . . . where else? "I love this so much."

"Thank you. You don't think it's too much?"

"Not at all." Emma shakes her head, still looking around. "This entire shop deserves to be in a magazine. You and Racer did an amazing job."

"Thank you."

Madison pops back into the main space and squeals when she sees Emma and Adalyn. "Our first customers." She hands me my Coke before clapping her hands in excitement.

"Not customers, just here to see if you need any help."

"I think we're good," I say, looking around. "Tomorrow we're taking care of inventory so we might call it an early day today. We finished faster than I expected."

"It's because we don't jack around. We're efficient."

"You really are," Emma says before turning to me. She looks nervous to ask me something. I wonder if she wants to try a dress on.

"What's on your mind?" I ask, hopefully making it easier on her.

She glances at Adalyn and clutches her purse close on her shoulder. "I know we're not supposed to ask you this, but I can't help it. I need to know. How's Racer?"

Nervous sweat starts to creep up my back. Why is she not supposed to ask me this? "Uh, he's doing fine. Still up in Syracuse. I hope to talk to him tonight."

"What do you mean still up in Syracuse?"

"For work . . ." The girls share a look. "He's been there for a few days. I haven't seen him."

"Uh, Emma, crap we forgot about that nail appointment we have. We're going to be late if we don't leave right now."

"What nail appointment—?"

Adalyn whacks her with her purse and stares her down. "The one I scheduled two seconds ago when you got a clue."

Okay, something is going on and it looks like I have two people in the know to give me all the details.

"What's going on?"

"It's really not our place. I never should have brought it up." Emma looks really apologetic but that's not going to stop me from probing her.

"Emma, tell me."

"Yeah, tell her or else she will tear your wedding dress on your wedding day." Madison crosses her arms over her chest as if she's in the mafia, making death threats.

"I won't," I say, "but please just tell me. You're worrying me. Is he hurt?"

Emma bites her bottom lip and turns to Adalyn who throws her arms up in defeat. "Just tell her. She's bound to find out somehow. I was hoping it wasn't us, but look how great that went."

Emma lets out a long breath. "Racer was fired from his job."

"What?" I shout, my eyes wide, worry immediately enveloping me. Dread fills my entire body. No, this has to be a sick joke. My throat starts to seize on me. "He was fired? Why?" Please don't let it be connected to me. Please . . .

"Um . . ." Emma pauses as she wrings her hands together.

"Oh, for fuck's sake." Adalyn steps in. "He got into a fight with your dad here the other night. Your dad went to Julius and told him to can Racer or else he would be taking his business elsewhere."

"My dad was here? What?" I'm going to be sick.

Adalyn nods. "Racer said you were out getting food when your dad stopped by. I guess your dad wanted to shut you down, but Racer told him off and said to not fuck with you or he would make him pay. It was knight-in-shining-armor type stuff. But he kind of forgot who your dad was, and because of that, he was fired." *Oh God. I am going to be sick.*

"Oh my God. Why didn't he tell me?"

"The shop." Emma steps in. "With its opening in a few days, he didn't want to distract you."

Adalyn smacks Emma in the arm. "Yeah, glad we were able to see through his plan. God, Emma."

"I'm sorry. None of us have heard from him. I had to know if he was okay."

I can't even focus on their bickering. I can only think about Racer and what he must be feeling, what kind of pain and heartache he's going through. And he's going through it alone. He once again stuck up for me, defended me against my dad, a horrible man, and then took the brunt of it all. For me.

I need to get to him.

Without even thinking, I grab my purse and bolt out of the shop, hoping Madison remembers to lock up. The drive to his house is treacherous. I can't go fast enough without being sent to jail. And of course, I keep hitting every red light there is from Limerence to Racer's.

When I finally arrive, I slam on the brakes from the sight in front of me. I've never experienced such heartbreak as I'm experiencing at this very moment.

This can't be real.

Plain as day, there it is. A For Sale sign.

"No," I whisper as my heart shatters into a million pieces. "This is all my fault."

As I pull into the driveway, Racer comes out of his house wearing khaki pants, a button-up shirt, and his hair combed to the side. He looks professional, ready to look for a job.

Crap.

I put the car in park and hop out quickly. Racer doesn't even look in my direction as I approach him. Once again, I feel like we've come full circle, him getting in his car ready to leave, and me pleading for him to stay.

"Racer, why didn't you tell me?"

Gripping the steering wheel, he asks, "Who told you?"

"It doesn't matter. What matters is why didn't you tell me?"

He shakes his head, defeat heavy in his broad shoulders. "You didn't need to know. You have bigger things to think about right now. Get back to the shop, Georgiana."

Georgiana.

He uses my full name in two ways: when he wants to get a serious point across, or he's lost in sweet bliss. There is nothing blissful about this situation.

He goes to shut the door to his truck when I stop him. "You're important to me, Racer. I want to make this better."

"This isn't your battle."

"To hell it isn't. My dad did this to you, so that makes this my battle. Now stop pushing me away and let me help."

Looking up at me for a second, I notice the dark circles under his eyes, the worry in his features, the utter devastation in his beautiful, non-existent smile. "There is nothing that can be done. So drop it." He starts his truck and pulls on the door but I resist.

"What about the house?"

"I can't afford it. I have to move on . . ."

Two words no one ever wants to hear. Two words that bring tears to my eyes and break my heart even more.

Because I get the distinct feeling that when he says moving on like *that*, it's not just the house.

"Move on from what? Move on from us?" My words are barely audible.

He lets out a long breath and leans his head against the seat. "Georgie, your dad tore my life apart. He has made it impossible, and I'm not being dramatic, but fucking impossible for me to get a job in any field relating to construction within one hundred miles. I can't even score an opportunity with a fucking paint store. He's put a black mark on my name, and it's fucking me over. I'm already drowning in debt, and without a job I can't keep up. Do you really think if we stay together he's going to relent? It's pointless. From the beginning I knew we were worlds apart." He runs his hands over his face and turns toward me. He cups my cheek and brushes his thumb over a tear rolling down my cheek. "Fuck . . ." He takes a deep breath. "I love you, Princess"—my heart catches in my chest —"but it's never going to work. If I have to give you up to make sure you're successful, to make sure your every dream for Limerence come true, I will. He can't hurt you that way. He can only hurt me."

"He's destroying me," I say as a sob escapes me. "He's hurting me by taking you away. Don't leave, Racer. Don't let him drive a wedge between us. We can make it through this."

His thumbs continue to caress my cheeks so I grip his hands and hold on to them tightly. Tears stream down my face. He leans forward and places a soft kiss on my lips. When he pulls away, he tugs my heart out of my chest with him.

"We can't." He answers with such certainty. I know he won't back down. *For me.* He's letting my dad win. *For me.* "I'm going to Pittsburgh for a few days. Tucker knows some guys down there who might be able to get me a job."

"Pittsburgh?" More tears fall. "You can't move, Racer." His name comes out as a choked sob. "What about us, what about the grand opening? You're going to miss it. I want you there, I need you there."

He grips my face tighter and tries to smile, but it's lackluster, missing his contagious spark. He looks so . . . broken. This man should never, ever look broken. He's my hero. My beautiful, talented Racer. "You don't need me, Princess. You've done everything to get you where you are today." *He's wrong. He's so, so wrong.*

"Don't do this. Don't leave."

He puts more distance between us, his hands leaving my face. Gently, he pushes me back so he can shut his truck door. When he rolls down the window he pinches my chin in his loving way. "You'll do great, Georgiana. Have faith in everything you created." He pauses and takes a deep breath. "I love you."

With my heart shattered into pieces in his driveway, Racer takes off, leaving a trail of heartbreak in his wake.

"I love you, too," I whisper, watching through blurry eyes as his truck get smaller and smaller in the distance.

From the beginning I knew we were worlds apart...

From the very beginning . . . I've never seen it that way. I've seen Racer as my equal counterpoint, as someone to push me, make me believe in myself, and help me learn how to trust my own decisions.

How can he drive off and let my dad win?

Because he doesn't believe there is another way.

Why is he not fighting?

Because he's been fighting ever since his dad died, and I've made it harder.

If he loves me, he should fight.

He loves me enough to let me go.

I sit down in his driveway and bring my knees close to my chest as I stare at the road, willing him to come back, willing him to change his mind.

But I know he won't change his mind, because he is loyal, fierce, kindhearted, and magnificent. *"Have faith in everything you created."* I do. I do because *he* helped me have that faith. I have faith in what we created together. *Us.* I want him by my side. I want him to have the same faith. I don't know how I can physically change this situation, but I won't lose faith. I refuse to lose him.

The sun begins to fall, the breeze begins to pick up, and Racer is nowhere in sight. He's gone, maybe for good.

I wipe away the constant stream of tears and take a deep breath. He's put everything on the line for me. It's about time I do the same for him. At least stand up for the man I love.

∼

"Where is he?"

"Georgiana, you startled me." My mom stares at me as her hand is pressed against her chest.

"Where is he, Mom?"

"That is no way to greet your mother. Maybe if you calm down, we can—"

Losing patience, I slap the table my mom is working on and lean forward. "Where the fuck is Dad?" I don't swear, and I surely don't swear at my mom, but there is no stopping what will come out of my mouth right now.

She's so stunned, she doesn't answer me, she just stares at me, mouth agape, and a ridiculous look on her face.

"Useless." I throw my arms up in annoyance and walk toward his study. I shouldn't have bothered talking to her; there really is only one place he could be.

As I approach his grandiose office doors, I can hear him talking on his phone. Hopefully it's no one important because my dad is about to get a very rude awakening.

I fling open the door to find my father with his legs kicked up on his desk, his phone in the crook of his neck, and a pen twirling in his hand.

"Wh—"

He can't even get the words out before I reach over and press the hang-up button on his phone. I then tug the cord, causing the phone to slip from his grasp and I slam it on the console.

"What on earth—"

"You bastard." I lean over his desk and stare directly in his eyes.

"Georgiana."

"I suggest you save your breath, Donald." I don't even give him the dignity of calling him Dad. He doesn't deserve the title. "It's my turn to talk. I have spent my entire life appeasing the absurd requests you put on me as your daughter. I never got dirty. I sat prettily at parties and didn't play like the boys. I went to college, got straight A's, and I spent countless hours helping Mom with her charities. I've done everything you've asked me to do up until I decided I was ready to branch out; I was ready to truly make you proud." Never losing eye contact, I continue, "You're a businessman, and you've made a wonderful life for us by thriving in the business world. Why wouldn't you want your children to follow in your footsteps? Why wouldn't you want to brag about your children who are putting their careers on the line like you did so many years ago and trusting their instincts? You, out of anyone, should know the kind of courage it takes to start a business and grow it, so why would you admonish their plans to do the same?"

Removing his feet from his desk, he buttons up his jacket and places his hands on his desk. "I'm going to ignore your outlandishly rude behavior and try to speak to you as an adult." He clears his throat, only making me want to punch him directly in the larynx. "This world is ruthless, and unfortunately, it's run by men, men who will do anything to get to the top. As a father, I've wanted to shield my children from such men, especially my daughters. Because of your naiveté, you can't comprehend the kind of private meetings I've had to sit through, the vile and disgusting things I've witnessed. Business has gotten me to where I am today but it's not from outsmarting my opponent, it's from keeping my head focused and making sure I have an iron-clad stomach." He shifts his pen to the side and folds his hands together. "My sons have been ruthlessly prepared through their studies with me, they've been warned of inappropriate behavior and when it comes down to it, in the business world, they're not going to be walked on like women. I'm sorry to say, but despite your courage, there are pathetic people out there who will do anything to get ahead of you, and I won't apologize for not wanting that to happen to you. You're my little girl. I will be damned if I allow for you to get tossed around."

Stunned, I flop down in one of the chairs that face his desk. That's what he thinks is protecting me? Squashing my hopes and dreams. He really should learn a lesson from Racer.

And men run the business world? Screw that.

We're living in a world where women can flourish, where we can seize an opportunity and make the most of it, a world where despite gender, religion, ethnicity, or sexual orientation every person has the right to succeed, to strive for a better life. All it takes is encouragement, determination, and the helping hand of an adoring fan.

I'm not the naïve one. My father is.

"You're wrong." His brows rise from my brazenness. "I'm sorry, but you're wrong, and it's time you realize it." I stand now, gaining more courage. "Life is bigger than the typical stereotypes you choose to live in. There is a world of freedom right outside your front door that you've chosen to ignore. Instead of looking past your blinders, you've accepted an old adage of women doting on their men, and men being the supporters of the family, the rulers. That's not how it is anymore. You're living in the past, Dad, when you should be looking toward the future. A future where women are paid the same in the workforce, a future where entrepreneurs just aren't men, but they're women, they're African Americans, they're a married couple of the same sex. Be a part of that world, Dad. Be the difference. Because if you don't, you're going to miss a lot. I will be damned if I get married one day and my children are exposed to your 'values'. They're skewed, ancient, and frankly insulting to what freedom stands for."

I start to walk away, when I realize there is one more thing I need to address. With my hand on his door, I keep my eyes trained on him. "And what you did to Racer McKay is abhorrent. Using your *influence* for such a dishonorable and despicable purpose is one of the most monstrous things I have ever seen. I am so ashamed that the man who shares my DNA is capable of such *vile and disgusting* behavior. *Your* words. Racer, on the other hand, has worked tirelessly to preserve his father's legacy, to keep the one thing that mattered the most to him. And without even blinking an eye, you ripped that away from him. You also ripped him away from me, because he left believing *he* would shame me. You might not have liked what Racer had to say to you, but I will tell you this.

Racer is and will always be a better man than you. He doesn't have the flourishing bank account you have, or the status, but he has heart, he has compassion, and he has been the unyielding force behind me since the moment I met him. *He* has driven me to be better, to be the woman I've always dreamed of. I'm the person I am today because of him, not because of you. You used *your* influence to hold *me* back. Your daughter. I love that man with everything I have, and despite your feeble attempt to break him, I still believe you will never be half the man he is."

With my head held high, I leave my father's office, adrenaline pumping through me, my heart beating uncontrollably, and the unknown resting in front of me.

Fuck. Him.

How can I possibly fix all of this?

I'm certain of one thing, though. Standing up to my father was task number one.

CHAPTER TWENTY-FOUR

GEORGIANA

"G, come on, you have to eat something."
"I'm not hungry." I bring my knees to my chest as I stare at the wedding dresses in front of me.

"You haven't eaten anything in two days." Madison pokes me. "Look, I can see your bones."

"You can't see my bones, and I had a cheese stick this morning."

"Oh well, Jesus, look out, Thanksgiving Dinner, we have a new gorging session." Madison pokes me again. "Come on, eat this doughnut for Mommy."

I cringe and look at my friend. "Don't call yourself Mommy."

"Well, I've acted like one the last few days. Besides wiping your ass, I've done everything for you." As she prattles on and on about Russell Stover chocolates and alcohol-infused God knows what she thinks I owe her, I start to feel angry. I miss Racer so much.

I'm really not into Madison's antics today. I know she's stayed by my side the last week, but even with the grand opening of Limerence tomorrow, I feel hollow. I haven't heard from Racer since he left. That doesn't mean I haven't sent him multiple text messages.

I haven't been pleading with him. I haven't begged him to come back. Instead, I resorted to one thing that has brought me joy over the years: my book.

Madison starts going on about what kind of booze she wants as I scan through my messages I've sent, all of them going unanswered.

Georgiana: Heimat – a place you can call home. Let me be your heimat, Racer.

Georgiana: Rutilant – glittering with gold light. I miss how your eyes would rutilant when you stared down at me.

Georgiana: Sobriquet – a nickname. I just want you to call me my sobriquet one more time. Call me Princess, call me Georgie, just call me.

Georgiana: Dalliance – a brief love affair. I don't want this to be a dalliance. You're my forever.

Nothing. I've heard absolutely nothing. And with each moment of his silence, a little piece of me breaks, a little piece of me dies. I've never relied on another human, but Racer brightened my day, he made the bumps in the road seem non-existent, and he made my accomplishments feel like I had the power to do anything. He made me feel warm, protected, loved.

But now . . . all I feel is hurt.

I hurt myself loving him.

Knock, knock.

I look toward the door, a flash of hope fluttering in my stomach, but when Aaron peeks his head into the shop, my hope vanishes.

"Is it all right if we come in?"

"Only if you take your shirt off," Madison teases. At this point, Aaron gives no thought to Madison's requests.

He opens the door wide and is not alone. He's joined by Tucker, Emma, and Adalyn, a group of friends I never thought I would have, but ones I've come to love. Tucker is carrying a bouquet of flowers and Adalyn has two six-packs in each hand while Aaron holds another two.

"We came to celebrate." Emma holds on to Tucker's arm as she speaks, looking sad, but also excited if that's possible. "We thought before everything gets crazy tomorrow, we could have an intimate night of just friends."

"That would be lovely," I say, putting on a good face, speaking past the lump in my throat.

"These are for you." Tucker awkwardly hands me the flowers and then steps back and puts his hands in his pockets. He can't even look me in the eye, and I know why; Racer isn't coming back.

Just the thought of him not returning brings a fresh batch of tears to my eyes.

"Crap," I mutter as tears fall down my cheeks and I try to wipe them away. "I'm sorry. Um, excuse me for a second. Pop open the drinks, I'll be right back."

I walk to the bathroom and grip on to the sink. staring at myself in the mirror. I look horrible. I'm surprised everyone didn't take one look at me and leave. My eyes are drained, my face white, devoid of any life, and my hair is plastered to my face. It's not a good look. I splash my face with water, trying to bring a little color back into it when there is a little knock at my door. Emma pops in and before she says anything, she reaches in and gives me a hug.

I lose it.

Everything I've been trying to hold in spills out. That's all it takes, a knowing look and a hug. I sob into her shoulder, ugly, snotty sob, the kind of sob you can't control, the kind of sob that causes all different things to happen to your face so you're the most unpleasant person to look at. But right now? I don't freaking care. *This. Hurts. So. Much.*

"It's okay," Emma says, rubbing my back. "I've been there. I know what you're going through, and you have every right to cry."

"Why won't he call me? He won't even text me back."

Emma sighs and pulls me closer. "He's in a tough spot, sweetie. Just give him time."

"Give him time? How can I give him time when he's looking for a job in Pittsburg and selling his house? He's leaving, Emma. And it's not like I can go with him. I'm opening a business tomorrow, a business that will be almost six hours away from him."

"I know it's hard right now, but you have to let him find his way. Right now, you need to focus on one thing and that's your shop." She pulls away and grips my face. "Tomorrow marks the day your dreams come true, and you need to relish in them."

"My dreams have changed."

She shakes her head. "No, not possible. One man can't change everything you've worked for. It may hurt right now, but you will get through this, you both will. Let him find his way. Have faith in what he's doing. Have faith in his plan."

His plan?

I search Emma's eyes, looking for any kind of tell. When her eyes dart to the side, I know there is something she's not telling me.

"Have you spoken to him?"

"No. I haven't."

I study her some more and this time she fidgets in place. "What aren't you telling me?"

She takes a deep breath and grips the door to leave. "Just have faith and focus on tomorrow. Promise me that. Promise me you'll soak in every minute tomorrow because you've worked so hard to get here, to make this dream a reality." She cutely points her finger at me. "Promise me."

Some of the tension in my chest eases. "I promise."

"Good." She smiles brightly. "Now come watch Tucker drink Angry Orchard. It's hilarious. He pretends not to like it, but I've conditioned him enough to love it. You can tell when he casually licks the top of the bottle. It's his tell." She winks and takes off toward the main part of the shop.

Have faith in his plan. Please let his plan include me because I need him, I need him bad.

TANGLED TWOSOME

～

"We should have bought more champagne," Madison says into my ear. "We only have five bottles left. I'm pretty sure it will be gone in an hour."

"Are you serious?" I twist my hands together and look around at the bustling shop, champagne glasses in almost everyone's hands, red velvet ropes blocking off the dresses so said champagne isn't spilled near them, and the look of pure awe in every face.

I couldn't be more proud.

"Yes. Should I ask Emma and Adalyn to go get more?"

"Do you think they would mind?"

Madison shakes her head. "No, they just asked me if they should get more."

"They're life savers. Tell them I will pay them back after the party."

Thank God I have Emma, Adalyn, and Madison. They've been amazing all day. Naturally, my mother hasn't shown her face. Coward. While I talked to potential clients, *my squad* has been bustling around cleaning up, refilling plastic champagne glasses, and making sure to point me out to anyone interested in setting up an appointment.

So far, I'm booked out for a month. A month! I still can't believe it. This all seems so crazy and yet, something is missing.

Not something.

Someone.

Even though this shop is filled with women, as I hoped it would be, *my someone* isn't here.

Racer.

I've tried to not think about him all day, I've tried to push him out of my mind, but every time someone compliments the shop, I immediately think about the long nights Racer and I spent together bringing Limerence to life. It feels wrong that he's not by my side, receiving compliments with me.

"Are you the owner?" A pretty woman with short blonde hair walks up to me, a folder in her hand and a smile on her face.

"Yes. Hello. I'm Georgiana Westbrook." I hold out my hand.

"Nice to meet you, Georgiana. I'm Sunny Dubois from NY Bride magazine." And just when I thought my heart would never pump again, Sunny jump-starts it.

"Sunny, what a pleasure." I try not to show how excited I am inside.

"I've had a chance to walk through your little shop and take in everything. I have to say, Miss Westbrook, you have a little gem here." Don't kiss her, for the love of God, don't kiss her out of excitement.

"Thank you so much. I've only been able to make it happen because of my amazing support system." And that's the truth. Waverly and Abe were here earlier, taking the first shift of chatting with visitors, and Emma and Adalyn have taken the second shift while Madison has been with me from the beginning. There is no way I could have done this on my own.

"It's such a beautiful thing to hear someone acknowledge the community around them. I'm wondering . . . would you be interested in being interviewed for a feature in the magazine?"

"Are you serious?" I feel like my eyes are popping out of their sockets. "Of course, I would be honored."

"I was hoping you were going to say that." She winks at me and pulls a card from her folder. "Give me a call on Monday to set up a time. I would love to have a personal tour where we can take pictures of the shop and have a little behind-the-scenes look. How does that sound?"

"Like a dream."

"Perfect. I look forward to hearing from you on Monday. Congratulations, Miss Westbrook. You should be very proud."

We shake hands, and I watch her work her way through the crowd to the front door. I can't believe NY Bride wants to—

What?

Anxiety starts to wash over me when an all-too familiar man

walks through the doors of Limerence. The last person I ever expected to show up. I watch him like a hawk, examining my hard work, taking in the crowd, and working his way around everyone. Casually, he scans his surroundings but when he spots me, he makes a beeline for me. I hate that my high is already slipping. *How dare he?*

I swallow hard. "What are you doing here?"

He adjusts his tie and clears his throat. "I thought about what you said." He fidgets with his tie again. My dad is a powerful man, one who never shows weakness, but right now, I'm seeing a completely different man. "I want to be the difference."

My words repeated out of his mouth sound strange, almost like he's on autopilot being controlled by someone else.

I don't know what to say. I honestly don't know how to react so I just stand there, unsure of how to act.

He continues, "I'm . . . sorry, Gigi." Three words I never thought I'd hear from my father's lips.

"Perhaps today isn't the time to say this to you, but I wanted to show my . . . support for your business venture." *My business venture.* Not exactly words of praise, but not a dismissal.

"Wh-why now?" I ask. I know my father, he's a prideful man, and even though I hoped my speech could change his mind, when I left, I had the impression everything I said to him went in one ear and out the other.

"Someone with remarkable aptitude approached me. Not just you." Before I can ask who, my dad holds out a letter to me. "Read it, Gigi. You will understand."

With a shaky hand, I open the letter, and my eyes immediately start to tear as I recognize the chicken-scratch handwriting.

Mr. Westbrook,

I'm sure I'm the last person you want to hear from right now, given our previous unpleasant conversations, but you're a smart man, and I don't want to undermine you. I want to help you understand me.

I was blessed as a baby. I was born into a broken

marriage. Some might think that isn't a blessing, but it was where I was concerned because from the broken pieces of that marriage rose a strong, loving man who would do anything for his child.

My father was a great man. He wasn't the richest, he wasn't the most educated, nor was he the most skilled, but what he didn't have in professional attributes, he made up for in love and dedication. He loved me, he loved me every damn day of his life, and he never hesitated to make that known. He wasn't afraid to kiss me in public, he wasn't ashamed to hold my hand when I let him, and he wasn't embarrassed to express how much I mattered to him. He loved me wholeheartedly. He died two years ago, and I miss him terribly.

But he was also hard on me. His motto was: make mistakes, tell the worst truth rather than the best lie, love hard, and be the better man. So I want to pass on some of his wisdom.

Make mistakes – I made a mistake by talking to you the way I did. Instead of taking the high road, I made threats, called you horrible names, and disrespected you. I see that now.

Tell the worst truth rather than the best lie – There is no doubt in my mind that if I was given the opportunity for a redo, I would say the same exact things to you. Despite how ugly that sounds, I meant every word I said.

Love hard – I've never been in love before. I didn't know what love really was until your daughter fell into my life. I didn't think I would fall for her, we are like water and oil knocking heads, but we also balance each other beautifully and for that, I love her . . . hard. I love her so fucking hard.

Be the better man – I don't want my job back. I know that's a moot point by now and that's not what this letter is about. This letter is to plead to you one more time . . . cherish Georgiana. She's an amazingly smart and beautiful indi-

vidual with the strength and courage I only wish I could obtain.

Give her a chance, reconnect, show her your love, because you don't know when you will take your last breath. Make every moment count. I would give anything, and I mean anything, to have one more hug from my father, to have him grip my shoulder, look me in the eyes, and hear those four little words that always seemed to alter my universe: "I'm proud of you."

I've told Georgiana this before, but with heartfelt encouragement comes monumental accomplishments.

Be a part of her accomplishments, not someone ready to point out her failures.

Because there is no denying it, your daughter is ineffable.
Sincerely,
Racer McKay

I wipe away my tears as I look up at my father. He holds out his handkerchief and dots at my eyes. "I want to be part of the accomplishments." My phone dings in my hand and my father nods at it. "Read that."

My heart hammering in my chest, I feel uneasy as I look down at my phone.

Racer: Ineffable – too great to be expressed in words.

Tearful joy blankets me as I read his text over and over again. When I look at my dad, he opens his arms and pulls me into a hug. His unfamiliar embrace holds me close to him. It's strange, different, but comforting. I squeeze him back before he holds me at a distance. He hasn't said many words to me today, but somehow because of that, I know he is sincerely sorry.

"Go on," he nods toward the street, "there's someone waiting for you."

I look past my dad's shoulder and see the tail end of a rusty, beat-up truck on the street.

He's here.

I smile brightly at my dad and head out the door but not

before he calls out my name, a timid smile on his face. "I'm proud of you, Gigi, so very proud of you."

My breath catches as I bring my hand to my chest. Through tears, I mouth, "Thank you."

With a renewed sense of joy, I make my way to Racer, who's leaning against his truck with his arms crossed, and one leg propped up. I can't even contain myself. *I refuse to.* I throw myself at him, and he catches me in the air just in time for me to wrap my legs around him. I grip onto his neck and press my forehead against his.

"You're here."

"I'm here," he whispers and presses a light kiss on my lips.

Before I can deepen it, he looks past me at the shop, admiration in his eyes. "Fuck, I'm proud of you, George."

My nickname sounds like absolute heaven coming from him and fills me with so much joy.

"You made this happen."

"No, you—"

I stop him with my finger to his lips. "We both made this happen."

He smiles against my finger. "I can take that; we both made this happen." He kisses my finger and spins me around so my back is pressed against his truck. "I missed you."

"I missed you. Why didn't you call?"

"I had some things to figure out."

I'm almost afraid to ask, but I need to know. "Are you moving to Pittsburgh?"

He presses his lips together. "I did get a new job." My heart falls, and I try to release my legs from around him but he won't let me as he pushes me harder against the truck.

"Racer . . ." Once again, more tears escape, but this time, it doesn't look like sorrow in Racer's eyes.

"Funny thing, Georgie. I happen to know a very interested investor keen to fund the beginnings of a new construction company."

"What?" I perk up.

"Tucker, Smalls, and I have wanted to start our own company for quite some time, and like you, we just needed a little push. Tucker and Smalls quit shortly after I was fired, taking at least a dozen men with them . . . and contracts as well. All we needed was an investor to keep us steady."

"Abe." Of course he would help, he always finds a way to do good.

"Not Abe." A giant smile crosses over Racer's face. "Your dad called me last night and said he was looking to start a construction company, but didn't have anyone he could trust to run it."

"You're kidding." *Did an alien just come and replace the man formally known as Donald Westbrook – asshole father of the century?*

"Nope." He nuzzles me. "I'm staying, Princess."

"Oh my God," I cry out and hug him, but then my happiness falls short. "But what about your house?"

"That's the best part." He wiggles his eyebrows. "Our little company needs headquarters. Your dad is paying me rent to house the business until we can figure out a more central location. But it will work for now."

"I don't believe it."

"Believe it, Georgie, your dad and I are best friends now."

A laugh pops out of me. That thought alone should make the world slip on its axis. And here I thought Racer and I were complete opposites. Racer and my dad, now that is the weirdest combination I could ever conjure up.

"Are you going to wear matching shirts that have arrows that point to each other and say, 'I'm with him'?"

"Um, we were leaning toward friendship bracelets, but the shirts are a good idea."

I press my forehead against his. "God, I love you so much, Racer."

He sighs into me. "Fuck, I've been dying to hear you say that. I love you, Georgiana, more than fucking anything."

I press a kiss against his lips and ask, "Do you love me more than Little Debbie?"

He pauses in his pursuit to my lips and sits back on his heels, staring me down. "Let's not get hasty, Georgie. You know Little Debbie will always be number one in my heart. That broad will live on in my heart forever."

I laugh and shake my head. "I guess I can settle for second best."

"Maybe you two can be sister wives."

Now I roll my eyes. "She's a fictional baker in blue gingham, never going to happen."

"Judger. That gingham is becoming on her."

"Just love me." I peck his lips.

"Always, Georgie . . . always."

EPILOGUE

RACER

O*ne year later...*
"You're a little too smooth, have you been practicing?"

"I was born with this talent." I spin Georgie around the dance floor and hold her close to my chest.

"I'm not buying it. You haven't stepped on my feet once."

"Princess, do you not remember the amazing strip dance I gave you when I first stopped by Limerence? I have moves."

"Your frame is too good, and I keep hearing you count your steps under your breath."

Busted.

"Fine, Tucker and I took dance class together. He wanted to be able to dance properly with Emma on his wedding day."

"Lie," Tucker says as he leans into our private conversation. "Racer begged me to go to class with him so he didn't look like a fool today."

"Dude. Come on. You're blowing up my spot. You're already married, you're a done deal. I'm still trying to win this little peach."

Tucker spins Emma in her beautiful lace gown she bought from

Limerence. It was Georgie's first sale. Even though it was her friend who bought it, she still celebrated that night. It was fucking adorable.

Emma hired Georgie for the works from flowers to venue, to photographer to the men's attire, which dare I say, I look quite dapper in. I really can rock suspenders. I'm just putting that out there. They were made for me. Not for Smalls. Imagine a six-foot-four, two-hundred-pound giant picking his pants out of his ass all night. *It's so not pretty. Something you can't unsee.*

I couldn't be prouder of my girl though. She's done a beautiful job with the entire wedding, truly listening to Emma, and helping her execute everything. Of course, since Emma was Georgie's first client and is her friend, she gave Emma a steep discount in exchange for use of wedding pictures. It was a done deal.

Limerence is rocking Upstate New York, especially after her spotlight in NY Bride. She's been busy every day and loving every second of it. It's a beautiful thing to watch someone enjoy what they do, to see their dreams come true right in front of their eyes. Not from luck, or rich-people associations, but from hard work and dedication.

"You know you don't have to try to impress me anymore, you already won my heart."

I kiss the top of her head right before I dip her. I pause while she giggles and hangs on tightly. "My goal is to try to impress you every day, and that will never change. Now tell me, are you impressed?" I wiggle my eyebrows at her, which causes her to giggle some more.

"How can I not be impressed?"

"Good answer."

I lift her back up and spin her around the dance floor some more, loving the way her navy dress flares out with each spin.

When I bring her back to my chest, she says, "Maybe we'll have a day like this of our own someday."

A small smile peeks past her lips. Little does she know, I already talked to her dad about taking her hand in marriage. I thought it would be the proper thing to do especially since we've developed a high level of respect for one another. I was fucking terrified to ask him if I could marry his daughter, but he didn't even give it a second thought. He said he would be honored to call me his son-in-law. So now I just have to find the right time and the right beautiful word to propose with. It's been in the works, but it will take some time, because I want it to be perfect. Proposing isn't something you half-ass, especially with a girl like Georgiana. She deserves something epic, and I will deliver it.

"Ah, I don't believe in marriage."

She slaps my chest as I throw my head back and laugh. Such a lie, and we both know it.

"One day you'll make an honest woman out of me."

"One day." I kiss her lips and then say, "But sorry, Princess, that white wedding dress won't be worn, not after the serious boning you gave me last night."

"Oh my God!" She pinches my side.

"Just being honest." I laugh.

"Don't talk about our sex life at a wedding."

"He has no class," Smalls says as he puts his arms around us when the song ends. He guides us to our table where we sit down and take a breather.

"Where's your date?" Georgie asks, looking around.

Smalls points to a small table across the dance floor. "Ditched me for another guy."

"Ouch." Georgie cringes. "That can't feel good."

He shrugs his shoulders and takes a sip of his drink. "The girl knows what she wants. I can't blame her. He lured her over with crayons and a coloring book."

We all stare over at the kids table where Smalls' *date* sits with a little boy her age, sharing crayons and coloring together.

"They're so cute though."

Smalls nods. "Reminds me of me when I was young. That boy better treat her well. She's a good girl, and you can't let the good ones get away."

Slowly Georgie turns toward Smalls and places her hand on his arm. "Are you opening up right now?"

Jesus, here she goes again. Georgie is obsessed with finding a woman for Smalls. Too bad every girl that walks into her shop is already taken. She tried Madison, which wasn't a good match, talk about an awkward night. I won't even get into it. Georgie also tried setting Smalls up with Adalyn, which was a disaster since they consider themselves to be brother and sister. That's the kind of relationship they share. Plus, if I didn't know any better, Adalyn has her sights set on someone else, it's obvious by the way she's holding his hand right this minute.

Instead of playing into Georgie's info trap, he pats her hand. "No need to focus on me, pretty lady. I'm good."

When he's out of earshot, Georgie turns to me. "You need to find out what his type is so I can set him up with someone."

"Is that so?"

"Yes."

"And what do I get in return?" I pull on her hand until she's sitting on my lap. She wraps her arms around my neck and kisses me softly.

"I'll do all the naughty things to you."

"I do like naughty things. Does that include a little taint tickle?"

She rolls her eyes. "It does not include a taint tickle."

"What the hell? What does a guy have to do to get a little taint tickle?"

An evil smirk crosses over her lips. "Propose."

Fucking smart-ass.

Fine. I drop to my knee and place her on the chair, I hold her hand and I'm about to ask her when she playfully pushes me away. "Get up, you fool."

Loving this woman so fucking hard, I pull her out on the dance floor and show her my best moves. After all, they're one of the *many* reasons this beautiful woman is in my life. Who knew the girl who drank and ate chicken "nuggies" poolside would become the love of my life? Who knew the woman I sparred with on a daily basis, the woman who drove me crazy day in and day out, would steal my heart? *No. She didn't steal it. I entrusted her with it. Loving hard.*

I guess the old adage is true: there is a thin line between love and hate.

And fuck, do I love this woman. I think it's correct to say she's a faodail: one lucky find.

My faodail.

THE END